THE RAVEN WATCHED

✳ ✳ ✳

KARIN E WEISS

Cover Photograph by
Gothicrow
Library of Congress Control Number: 2014916858
CreateSpace Independent Publishing Platform
North Charleston, South Carolina

DEDICATION

I dedicate this work to my little furry house-mates and companions who have kept me company all the ten or more years that I have labored, cursed, and cried over the writing and rewriting and revising of this book. They have patiently sat at my feet and on my desk to give me encouragement.   And although some have passed away during these years, their small contributions are memorialized in the depictions of their fictional counterpart, the mysteriously magical cat in this story.

ACKNOWLEDGMENTS

Although the rituals and incantations in this book are of my own invention, all information about the Italian witchcraft tradition called *Strega,* comes from *Raven Grimassi; WAYS OF THE STREGA; Italian Witchcraft: Its Lore, Magick and Spells.* Copyright 1995, Llewellyn Publications. For the existence and wonderful information in that book, I am most grateful. Were it not for the information contained there, my own imagined ideas of the practice and experience of "white magic" and "Green Witchcraft" would be pale indeed.

Ideas for the 'ancestor stories' are drawn from reading of volumes of history written from the perspective of women throughout the ages. The stories as told here are my own adaptations. I have drawn much of my imagined "ancient heritage" of the Rimini family's lineage of mystical and powerful women from "ORIGINS OF MODERN WITCHCRAFT: The Evolution of a World Religion" by Ann Moura, copyright 2000, Llewellyn Publications. This is another fascinating book which I am very grateful to have found. Without the scholarly information it provides my story would lose its backbone entirely.

For her delightful overview and stories of strong independent women throughout Ancient and Medieval history, I am grateful to have found Vicki Leon's "UPPITY WOMEN OF ANCIENT TIMES" copyright 1995, Conari Press, Berkeley, CA.; and "UPPITY WOMEN OF MEDIEVAL TIMES" copyright 1997, Conari Press, Berkeley, Ca. Beside expanding my imagination of those long-ago times, these books gave me courage and creative inspiration for composing my fictional tales of the 'Rimini ancestors' that are interspersed throughout my novel.

And, especially, I am grateful to friends from my women's groups over the years who have encouraged me with their feedback and support of my unconventional ideas about women's spiritual history.

CONTENTS

PROLOGUE: CIRCA 1600 AD

*** * ***

Set among sun-bleached cliffs and wind-shorn pines, the tiny stone and wood cottage seemed hewn from the craggy slopes on which it clung. A well-trodden foot path wound from its single sturdy door, through a sparsely wooded meadow, to a rock-strewn stream winding into a denser forest forty yards down-slope. Behind and above, rose the purple-shadowed summits of the Apennines, still snow-capped in June.

The flame-haired woman hummed to herself while holding up her skirt and stepping barefoot along the bank of the stream. Obviously accustomed to the rugged terrain of the mountain, her feet, though shapely, were hard with calluses and she sprang among the rocks like one of her goats who grazed farther up the mountainside. Her work-toughened hands quickly plucked shoots from the icy water and placed them in a basket on her arm. She stopped to tuck an errant curl into her braid, and inhaled deeply of the bracing mountain air.

A large carp surfaced and dived. She knelt to watch the old fish skim downstream, and in the ripples of its wake saw a bird's reflection peering down on her. Shading her eyes from the blue brilliance of a mid-morning sky, she turned to address a large raven sitting on the withered tip of a storm-bent cedar. "Good day to you, Melanthus," she said with a laugh. "Were you intent upon snatching some fish-guts, should I have been fishing? Sorry to disappoint you, but it is not fish we're having today. It will be sour bread and cheese."

The raven cackled and hopped to a lower branch to preen itself. Suddenly it opened its sharp beak and gave a long hacking cry before flying off to settle in a copse of aspen lower on the mountain. The woman followed its flight with her eyes, peering deeply into the rift between hills. Nothing could be seen yet, but there was the faint sound of horses neighing and snorting as they scrabbled up the steep trail.

"Who will this be now, Esmeralda? Friend or foe?" she whispered to an amber-eyed brown tabby who had been prowling the stream at her side. Collecting her basket of herbs, the woman tucked a small crescent-shaped knife into the waistband of her apron and turned back to the cabin.

A tidy garden plot and rock-fence corral for milking goats, plus a small latrine behind a trained grape arbor, made up the surrounding yard. The cabin itself backed against a steep slope, overgrown with patches of lava-nourished grasses and wildflowers.

As she hurried up the path, she was joined by two huge mastiffs with the look and manner of stealthy wolves. They silently dogged her through the door. The cat followed, springing quickly over the threshold to find a secure perch away from her lupine co-habitants.

Inside the tiny shack, appearances shifted subtly to camouflage articles and evidence of a healer's Craft. Only the simple accouterments of pastoral living could be perceived: a sturdy stone hearth and fire pit, with a smoke hole through the thatch roof; crude wooden benches flanking a trestle table; cooking utensils and drying herbs hung from rafters; a neat pallet against the hearth_ all gave evidence of a peasant woman's quiet existence.

The animals assumed a casual air posing lazily about the hearth, while the woman busied herself with a broom at imagined dust on the spotless wood plank floor. A raven's belligerent call sounded from a clump of tall pines outside the window. Soon there came boot-stampings up the path and a pounding at the door. The woman stood before the hearth, facing the door. In a voice of calm command, she said, "The door is not locked, you need not break it down. Enter at your will."

The door opened to reveal two armed soldiers, flanking a skinny old man wearing a cleric's collar. "Cecelia, we are here at the command of the Bishop, to arrest you for heresy. If you come peaceably, you will not be harmed." The three men stepped into the cabin, stuffing the room with their ominous presence.

Cecelia's raised eyebrow and scornful smile barely suppressed a laugh. Her eyes flashed, as if daring them to lay hands on her. Her dogs stood at attention with hackles raised and teeth barred. She signaled the wolf-dogs to stay back. Their rumbling growls echoed through the room. The cleric pulled nervously at his collar. His guards backed up several paces.

"I will come with you to see the Bishop," said Cecelia softly. "But you must first allow me to get my cloak and put away the food I've just begun to prepare."

"I suppose that should be all right," answered the cleric in a tremulous voice. "But call off those wild hounds of yours, or we will be forced to shoot them."

Cecelia nodded and motioned to the dogs to follow her to the back of the room, where she made to attach chains to their iron-studded collars. They bowed their heads submissively. The men breathed an audible sigh in unison.

Carrying a mixing bowl and a pot of vegetables, Cecelia went to a small door in the corner. "I will lock the dogs in here too," she said over her shoulder, "so they can't follow us when we leave." She led the animals into the pantry with her, and closed the door. She gathered up a hooded cloak, a tall walking stick, and a pair of heavily lined leather boots. She quickly packed a knapsack with a few provisions. Then she unchained the dogs and gave them each a hug.

A bank of shelves in the pantry's back wall slid aside noiselessly at her touch, disclosing a room-size cavern carved into the sandstone bluff that backed the house. Cecelia slipped quietly into the sanctum of the mountain and disappeared as the shelving slid silently back into place.

After some minutes of waiting, the men glanced warily toward the quiet pantry. "Cecelia, come with us now. No more time for housekeeping today." joked the cleric nervously. When there was no reply, he beckoned the guards to go open the pantry door. They did.

Instantly each guard was laid flat, a snarling, snapping mastiff at his throat. Just as fast, the cleric found himself trying to fight off a clawing, slashing cat. Her hisses and shrieks blended in a gruesome duet with his screams as the cleric stumbled down the path, blood streaming down his robes from gashes in his face and eyes. Blinded and terrified, he ran until he fell unconscious into a deep ravine at the edge of the wood.

Searchers found him dead there about a week later and deduced that he had been chased by a boar or cougar. The husky wolf-dogs dragged the corpses of the armed guards down the mountainside and deposited them near a road where those who found them assumed they had been attacked by ravenous wild wolves.

Some nights later, Cecelia's followers brought tales to her cabin of further denunciations made against her by local authorities. The cries of witchcraft and devil worship had begun to grow shriller, but to these had been added another: Werewolf!

Meanwhile, the cat and two hounds lounged on the porch. Self-satisfied grins flashing on their muzzles, ears twitching humorously, they exchanged accounts of that most gratifying escapade. The raven, on his favorite tree branch, laughed with them. He had witnessed it all and knew when they exaggerated their tales; but he rejoiced with them at their successes and cheered them on for future battles to be engaged.

1

SPRING EQUINOX CIRCA 1970 AD

S ophia and Gina Stood beside a clear pond in which was cupped a perfect reflection of the moon's full orb. The breeze billowed their gossamer veils and fluttered them about like enormous fairy wings. The two women faced each other an arm's length apart, mirroring each other's grace as two versions of the same individual. Sophia was a seasoned Crone, Gina a mature Matron. There was no innocent Maiden here, but two well-ripened women, wise in the ways of this world and of the Otherworld.

A raven watched from a high branch, its indigo feathers iridescent in the moonlight. It was the fourth Treguenda in the Witch's Wheel of the Year_ March twenty-first, Spring Equinox_ time of the Goddess annual return from the Underworld. The Witch's Coven gathered in a Grove ringed by a dance of ancient trees to celebrate a secret Rite that had survived thousands of years, passed through the lineage of a few clans of women whose origins lay in a time before Time was marked by men.

Shielding its charmed circle of celebrants from prying eyes, the sylvan meadow thrummed with muffled nocturnal murmurs. The scents of seaweed and hillside bracken mingled with the aroma of burning incense and the fragrance of a budding forest. Around the perimeter of the time-honored glade, other celebrants observed the metamorphosis of the Moon Goddess in silence.

Sophia and Gina dropped their veils. They stood suffused in an aura from a place outside of time. Their bodies were illuminated, vibrating with the pulse of magic. Like the two-faced sphinx who stands between yesterday and tomorrow, the two women were caught between moments of time.

A dagger-blade flashed in the old woman's right hand as she raised her arms, arching the Athame above her head to join with the Wand of carven oak in her left hand. Holding the sacred objects crossed, like hands in prayer, she called down the Moon.

"Come join with us, our Holy One, and let your glory reside in our midst. Come down to bless our offering this night so that your truth will live on in this Grove forever."

From around the glade, the voices of men and others, seen and unseen, chanted in response to Sophia's paean to Luna-Diana-Aradia, Goddess of the Moon and Witches:

"To you, our Mother and Sister, our Protectress and our Guide, we come in celebration this night. You have traveled to the far places, the dark places, the lonely places and comforted those who tarry there. Now you return to us bearing the seeds of new Life with renewal of Spirit for all Earth's creatures. We welcome you and salute you."

✳ ✳ ✳

Sophia continued the chant:

✳ ✳ ✳

"We come in supplication as well, for our small circle seeks one who is lost to us, but who we dearly desire to have return. We are come to ask your guidance as the Wand passes from past to future and your Wisdom is carried forward. Blessed be."

✳ ✳ ✳

Quickly the Crone brought the blade and the wand down together so their points rested between the breasts of the Matron standing before her. The tip of the knife nicked the younger woman's throat and a trickle of blood glistened like a ruby on her pale skin. Then the old Priestess pressed the dagger gently against her own breast, making a shallow cut to draw her own crimson bead. When the women knelt and embraced, their droplets mingled to forge a bond to last through time.

Once more, the Crone raised her face to the Moon and chanted:

✳ ✳ ✳

"The Lady of the Evening appears in the heavens
    The people in all lands lift their eyes to Her and rejoice
    The four-footed creatures of the high steppe
    gaze up at her in wonder
    The small creatures of the forests stop their scampering

to look at her with delight
The horned and hoofed beasts of the mountains
bow to her with humble gratitude
The fur-coated hunters and predators halt their hunt
to sing her songs with howls and growls
The birds in the sky rejoice in her magnificence
All bow before her."

Now, standing naked in the midnight glade, enfolded in a shawl of moonbeams, Sophia placed the carved Wand into Gina's hand, saying, "This Wand now passes from Past to Present. Take the Power it holds and use it for the good of all."

Although silver-haired with age, Sophia radiated a fey grace that was mirrored in Gina's dark elfin beauty. Transformed in the Spring Rite, they together embodied the Moon Goddess in her waxing and waning aspects. Sophia, the old Priestess, passed the Wand of Authority to Gina, her niece. An era was ending, a new era begun.

At this point, Gina took up the chant, singing:

"She is Luna, our guide
She is Diana, our huntress
She is Shakti, our lover
She is Aradia, our teacher
She is Enheduanna, our muse."

Voices from around the Grove replied:

* * *

"She is the spirit of our Ancestors
    She is the soul of our lovers
    She is the hope of our children
    She is the grace of our homes
    She is the Great Mother's Eye upon us
    She is the sustainer of our Living Earth
    She is the Male God's own mother and sister
    She is His lover and his bride and his wise counsel."

At last, Sophia finished the chant, singing:

"She is Inanna, Ishtar, Isis, and Astarte
    She is Hera, Artemis, Athena, and Aphrodite
    She is the venerable, the feared, and the adored
    She is the long misunderstood and denied Goddess
    whom we honor forever.
    Blessed be."

* * *

As the ritual drew to a close, the two priestesses took their seats side by side upon a pair of throne-shaped boulders at the edge of the Grove. Sophia lay the sacred Dagger upon her knees. Gina beckoned to the surrounding celebrants with the sacred Wand. The trees bowed and whispered their benediction. The raven flew down and settled on the Crone's shoulder while an orange tabby cat curled at her feet and a huge silver-coated wolf stood guard at her side.

    Four men emerged from the perimeter of the Grove. Mario draped a fur-lined cape over Gina's bare shoulders, kissing her gently on the forehead. Heironymous did the same for Sophia.

Anthony brought a carved Staff to Sophia and bowed before the women, gallantly kissing each on the back of her hand. Finally, Giuseppe brought a large silver Chalice of wine which he offered first to Sophia, then to Gina, with a wink and a grin.

Gina then passed the cup of wine around to each of the men while Sophia made a closing prayer for protection, peace, and preservation of power. But everyone in attendance knew that the ultimate succession of Shaman-Power had not occurred here, from Sophia to Gina. Another was intended to inherit the greater legacy, but she had not yet arrived.

2

PREPARATIONS

The notice tacked to a tree said, "ATTENTION: To all inhabitants of the area: An EDICT is hereby given through the Cultural Affairs Ministry to immediately CEASE AND DESIST all Bonfires, Revels, and other Satanic Rituals on the upcoming night of BELTANE/MAY EVE."

"Befana!" swore Sophia, "protect us and banish this evil that masquerades as good in our midst."

The old woman sketched the sign of a pentagram inside a circle with her left hand, and ripped the poster from the tree. She cursed as she tore it to shreds and put it into her pocket with the others. Sophia had come across these hateful notices posted throughout her villa's land as she made her final rounds to cast spells of protection. She intended to burn them as soon as she returned to the house.

Travelling the woodland paths on foot, using her yew-wood staff for support, Sophia was accompanied by a sleek orange tabby, who sauntered at her side, batting at bugs and pouncing upon beetles. A king-sized Raven hovered around them, darting from tree to tree, scolding and gossiping.

As she performed quiet rituals in certain sacred places, the old woman set out charms, amulets and talismans. Her eyes misted with tears as she prayed their intended recipients would find them when needed.

One still evening, in the hush of twilight, Sophia settled herself on a fallen log in a meadow overlooking the sea. An unlikely group gathered to pay her their respects. The fierce congregation who met here in good fellowship included a noble stag, a gruff brown bear, a regal mountains lion, and a cunning red fox. A stealthy silver wolf lounged at her feet, while the trickster raven preened, sitting on her shoulder. A great white owl huffed in the branches above them, casting wise somber eyes upon all.

The tabby curled in her lap, unperturbed by the wild company they kept. Sophia spoke to the feral gathering: "Thank you for your constant watchfulness, my old friends. After I'm gone, I ask you to keep faith and stand by those who need our help. You know I will be with you in spirit always." Again tears clouded her eyes and she sighed, painfully aware of a great task left unfinished.

The next morning, Sophia climbed the stairs to the tower-room of her mansion. She searched the dusty book shelves in the turret and placed several tomes on a table in the center of the room. She laid a broom, with its brush-side up, against a wall behind a chair, and draped an old jacket over the back of the chair. She chuckled at the ridiculous superstition, but she honored this little ritual as a symbol of the Goddess' presence and protection.

Then she selected one ancient tattered journal and, clutching it fondly to her breast, carried it to a shelf of books in the downstairs front room. There she wove a spell to conceal it from all but the one it would choose.

That afternoon, Sophia followed a faint trail about a hundred yards down the mountain from the villa's east-facing walls.

Carefully balancing on her yew staff and making a slow, but certain descent down a hidden set of rock-hewn steps, she came to the squared-off entrance of a well-preserved Etruscan crypt.

Below her, the small fishing village, with its colorful stucco houses, hovered above boats bobbing at anchor in their cove. The familiar sight and its associated scents of the sea brought a powerful tinge of nostalgia. Then she entered the crypt and went to work on her preparations for the family gathering to come.

Late afternoon sunlight pierced the dark cave, etching sharp shadows and illuminating the ancient, but still brilliant, painted murals on the walls. In her long lifetime, Sophia had spent many hours here, communing with her ancestors. She stayed now for one final visit.

She recalled that she, herself, had been one of those ancestors, and that she had made some of these paintings in that remote civilization ages past. Now she added another small painting to mark her return in this current lifetime.

Leaving, she prayed, "Dear Goddess, I know not why you have set it this way, but it is your will which must prevail. I yield to your wisdom and benevolence. Let love bloom here again, in hearts reunited, to heal the scars of past hatred and hurt."

One late April afternoon, she visited a run-down cabin higher on the mountain, where a family of wolves made their den. "I am leaving you now, my wild brother and sister, but the raven will keep in touch. If my girls come to you, please protect them as you have protected me all these years." A sob forced itself from her throat when the big silver-coated male nuzzled her hand.

She removed a sacred talisman which had hung on her neck since she was seven years old. In a delicate silver casing, the amulet bore the carved ivory figure of a woman in hunting attire, accompanied by a wolf. Sophia wrapped the figure in soft doeskin and buried it securely in a rock cairn by the far back wall of the hovel. The wolves sat in silence, observing her ritual. When she left, they made sure to protect the treasure as the mother wolf moved her cubs and set their feeding nest against the rock cairn.

In the next few days, Sophia visited several other sites of ancient spiritual and mystical resonance around, and deep within, the Tuscan mountains of her villa. In each one, with incantations, spells and prayers, she left significant artifacts of the Craft.

Often in her wanderings, she heard the faint tinkle of miniature bells and saw the fluttering-sparkle of a familiar magic_ Fairies. She smiled to know the ancient small creatures would help bring her wishes to fulfillment. Toby mischievously batted a paw at the twinkling lights and was met by a scolding chatter, after which he put his whiskers forward in a cat-grin but left the invisible sprites alone.

In her final foray, Sophia visited a cathedral-size cavern deep in the mountain. Here, she hid her Athame, or Spirit Blade. The sacred dagger had been handed down from generations of Priestesses in the Rimini clan. As she left this powerful object behind, Sophia felt a stab of fear for Tuscan witches believe their legacy must be passed directly from one generation to the next in order for its magic power to survive. Sophia still did not know which of her progeny would have the strength and courage to carry this most powerful tool of Strega, Italian Witchcraft.

A small figure observed them from a perch on the rock ledge above a cascading waterfall. Toby eyed the fairy and blinked twice in recognition as it flew to Sophia's shoulder, where it shed tiny tears onto the old woman's shawl. Sophia stroked the fairy person's wings gently with her finger and murmured assurance. "We will meet often yet, my little sprite. Just keep watch for me."

But her own tears mingled with those of the little creature.

3

DEPARTURE

A few days later, the raven watched the old witch die. Perched in the ancient oak that splayed protectively over the cracked stone wall of the villa's courtyard, it observed death rites only a very few fortunate souls are given to commemorate.

An aquamarine and tangerine sky displayed a few pillowed clouds on this late-April afternoon in the Apennine Mountains of Italy. A soft southerly breeze wafted loamy earth and salty sea breath through the courtyard and birdsong piped from vine-yards on the sunny slope behind the house. Beyond the garden wall, in the olive orchard, several wild creatures attended her death vigil in solemn silence, but for a mournful series of hoots from an owl.

Sophia shifted on the canvas cot that had molded to her shape from decades of afternoon naps. The marmalade tabby stretched and rearranged himself in the crook of her arm and she was amused to see the cat grudgingly acknowledge the raven with a blink. Then he shut his eyes, rumbling a soothing purr.

Inside the courtyard, one huge bear of a man, Heironymous, plucked notes on a minstrel's lyre. He lounged comfortably with two younger men beside the fountain. Anthony, who reminded Sophia of a tall stag, thrummed heart's rhythms on a frame drum. Next to him, Giuseppe, reminiscent of a wiry ram, piped a gentle refrain on a flute.

"Our men manifest the Goddess' animal consorts near perfectly, don't they?" said Sophia, chuckling and looking up at Gina, who sat by her cot, humming along with the men's music.

"You mean the stag and the ram? You are right. But it seems a disturbing thought, given the fate of those horned gods in our myths," Gina lovingly fluffed the pillow and gently brought the old woman's long braid to lie over her shoulder.

Sophia eyed her niece teasingly. "As the sitting priestess of our Grove, you need to develop a more hardened attitude toward those old tales. The goat and stag are far more than mere sacrificial victims, you know_ being the symbols of the goddess' lover and her positive male escort." Sophia's chuckle caused the her to cough, so Gina gave her a sip of wine from a goblet by the cot. "And the bear is foster parent to all young acolytes." Sophia continued after she caught her breath. It had always amused her how the old myths gave animal forms to the male gods.

Gina shrugged. "Nonetheless, those old tales make me feel a bit uncomfortable. Maybe I'm just superstitious, but given the recent animosities between the Old Religion and the newly formed vigilantes of the Church, I worry about the safety of those two boys. After all, Tony and Giuseppe are involved in heretical underground and insurgent activities."

"Nonsense!" scoffed Sophia, "We no longer sacrifice our consorts. Look at Heironymous there. That old bear has been with me since the war when we rescued him from his downed airplane. I wouldn't dream of sacrificing him to some younger beast!"

"Yes, if it weren't for his covert position, we might all have been cited for heresy or worse, during the increasingly narrow-minded regimes of the past few decades." Gina laughed, but she looked troubled.

"Have we heard anything from Barbara and the girls yet?" Sophia changed the subject and her mood switched to one of worry. "Oh, why don't they come? Where are they?"

"Sta bene, Nana," soothed Gina. "Mario is calling them again at this moment."

Sophia leaned back and let her mind wander. Although she had long counseled that "death is but the doorway to the next life," she was terrified to cross the threshold when something important remained unfinished. She reviewed her preparations. She had warned Mario to guard against interlopers on the coming Beltane and May Eve festival nights. She had put records in neat order, so Gina, Giuseppe, and Anthony could continue managing the school without her. Heironymous had promised to keep close watch on all of them. And she knew they would do their best to guide her three grand-nieces_ Kara, Mimi, and Joanna_ in learning the lore and ways of the Strega.

She must trust to their skill and the Goddess' guidance. She must let go. Sophia's mind roamed between the present and the past.

Being childless, Sophia's greatest fear had always been that she would fail to pass on the ancient heritage to her own kin, a tradition going back for many centuries. Although the revered teachings would survive her, the wand of Strega Holy Priestess, so long having passed through the Rimini line, may now have been dropped.

Gina was skilled in casting spells and performing healings, and Barbara once showed talent in teaching the lore and telling the tales, but neither Gina nor Barbara had the warrior gifts required of the High Priestess. Sophia heaved a sigh of frustration and near despair.

She smiled at the memory of their fortuitous meeting with Heironymous. It turned out he had been an archeologist working on Etruscan burial digs before the war. He was trained in the mysteries, so he joined the Grove and soon rose to the position of High Priest in consort with Sophia as High Priestess.

He lived a double life, however, for he also attended seminary and became a Catholic priest in a small village church near Sophia's villa. In this position he was able to avert a good many threats to the mystery school from a self-styled band of reformists led by a man who posed as a church official, but was a practitioner of black magic.

Sophia sighed again. Although the Inquisition was long past, remnants of the hateful interrogations remained alive and well within the patriarchal branches of some religious orders. Gina had good reason to worry about the men's safety, she thought, but did not say.

At this point Sophia's reverie was interrupted by Mario, who strode into the courtyard from the house. He stopped at Gina's side. With an arm across his wife's shoulder, he leaned close to Sophia and spoke softly. "Scusi, my dears, I finally reached Barbara. They have been vacationing in Maine and had no phone there. They will be taking a flight tomorrow evening from New York City."

Sophia breathed a sigh of relief. "Grazie, dear Mario. Now perhaps I can let go of the burden and trust you all to finish what I have left undone."

Mario flashed a broad smile. "Va bene! No need for you to worry, Sophie. We are well rehearsed for the big show to come."

Gina frowned and muttered, "Barbara should have come months ago. It's that husband of hers, curse him."

"We need not blame John," Sophia said. "Barbara made her choice. And if I had been more insistent on her coming for visits with the girls, she would have found a way. I don't believe John could have stopped her if only I had stayed in contact. Instead, I pushed her out and turned to my work."

She glanced up at the raven, still watching from the oak tree. "Now you have another chance to repair the rift I failed to mend for all these years." Tears spilled and sprinkled the cat's coat. He casually licked them, shaking his head as if to dismiss her grief.

This made Sophia chuckle and she relaxed. Closing her eyes once more, she breathed raggedly, but deeply. A vision came to her of herself and her sister Dianna, with their great-aunt Iona. They were doing a ritual burial for a pet kitten who had died from wounds inflicted by a large hawk. While in the secret chamber underground, Sophia_ then about age nine_ saw an image of a tawny lioness standing at the entrance to the chamber. When she called out, the apparition disappeared, but Iona explained it was a spirit incarnation of their kitten and meant Sophia would be provided protection by the wild animals.

Eventually she found that her own pet tabby, Toby, was a shape-changer who transported the power of the mountain lion. But she also discovered her greatest enemy in this lifetime, an evil Melandanti wizard who folks called 'the Vulture,' controlled a vicious hawk with which her cat had more than once had to match powers. Heironymous was aware of the connection between the Vulture and John's family. She knew she could count on him to use that information most constructively in days to come.

These recollections helped her feel reassured that her lineage would be transmitted appropriately to the girls. The faithful animals would carry her messages to her family in her absence. She looked at the cat curled by her side who returned her gaze calmly, blinking twice to affirm her thought. Then he licked her cheeks dry of tears.

Sophia breathed another ragged gasp from deep inside. Struggling for air, she glanced up into the oak tree, and said to the raven, "Si, Melanthus, it is time now for us to fly."

She turned a loving gaze to her attending coterie. "Arrivederci, my dear ones. Each of them came and kissed her brow, and although tears glistened in their eyes, no one murmured sad regrets. They spoke good wishes for her journey and the promise to meet again and keep in touch.

Stroking the marmalade cat, she admonished, "You watch after them while I'm gone, Toby. You know how to reach me if needed."

Then, as the sun dropped into the sea, Sophia's soul flew away with the raven over the mountains. When she died her descendants inherited her legendary villa, her sacred Grimoire, a magic raven, a pet wolf, and a shape-changing cat to help them carry on her sacred mission.

4

TRANSITION

For a few moments Sophia can't decide if she is dreaming or if she has really died.

The divine Circle convenes at a crossroads where global, galactic, and celestial worlds converge. Here, in a fold of the universe, lives pass from one to the next and past meets future. This hallowed genealogy has bred progeny of mythological and supernatural strains as well as those of simple pagan stock. Sophia stands in the company of immortals.

Circling the ring of Beings, Sophia espies figures from vanished matriarchies, fabled kingdoms, and renegade tribes. The renowned, the notorious, and the deified all stand together here to welcome her into their midst. Many are legendary heroines and heroes of their particular sect, worshippers of Goddess and God - female and male deities - whose lineage and traditions weave back to the beginnings of civilization, and perhaps to the very origins of life on earth.

A profound serenity prevails over the group, which seems intimate in spite of its numbers. Individuals arrive while others leave intermittently, going about errands, passing between lives. Sophia has been here before and knows these momentary appearances or departures to and from the Circle can represent entire lifetimes in earth perspective. The Circle exists outside of time, in all-time and no-time.

At the center of the Circle, an altar of ebony and amethystine holds a clear crystal bowl flanked by silver candelabra. There, dressed in pure white robes with a simple silver circlet crowning her flame-red hair, stands the High Priestess of the Circle, Artemis-Diana-Aradia, Moon Goddess, the goddess of witches, gypsies, and pagans.

Sophia kneels before the great matriarch deity. "Dearest Goddess," she intones softly, "I come with heavy heart, for I have failed in my charge to bring my kin into the Circle. My grief burns my soul." Tears spill and puddle at the feet of the goddess, who grasps Sophia's hand and bids her rise.

"Grieve not, dear Sophia, your sacred Grimoire is, at this moment, in the hands of one who will inherit your sacred trust." She leads Sophia to the altar where they peer into the crystal bowl and see that Barbara and her family of daughters are newly arrived at the villa.

"Your Raven messenger is already there," the Goddess assures her. "You must trust in your companions on Earth to relay your instructions, as you guide the girls to discover the magic through dreams, and writings."

Sophia gazes around the circle and smiles. She was not dreaming. Happily, she knows she has really died. Once again.

5

A BIRD'S EYE VIEW

An enormous raven, gliding on warm updrafts from the sea, soars above the wave-torn coastline of a land steeped in history's mysteries.

Sun-shards, like faerie-beacons, spark off the azure waves stretching relentlessly westward. A storybook village clings to cliffs burnished orange in the sunlight. In the harbor turning tides lift sailboats like floating fragments of a torn letter. Gnarled trees grip their volcanic mountain like aged Mages perched upon a dragon's spine, and deep beneath their roots thrums the heart of the land; a secret Grotto steeped in Magic.

Now the bird veers eastward, aiming toward a turreted villa set in the hills above the town. Sitting high upon the mountainside overlooking the sea, the mansion nestles into its surroundings as if it grew right along with the ancient cypress, oak, and cedar woods surrounding it. A virtual citadel, the estate sprouted and spread its girth of pillared porticoes, walled courtyard, balconied gables, and crenellated tower from the seed of a primeval stone hut that survives at its core, still guarding ageless secrets.

The raven swoops over the countryside to survey what he knows lies there. Like a spider centered in her web, the villa casts forth tendrils in the form of hidden pathways, subterranean tunnels, and deep-cut ravines, to weave a network harboring a world of magic within the world of perceived reality. Concealed portals are situated at various positions on the villa's web: caves in rocky out-crops, a spring in a gully, a venerable Grove surrounding a crystal pond, the ruins of a temple to a Greek goddess, and higher in the mountains, an abandoned and partially demolished alpine cabin.

Each of the portal sites has its own strand in the web, linking the villa to the true heart of this volcano-sculpted seaboard, the Grotto that sprawls within the bosom of the land, far beneath its spine of mountains.

From the Grotto, a sacred spring sends arteries of meandering creeks and veins of tumbling cataracts bound for the sea. The same sea that once carried ancient mothers to this sun-baked peninsula to seed the land with a wisdom older than god.

A wolf howls nearby. Another answers from somewhere farther in the hills. The shadows of morning grow shorter with the climbing sun. The raven calls twice in reply to the wolves.

Then its attention focuses on a glimmering movement below. The bird flies above the sleek silver sedan as it skims along the coastal highway and watches it turn off to ascend the zigzag mountain road.

Finally the raven settles at the top of a hoary oak that shields the villa from the road below.

The bird, the tree, and the landscape all derive from primordial stock that echoes in the bloodlines of the car's occupants.

6

ARRIVAL

Kara shuddered and tried to analyze the source of her unease. Gnawing on her thumbnail, she gazed out the open sunroof of the Mercedes at a big black bird spiraling in the clear sky above them. It had kept pace with their car for the last quarter hour and she had the eerie sense that it was watching them. *Of course that's silly*, she told herself, *it's just a bird hunting prey, not us.*

With a vigorous swish of her pony tail, she brought her attention to the scenic Italian countryside they were passing through. Kara rode in the back seat between her two sisters, Jo and Mimi, all wedged amid a jumble of luggage.

Nine-year-old Mimi bounced with eager impatience, exclaiming over everything they passed. She waved vigorously at a donkey pulling a cartload of dried twigs. "The donkey smiled and waved his ear at me!" Mimi insisted in all seriousness. Kara laughed and tweaked her little sister's ear.

Every turn in the road revealed a new vista. Rounding another sharp curve, they came upon the sun-splashed ruins of a Greek temple perched on a bluff. At this, Kara's seventeen-year-old sister, Joanna, who had stared sullenly out the window for the past hour, looked at the tumbled shrine and murmured, "Oh! That is so lovely and romantic. But it is sad too."

Kara knew Jo was nursing resentment at having been uprooted from her busy social life in New York City. On this point Kara could empathize with her older sister for once. It had been hard for her to leave friends and miss a scout wilderness trek this summer.

In the middle of the front seat, their mother, Barbara, chatted with Uncle Mario as they passed ancient ruins overlaid by markers of modern habitation. A confetti of sailboats bobbed in a cove flanked by cave-pocked cliffs below.

"Scusi, John. We now come near the alleged Cave of the Cumaean Sybil." Uncle Mario pointed this out to their father, who sat on the passenger side grimly staring straight ahead. "Legends say one such prophetess was an ancestor of Sophia's and of our lovely wives." John grunted at Mario's banter, but said nothing.

As Uncle Mario maneuvered the car over the tortuous coastal highway, Kara saw the raven soar higher into the mountains to their left and swoop over a cluster of tile roofs. She guessed that must be the villa, wondered how long they would have to stay there.

Although her mother and Aunt Gina inherited the estate together when Sophia died, Kara knew her father wanted to give the whole thing over to Gina and Mario and get back home to the States soon. Kara was of two minds about this: It could be fun to stay and explore the old country, she thought but I think I'd rather get back home sooner."

The car snaked over steep hills and precipitous curves until it nosed its way into the bramble-hedged driveway of the villa. Wisteria and roses bloomed against crumbling stone walls. Their scents mixed with those of the churning sea-spume on the beach below and the lava-scorched earth of the mountains looming above. Kara's mouth felt dry. She tasted road dust blended with sea salt, fish, and wild onion. Not a bad taste, but oddly discomfiting_ like the combination of apprehension and curiosity that knotted her stomach.

A delicately sculpted life-size marble faun reached out to them from among rotting grape-vines on a garden slope. Kara frowned at the nude figure with its horns, erect penis, and smirking face. *It's not like I've never seen a guy without clothes on*, she thought, *remembering a few times at school when she and a couple of girlfriends spied on the boy's locker room.* That memory made her grin to herself. *No, I'm not a prude. So how come that horny little fellow gives me the creeps?*

"Demonic relics," growled her father, as if answering her silent question. These were the first words he had uttered since they began the drive from Rome to her mother's deceased aunt's villa. No one paid him any attention as the car came to a halt a few yards from the pillared portico of a saffron-toned stucco mansion.

Mimi, a freckle-faced gamin with a mop of strawberry blond curls, hopped out of the car immediately. "It's a totally magic place!" she exclaimed, turning in circles to take in the entire scene with bug-eyed innocence. "It's even got a tower just like in the fairy tales!"

A big orange tabby cat sauntered over to rub against Mimi's bare legs. She squatted down to pet it. "Hello puss! Will you be my guide to the magic castle?"

Kara noticed how the cat's green eyes mirrored the keen impish wit that sparked in her little sister's blue ones. She felt a twinge of envy at Mimi's already having found a friend in this strange place.

Mario confirmed Kara's impression when he said, "That's Toby. He was Sophia's constant companion, and he sure misses her. Looks like he's found a new friend." He winked at Kara and added, "Buona! He will be a good guide for you, Mimi."

Mimi gave Mario a dimpled grin. Then, with Toby leading the way, she skipped toward the house before others had even begun to disembark.

Kara clambered out of the car and grabbed her backpack. Slinging it over her shoulder, she took off at a trot after her sister, calling back, "She has no fear, the little scamp. I'd better go with her to make sure she doesn't scare up any other goblins." Kara said this jokingly, but a foreboding stabbed her gut as she caught up with Mimi on the pillared porch.

A horned faun's face stared at them from the carved oak door. Kara shook her head to clear the impression the thing had winked at her. But Mimi, unimpressed, stood on tiptoe to reach the brass knocker. Its loud clunk reverberated through the house, but no one came to answer.

Mimi tried the latch and the door opened soundlessly. Toby padded over the threshold and turned, beckoning them inside.

Kara followed Mimi and the cat into a room of astounding size and grace. Stale air and dim lighting at first made her hesitate, as if the place held danger or bad memories. She hurried to the south wall and unlatched tall shuttered windows that stood sentinel over the cliff-side. A magnificent view to the sea admitted a fresh mountain breeze carrying scents of cedar and pine mixed with ripening grain.

Below, the mid-morning sun burnished the red-tiled roofs of a quaint fishing village. For a brief moment Kara had the impression this entire scene was familiar to her, as if she was living in a distant past.

As she blinked and shook her head to clear the strange sensation her attention was diverted to a raven perched on a high branch nearby. Jet purplish-black feathers. Fierce looking talons. Sharp beak and beady eyes. It seemed menacing; an alarmingly large bird. It peered at Kara for several seconds before it took off with a harsh cackle that almost sounded like it was laughing at her. She tossed her pony tail. *Don't be silly. It's just another bird*, she muttered to herself, and turned to see what Mimi and the cat were up to.

But she was alone in the room. Mimi and Toby were gone! Her heart slammed against her ribs. "Mimi! Come back here! Don't go wandering off without me." Her voice was shaky with fright.

Trying to guess where they might have gone, she turned to go to a door in the far opposite wall when she ran smack into a woman who stood just a few feet from her. *I'm certain there was no one else in the room just a second ago.* This thought fueled the creepy sense of dread she had been feeling.

But the small dark-haired woman smiled as she grasped Kara by both arms to steady her. "Aspetta! No need to dash off, my dear. Your little sister is in no danger. I'm guessing you must be Kara?"

Kara could only nod and gasp to catch her breath. The woman's gentle voice soothed her, even while her mind screamed that something seemed very weird here.

Just then, Barbara came in from the porch. "Oh my! I feel as though I've just walked back into childhood." Kara saw her mother's eyes grow misty as she stepped gingerly from the vestibule into the big living space. But then she stopped in mid-step. Her mouth opened, but no words came out. For a long minute she stared at the woman standing with Kara. Then she said, "Gina? Is that you? For a minute I could have sworn you were Sophia."

Gina met Barbara's dumbfounded stare with easy laughter. "Ciao! Everyone says I look like her. But she was nearly a hundred years old when she died you know! I hope I don't look that old yet." The two sisters embraced a bit awkwardly. "It has been much too long. I still think of you as the adolescent wraith you were when you left with John. Age eighteen, was it?"

To Kara, the sisters appeared opposite images of each other. Her mother, tall with a slim athletic figure, had a fair freckled complexion, long curly reddish blond hair worn loose, and twinkling green eyes. Aunt Gina, whom Kara had only seen in pictures before, was much shorter with a petite sensuously-rounded figure. She was tawny complexioned with blue-black hair bobbed neatly in a classic shoulder-length style. Her deep brown eyes twinkled with a glint of amber. Kara thought both were strikingly handsome women.

Barb and Gina walked arm in arm, admiring and exclaiming at assorted objects decorating the room. An exquisite portrait of a woman in a Grecian gown hung in the west corner overlooking a stately grand piano. Kara thought the portrait bore some resemblance to her mother.

Aunt Gina affirmed Kara's impression when she said, "I always thought you look like our great grandmother, Selena, as she appears in that portrait."

Nearby, a spindle-legged console held a reading lamp and tea-tray next to a high-backed wing chair. Barbara's hand caressed the fringed shawl draped over the chair as she reached to pick up a small ivory figure of a bare-breasted woman in a flounced skirt. Snakes twined on its arms. "Sophia's collection of artifacts must be priceless," she said, gazing tenderly at the figurine.

"You know, most of this stuff was here before either of us was born, Babs." Gina chuckled, a throaty warm voice. "Who knows what surprises we'll find in this haunted treasure trove." But Kara thought her aunt sounded a little tense when she added, "I am so glad you got here at last!"

"I'm so very sorry." said her mother. "I know it's been hard for you dealing with everything. I feel terrible that you couldn't reach us sooner." She put her hand to her mouth, stifling a sob, as if she just now realized the fact of Sophia's death. Gina held out her arms and the two women embraced, crying on each other's shoulders. Kara busied herself looking around the room.

Bookshelves covered three walls from the polished wood floor to the high beamed ceiling. More ancient artifacts nestled among stacks of well-read volumes. Kara admired a hand-carved stag, a pair of wolves, and a mountain lion arranged in a group together. There were many female figurines in odd costumes, or wearing nothing at all, their protruding stomachs and big breasts exposed. And, on a high shelf, an exquisitely sculpted bird, its wings outspread ready to take flight. It made Kara think again of the one she'd just seen. She shivered with a vague sense of confusion.

Her mother's laughter caught her attention. "Your father will be incensed by all the artifacts of pagan worship in your great-aunt's home," Barbara said with a wry grin, holding up yet another horned faun figure_ this one a miniature in black marble offering forth a tiny silver cup. Kara returned her mother's smile, but she secretly shared her father's chagrin at the heathen reminders of their heritage.

Gina looked at them both questioningly. "Is John so against the old ways then?"

"It never sat well with John that I come from ancient matriarchal stock. I've always kept my personal beliefs quiet because of his staunch devotion to church dogma." Barbara laughed and winked at Kara. "We kid him about his family of wicked women sometimes though, just to keep him on guard."

Kara felt uncomfortable pretending to go along with the joke. Whenever Mom mentioned her early life in Italy, Dad made disparaging remarks that left Kara feeling very confused. She detested feeling muddle-headed. She shook her pony tail irritably.

Browsing absent-mindedly among the voluminous bookshelves, Kara selected a worn tome at random and began turning pages. Strange signs were drawn in an archaic script. Yellowed sheets of parchment held artfully drawn sketches of plants, trees, flowers, animals. A lot of the writing was in English, although some was in Latin, which Kara had studied a little in school. Fascinated, she tucked the old notebook into her backpack, intending to look at it later. Then, while her mother and Gina sat talking on an overstuffed floral chintz sofa, she set out to explore the villa's grounds.

7

KARA'S FIRST SURPRISE

Kara wandered through the orchard behind the courtyard wall. The redolent mountain air smelled pleasant, but foreign to her city-bred senses. She saw unfamiliar plants, elongated cypress trees, and gnarled olives and oaks, many of them hundreds of years ancient. She touched the rough bark of one wizened specimen and a shiver ran through her fingers. A slight electric charge vibrated her finger-tips, as if the tree responded to her touch. She shook her hand, wiped it on her jeans.

For just a fleeting moment Kara imagined quiet laughter and a pair of eyes peering from high in the tree. She walked a little faster without looking back. *Fairy magic*, she murmured, then wondered at such a silly idea. *It's just the magic tales I have always associated with this place. My imagination is playing tricks on me.*

She followed a well-traveled foot path farther up the landscape of volcanic rock and scrub pines on the mountainside. At a clearing, Kara sat down on a fallen log and leaned against a cedar tree facing toward the sea. Its rough bark pressed on her back, a gentle reassuring presence. She listened to the lap of perpetual surf on the beach below.

Breathing deeply, she realized something about this country felt comforting to her despite her underlying sense of disquiet. *It's as if I have returned after an absence, even though I have never been here in my life.* "Mom would call it an ancestral past-life memory, but I have never taken that stuff seriously." She spoke to herself aloud, almost as if there was someone there to hear her, which seemed natural in this wild place, not silly as it would back home.

"Kara Selena Marini," she chanted. She liked the lilt of her name and was reminded of a ballad her mother used to sing to them about a gypsy girl who became a Priestess of her tribe in an age when people worshiped a female god. When she was little Kara sometimes imagined being that priestess, loping long-legged through the wilderness with wolves for companions. But now, at age fourteen, she fancied herself far too reasonable to believe in fairy tales. In fact, Kara prided herself on being the realist in her quixotic family.

Relaxing against the tree, she recalled a dream she had on their flight to Rome last night. *Or was it yesterday morning? Time has become kind of erratic since we left New York City.* In any case, a bird, like the one she had seen from the car, spoke to her in the dream, though Kara could not understand its language. Whatever it said left her feeling both scared and excited, the same mix of feelings she had about the villa where Mom and Aunt Gina grew up with their Aunt Sophia.

The Witch. That's what they say the old woman was, but a good witch. Mom insists that witchcraft is about healing and preserving life, not evil spells like in the fairytales. But Dad calls it devil's work and gets angry at Mom for teaching us about our ancient Italian Strega heritage. Kara often felt caught in a tug-of-war between her parents.

She was the sensible one, the responsible one of the three girls. Or, so her father often told her. She took pride in playing that role, although at times she longed to be as free-spirited as Mimi.

She grinned at another thought: *Wouldn't Dad be horrified if I told him I thought I saw a fairy in that tree. He believes in devils and evil witches, but not in the possibility of good witchcraft and fairies like Mom does.* Gazing at the water-colored sunset, Kara wondered why her father could believe in the evil kind of magic, but not the good kind.

She leaned back to watch a murder of crows settle into some pines higher up the mountain. Listening to their chatter, she imagined their conversation might be about the new visitors at Sophia's villa. *Do they know she died? Do they miss her?* Ignoring the foolishness of these thoughts, Kara regretted that she had never known her great-aunt in person. Wistfully, she pictured how the wise old woman might have helped resolve her bafflement over her parent's opposing views of life.

Reminded of the journal she'd hidden in her back pack, she pulled it out. Flipping pages at random, she stopped at one with a drawing of the horned faun like the garden statue and those she had seen elsewhere around the villa. Beneath the illustration was a caption.

FAUNUS, THE HORNED GOD:
CONSORT TO THE MOON GODDES

Faunus is the consort of Diana, Goddess of the fairies and Queen of the Moon. Faunus, (also called Pan,) is the Beast-man of the Grove, and the Green-man who rules over wilderness and vegetation. He is horned and hoofed as a goat, and shares, with the great stag, the honor of becoming a sacrifice for the returning cycle of life. The Horned God reigns in the Grove for a year, when at an appointed time, in the Full of the Moon, he lays down with the Goddess to conceive his own successor. Then, at year's end, he is brought down, sacrificed, in order that the new king may be born and reign in his time. It is Nature's way, the way of all vegetation and wild life that Witches honor with seasonal ceremonies called Sabbat.

✳ ✳ ✳

Strange though this all sounded to her, Kara thought the Horned God certainly did not seem like a devil or anything terribly evil. *At least the smirking little guy can't exert much serious power since he only holds his crown for a year.* She grinned and shook her head.

The symbolism of Nature's cycles did not escape her, for Kara often reflected on the cyclic nature of Life. She saw how sometimes things that end actually reappear in a different way at a later time. *Like Joanna's boyfriends*, she joked to herself.

Dusk crept across the mountains. She tucked the fragile old journal into her pack and rose to leave when, from the corner of her eye, she glimpsed a movement and froze in place.

A very large dog, *or could it be a wolf?* sat in the shadow of a bush about six feet away, watching her guardedly.

Is it dangerous or merely curious? Kara's heart pounded as the beast rose from his haunches and ambled over to snuffle her back pack. And then, the handsome animal turned his golden-eyed gaze directly toward her, his tongue lolling and sharp teeth showing.

Is that a friendly smile or a wolfish grin?

A comic-book vision of herself as Little Red Riding Hood (with grandma already eaten) flashed through her mind.

Wake up! She scolded. *This is real, not a fairytale.*

8

SISTER REUNION

Barbara found it hard to believe she was home after being gone so many years. She and Gina sat side by side on the floral chintz sofa, haloed by the afternoon sun. They held hands, their fingers entwined automatically in the secret signal they'd invented when they were little girls.

Barb regarded Gina, two years older than herself, girlish in her petite size and pixy-like features. "Even at forty-six, you still look like a kid!"

Gina laughed and squeezed her hand. "Just a while ago you mistook me for our aged aunt!"

"You do look a lot like I remember Sophia during the war years." Barb gazed out the window at a cloudless azure sky. *Twenty-two years since I left,* she calculated. "But Sophia would have been in her mid-seventies by then! Nana never showed her age, did she? She always looked young, even to us kids."

Gina nodded. "Nana was ageless, as they say. But you know it's in our blood." She looked into Barb's eyes, her own twinkling with brown and amber lights. "Faerie blood, they say. You don't look much older than the kid you were when you left here either, only more world-wise perhaps?"

Barb thought ruefully of the years during which she'd lost contact with her family and heritage. "Worldly, but not very wise, I'm afraid. Oh! Gina, I'm ashamed for not getting back sooner. How can you ever forgive me? And, more to the point, how can I make it up to dear Sophie?"

Gina unclasped her hand, patted Barb's shoulder and got up to walk to the window. Barb stayed sitting on the sofa.

"The faerie blood thing. I am intrigued by the idea, and I've used the theme in my writing and painting. I told the girls many of the old tales over the years, much to John's displeasure. But, Gina, I must admit I find it hard to believe anymore, at least about myself and my daughters."

"Oh, Baba! The girls, they all three have the Rimini magic blood in full force. Perhaps even stronger than you and me. I could see it as soon as you arrived, and I thought how pleased Sophia must be to see them here."

Gina turned back from the window, walked to the bookcases, began searching through them. "Funny, I expected to find the old Grimoire, but I haven't been able to locate it since she died."

Barb watched her sister and thought *She may look young, but she speaks with the wisdom of centuries.* She shook her head. *I have been gone too long. John's accusations pierced me too deeply and I have become a doubter. I will need to work hard to regain my faith if I'm to be of any use around here.* Aloud, she said, "You sound so sure. About the girls, I mean, and Sophia knowing they have come. You haven't even met any but Kara so far!"

"But I observed you from Sophia's loft, as you arrived. To one with eyes to see, the light of the Gift shines brightly even in noonday sun."

"I've got a lot of catching up to do, Gina. How can I overcome the poison of guilt and doubt so I can be of help to you with the school, or anything else?" Barb got up and went to join her sister at the shelves of books and artifacts. "Perhaps just immersing myself in the memories will bring my faith back," she murmured.

Gina put an arm around her shoulder. "When you open yourself to the Goddess, she will return very quickly. Yet, to retrieve a lifetime of magic wisdom could take a bit of work. Doubt is the worst enemy we have, so hard to eradicate once it takes hold. Doubt has been the most potent weapon of our enemies throughout the centuries, for it erodes the heart and silently steals faith."

Barb felt shy with her sister as she listened to her speak the Teachings.

"You are the Priestess of our Grove now, aren't you? Sophia must have passed the Wand and all to you this spring?"

"The Wand, but not the Spirit Knife. That she put aside for another."

Gina glanced toward a pair of French doors on the adjoining wall. "Oh, look. Your elder daughter is in the courtyard. Perhaps we should go out and have introductions."

Barb stepped quickly to the French-doors leading to a dusky walled patio. The familiar old fountain and its goat-footed statue surrounded by potted hibiscus and roaming honeysuckle brought a new lump to her throat. But Barb stopped without opening the doors.

Watching through the glass panes, Barb saw Joanna, who had been sitting dreamily on a mosaic bench, suddenly jump up and stare across the courtyard. The girl took a step backward, apparently surprised, and then broke into her flirtatious cover-girl smile.

From the dappled stand of olive trees behind the stone wall, a stocky dark-haired youth entered through the garden gate. He flashed an equally disarming smile, and the two young people fell immediately into conversation.

Barb turned to Gina. "Someone else is there. Who is that young man?"

Gina came and stood by her. "Oh! That's Giuseppe. He's the fellow who helped Sophia with the grounds and upkeep of the villa for the past few years. He is also a disciple of hers and a loyal member of the Grove. He was one of the orphans Nana took in after the war."

Barb grinned wryly. "I surely don't recall anyone that handsome coming here. I think I might not have gone away, had he been around!" she exclaimed, joking. "But, of course, I gave little attention to things going on at the villa when I was in my late teens."

Gina laughed heartily. "Giuseppe was a mere toddler of two or three when he arrived here, just shortly before you left. You would've hardly had any reason to notice him!"

Barb laughed too. "Oh, I'm relieved to learn he is only in his mid twenties then. He looks older." As she watched Jo chatting amiably with the roguish-looking fellow, she scolded herself for feeling a twinge of envy.

"Well! It didn't take my daughter long to find a new boyfriend. Kara thinks her elder sister is a fool for chasing after boys, but I can identify with Jo. She is much like me at seventeen, I'm afraid; very flirtatious and romantic and more sophisticated by far, than her age would merit."

Barb turned away from the doors.

"Let's get outside for a bit while the day is still bright." she needed to be out of the house where memories were encroaching on her too quickly.

Gina strode toward the front doors and Barbara followed, "I understood you to say Joanna is talented in music and dance. Has she performed professionally yet?" Gina asked.

Barb sat down on the portico steps, leaned against one of its Corinthian columns. Breathing in the fresh spring warmth, familiar scents she'd known as a girl wafted around the mountainside.

She sighed with some exasperation, "Joanna had bit parts in a couple of off-Broadway musicals, and she is a dedicated performer, but she lacks a personal vision. In fact, she's been neglecting her practice and studies in favor of a rather rebellious social life."

A squirrel chittered at them from a tree by the corner of the house and Barb watched it scamper down a tree limb to the ground.

She continued, "Jo has become quite defiant of convention lately, which I can identify with too, of course. But we worry where it may lead in this day and age in America."

She bent to pick up a pinecone and tossed it to the squirrel.

"I'm relieved to get her here for the summer, away from those temptations." Barb stopped to reflect. "So far, she has not gotten off on too bad a track, no drugs or such at least. I think she takes care of herself sexually too, but what does a mother know?" She sighed again. "You are lucky, Gina. Boys must be much easier to bring up."

The squirrel ducked into a hollow of the tree with the pinecone.

Gina sat on the ledge of a stone planter, her legs crossed at the ankles. "Anthony is a good kid, but he's been in his share of trouble. He takes after his father as a daredevil, and very involved in our country's current political struggles, which never end of course." She shook her head. "I do worry about him. Our national group lost three members last year when a rally was bombed in Milan."

"Goodness! It reminds me of when Sophia and her friends were partisan resistance fighters during the war. Their movement helped to defeat Hitler's forces in Italy, but so many lost their lives." Barb shivered at the memory. "I remember that Nana would not let us join, even though we were old enough."

"But we had plenty of excitement at home, hiding the refugees who came from around the countryside," Gina added.

Barbara saw the squirrel leap between branches to another tree in search of nuts. "I'd forgotten how dangerous it was in those years, but how thrilling for us kids."

Gina nodded solemnly. "Even though the partisans captured and executed the Fascist, Mussolini, Italy continues to be harassed by crooks in government, the Mafia, and the corrupted factions of Church leadership. Things have grown worse again in the past decade. And a resurgence of anti-paganism has taken hold pretty strongly in our district."

Gina stroked the head of a sculpted lion on the stair-post while she paused to think. "Sophie had some rather contentious interactions with a particular minister at the Vatican." She shrugged her shoulders, shaking off bad vibes.

Barb tried to change to a more pleasant subject. She wasn't ready to hear about the problems facing them with Sophia's villa and school yet. "Gina, do you remember the tunnels that led to that grotto where we stayed, during the bombing?"

"Of course" Gina raised an eyebrow. "The passage from the cellar was boarded up some years ago, but it is still viable. I think Sophia had it covered by wine racks to hide it from some nosey archeologists who came visiting one summer. They claimed to be from a university in France, but she suspected they were spies of the church or the mob."

Gina chuckled, shaking her head. "Poor Sophie, she was so paranoid in the last years that she did not even use a telephone. She communicated mostly by telepathy or through the underground. But, then it turned out that she had good reasons to be paranoid."

Gina jumped down from her perch and stretched her arms. "Come on, let's take a walk to the Grove before we make supper."

A raven cawed from the top of a tall pine nearby. The squirrel was back at its hollow tree with an acorn.

Barb got up and followed her sister along the driveway and to a path leading off the side, up the mountain. "Surely the Church isn't still witch-hunting," exclaimed Barb in mock horror. But a shiver of fear snuck into her as she recalled how John's family hated the Strega.

"A strong anti-pagan faction has been building propaganda against us for several years now," explained Gina, frowning. "Anthony is with a theatrical underground movement that works to promulgate the old traditions through the arts. They are being harassed more and more. It terrifies me to think how close he came to being killed once in a so-called police raid against a mime troupe he works with. And he has been arrested more than once on trumped up insurrection charges against the government. It used to be subtle, but lately a local group of vigilante's have become overtly threatening."

"What about Giuseppe? Is he one of Anthony's rebel group too?"

"Not exactly. He seems to be a loner and doesn't join the demonstrations or anti-establishment activities. In fact, although the two boys grew up pretty close, they've developed a kind of rivalry lately. I'm not sure what it's about, except that Anthony speaks of Sep as a 'fox', meaning someone who is tricky, unpredictable." Gina shook her head. "I can't pretend to understand the permutations of Anthony and his group. I do know that both boys are loyal to the Strega, but each in his own way."

Barbara kicked at a clump of toadstools absent-mindedly. Then she remembered toadstools were sacred to the fairies, and she made a silent apology by dropping a small token from her shirt pocket, a piece of mint candy.

Gina smiled at her. "Glad to see you haven't forgotten the fairies, Sis."

Barb resumed their former conversation. "I had no idea there is still so much intrigue around the old traditions. In America the Wiccan movement and other New Age spiritual groups are all the rage. No one questions the use of psychic and other divinatory techniques. In fact, there is a kind of craze for all sorts of pseudo magical beliefs these days."

"But you don't hear about the real stuff much, do you? Here, and all over Europe, there is the same kind of New Age psychedelic mania for Tarot, Astrology, I Ching, fortune telling. You name it. But where the real mysteries are practiced and taught, few know and fewer will take the trouble and risk to learn," said Gina. "The truth is, they are still afraid of the ancient pagan spiritual knowledge since the distant days of the Church's first cursed persecutions and vile lies."

Barbara slowed her pace. Her thoughts were troubled. "All this will surely feed John's contempt of our family tradition and fuel his scorn of the school. I'm going to need all the help you and Mario and the others can give me to persuade him to let us stay for the entire summer. He would rather I leave it to you and return to the US in a month."

"We are prepared to deal with John's animosity, Baba. It could be no surprise to us after these many years. Sophia left clear instructions. It is important that the girls remain here long enough to be introduced to the basic mysteries at least." Gina sounded determined, but not angry.

A familiar pang tugged Barbara's gut. "I failed so miserably, haven't I?"

"That's no longer important. We all failed in a sense," Gina smiled. "We have new opportunity before us, so let's make the best of it. Perhaps this is as it should be, who knows? Only the Fates, and they don't tell." Gina patted Barbara's back.

Barb's mood lightened a bit. "We may be able to initiate Jo in the mysteries quite easily. She is inclined to romanticize things, but she's a quick study, and she's got a definite mystical side to her.

The squirrel was following along in the near-by trees, searching for more nuts.

"Mimi is already a bewitching little charmer. But don't you think nine is too young for the mysteries?" Barb glanced at Gina.

"You were five and I was seven when we came to live with Sophia." Gina reminded her. "Didn't take long for us to catch on to the basic ideas of magic, did it?" They both laughed, and Gina added. "In fact, we know a younger mind is always more open to unseen possibilities, yet less vulnerable to the dark side, because of freedom from the doubt that plagues older minds."

Barbara nodded. "But Kara, she's another case altogether. Very incredulous, skeptical, hardheaded since she turned teenage. She tends to sympathize with her father in judging magic as foolishness."

Barb watched the squirrel precariously swing between branches, reaching for another nut.

"It's not up to us, Baba. Other forces are directing things here, you know. We must let go and be alert to all possibilities." Gina stepped over a fallen log, stopped to brush some thistledown off her slacks.

Barb saw the squirrel, now with the new acorn in its mouth, catch another branch and head back toward the house.

Gina stopped at a stand of large age-weathered trees surrounding a clear circular pond in a quiet meadow. "Before we enter the Grove, let's take a moment to get centered. Our conversation has roused distress that should not be carried into the sacred space. We need to do a spell of cleansing and grounding."

They knelt together at the base of a large oak, took a few deep breaths, laid their palms flat to the ground.

"Goddess, lift away our negative thoughts and open our minds to your beauty here in this sacred space." Gina spoke softly, her face raised to the sky. Then she bowed her head. "Mother Earth, guide us and let your wisdom prevail. Blessed be."

They stood up and walked hand in hand into the Grove.

But they came to an abrupt halt at the sight before them. There, marring the pristine beauty of the bower, lay a dead owl. Its neck had been snapped so sharply that its magnificent head was twisted upside down and turned backward. Its huge eyes starred up at them blankly.

Barbara stifled a scream.

Gina ran and knelt by the bird, but did not touch it. "Malandanti did this. Such a big owl is a vicious fighter and has few natural enemies. This is meant as a warning to the Grove. We need to tell the men right away."

Barb came and knelt by Gina. She reached out to stroke the beautiful mottled brown and white feathers.

"No!" Gina gently pushed Barb's hand away. "Don't touch it. Vile energy still surrounds the bird's body." Gina reached into her pocket and took out a handful of dried herbs, scattering them all around the mutilated corpse while she murmured a spell of protection.

"We will come back to get the owl before the burial service for Sophia tomorrow evening.   It must be intended as her soul-companion in this passage. We have been troubled at the prospect of selecting a sacrificial soul-mate for her interment ceremony. Looks like the Malandanti solved that problem for us." Gina's chuckle sounded grim.

Barbara realized at last how serious the challenge to the school was, and what a great task lay before them to convince John, guide the girls, and save their heritage.

Would she be able to rebuild her own faith in magic soon enough to do her part? She spoke none of these doubts to Gina as they hurried back to the villa.

9

MIMI EXPLORES

Sophia's villa whispered secrets and beckoned Mimi to follow the cat through the house's labyrinthine spaces. A dim
hallway zigzagged past high-ceilinged rooms inhabited by
shrouded shapes. Dust-mote phantoms and spider-web wraiths
revealed themselves in dingy daylight. Toby scrabbled at suspect mouse-holes, while Mimi inspected mounds of sheet-cov-
ered furnishings.

Echoes of a long-ago piano recital seemed to hum in the
walls of a music room, where a big bass viol leaned, like a congenial host, against a corner wall. Mimi plucked a couple of its
strings. The thing was badly out of tune and made a sound like
the moaning of a very sick ghost. Mimi giggled and scurried
out into the hallway to the next room.

Here, a telescope peered blindly through a large, but sooty,
skylight into the blue-sky afternoon. A pair of binoculars rested
by a bay-window that overlooked wooded hills. Mimi held them
to her eyes and watched a large blurry black shape lift off from
a tree beside the side gate. Toby perched on the window-seat,

chattering at the bird. Mimi patted the cat on his head. "Stick by me, Toby. Like Kara said, we don't want to scare up any old goblins!" She laughed when he put his whiskers forward in a cat-grin.

At the end of one hallway, a large room brightly lit with tall banks of windows on two walls proved to be Sophia's studio. It held a desk the size of a single bed covered with piles of yellowed papers, boxes of old photographs, and containers holding tubes of oil paints and brushes. Mimi started to flip through the photos, but Toby dashed to a door at the corner wall. "Mrorow," he called, looking back at her. She followed him and found a broad vestibule with stairs winding upward.

"Why, Toby, this must be the tower," Mimi exclaimed, dashing up the steps, the cat at her heels. The second floor housed an elegant master bedroom suite. Toby eagerly leapt onto a great canopied bed and began kneading the pillow. "Was this where you slept with Sophia?" Mimi tickled him behind his ears, and left him to his memories while she tiptoed around the room. She felt a bit naughty snooping into Sophia's private space, even though Sophia was no longer alive to care. *Maybe her ghost is watching us,* thought Mimi, with a shiver of guilty excitement.

On a reading table in the adjoined sitting room, she examined a photograph of two little girls. One wore a sailor's hat cocked jauntily on her curls. There was a cat, very much like Toby, on the other girl's lap. Mimi guessed the picture was of her Mom and Aunt Gina when they were about her own age. She returned to the vestibule, and forgetting Toby, cautiously took the stairway to the next level.

Glancing briefly into a room with two single beds hung in frilly flowered canopies, Mimi was compelled to continue upward. She hesitated-- *what if someone is up here?* She shook her head. *No one came up while we were downstairs or we would have heard them.* Nevertheless, she crept up the last steps stealthily and stopped to listen for sounds on the other side of the heavy door to the upper room. She tapped lightly, then pushed. It groaned on its hinges, scraping against the slate-tile floor, and opened onto a stark stone-walled room with narrow windows on all four sides.

She stopped with an intake of breath. Someone was standing silently in the far corner! The light in the room was dimly shadowed, but she thought she could make out the head of a person peering at her from behind a chair. "Oh, excuse me," whispered Mimi. "I didn't think anyone was here." But there was no answer, so she hesitated at the doorway and let her eyes grow more accustomed to the dusky light.

Gradually Mimi was able to distinguish the shape of a broom made from a tree branch and straw twigs. It had been left propped in the corner with its twiggy brush-side standing up so it looked like some wild-haired creature. An old coat was draped on a chair in front of it, so it did kind of resemble a person if you peered through foggy eyes. Mimi laughed at her own startled fright. Toby came and bumped against her leg, which encouraged her to keep exploring.

A round oak pedestal table and two wooden ladder-back chairs sat on a faded oriental rug in the center of the room. Some books had been placed by an oil lamp on the table. She glanced at the titles: 'A Guide to the Central Apennines: Abruzzo and Molise'; 'The Art of the Etruscans'; 'The Young Italy Movement and Garibaldi; 1830-1870'. Mimi quickly flipped through some colored pictures, but left the books as they were.

A large pine armoire stood in an alcove, one of its doors ajar. Mimi peeked in. It smelled of mothballs and held a worn green wool cape and a pair of smelly rubber boots. Tucked into one end of the roomy cabinet was an old fold-away cot and mattress. The only other furniture in the room were two bookcases that leaned crookedly under the weight of their over-stacked shelves. Niches in the stone walls hoarded more stacks of dusty volumes, and deep window ledges were cluttered with collections of rocks, feathers, birds' nests, jars of herbs, dried flowers, and seashells.

Mimi dragged and clambered onto a chair to look through each of the four windows. Eastward, a burbling stream carved a rocky ravine. Deep-forested mountains climbed northward. A flower-strewn meadow lay on the west, guarded by a stand of tall trees. To the southwest, sparkled the wide sea. Mimi's mind imagined it through a haze of fantasy as a genuine fairytale world.

A soft sound startled her from her perch. She scrambled down and turned to find Toby scratching at yet another door off the stair landing. "So, there is still more you want to show me, my little guide?" Opening what she had assumed to be a closet door, Mimi followed the cat up one more flight of stairs and found herself on the battlement of the tower. Its tall crenellated walls surrounded her. "Wow! This is really cool!"

She noticed Toby was staring pointedly at one corner of the parapet. Mimi peered into the corner but saw nothing remarkable except a rather large cobweb clinging to the stone.

"Well, it's about time you got here. We have been waiting for ages and ages!" A small bell-toned voice scolded from somewhere just above Mimi's head.

She turned toward the door, but no one was there. Toby continued to stare at the corner, so she looked more closely at the cobweb. Gradually, it took a shape, solidifying as it shivered in a breeze that Mimi could not feel. She stared and blinked her eyes. Toby sat licking his paw nonchalantly.

Mimi again turned to the cobwebbed ledge, where there now sat a tiny creature. It was about the size of her Barbie dolls, only chubbier and not so stiff-legged. It wore an iridescent robe in shades of green over a plain amber colored tunic. Silvery white hair cascaded over its back in a mist. Suddenly, the creature's robe flared into a pair of wings and the fairy-person fluttered down, like a moth, to alight on Mimi's shoulder.

"She has been expecting you ever so long, you know." The fairy continued scolding. "But now it will be a lot harder for us to get you there." The fairy tweaked Mimi's ear. "She waited as long as she could, but she finally had to leave it up to us."

Mimi felt chastised although she had no idea what she had done wrong. Looking into crystal green eyes that stared at her with wily mirth, Mimi found her voice. "Who is this 'she' you're talking about?" She fell into conversation as if it was an ordinary event for her to speak with fairies. Mimi often did talk to her imaginary friends, in fact, but she had never seen one of them in the flesh before.

"Why, Sophia, of course, silly. Who else would be waiting for you here?" Mimi was baffled. "My great aunt Sophia died last week. I never even knew her. How could she be waiting for me? And, why?"

"Because you are the only one who can hear what she has to say," answered the fairy impatiently. "My name is Tinklebell, by the way."

Mimi laughed out loud, "You have to be kidding me. That name is right out of Disneyland. It's too obviously fairytale. No one will believe me when I tell them about you." She looked into eyes hugely glaring in the tiny face, and demanded, "Make up another name for yourself."

"Why should I? It's the name Sophie gave me years and years ago. I like it." with a toss of her hair, Tinklebell stared defiantly back at Mimi. "You aren't s'posed to be telling others about me anyway. We are a secret." She squinted her eyes suspiciously. "Can you keep a secret? If not, Sophia must have sent me to the wrong girl."

"Oh, don't worry. I like secrets. I'm very good at them, so you needn't worry." Mimi realized the two of them were arguing in the way she argued with her sisters sometimes. It felt familiar, yet disappointing. *Aren't fairies supposed to be sweet and nice and purely good? Maybe I have them confused with angels.*

Tinklebell read her thoughts. "I'm not any angel," she exclaimed rather disgustedly. "Sophia is kind of an angel now, but not really either," She thought for a minute, "Anyway, who wants to be sweet and nice all the time. It's much more interesting to be a sassy trickster. That's what Sophia says I am." She aimed a smirk at Mimi. "So are you."

Mimi had to grin too, thinking how she enjoyed playing little tricks on people and challenging adult's rules. Kara called her their imp, or scamp, meaning she often got into trouble that worried others, but not herself.

Mimi frowned and looked at the fairy, then at Toby. "But how can I keep this tower a secret? Everyone knows it is here, and Kara will want to come up to see it for sure."

"We will meet in another secret place, where I can show you something Sophia left for you," said Tinklebell mysteriously. "Toby will see that you find me again soon." Then the fairy flitted back to her cobweb and disappeared with a tinkling laugh.

Mimi picked up the cat and hugged him. "What a wonderful place this is, Toby!" He wriggled to be put down, but purred loudly. "I wish we could keep the tower room a secret. But Kara is sure to find it anyway, so I guess we will have to show her. That way, I can claim first rights to it." Mimi smiled happily as they hurried back to the main floor.

10

INTRODUCTIONS

B ack downstairs, in Sophia's studio, Mimi took more time to explore. She uncovered a painter's easel supporting an unfinished oil painting. Rendered in the muted colors of opalescent moonlight, it featured a horned faun, like those in the yard and garden. Behind the faun stood a blue-robed woman holding a curved knife, and behind that figure rose a full moon shadowed by the flight of a huge bird. The image caused Mimi to shiver, but she felt drawn into it, rather than repelled. Standing mesmerized by the painting, she didn't notice when someone entered the room.

She was startled by a pleasant baritone voice at the door. "Sophia was a well accomplished artist, you know." Mimi turned to see a wiry fellow with gray-blue laughing eyes casually striding across the room. He stood next to her at the easel, silently contemplating the picture for a moment. Then abruptly he brought his attention back to her and said, "Buona sera, Signorina. My name is Giuseppe."

The stranger bent down to meet her face to face, and gently took her hand in his. "I have been the caretaker for Sophia's home and school for several years." His eyes clouded a moment and he glanced at the painting again. "I miss her so much," he murmured with a sigh. But then he smiled wickedly and added, "But I am pleased her death has at least brought us the visit of two such charming young women to our country."

Behind Giuseppe stood Joanna, staring about the room with a look of rapture. Mimi immediately deduced her older sister's rapture was directed toward the handsome young man, rather than toward the ancient artifacts surrounding them. Tickled by his flattery, Mimi teased back. "There is a third young woman too. Wait 'til you meet our sister, Kara. She's the most charming of us all!"

That comment brought a look of stunned disbelief to Jo's face, which sent Mimi into a spasm of giggles. Then, picking up Toby, who was impatiently winding around her legs, Mimi bounced out of the room and headed for the next door along the hallway.

"No! Don't go there!" Giuseppe shouted just as Mimi reached for the knob. She pulled it open a crack before heeding his cry. Glimpsing a rough-hewn staircase leading down a cobwebbed archway of stones, Mimi sensed the allure of another secret. She closed the door.

"Why? What's down there?"

"It's really nothing. Just an old wine cellar. But it could be dangerous because there is no light," Giuseppe said. Then he laughed lightly and added, "I would not want one of my pretty new friends falling and getting hurt."

Mimi resolved to investigate that mystery later. For now, she was content to move on to the next doorway, an open arch that led into the kitchen and dining area. At the far end of the long narrow room, sliding glass doors opened into the courtyard.

They found her father and Uncle Mario standing before a huge stonework fireplace, its soot-blackened cooking hearth cluttered with well-used pots and pans. The two men were in a heated discussion with their backs to the doorway and did not immediately notice them.

"It's pure devil's work, all this paraphernalia," John was shouting as he gestured to nearby cabinets filled with vials and jars of unnamed contents. Dried bunches of herbs hung from rafters in the high ceiling. Wall shelves held shapes of braided straw, sachets of colorful rags, baskets of stones, shells, and the skeletal remains of small animals. From a sconce a dried snake-skin twisted in elaborate furls.

"Now, John," said Mario, his voice in a level but authoritative tone. "You know the old woman was a shaman. There's no deviltry in that. It's an age-old healing art well respected in some circles. Your own wife grew up under its influence. Would you call that devil's work?"

"If I'd known what Barb believes in when I met her, I would never have married her," John growled. "Of course, once I fell in love with her it didn't matter," he muttered, sounding pensive. He shook his head and resumed his diatribe with scathing bitterness. "But I won't stand for her getting involved in this damnable school you want to run. Better it should die with the old woman."

Her dad's face was flushed and Mimi saw the veins at his temples standing out like warning flags. She realized this was not a safe time to intrude, and began to back out of the doorway, bumping into Giuseppe right behind her. The sound caught the attention of the two men and they turned in unison to greet the trio of young people who had just witnessed their dispute.

"Ciao!" said Mario, shrugging a shoulder as if to discount what they had just heard. "Is Giuseppe giving you girls a good tour of the place?"

Mimi's father made a weak attempt to cover up his anger, "Quite a spooky old joint, huh kids? I wouldn't want to get left here alone in the dark, would you?" He laughed, pointing to the snake skin.

"I think it is totally wonderful!" said Mimi. She was suddenly determined to defend her castle and its magic from her father's disdain. "Toby has already shown me the tower room where I am going to sleep. There is nothing spooky about it." She stamped her foot in defiance.

Mario laughed out loud and Giuseppe went forward to shake John's hand and introduce himself.

Jo winked at Mimi, so she relaxed and forgot to be angry for the moment. But she definitely did not like what she had heard her father say, and she felt bound to protect her fairy friend's secret.

Toby's whiskers tickled her leg, and she bent to stroke him while the others conversed. She thought her father looked very uncomfortable, and she didn't care.

11

SHARED DISCOVERIES

While the others continued their casual conversation, Mimi and Toby went looking for Kara. They met her returning from her walk. She came through the front door into the vestibule of the main room and stamped some mud off her sneakers before entering. "Hi Mim! What have you two been up to?" Kara bent to stroke the cat. "I thought I'd lost you earlier, but Aunt Gina assured me you were okay."

"Oh! Kara, I have something wonderful to show you. Come with me, right away." Mimi turned back into the hallway and led Kara into Sophia's studio. Kara looked around the cluttered room with interest. "Wow! This is neat. I bet Mom could enjoy using this room to do her art work!"

Mimi was relieved to see her sister's mood had grown more cheerful and less anxious from how she'd seemed when they first arrived. "This house is just full of neat things!" Mimi exclaimed. "There's a music room that Jo would really enjoy for dance and stuff. It even has a little stage for performances.

And, there is an observatory room with a skylight and telescope I bet you will really get into!"

She looked back and flashed her sister a grin. "But that's nothing compared to the other cool place I have to show you." Hesitating briefly, she added, "but you have to promise to let me have that room because I found it first, okay?"

Kara laughed. "Oh sure, honey. Whatever it is, finders keepers is okay with me." She hooked her backpack over her shoulder. "So what is it? Lead on! I have a bit of an adventure to tell you about too."

The two girls trooped up the tower stairs with Toby leading the way. He swished his tail rather sharply a few times, and Mimi took that as a reminder to her to be careful what she said to Kara. She had to be sure not to give away Tinkle's secret. But it would not be easy, especially if Kara had a secret to share with her too.

They looked into the rooms on each level, but headed quickly to the roof of the tower. As they came up to the roof, Mimi darted a glance toward the corner. The cobweb hung unmoving and empty. She felt a little disappointed, although she had not really expected to find the fairy still here.

Kara seemed duly impressed with the watchtower. "What a great hideaway! I'd love to come up here to read sometimes," she looked questioningly at Mimi. "Would that be okay with you?"

"Of course," Mimi assured her, "but I want the tower loft room for mine."

"No problem on my account. You might have to persuade mom and dad though." Kara laughed.

Mimi shrugged. "I'm mad at Dad. I heard him say some really mean things about Aunt Sophie. I hope he lets us stay for the summer like Mom planned."

"Me too," Kara said. "I wasn't sure I felt that way before, but I've run into some things that make me want to stay around and learn more about this place and its history."

"What have you found?" Mimi was intrigued. She knew her sister had endless curiosity about all sorts of things, so it was not surprising if she had been hooked into wanting to know more about this fascinating place. Something about the flush in Kara's cheeks and the eagerness in her voice when she said she wanted to come up to the parapet to read gave Mimi a hunch there might be more to it than simple curiosity. *Why read in secret?* But Mimi did not ask. *I have my secret to keep, so she can have hers.*

When the big black bird landed on one ledge of the tower roof, however, Kara visibly startled and frowned.

"What's wrong Kara?" Mimi asked.

"That bird. It seems to be following me around. Or, at least I keep seeing one like it everywhere I go." She shivered and looked away from the bird. "Gives me the creeps."

Mimi saw Toby and the bird eyeing each other. It did not look to her as if they were menacing, more like the two creatures were familiar with each other, maybe even friends.

"I don't think the bird is creepy at all," defended Mimi. "Toby seems to know him and be perfectly comfortable." The bird cocked its head from side to side but made no sound.

"Yeah." Kara scoffed. "You would imagine that. You always think everything's friendly. I bet you would have tried to make friends with the wild dog I ran into in the woods too. But you just can't be so trusting, Mimi. You never know about some wild animals, so it's best to steer clear of them."

"What wild dog, Kara?" Mimi ignored the scolding.

"Oh, I was walking up along a path in the woods behind the house and sat down to r..., to rest. There is a cool view of the mountain and sea at one overlook that I want to show you sometime soon."

She glanced at the bird warily. It perched silent and still. "Jeez! It seems to be listening to us!"

"Maybe it is," Mimi countered casually. "I know Toby can understand what I'm saying, and I don't think it is at all odd if the other animals can too. Especially around a place like this where everything is so magical." She caught herself before she said any more about the magic.

"Yeah. Magic." Kara shrugged. "I used to believe in those stories when I was your age. But now, I know everything has a practical and logical explanation. Magic is just a word."

"CRAWK" said the bird. It ruffled its feathers vigorously, and lifted off over the trees. They watched it until it disappeared into the hills. "Well, I guess if it does understand, it got the message that I'm not going to be available for any conversations!" Kara laughed.

Mimi hated to hear Kara speak that way. She had hoped to get her middle sister to join her in whatever secret things Tinklebell was going to tell her or show her. But now Mimi vowed to keep it to herself. She felt sad and alone with it until she remembered she had Toby's help, and maybe this strange bird too? Mimi sent a silent apology to the bird. But all she said to Kara was, "I wish you hadn't said that."

"I must admit, though," Kara's voice sounded softer, more thoughtful. "The animals I have seen so far around here are very unusual." She reached over and fondled Toby around the head and neck. "Like that wild dog. He seemed as if he almost recognized me and wanted to be friends."

"So, what happened?"

"I did not know what to do. I just stood still until he finally wandered away." Kara looked up into the sky and frowned. "He was so big. Really looked more like a wolf than a dog, but wolves don't come that close to people. At least not that I have ever heard of." Kara's voice drifted off and she gazed over the parapet awhile. "Maybe I will go back to that meadow and see if he's still around there tomorrow. If it is a stray dog, it's probably lonely. I wouldn't mind a companion in this place, like you have in Toby."

Mimi still could not forgive Kara for scaring away the bird. *It shows me that I can't trust her with the secret,* she thought.

Kara does not want to believe it, but I know the animals and lots of other things around here are magical!

Kara reached over and gave Mimi a quick hug. "We'd better go down and claim our rooms and get settled before dinner." She didn't notice that her little sister hadn't returned her hug.

12

FIRST NIGHT- BARB

The family settled into the tower that nestles on a border-land of wild growth at the northwest corner of the house. Legend has it that its bottom level and foundation were from the original hermitage built by Aradia, legendary early ancestress of the Marini lineage, in the 1300's. Certainly that portion of the house was hewn right out of the hillside's primordial rock. Used primarily as a wine cellar in recent years, it harbors hoary cobwebbed apparitions within its murky decay.

But above that ancient edifice a descendant, (some say Aradia's granddaughter, Karamena, who was a warrior witch) in a later century, constructed the square tower with its four levels of airy high-ceilinged rooms and its roof watch-station battlement. This is the part of the house that Sophia had retained for her private quarters. The upper room had been her sanctuary. She called it her 'loft' and spent many hours there in meditation, sending and receiving messages to and from others including some in forms and states of being unknown to most mortals.

The rest of the house had always been open to friends and strangers alike. It served as school, health clinic, restaurant and hotel, as well as retreat for those with troubled souls. And at times of persecution, it provided sanctuary for refugees.

In recent years, the villa became a healing center where Sophia produced, administered and sold or gave away herbal remedies from recipes passed down through centuries of shaman healers. The house was also the site of a mystery school where Sophia taught a few chosen students the arts of natural healing. It held a monumental library and enough artifacts and artwork from around the world to constitute a fine museum of esoteric antiquities.

For Barbara and Gina, growing up there, the villa and its surroundings had been a place of constant adventure, intrigue, and genuine happiness. Returning now, after twenty years in America, Barbara was overcome with nostalgia. This entire day felt unreal to her because she had long dreamed of coming home, but had believed she never could.

Now, lying in Sophia's large down-covered bed, Barbara could not fall asleep. John lay next to her, snoring his usual death-deep slumber. *I've grown so accustomed to his night sounds I would probably have trouble sleeping without them,* she mused as she adjusted her position. *But marriage to John has not been as happy as I expected when we first met. Even though we share interests in similar subjects: history, philosophy, the arts, music, it turns out that most of our individual beliefs are in conflict with each other's. We embrace world views that are diametrically opposed, even though we can both trace ancestors back to this country's very founders.*

Lying here, in the room Sophia occupied for nearly a century, Barbara felt a sense of calm and protection that she'd missed for the past twenty years. She turned on her back and watched shadows waver across the ceiling. *It is as if Sophia's energy still watches over us here. Or, is that just another childhood fantasy?*

Barbara had to admit she was often afraid of John. But here, in her childhood home, she found herself more willing to risk a confrontation with him. She shuddered with foreboding for she realized that she was about to engage in her personal struggle against those opposing forces at last.

Tears welled again in her eyes and she got up quietly, tiptoeing in slippers and bathrobe to the little sitting room adjacent to the bedroom. Snuggled cozily into the worn overstuffed Morris chair with its big nurturing cushions, she became acutely conscious of a familiar scent: Sophia's unique blend of herbs and flowers lingered in the cushions and air of this little room. That fragrance had comforted Barbara often when she was sad and lonely or scared as a girl. Barb lay back against the cushions into a dream-memory.

On the sun-dappled stone-strewn beach two little girls, Gina and Barb, cling to each other, sobbing. Strangers surround them, trying to talk to them, to console them. The girls cling together refusing help from the strangers.

Out on the glittering sea, a sailboat lays capsized, its mast broken and its sails drifting limply upon the waves. The hull is slowly sinking, bow first, into the deep dark water. Other boats with sails fluttering circle the capsized craft. Divers surface, hauling first one, then the other lifeless body. She had been hit by the falling mast, knocked unconscious. He had been caught in the rigging, strangled. Both were expert sailors and swimmers, so it was a terrible and mysteriously inexplicable accident.

(It was rumored that a giant shark mysteriously rose from the sea and rammed the lightweight craft, then disappeared as the boat capsized. Sharks did not normally travel these waters, nor was this one ever seen again.)

In stunned disbelief, the girls watch their parent's bodies carried to shore in the dinghy of a larger ship. The harbor is abuzz with the commotion of emergency. Ambulances arrive and take the beautiful couple away, who had just hours earlier been so full of life, so vibrant with the joy of living. The girls, five and seven years old, had been watching the race in the company of their parent's good friends, who are now become strangers in their eyes.

Then Aunt Sophia arrives. She takes them into her safe embrace, reassures them, and brings them home to live with her at the villa where they have so often enjoyed summer vacations while their parents traveled the world.

Later, with Sophia, they return to walk that beach in the moonlight. It is deserted now, by the sailing crowd, and only the boats quietly drift, sighing in their slips. The foundered craft has disappeared into the deep, although parts of the sail cloth can still be seen floating in the calm water. They have come to receive any gifts sent by the spirits of their mother and father.

A perky white sailing hat, only slightly mussed, lays bouncing gently in the surf at Barbara's feet. It was her mother's cap. Reverently Barb picks it up, sets in on her red curls, and then wears it almost constantly for the first year or two afterward.

Gina gathers a few pieces of the boat's décor, but nothing of real significance. She shows her disappointment with silent angry tears. Then she spies her father's marine toolbox adrift near a buoy, and insists upon swimming the short distance to retrieve it. She caresses the little box of implements to her heart, and then puts it under her bed where she will pull it out to lovingly handle its contents whenever she feels lonely. It still retains the scent of her father's cologne as well as a little pouch of his pipe tobacco.

Sophia interprets their individual 'messages' as directing the roles each girl would play in carrying forth their parent's memory and vision. Barbara was to keep alive her mother's creative dreams, while Gina would carry their father's practical skills in implementing those dreams. That sounded good, but in later years Barbara lost the hat, while Gina has the tool box, still.

✳ ✳ ✳

Barbara woke from her memory dream feeling, once again, guilty. *I have failed, not only Sophia, but mother and father too, she chastised herself.*

Disturbed by the direction her thoughts were taking, she got up to do a cleansing ritual. She lit a small candle on a side table that was draped in floral and fringed shawls. Next to the candle she placed a small female figurine. She raised her arms, turning to the four directions and asked for blessing and forgiveness from the Goddess. The familiar words of an old chant came back to her with surprising ease.

"Diana, beautiful Diana, Goddess of the Moon and beyond,
Queen of all witches, Goddess of the dark night and of all Nature,
If you will grant me your favor I ask a token sign from you..."

But, speaking the words silently in her mind, she was not yet entirely invested in what she was saying. It was like repeating a childhood verse that felt reassuring simply because it was so familiar.

13

FIRST NIGHT - KARA

Late that same night, thinking others fast asleep, Kara got out of bed to read more of the old journal. She sat in an overstuffed armchair by the window that faced toward the sea. The room she shared with Joanna, on the third floor of the tower, stood above the roof line of the main house and gave views in three directions. (Had she chosen the opposite window, she might have seen she wasn't the only one up and about.)

Turning the book's brittle pages with care, her heart accelerated and she held her breath. She felt as if she were entering a secret hidden place. So far, she had not shown or told anyone else about the book for she had a vague intuition that its mysteries were meant just for her. At the same time, her rational mind told her it was a sacred relic that probably *she* should not be reading either.

Flipping pages at random, she stopped at one embellished with a drawing of a woman in a cape looking out over a moonlit sea. Beneath the illustration was the caption: <u>Aradia, Daughter of The Goddess</u>. A story followed, written out in careful longhand.

Kara was surprised at how easily she read the old fashioned script, and that she had no trouble understanding the Latin in which it was occasionally written. She wondered who this enigmatic woman might have been, but decided she would read it at another time.

She turned back to the beginning of the notebook, examining its cover and construction more carefully. The cover was of a soft deer-hide, beginning to stiffen slightly with age. Several leaves at front and back were translucent parchment, but the main pages were of a heavier pressed paper, perhaps of some cotton-flax mixture. It seemed to have been made by hand, for the book was bound with strips of tough braided hemp threaded through the centerfold of all the pages. Kara marveled at its fine condition. *Whoever kept this has taken precautions to protect it, even if they used it a lot.*

The book felt almost alive in her hands, as if it were imbued with a power of its own. But the sensible voice in Kara's head chided her. *It's only an old notebook! Must have been someone's diary. Seems too old to have been written by Sophia, though. So who did write this?* She searched for a name on the cover flap, but there was nothing to identify either the author or the age of the thing.

There was, however, a drawing in ink of a large black bird perched on a tree branch. This drawing was titled

MELANTHUS: WATCHER RAVEN.

Beneath the illustration, the inscription read:

The Raven is the symbol of the Teacher of Hidden Knowledge. He is the first of the Watchers --the Messengers of the Gods-- and

where he alights, he brings news of beginnings and endings. His Call announces a secret Path which only a select few will stop to attend and follow. He then accompanies such a Witch in all of her travels, even unto Death.

✳ ✳ ✳

Kara shuddered, trying to shake off a spasm of nervous excitement. Tickles of energy ran up her spine, and she couldn't rid herself of the notion that she had trespassed into a world outside of her own time. She decided she would have to read the whole thing from cover to cover and see what it could teach her about the weird world she and her family had wandered into. She tossed her pony tail and settled herself more comfortably into the big chair, glancing toward her sister, Joanna, in the bed on the other side of the room, to be sure she hadn't woken her.

The first entry gave a hint of things to come. Beneath a sketch of oak trees in a meadow by a lake was the caption:

THE HISTORY AND TEACHINGS OF STREGHERIA.

And this caption bore a signature with a date. In furled calligraphic penmanship it read: *Cecelia, 1675*. Almost exactly three hundred years ago, Kara marveled. She became engrossed in reading.

✳ ✳ ✳

I write to record the history of the Stregheria Witches of Italy, especially that of my own clan, the Rimini, who first planted their roots on the Campania Coast between Rome and Naples, where our seed contributed to the growth and legends of those two great cities.

Our line casts back into the farthest reaches of memory and place, for we come of the ancient First Stock, matriarchal clans migrating from the Far East, to escape captivity by hordes attacking their homeland from across the great northern mountains of Asia.

By ship our foremothers traveled and settled all the sun-drenched countries around the blue Mediterranean Sea. Our own clan found its way to Italy's warm untamed shores around a thousand years before the Christian era. The peninsula was then inhabited by only a few indigenous tribes and teemed with wildlife of every manner.

There, after generations of intermarriage and strife, we helped evolve the great Villanovan and Etruscan civilizations of antiquity.

✳ ✳ ✳

Kara stopped reading and gazed at a star-pierced sky. The moon-shadowed flight of a large owl crossed the roof of the main house below her. She pulled the window open a crack and breathed in dewy night air, listening to the far-off sloshing of waves on a beach. *How long have our ancestors lived in this very place, on this very parcel of ground?* It gave her a shivery feeling to imagine all the centuries of lives lived, deaths died, and to sense the spirits of those who had walked these lands, fought to tame them.

And what of her Great Aunt Sophia, herself? Might that old woman's spirit now hover near, watching and somehow be affecting what they would do at the villa? Such thoughts, which would normally seem foolishly fantastic to Kara, suddenly seemed quite reasonable in the star-studded silence.

She turned another page and read on:

✳ ✳ ✳

The Stregheria believe that every witch must pass her Dianic legacy on to at least one daughter of her own line before she dies.

This is because a Tuscan witch is reborn to her own descendants. The sacred lineage must not be broken, for it is the very web-work that holds life on earth together.

This is the deepest power we hold, yet it hinges on such fine threads. A single woman, rejecting her heritage, can bring great devastation. It has happened many times in history that a priestess dies without progeny or that an acolyte rejects her mission. And, each time, a rift is torn in the fabric of the world, which costs great pain and sorrow to mend. This is the hidden catalyst for nearly all wars and other human-born corruptions suffered on the earth: the Power of Woman denied or defiled.

Wow! The power of woman, thought Kara. *Now that is something I can relate to.* She reflected on her own family of independent women: her sisters and her mother, and now, meeting her Aunt Gina as well as learning about Sophia and her school here in Italy. *No wonder dad seems always on the defensive around us,* she joked to herself.

Yawning, she marked the page and set the book on her lap, curled up in the big chair, and dozed off. She dreamed of running freely through the woods with a motley crew of animal companions at her side.

14

FIRST NIGHT - MIMI

Mimi slept in the loft as she had wished, despite objections from her father. With tolerant caution from her mother, Mimi moved her bed-roll and bag of clothes to the top floor of the tower. She carried a battery-powered lantern, since Barb drew the line at her lighting candles.

The comical 'broom person' that had given her a fright earlier now seemed a comforting presence. Mimi pretended it was Aunt Sophia, in disguise, watching over her.

Mimi laid her bedroll on the tile floor, under the south-facing window where she could look up to the night sky. Toby curled next to her, purring loudly, as she fell asleep counting stars.

"Rat-a-tat-tat. Swshh, swshh, tat-tat-tat,"

Shortly after midnight, Mimi woke to loud tapping at the window. She got up to investigate while Toby watched with an amused expression. A bare oak branch rubbed against the turret's stone wall, swaying in the steady southeast breeze. On the branch sat a big black bird, pecking at the glass.

Mimi stood on tip-toe to reach the windowsill. The bird hopped onto the outside window ledge, cocking its head from side to side. Opening its wicked looking beak, the raven gave a shrill cry: "RaCaw!" It looked directly at her for several long seconds. Then it flapped its wings excitedly a few times, and flew away into the hills.

"Is that bird a friend of yours, Toby?" Mimi asked the cat. "Is it the same bird that Kara made angry when we were on the tower?"

Toby yawned, stood up, fluffed his fur, stretched, and then began pacing to the door. He stopped and looked back at her as if to say "Come and see for yourself." Mimi instantly understood this to be an invitation to adventure.

Pulling on her jeans and sweatshirt over her pajamas, she tied a scarf around her hair, grabbed her tennis shoes and picked up the lantern. Padding barefoot down the stairs, Mimi passed her sisters' room on the next level where she heard only the soft breathing of sleep. Down another level, she neglected to stop in the bathroom for fear of waking her parents. The snoring from that bedroom remained uninterrupted, although the floor creaked a little as she tiptoed by.

Down one more flight and through the hall to a side door into the courtyard, Toby led the way to the gate in the garden wall. The old iron hinge grated loudly when Mimi pushed on it. She stopped and held her breath, but no one in the house stirred. After slipping out and shutting the gate, she sat down on a stump to put on her shoes. She turned off the lantern to let her eyes accommodate to the dark and was surprised at how brightly the stars lit the woodland glade.

Toby waited by a gnarled tree whose trunk was about five feet wide. He patted the trunk with one paw and Mimi got the distinct notion he was talking to the tree. "Is this old tree a friend of yours too, Toby?" Stooping next to the cat, she felt the tree vibrate ever so slightly when her hand touched the rough bark. Looking into the branches, she spied a beady eye peering down at them. A big beak opened, hilariously calling, "RaCaaaw! RaCaaaw! RaCaaaw!" Toby nodded, whiskers pulled forward, smirking a cat-grin. The two animals were clearly having a little joke at her expense.

The bird took flight, and Toby immediately took off on a path in the same direction. Mimi followed without hesitation. They took a narrow winding trail into the hills behind the villa, until they came to a meadow with an outcrop that opened onto a starry view of the sky. Mimi sat down on a fallen log, inhaling the salty breeze and listening to the sounds of a timeless world: waves forever lapping against the seashore, gentle winds sough-ing through ancient trees. An owl hooted somewhere farther up the mountain and was answered by the howl of a wolf. Mimi turned her lantern on low beam, enjoying the exhilaration of a new adventure.

A tap on her shoulder made her jerk upright, startled. "Oh!" Toby was patting her with his paw, reminding her of their myste-rious destination. He bounded across the meadow and stopped to wait for her at a pile of boulders shaped rather like a sleeping dragon. A tangle of shrubs and wild flowers grew in profusion around the stones. When she reached the rugged bank, the cat seemed to disappear into the face of the rock.

Groping her way through brambles of a dormant grapevine, her lantern revealed a wide crevice in the rock-wall. "A tunnel!" she whispered to herself, delighted, as she eagerly pursued a narrow passage between granite boulders.

A bat swooped overhead, screeching as it flew out of the chamber. Mimi froze on the spot, her heart pounding in her ears. "Toby! Where are you?"

The cat reappeared from behind the limestone wall, saun-tering nonchalantly, his whiskers sparkling with cave-dust. His calm and comical manner soothed Mimi's fright and they resumed their exploration of the underground passage. Soon the narrow tunnel gave entrance to a small, low-ceilinged cave on one side, while the main shaft continued deeper into the mountain. Toby, however, stopped and sat down at the entrance to the small cave. He looked at Mimi as if to say, "Well, here we are." And then he began grooming his ruffled whiskers.

Mimi's lantern beam fell on a petro-glyph carved above the archway. An elaborate scrollwork of vine and floral shapes encircled the form of a woman in a long gown riding on the back of a wolf. The figure rested one hand on the animal's head and in the other she offered a chalice to the onlooker. Mimi gave it only a brief notice and then aimed her light-beam into the cave.

She was delighted to see the walls and ceiling adorned with paintings! Mimi stared about the small space wide-eyed. Little images of animals, birds, flowers, trees, and a few stick-figure women covered the yellowish brown interior in a colorful hap-hazard design. Among the figures were spirals and other abstract shapes like thunderbolts and flames and stars. Over a crevice to the side, her attention was caught by a particularly amusing por-trait of a girl with a cat and a bird. She stood mesmerized.

Mimi was greeted by a familiar voice. "Good! You got my message!"

Looking up toward the curved ceiling, she saw the fairy sit-ting cross-legged on a narrow jutting piece of rock. When Mimi hesitated at the threshold of the little chamber, Tinkle taunted her. "Come on in. Don't be such a fraidy-cat. There's stuff here for you to find."

Mimi ducked into the cubbyhole, which proved to be roughly circular, about ten feet in diameter, with the ceiling just tall enough for her to stand up at the center. She stayed hunched down and then sat in the middle of the floor, crossing her legs in imitation of the fairy. "I am not a fraidy-cat!" she grumbled, arguing again with the fairy. "So, what is it you want me to see?"

She looked around again and noticed that the little cave seemed to be unnaturally tidy. There were no signs of animal droppings or other grunge she would have expected in a moun-tain cave. Not even any cobwebs or musty smells. "Who uses this little cave? It seems too clean for animals," she remarked more to herself, than to the fairy.

"And what makes you think animals are dirty?" taunted the fairy. It seemed determined to argue and tease her. However, Toby also looked miffed at her comment, and Mimi apologized.

"Oh, I didn't mean dirty, like icky. I just meant, there is no fur or spider webs or stuff like that. Not even any dried leaves." She looked at the fairy. "Is this where you live? Is it your house?"

"No, not exactly," replied Tinkle, with a wink at Toby. "You might say it is a community meeting room, a place where we come to talk."

"You fairies meet here to talk? Like what do you have to talk about and can't you just send messages by magic?" Mimi felt a bit defensive, as if she were being teased and didn't see the joke.

"Not just us fairies, silly. It is a meeting place for all of the mountain creatures to come and talk with those who have gone away." The fairy did not look like it was teasing her now at all. It looked a bit cross, as if it was getting impatient with her and scolding her for being stupid.

"I don't get it," said Mimi. "Who has gone away? You mean, like you have some kind of telephone thing here, that you can call people far away?" She looked around again, and this time she spotted a niche in the wall beneath where the fairy was sitting. She crawled over to it and peered inside to see if it held a telegraph device or something.

"Oh pooh!" The fairy flew down on her shoulder and tweaked Mimi's ear. "You are even more bone headed than I thought. You are supposed to believe in magic, Sophia said. She must have been mistaken."

"I DO believe in magic! I believe in YOU, don't I? But you haven't shown me any other magic here yet. All you've done is scold and tease me."

Mimi scrunched down and aimed her light into the niche in the cave wall. She saw a bundle in there and reached for it tentatively. "This must be what you want me to find." Tinkle

71

remained perched silently nearby. Mimi gingerly pulled out the package which was wrapped in a coarsely woven cloth. It was a rather awkward bundle, about the size of a baby doll. For a moment she hesitated, imagining that it could contain some gruesome animal remains or even a human skeleton.

"Go on," prompted the fairy. "It won't hurt you, and don't go thinking it's anything bad to scare you either."

The cloth unfolded to form a good-sized shawl or blanket that could be useful on a colder night than this one. Within the blanket bundle, another smaller package was wrapped in leather. "This is fun! Almost like opening birthday presents or something!" Mimi laughed.

Inside the leather packet she found some partially burned candles, some matches in a little tin box, a small, but sharp knife and a forked stick with some carved figures on it. She examined each of these somewhat perfunctorily. "Well, it looks like an emergency kit for in case someone has to hide out here or something. I wonder who used it?" She spoke to herself, expecting no answer from the fairy, so she was surprised when she got one.

"This cave has been used many times by different people. Some hide from vigilantes, and others just get away for time alone. Sophie came here sometimes just to visit with us fairies." Tinklebell looked sad. "We miss her a lot. She used to leave us little cakes and sweets."

Mimi made a mental note to bring some candy with her next time she came. Now she went on to examine the rest of the bundle's contents. A small leather pouch held an assortment of shells, stones, and seeds. "You are supposed to hang that around your neck and wear it for protection," explained the fairy.

Mimi looped the thong over her neck and let the pouch fall against her breast. She liked the idea of wearing it, but then realized she did not want it to be seen by her family. "I can't wear this, the others will all want to know where I got it and then I would have to either lie, or give away your secret."

"That's true, but you are only to wear it when we go on our secret trips. We will always meet here before going anywhere else."

"Oh? Are you planning to show me more secrets?" Mimi felt excited, but also a bit nervous. What was she getting into? "I have already been gone too long and need to get back before they discover I'm out alone."

"We don't need to do everything tonight. We will do some more tomorrow afternoon. Now that you know where to find us, Toby will tell you when to come." Tinkle flew back to her ledge. "It probably is time for you to go back now."

Mimi tucked the bundle and its hidden objects back into the crevice, picked up her lantern, waved a salute to the fairy, and followed Toby back out of the cave, through the tunnel entrance, and down to the villa. They snuck in by the side kitchen door and found their way up to the loft with no one in the family seeing or hearing them.

15

JOANNA: MORNING, DAY TWO

* * *

The quarter moon shone brightly down on the mountain meadow where Tana danced alone. She wore only a very soft sheer gown over her nakedness, and she relished the gentle breeze wafting from the steep vale at the other side of the stream. Long grasses tickled her legs under her skirt, and her bare feet made soft slapping sounds as she leaped and spun over barren turf. All at once, she sensed someone watching her.

She stopped dancing and saw a great stag with a huge rack of antlers standing at the side of the hill by the stream. They watched each other for long minutes until the stag stretched his right hoofed leg out straight before him and bowed his great head deeply to the ground. He seemed to be bowing down to her, genuflecting worshipfully. Was he offering himself to her for sacrifice in the season's Solstice festival the following day?

She couldn't bear to see this magnificent animal slaughtered in the barbaric religious tradition of this country.

She was a captive princess, yes. And she knew she was expected to lead the ritual dances the following day. But she could not, would not, take part in the brutal sacrifice to their war-god. She struggled with her conscience. Could she desert this tribe and try to find her way home on her own? Better yet, could she coax this gorgeous creature to come with her and thus ensure his survival for another year? Tana knew she had to try even though it may cause more strife between their tribe and her own. How long would it take to discover her absence? Probably not until tomorrow night when the festivities would begin. That seemed like plenty of time for her to be well on her way home.

She took a few cautious steps toward the buck. He remained bowed as he had been, but watched her very carefully come toward him. She crossed the little stream, easily stepping over stones that felt slippery and deliciously cool on her feet. When she came close enough, she reached out and gently stroked his nose. He snuffled her hand, then rose to his full height and lifted his front left leg in another posture of homage. She took hold of his leg as she would to shake hands, and she felt him gently tug at her, pulling her toward him. She allowed him to snuffle her legs and up the front of her gown and found herself becoming strongly aroused. She stroked his neck and his haunches, then rubbed him vigorously all over his body, as she would when grooming her horse at home. But her horse was not with her here, for she had been snatched from bed, abducted upon the back of an enemy warrior's horse.

She whispered into the stag's ear, asking him if he would let her ride on his back and take her home. He immediately understood and knelt next to a large boulder so she could climb up on his broad shoulders. She clung lightly to his forelock and turned him toward the other side of the mountain. They made slow but easy progress through the wooded copses and down the craggy slopes to the valley below, following the river to her tribe's settlement.

The trip was long, and Diana made the stag stop every night so they could rest and forage something to eat among the roots and berries of the forest. On those nights they slept side by side, and when she would wake in the dark, she found the stag transformed into a handsome prince. They made love, but in the morning neither of them recalled it, and they travelled on as before: he in stag form and she riding on his withers.

When they came within an hour's travel to home, she stopped him at another mountain creek. They drank together and she reached out to touch his face and spoke to him. She told him he could leave her there and find his way to a normal life in the wilderness. She promised him that she would visit the stream often, and he could come and be with her there. He bowed to her as he had done when she first saw him, then turned and walked back into the woods a short way. There, he stopped and watched her as she made her way the last few miles home. But she did not have to go and meet him at the stream, for he would visit her every night in her cabin where she lived alone as a witch-healer for the tribe.

Joanna awoke at daybreak from a night-long slumber in which she dreamed of a strange and exotic life. The part that stayed most vivid in her mind was of a magnificent stag for whom she had danced, taming him to become her lover.

Now she took a moment to orient herself, for the bedroom seemed almost as strange to her as her dream. Then, gradually, events of the previous day came rushing to her mind and made her fairly leap from the bed with joy. *I have really met Giuseppe and Anthony! They are not just a dream, she assured herself.*

Joanna nearly burst into song as if she were starring in a romantic opera. She often did sing when she felt happy, but she remembered that her sister, Kara, was asleep in the other bed, so she stopped herself from serenading the household.

Instead, tiptoeing quietly to the bathroom on the second floor, she took a quick shower and got dressed. Wearing her favorite red silk midi blouse, matching sweater and black cotton shorts with red strap sandals, Joanna practically flew downstairs to the kitchen where she grabbed an orange from a bowl on the table and poured herself a glass of milk.

Taking these to the courtyard, she settled expectantly on the cool marble bench by the fountain. She recalled how girlfriends back home had warned her that Italian men could come on kind of strong, so she told herself to cool it. *Don't look too eager, Jo-girl, even if you can hardly refrain from throwing yourself at him.* She was already in thrall with Giuseppe's ready grin and quick wit. *He's really not exactly handsome, but kind of inscrutable with his dark curly hair, laughing brown eyes and that great smile.*

In her vivid imagination, Jo thought about the stag in her dream and immediately saw a likeness. *Giuseppe does seem a bit wild and roguish, but there is something kind of deep and hidden, a sad-feeling that makes me want to comfort him, soothe the enigmatic beast in him.* She liked that idea but she realized she was letting her imagination run away with her. *Hey girl! He's just very charming and a somewhat mischievous guy. Not some mysterious tragic hero*

She got up and casually wandered around the courtyard, stopping to examine curious artifacts such as the funny little 'house' in one corner of the garden wall. She had assumed it to be a bird-feeder but was surprised to see it held a beautiful silver chalice etched with mystical symbols, one of which was (no surprise) the horned faun. Looking into the goblet, she was astonished to see her own face mirrored and animated, as if her twin was looking back at her. For a moment it seemed the face winked at her when she was certain she, herself, had not winked.

As she put the goblet back in its place with a shaky hand, her finger grazed a soft object behind the goblet and this startled her so that she pulled her hand back, knocking the small pouch off the perch and it landed at her feet. She picked it up cautiously.

The pouch was carefully crafted of soft leather, dyed red and beaded with lovely blue and gold patterns. She tugged its thong open and looked inside at a curious assemblage of items. There were some small stones of different colors, a feather, a shell... But just then she heard the car rumble up the driveway, and she hastily tucked the little bag back into the shrine.

Quickly, posing herself and sitting on the bench with her cardigan sweater draped over her shoulders, she tried to appear relaxed, but her heart was racing. She was a bit nervous about seeing Giuseppe again, but more stunned by her discovery of that goblet and the little bag. Should she show them to Giuseppe? She decided to wait until they were better acquainted. After all, she really did not know anything about him yet. He might even be angry at her for having snooped into Sophia's private house shrine, for that is what she suspected it was.

He had borrowed Mario's sport car convertible on the promise they'd be home before nightfall. Now Giuseppe strode casually into the courtyard from the side entrance and flashed a smile. "Buon giorno, Signorina! You are truly a vision of the goddess," he exclaimed, holding out his hand to her.

His easy stride gave the impression of supreme self-confidence, though he was a small man, only about five-foot-six in height, with the wiry muscular build of a hard-working laborer. He looked to be of peasant stock and seemed to have few pretensions, if any, toward glamour or worldliness. Yet, in the short time she had spent with him, Joanna sensed Giuseppe had a natural understanding of the world around him and could handle himself anywhere.

She took his hand and joked to cover her awkward embarrassment. "What goddess? I have heard there is one who is supposed to run wild in the woods with wolves. Do I look like her?"

Giuseppe winked and said, "The Goddess has many faces, some more terrible than others, but all are beautiful." Then, taking her arm, he led her to the little red Ferrari and held the door as she climbed into the convertible.

After some light banter, they drove in silence for several miles, winding down the curving mountain road to the autobahn. Joanna gazed at the sun-glazed countryside, uncertain of what to say. She didn't want to sound like an ignorant tourist. She busied herself with tying a red bandana over her hair, peasant fashion.

Giuseppe broke the silence. "Have you heard the story of how Sophia's villa was built? It was originally but a small stone hut!" He glanced at her as she pushed a flyaway lock of hair out of her eyes. "That is a hard thing to picture now! Is it not?" He grinned at her as if he considered it a marvelous thought.

Joanna felt no particular interest in her great aunt's house, but in the devious manner of any young woman seducing a man, she pretended fascination with anything he had to say. "You're kidding! That big old mansion started out as a measly peasant's hut? That's amazing!"

But she immediately regretted her choice of words when she saw him frown. *Of course he wouldn't think a peasant's cottage was measly,* she scolded herself. *How snobbish I must sound.* She quickly tried to repair the damage. "I really find the small houses of the village much prettier than that big old place." She grabbed the scarf that threatened to blow off of her head, and retied it. "Mimi calls it a castle," she added with a merry laugh.

Giuseppe grinned back at her. "It could well have been a castle at some time in its long history. That measly hut, as you call it, was built way back in the thirteen hundreds. At that time it would have been considered quite luxurious. Most country folks' homes were made of mud bricks and stucco, like those we can see in the hill country today. They don't stand long without constant repair. The ancient stone structures lasted even through earthquakes."

Joanna resumed watching the scenery speed past them and let the subject drop, since she'd stuck her foot in her mouth already. Besides, she was more interested in having a romantic excursion to Rome than in discussing her weird family history. The car turned off the main road onto one that wound through beautiful hills redolent with the scents of spring flowers and newly leaved trees. She could see a tiny lake glimmering in a valley, and on a hill nearby were the ruins of another small temple.

"This is one of the oldest sacred sites in Italy," said Giuseppe. "Lake Nemi, down there, was where the early Dianic groves were sanctified, back in around the seventh century BC." He glanced at her and raised an eyebrow teasingly. "Your own ancestors were among the first priestesses in those ancient magical times."

Joanna's stomach tightened and she clenched her teeth with a familiar feeling. She reacted testily, "You don't actually believe in all that witch business, do you?" She looked at her escort, but could not discern if he had been joking or not. She babbled on. "I have heard mom tell stories about it all my life, and it just seems like a kind of family fairy tale to me. My father calls it the Rimini witch delusion." She tried to make her voice sound playful, as if they were sharing a joke. But she saw another frown cross Giuseppe's features. *Now I have really screwed up. I want to be cool, but I seem to keep offending him, she thought.*

He pulled the car into a gravel lot next to a public park and stopped. "Look, Joanna, you and I may have some very different ideas about who Sophia was and the importance of her life and work. Maybe today is not the time for us to debate it, however." He took a deep breath as if to calm himself, then continued, "I would like to show you some things I enjoyed as a kid. Since

you study theater, you might enjoy them too." He looked hope-
fully at her, waiting for a response.

Joanna realized she was acting childishly. *I'm being stupid,
she chided herself. I'm pretending to be sophisticated, when he
is trying to be friends.* She said, "I'm sorry, Giuseppe, I'm acting flip about stuff that just baffles me, I guess. It's just that any
talk about mysteries and magic surrounding Sophia has always
made me uncomfortable." She stopped to gather her thoughts.
Giuseppe sat quietly watching her and waiting.

She decided to be completely honest. "No. In fact, those
ideas really scare me. Whenever they come up, my father gets
mad and acts mean to my mother. I've got so I just ignore the
whole subject, or I make fun of the Rimini witches to make
people think I don't care."

Giuseppe reached over and patted her hand. "Mi scusi, Jo,"
He squeezed her hand and she returned the pressure. "It must
seem far-removed from your life, but here in the Old Country,
you know, we live with the history every day. I should have realized this difficulty after we walked in on that argument between
your father and Mario yesterday."

She nodded. "That argument scared me. Dad sounded an
awful lot like he does at home, except that he probably doesn't
dare call Mario names like he does Mom." She swallowed.
Maybe I'd better grow up and listen to what you have to tell
me. I think I would rather hear about these things from you.
It scares me, but part of me really wants to know more, and I
feel I can believe you." She was surprised at her own honesty. It
was probably the first time she had admitted any of this, even to
herself. She smiled meekly at him.

He leaned over and gently kissed her cheek. *Not exactly the
passionate embrace of my fantasy dream,* she thought, *but it felt
very nice.*

"Va bene. I'm honored you trust me," he said," I promise I
won't scare you. We will only take in some happy entertain-
ments today, Okay?"

They climbed out of the car and went for a walk in the park.

Following a stone-paved path along well-tended hedges of yew and arborvitae, Joanna and Giuseppe held hands and said little. Soon they came to the top of an incline and looked down upon a view that made Joanna think of a picture-book image of paradise. It was a bowl-shaped valley with a crystalline lake sparkling in the center, also perfectly round. Trees ringed the lake and climbed the slopes of the valley in circular enclaves of regal cypress, wizened oaks, and bowing willows. Here and there circles of blooming fruit trees gathered like gypsies performing a round dance.

"We are standing on the rim of an ancient volcano," explained Giuseppe. "That lake is what remains of its crater."

Joanna exclaimed in wonder. "Everything is round: the lake and valley, because of the volcano, of course. But why are the trees planted in circles too?"

"It is part of the ancient traditions" answered Giuseppe. "The Witches believe that all of Nature moves in cycles and circles. They know that the circle is the most nurturing, healing form. It is also the best arrangement for protection and sanctuary. Even cathedrals, synagogues and mosques of later religions retain the form for their most holy places." He glanced at Joanna. She nodded with interest. He continued, "All sacred traditions began in settings where people found solace in Nature's magic. The rules and trappings of formalized religions were only added on as men tried to take control of Nature."

After a minute Joanna said, "That does make sense. The part about Nature, I mean. I remember I used to visit a little garden behind our flat in New York City to find peace and quiet. Somehow, even in that big metropolis, the green grass and trees gave comfort."

Resuming their walk down into the valley, Joanna found herself tuning in to the natural landscape around them. Although things were carefully tended, it was not a stiffly formal landscape.

Children played run and chase, and adults walked or sat casually, visiting on the grassy knolls. The park felt invigorating, full of life and vibrant with history. Joanna became aware of a shift of perspective occurring within herself. She felt as if she was waking from a long sleep and discovering things she had long forgotten.

They came to a statue similar to that of the faun in Sophia's garden, only much larger. Here the horned and goat-footed man played a lyre. He wore the same mischievous grin and big erection as the others she had seen, however. Joanna stopped to look at it and asked, "Giuseppe, who is this fellow? I've seen him in several places around the villa, and now again here. Tell me about him."

Giuseppe's grin mimicked the faun's as he sat down on the grass at the statue's base and made room for Joanna to sit next to him. "That, my dear, is Pan, god of wine and wicked revelry. He is a consort to the great goddess Luna, who is the moon. His stories are many, but I will tell you just one rather tender tale about him now."

Jo watched Giuseppe's comically animated face, delighting in his sudden resemblance to the statue. "Did you know you kind of look like him?" she said, with a giggle. He merely winked and proceeded to tell the tale.

Once upon a time a young god sat upon a mountain watching a beautiful maiden dance. He was transfixed by the supple movements of her lovely body, for she was dancing sky-clad in the moonlight, performing a ritual to honor the goddess of women.

It was a dance forbidden men to see. Any male caught spying on this sacred rite was supposed to be ritually killed by dismemberment.

The young woman had recently come into her maidenhood and had been chosen by her clan for a special fertility initiation ceremony on the following night of the full moon. She was practicing the steps of her dance, but she was also praying to the goddess for a kind and handsome lover to take the role of her partner in the dance.

The rite was for the midsummer feast of Cornucopia, depicting the union of the goddess Diana-Tana, who is the moon incarnate, with her lover, the great horned stag, Dianus-Tanus, a solar deity. In the rite, the female part is played by a virgin, and the male part by a man chosen by his victory in a mock battle held in the previous seasonal celebration of Summer's Eve.

The two are never to know or meet each other before the ritual performance.

Well, anyway. Here sits the young god, trespassing on this maiden's practice performance. He is so enamored with her that he just has to go and dance with her, (which means he wants to have sex with her, of course.) So he turns himself into a young goat, and goes blithely hopping down the mountainside to the moonlit valley where she is dancing alone.

As a goat, he scampers around her playfully, attracting her attention so that she stops dancing and goes over to pet him. She is equally enchanted by the pretty little animal, and soon they are romping around the glade together in seemingly innocent play. However, being a god, the goat is able to secretly engage with her spirit, so that the two of them actually end up making love when the maiden stops to rest and falls asleep. She wakes to find the little goat gone and assumes it was all a dream.

The next evening she performs the rite as planned.

The moon, however, observed the entire spectacle. The moon goddess is amused, but she is also perturbed at the young god for intruding in the sacred rites. She punishes him by making the horns and hooves of a goat remain a permanent aspect of his features.

Thereafter, the horned goat god came to play tricks on the goddess' followers whenever they performed her dance rites and love-making festivals. He could be found at other times cavorting in the moonlight, making love to the goddess herself, for she did enjoy his playful energy. She took him as her consort, Faunus, of vegetation and fruitfulness in summer celebrations.

Her other consort, Janus, the great stag, is Lord of the Shadows, and stands for much more serious rites of protection and rulership over the land. Ironically, both of these horned gods of the Old Religion have been combined into one so-called evil force by the church's teachings. Thus they accuse witches of consorting with the devil, or Satan. It is a sad twist to the essentially healing purpose of this happy little character.

Giuseppe stopped talking and looked questioningly at Joanna. She guessed he might be feeling embarrassed after telling her the evocative little tale. She decided to tease him a bit. "So that little guy is a symbol of sex and deviltry after all, just like my dad said!"

Giuseppe held two fingers behind his head like little horns and grinned at her. She laughed and added, "Yes indeed, the statues do make a girl wonder what he has on his mind with that wicked little grin." Wrinkling her nose, she playfully punched Giuseppe's arm and continued, "I liked the faun statues right away, but Kara says they make her feel weird. She never approves of my boyfriends either!"

"Well, I hope she will approve of me," laughed Giuseppe. "I want to be friends with all of you."

"Oh, I'm sure you will charm her in time," answered Joanna, with a bit of sarcasm, "but beware of her. She has always taken dad's side against mom on the witch business. Kara is so serious-minded I can't imagine her ever being interested in the kinds of mystical things you have been telling me today."

"Speaking of mystical things" Giuseppe changed the subject, "there is a dance performance scheduled at the amphitheater down by the lake about an hour from now. How about if we go get a bite of lunch at the café across the road and then take in the performance? It doesn't cost anything, and it only lasts for about half an hour. It kind of relates to the story I just told you. Being that you are a dancer and singer yourself, I think you might enjoy this."

She immediately agreed, "You don't have to convince me, Sep, You have already succeeded in getting me intrigued by the ancient mysteries. I'm ready for more!" She gave him a spontaneous hug and they walked back to the car with their arms about each other's waists.

The bistro was abuzz with young people enjoying a summer afternoon. Mostly they spoke Italian, but there were a few English tongues among them, and many seemed to know Giuseppe. He was greeted with great good humor, back slapping, and joking about the pretty American he had found for himself. He replied in kind, and held his arm around Joanna protectively. She reveled in the attention, and quickly caught on to the game, subtly flirting back, while still holding herself aloof in an attitude of disinterest, as a proper girl was expected to do.

Suddenly a commotion occurred at the back of the restaurant where three or four young men sat arguing loudly. They were brandishing their wine bottles and cursing at each other, threatening a fight. Giuseppe stealthily steered Joanna to a table far to the other side of the room.

They had just ordered their lunch of seafood salad, and were toasting each other with glasses of Coke, when they were interrupted by one of the young men who had been fighting. "Well, Giuseppe," said the rusty-haired youth, with a half-sneer. "What brings you out into the world from your fox's lair? Have you decided to join the real battle after all?"

"Hello, Anthony," said Giuseppe. "Maybe you should watch what you intimate in front of strangers. You never know where the magic infiltrates your so-called real world." The two men glared at each other, yet there was a hint of friendly banter beneath the surface of their words. It seemed to Joanna they were putting on a charade of antagonism, rather than being actual enemies. She watched the newcomer discretely through lowered eyelashes as she pretended to study the menu.

Just as Giuseppe was enigmatically charming, this fellow was strikingly handsome in a fey way. Both of them seemed to have an otherworldly quality about them. *Or, maybe that's just my imagination getting out of control on the magical mystery stuff around here,* she told herself.

The newcomer was tall and angular, carried himself with a cocky swagger that insinuated daring defiance. His red hair and freckled complexion tended to belie the belligerence, however, so that while he did seem dangerous, he seemed also vulnerable. *An animal with a soft heart,* she joked to herself, and found that she was quite attracted to him, but in a different way than she was to Giuseppe, with whom she felt utterly safe. *This guy would be like dating a tiger,* she imagined with some relish.

"Perhaps the two of you should be introduced." Giuseppe broke into her reverie.

"Anthony, meet our newly arrived friend from America, Joanna." He paused a moment, looking meaningfully at her, then said, "Joanna, meet your cousin Anthony. He is Gina and Mario's son."

Joanna and Anthony stared at each other, locked in mutual momentary surprise. "Well, Hi there!" they said in unison, reaching out to shake hands. All three laughed awkwardly, and Anthony pulled up a chair to join them, uninvited.

16

KARA: MORNING DAY TWO

Kara wandered into the courtyard, munching a piece of toast with honey. She strolled idly past whimsical bird feeders, wind chimes, candle holders, and hanging pots of herbs and ivy. Ignoring the little shrine that had so intrigued Jo, she stopped before a weathered cot that was angled across the shady south corner of the stone wall. She sat on the edge of the cot carefully, testing its strength, then she leaned back into the cushions. She pulled the journal from her back pack and turned to the story that had first caught her eye yesterday afternoon.

THE STORY OF ARADIA, DAUGHTER OF THE GODDESS.

Aradia was not only a witch. She was an Avatar sent to redeem the true Old Tradition from degradation and neglect; just as in every century others have been and will be sent to revive and maintain the sacred ways, which were passed from mother to daughter from the earliest times, to honor the God and Goddess.

Who was Aradia's mother? No one ever knew for certain, although many have imagined her parentage was of Amazon or even Faerie stock.

Regardless, Aradia was discovered abandoned or lost, a child of about three or four years old, wandering the hills of Alban in the year 1313 AD. She was adopted into the home of a wealthy couple who were strict religious Catholics, and who enforced rigid disciplines which grated against the girl's natural instincts toward freedom and independence of expression

While still living with her adoptive parents, Aradia occasionally walked alone in a secluded glade which was part of the wild lands used for hunting by her father and his cohorts. On more than one occasion, in these wooded hills, she came upon tiny creatures who spoke to her through the wind and trees in small voices of urgency and alarm. They cried out for help in preserving their sacred trees and hidden mountain havens.

Because her parents loved her, despite their rigid discipline, they humored her appeals to leave the fairy's homes alone. Her father set apart certain areas of his land as natural habitats, off-limits to farming, hunting, or building upon. Thus, even at a very young age, Aradia already began her work of retrieving and saving the Old Religion's sacred places.

When Aradia was about nine years old, she escaped the limiting confines of that home by agreeing to go to a convent. There, almost immediately, she gained her full freedom through the intervention of a kindly woman of the pagan traditions, who privately disagreed with the church's dogma against women. This woman took Aradia under her wing, teaching her herbal healing methods and secrets of ancient Etruscan magic.

✳ ✳ ✳

Kara was so engrossed in reading this tale she didn't notice someone come out to the courtyard from the house. A cough startled her, and she looked up to find her father sitting on the bench in front of the fountain.

"Hi kiddo," he said. "I was hoping to find you alone so we could have a little talk."

Kara got up, surreptitiously tucking the book inside her backpack as she pretended to straighten the pillows on the cot. "Sure, Dad," she said, walking over to sit next to him. "I thought you were on your way to visit your cousins in Naples this morning."

"I'm leaving shortly, maybe you would like to come with me?"

"Oh, I can't, Daddy. I, um, I made plans to go shopping with Mom and Gina in Salerno." Kara told this white lie, knowing her mother would cover for her if needed. They had talked about her and Mimi going along, but no actual plans were settled. Kara only wanted her parents to leave on their jaunts so she could quietly go back to the woods to read and maybe find the big dog again.

John looked uncomfortable as he fumbled to find words. "I'm worried, Kara. I have heard rumors of strange goings-on around here in the next few days because of those accursed festivals the pagans hold on the first of May." He peered bushy-browed at Kara.

"Why should that worry you, Dad? It's not as if we have to attend their celebrations. Gina and Mario said they won't be taking part in the fire rituals this year because of being in mourning for Sophia." When he didn't answer, she decided to break the ice with her own question. "I know you don't approve of Aunt Sophia's school, but why do you think we are in danger here?"

John coughed nervously again. "Yes, well," glancing sideways at Kara, he fumbled on. "I guess you are old enough to understand." He pointed to the statue of the horned faun positioned in the fountain. "You have noticed that this fellow with his lewd grin and indecent attire can be found all over this place, haven't you?"

"Sure. There's a statue in the garden in front, several smaller figurines inside, and even the knocker on the door is his face." She thought of the entry in the journal that told of the horned guy's strange fate, but she couldn't tell her father about the secret book. "He makes me feel a little uncomfortable, I admit. But so what? It's just a statue."

"Not just a statue, Kara," interjected her father. "This is a symbol of the Devil, himself! It is a sure sign that your great aunt and her followers worshiped Satan. It is Witchcraft that was taught in her school. And that is evil in the eyes of God."

He stopped to take a breath, for his voice was rising in the way it did whenever he encountered the pagan themes in Barbara's art and music. Kara always thought of it as his 'fire-and-brimstone' voice, and she cringed hearing it now. *You missed your calling, Pop*, she joked to herself in an attempt to quiet her own rising sense of resentment. The story of Aradia was fresh in her memory and she felt pulled in opposite directions_ the all too familiar feeling of being caught in the middle of her parent's arguments.

John cleared his throat and continued. "Your mother seems to think it is all very harmless. But there are still some people in the Church who hunt witches. Maybe they can't burn them like in the Middle Ages, but they can make life very difficult for anyone associated with those old pagan beliefs." He thought a moment, then added in his most ponderous voice, "For it is written in the Bible: 'Thou shalt not suffer a witch to live'!"

Kara gasped. "You can't mean that, Dad!" She stood up. "Maybe this little horny guy looks devilish, but I can't believe Mom's Aunt Sophia was evil." A sudden burst of defiance overcame her, and she looked her father in the eye. "You are simply wrong about that!" She turned and ran back into the house, realizing she was on the verge of giving away the secrets of the notebook if she stayed to argue with him.

17

MIMI: MORNING DAY TWO

Mimi slept late after her midnight excursion. Around nine am, Barbara came to ask if she wanted to go shopping in Salerno, but Mimi pretended to be too dozy and mumbled she wanted to rest up from traveling. Then, as soon as she heard Gina and her mother drive away, she got up and put on her outdoor clothes. She knew Jo had left early, but she was surprised to find Kara out of bed and gone as well. Making sure her father had also left for his trip to Naples, Mimi at last crept down the stairs. Toby silently padded after her as they snuck out the side door.

She'd originally thought to explore around the house a bit before going back to the cave, but something told her she should take advantage of the moment to escape undetected. She felt a thrill of excitement, knowing the fairy had more surprises waiting for her.

Tinkle met them at the big tree and directed them on a different path from the one that led to the fallen log in the meadow. Tinkle nestled on her shoulder and whispered to be quiet because there were others out and about this morning. Mimi guessed Kara might have gone for a walk, so she trusted the fairy to keep their whereabouts hidden. She felt like a scout on a hunting party, creeping through the woodsy brush, trying not to make a sound. For the most part she felt she did pretty well, but Tinkle rather frequently scolded her for snapping a twig underfoot or shuffling through leaves too loudly.

They arrived at the cleft in the rock from its back side, undetected. Mimi glanced through the brambles to get a look at the meadow, but a strange mist hid the meadow from view. Once inside the tunnel, Mimi found no need to turn on her lantern for Tinkle's wings emitted a halo that gave plenty of light to see by under-ground. It was dry and airy in the tunnel, the temperature pleasantly cool compared to the rather warm morning outside.

They stopped inside the little cave she had visited last night and Tinkle directed her to retrieve the bag of protection charms from the bundle. When Mimi found it and hung it over her neck they proceeded down the tunnel.

Then Mimi, Toby, and the fairy made their way quietly. It seemed the silence was almost palpable, and they were nearly gliding down a gently curved incline in a tunnel carved inside the granite mountain. After descending for a while, the tunnel leveled and widened. Then it converged with two other tunnels, coming from either side, to form a vestibule at the entrance to a circular domed grotto the size of a small amphitheater.

Mimi stared about her, awestruck by this hidden room in the mountain. It reminded her of a cathedral, only more inviting, less austere.

Light filtered into the cavern from some unseen source. Muted shades of rose-pink and burnished gold reflected from limestone walls imbuing a constantly dusk-like atmosphere. A slender waterfall cascaded from a cleft in a ridge by the ceiling. Its course tumbled over jutting rocks to splash into a swirling pool at the base of the cavern's far wall. From there, a meandering brook bisected the cavern and disappeared into a channel running through the opposite wall. Strangely enough, an elegant willow tree grew, in this underground cavern, canopied gracefully over the confluence of pool and stream.

The Grotto entrance stood several yards to the side of the water tunnel. Around the whirlpool were positioned some low flat stones that could serve as seats. Near the head of the waterfall, stood a group of larger stones arranged like an altar. Along the wall of one side of the cave were longer slabs laid out like sleeping pallets or benches, and on the other side of the stream, niches had been carved into the wall like shelves. A fire-pit was dug into the floor adjacent to the shelf-wall and more stone seats were scattered about at random. The entire grotto-room could easily accommodate a dozen or more people, although it had clearly been deserted for some time.

Mimi stood speechless, gazing about the room, until Tinkle flew up to sit on a ledge and called, "Come on in and see. There is no danger. Tinkle keeps watch, just in case."

Mimi stepped cautiously over the threshold, and began following the meandering stream through the middle of the large subterranean room. Toby casually leapt up to sit on the ledge by Tinkle. They seemed to want to observe her explorations, rather than tag along. "Just in case what?" Mimi thought to ask Tinkle after a few minutes of quietly walking around.

"Oh, nothing," answered the fairy. "I just like to see no one follows us in here. It is a very secret place, you know. Very, very secret." The fairy glanced at the cat, who blinked twice in affirmation. Mimi, watching their exchange, decided not to worry about it.

There were little stepping stones set into the brook at various points, so that a person could cross without having to jump or get their feet wet. Mimi knelt at the edge of the little stream, dangling her fingers in the water to feel its icy coldness. It was so clear she could see her face reflected at the bottom.

Then a reflection of a second face appeared next to her own, smiling at her. Thinking this to be a trick of the light, she pulled back from the water, glanced around and nearly fell into the water in surprise.

There, right behind her, stood another young girl! Or, at least, she seemed like a real girl, except somehow Mimi could see right through her. Mimi blinked. "Oh! I didn't hear you come in. d-d-d Do you live down here? I'm sorry if we've intruded on your place," Mimi babbled on, hardly knowing what to think, much less say.

The girl was dressed in old fashioned clothes, sort of like the hippies were wearing nowadays in San Francisco, but hers were authentic. A long flounced green skirt, held by a drawstring waistband, with a tucked-in blouse of white cotton embroidered in colorful floral designs. Over her shoulders she wore a heavy woolen cape, also of deep forest green. Its hood was thrown back, releasing unruly red curls, the color of Mimi's own hair.

The girl was very pretty, except she had a wicked scar beside her right eye. She appeared to be about twelve or thirteen years old. She was not ragged, exactly, but a bit shabby. *Like maybe she's had to go through some rough weather or something,* thought Mimi sympathetically. *She seems clean though, and she looks healthy enough. Not like a tramp or waif or anything.* Mimi, of course, had no idea what such people might look like except for pictures on TV of kids in war torn countries like Viet Nam. *But this girl does not look anything like those poor kids,* she thought.

"Are you lost or something?" queried Mimi after the girl made no reply to her previous questions. In her eagerness to make a friend, Mimi just kept talking. "My name is Mimi, and I've come here with my friends Toby and Tinkle." She indicated the two on the ledge who simply sat and watched her, unmoved. They didn't even acknowledge the newcomer.

Now, the girl held her forefinger to her lips, to hush Mimi, but still said nothing herself. Yet she continued to smile warmly, beckoning to two seats by the pool. Mimi glanced back at Toby and Tinkle. Both remained nonchalantly lounging on the ledge as if nothing unusual were going on, so she decided it must be okay to sit down with this strange girl.

The girl grasped Mimi's hand for a moment and looked into her eyes. Mimi felt a chill up her spine. The girl's eyes were so smoky-gray that they appeared colorless and almost translucent. The touch of her hand, while firm enough, felt strangely cool. unreal. like a touch experienced in a dream. A deeply sorrowful expression overtook the girl's face when Mimi drew back in a moment of fear.

"Who are you?" Mimi demanded, pulling her hand away. "Tell me your name. Say something!"

Mimi's raised voice drew the attention of her two companions, and Tinkle fluttered down to sit on her shoulder, while Toby remained on watch. "Don't be angry with her," counseled the fairy, whispering into Mimi's ear. "She can't speak, but she will show you things if you will just sit quietly and pay attention." The fairy then pinched Mimi a little meanly as if to punish her for her insolence.

Mimi felt chastised. "I'm sorry," she said to the girl. "I didn't mean to be rude." She smiled and held out her hand in friendship, and was relieved to see the girl smile again and accept her hand.

Sitting quietly side by side, Mimi and the wraith-like girl continued to hold hands as the girl leaned toward the water, commanding it with a motion of her free hand. Water splashed and eddied and whirled in the circular pond. With a flick of her wrist, the girl brought all the water to a standstill. The whirlpool cleared to mirror stillness. The girl drew Mimi to the edge of the pond to peer down fathomless depths into a haunted abyss.

Mimi had a flashing image of Alice falling down the rabbit hole, and held herself back in trepidation. But her friend's arm across her shoulders steadied her, and she ventured to peer more closely into the mirror of the pool. It was like watching a movie. Things were going on, events were unfolding in some unknown place, in some faraway time.

Mimi sat entranced, as history replayed before her eyes. A woman's soft voice narrated parts of the story, but it was mostly shown in pictures. Mimi glanced at her companion, but the girl remained silent. The voice seemed to come from inside Mimi's own head. She decided not to worry about it, and gave herself over to the enchantment of this new magic.

Two girls and a woman were gathered at the edge of a mountain stream. They were each wearing robes and tunics in varying shades of green. The woman wore a billowing white shawl over her hair. She stepped calmly into the stream bare-foot, and carrying a silver bowl before her. Her face was the epitome of serenity for her eyes were closed as if in trance or prayer

The girls knelt at her side, holding branches of herbs gathered from the meadow behind them. One wore a hooded cloak, pulled over her hair and hiding her face. Mimi thought she moved rather awkwardly, as if she was ill or hurt. The other girl's dark hair spilled down her back and shoulders like a cape, a bit like the feathers of a big black bird that sat above them on a tree limb.

The full moon shone behind them over a reckless landscape of stony hills, wild growth meadows, scrub pines, bent oaks and meandering streams. Beyond the meadow could be seen a small cottage nestled into a fold of the hills. Built of stone and wood, with a thatch roof, it blended quietly into the hillside. If moonlight were not pouring down upon it, Mimi would not have noticed the little house.

The voice in her head explained that the three were performing a ceremony to the moon, and that they were giving thanks for a recent healing. The voice moderating the scene told Mimi she was right, and that the smaller of the girls had been seriously hurt in an attack by a vicious hawk, but the woman and her sister had managed to save her life. She wore the cloak hooded to cover the scar on her face from the bird's talons.

The voice continued to tell the tale as Mimi observed the scene in the grotto scrying pool. The girls and their mother lived with their grandmother, in the mountain cabin, where they served the local pagans with magic potions and herbs. From the cabin, they could access this grotto from a different tunnel than Mimi had today, and they used it for a place of refuge from marauding bandits and local vigilantes on witch-hunts, and as a place for quiet meditation and healing.

But tragedy befell their little family when their grand-mother, Cecelia, was taken away and imprisoned on charges of witchcraft. She was one of the numberless women who were burned by the Church's Witch-hunts in the sixteenth century Inquisition. Great stories are told of how she foiled and fought the Church's conspirators from her little cabin in the mountains before she was finally abducted and executed.

While a sense of urgency accompanied the scene, the three acted with calm and unhurried demeanor. After the ritual, a gigantic wolf lopped in from the woods and began to playfully romp in the stream with the girls.

The image in the pool faded away. A moment of stillness kept Mimi spellbound until her spectral friend squeezed her hand. Mimi turned to her and said, "Oh! Juliet! I felt so sad for you, but I also see that you had some wonderful times with your family and animal friends. Thank you for showing me this picture from your life. I almost feel like I was there with you."

The narrating voice in Mimi's mind spoke again. "It is not to re-live those times that you are shown them, but to regain the mystery and wisdom of your family heritage to use in your life now." Mimi was about to ask who was speaking to her, but suddenly she did not need to ask. She knew it was their Great Aunt Sophia.

Tinkle flew to Mimi's shoulder and said, "Time for you to go back home for dinner with your family now. Remember to keep our secret though. We might come here again later tonight because Juliet has more to show you."

18

KARA'S NEW FRIENDS

K ara sat, lotus-position, on the sun-warmed log in the meadow, her back braced against a sturdy scrub pine. Breathing
the scents of sea and mountains surrounding her, she once again
opened the notebook.

Turning to the page she had marked earlier, she resumed
reading the story of Aradia:

As an adult, Aradia travelled and worked among country folk,
doing healings and teaching the history and wisdom of their
Amazon warrior, gypsy and Etruscan ancestors.

She had many confrontations with the authorities in her
travels. At last, she built a secluded "hermitage"_ a small hut on
the property she'd inherited, and lived there safely for a time.
But, eventually she was arrested, jailed and sentenced to die for
witchcraft. Yet she miraculously escaped in an earthquake that
destroyed the jail.

After this Aradia travelled far away, never to be heard from again. But many years later, her daughter, Karamena, came to live in the hut and added the tower and battlements to that original structure, which eventually became our own grand villa.

This young woman was a well-respected "war witch" and healer who was credited with helping to end the Black Plague in Italy. She was also known to travel with animal companions, including a pack of wolves.

✳ ✳ ✳

Kara felt an inexplicable shiver at seeing the daughter's name, so similar to her own. "It's just coincidence, not some spooky 'past life' sign," she scolded herself. "The history part is fascinating though. Hard to believe the villa's big house has some parts that were built in the thirteen-hundreds!"

She turned to another part of the book.

Here were several pages containing drawings of plants, with lists of their uses and what appeared to be recipes for healing potions. Kara flipped through these, thinking them of little interest to her. But she stopped to examine one drawing and its inscription more closely.

✳ ✳ ✳

FENNEL: A prodigious, fast-growing fragrant herb, found throughout the Mediterranean shores. Produces edible shoots and aromatic seeds and fruit. It has been used in protection amulets from earliest times, and is believed especially powerful against evil spirits and the black magic forces of the Malandanti.

For ages Benandanti Witches have periodically taken trance-journeys to engage in ritual battles with their arch enemies, the Malandanti. They fight with the stalks of fennel. In the material world, we too, must guard and fight against the Malandanti who appear often in the roles of high authority. Yet, our battles on earth, while still given protection by the herbal talisman, cannot be won by the use of herbal magic alone.

These battles often require taking great risks of imprisonment or even death by torture, for they are fought against the established systems of a civilization founded on denial of magic. When we engage in any struggle against the unbelievers, we are waging war against evil which is often disguised as friendship. Thus, the Benandanti witch is always challenged to stay on guard against the black arts, even while remaining open to the Mystery inherent in every soul. Thus it is that the battle is often first fought within our own hearts, for we must face our own illusions and sort out the true from the false in every new day's ventures and meetings

A packet of fennel seeds should be carried at all times on the person herself, most effectively in a pouch hung around the neck that also contains other protective amulets of special power to the individual. Then, when evil appears, or when in situations where evil may be lurking, a pinch of the fennel powder blown into the air, plus a seed taken under the tongue will assist in recognizing and engaging the adversary. Yet the perpetual battle between good and evil does not abate with any single victory or defeat.

Kara was struck by a sense of familiarity about this passage, as if she had known about this, even performed the ritual with the herb mentioned. *But that is ridiculous*, she sneered at herself. *I have never even heard of these Malandanti or Benandanti before, much less known of their cosmic battles. I'm probably getting it confused with some sci-fi book I've read.* She shrugged away the nagging feeling of significance and turned another page.

She gasped. On it was a sketch of the wolf-like dog she had seen yesterday at this very spot. In fact, she had come today hoping it would still be lurking around and she could try to make friends with it.

She examined the sketch and read the author's caption:

* * *

Gervain: The war-witch's guard and companion.

* * *

Oh great! What in the world is a war-witch, anyway? Heaving a sigh, she thought: *there seems to be no end to these mysteries and surprises.*

Kara propped herself more comfortably against the tree and shut her eyes, letting the warm sun caress her face. Before she knew it, she dropped into a brief catnap in which she was walking the woods with a pack of wolves and came upon a stone and wood cabin where they were greeted warmly by a woman wearing a long skirt and apron. A raven peered at her from the porch roof.

Kara woke with a sense of being watched. She opened her eyes cautiously, expecting to see that the big black bird was back. But, instead, the wolf-dog had returned and stood watching her from a few feet away.

Her heart took a big leap to her mouth, but she stifled the cry. He stood nearly three feet tall at his back, his huge head on an equal level with hers, where she sat. His paws were the size of desert plates. His sharp teeth gleamed above his lolling tongue. But Kara felt an almost irrepressible urge to run her hands through his magnificent silver-threaded ruff.

The wolf came to Kara, drawn by a familiar scent. The book in her lap evoked a memory of someone he longed to see again, and his heart warmed at the image. His normal instinct to flee from human contact deserted him, leaving him vulnerable to any danger the girl might represent.

But she looked as bewildered as he felt at finding this stranger carrying his old mistress' aura. Unsure how to make this new one understand his motives, the wolf simply waited for her to take the lead. Kara, her heart doing flip flops, waited to see what the wolf would do. They sat thus, looking at each other and waiting for a very long time.

Maybe five minutes later, as the yellow-eyed wolf gazed at the brown-eyed girl, they simultaneously made their first moves. Kara smiled and the wolf waved his tail. Kara slowly reached her hand, palm up, toward the majestic animal, as if offering homage to a divinity. The wolf muzzled softly,"whuff," and set its paw into her palm, as if to seal a pact between them.

Reaching out to let him snuffle her, she patted his head, at first tentatively, then with some zest. Suddenly she was hugging the animal around the neck, her face buried in his ruff and crying. He smelled clean, yet feral, a mix of danger and safety. Kara understood that she had found a friend, but one who would not suffer ambivalence. She must make the commitment to keep his trust, regardless any doubts she still harbored of such mystical possibilities.

This is not a fairytale, she told herself again. *This is real magic.* And that thought is what made her weep with joy and fear and sadness. *If I can allow a wolf to become my personal companion and guide, then I can no longer doubt the other mysteries that keep turning up around here either.*

How can I keep this a secret from Mimi, who would so love to meet him, she thought. And then a more troubling concern dawned on Kara. How to keep it from their father. He would surely shoot the wolf, believing any wild animal, making friends with humans, is either rabid or a spawn of the devil. For the second time in a day, Kara found herself vehemently disagreeing with her father's fanatical denial of the possibility of good magic.

She turned to the wolf and said, "I promise to be your friend. But I need to give you a name, or maybe you can tell me what you call yourself? I'm called Kara," and she laughed out loud to hear herself talking in all seriousness to a wild animal as if it would understand.

At her laughter the wolf raised its muzzle and gave a short happy bark. The bark actually sounded a little like he was repeating her name. "KaRah," he said again. Then he barked another sound, "RaarJerrr" and cocked his head to one side, waiting for her to get it. "RaarJerrr" Kara listened in amazement. She said, "Is that your name? Rarjer?"

He bounced up on his haunches, rested his forepaws on her shoulders, and licked her face in reply. Kara laughed again, and again he raised his muzzle in a happy bark, "KaRah! RaarJerrr!" Then he bounded off a little way down another path, and came back to her again. She guessed he wanted her to follow him. "Okay," she said. "Just a minute, I'll come with you. But where to, I wonder?"

She put the journal back into her pack, and together the girl and the wolf took off at a comfortable lope along the ridge of the hill, the wolf leading the way. They ran beside a stream that burbled through a stony field. When the stream angled downward again, the wolf jumped nimbly across. Kara followed, hopping a series of stones obviously set for that purpose. They entered a redolent old-growth forest, thrumming with muffled birdsong and bee-buzz.

Ascending the mountain along an overgrown trail that might once have been a well-traveled road, they came suddenly upon the burned out shell of a single-room peasant cottage. The roof was mostly gone except for a rear corner. Three walls yawned open to the elements in varying degrees of wreckage, but the entire back wall stood solid, a stark witness to the home's demise.

In the clearing, a line of broken fence posts marked a corral, and the weedy remains of a garden carpeted another patch of ground. It was within this shamble of a cabin that Rarjer made his home.

But he didn't live there alone. In the far back of the shelter lay a bitch with four newborn pups. The female wolf barred her teeth at Kara's approach, preparing to spring. The male walked calmly to his mate's side, snuffled her reassuringly, and stood looking proudly at the pups.

Kara froze, admiring the savage little family warily, although she felt protected by Rarjer. Shortly the bitch rose and paced cautiously to Kara, head slightly bowed in tacit submission. Kara allowed the animal to inspect her, taking care not to make any sudden move. The bitch was smaller than her mate, and fiercely elegant. She looked almost unearthly with a ruddy cast to her coat that shimmered with its own light. Golden sparks danced in her amber eyes. At last the female wolf gave her approval, inviting Kara, by a toss of the head, to come see the pups.

Kara took special care not to touch the tiny wolf-babies, but quietly murmured her reverent appreciation. Sitting quietly with the wolf family, time stopped in an otherworldly stillness.

Kara observed their surroundings. A substantial stone hearth stood intact, but cold, at the center of the single large room. Some bits of furniture-- an empty cupboard with its doors broken off, a chair with three legs, a weather-stained sturdy wooden table against the back wall. Two walls were open to the outdoors, grown in with weedy vines. The exposed foundation still held an outline of the threshold, although door and frame were gone. A third wall stood nearly whole with a shattered window overlooking the garden plot. The fourth wall remained firmly braced against the hillside into which the cabin had been built, thus securing the little sanctuary and sheltering its occupants from turbulent elements.

It was against this solid backdrop that the mother wolf had prepared her den. Kara noticed a door in the corner, behind the nest of pups, but assumed it to be an old pantry and gave it no further consideration. Lengthening shadows reminded Kara that time was not actually at a standstill and that she had better be getting back to the villa. She blew a kiss to the bitch and her babies and tiptoed out of the hideaway into the woods. Rarjer loped at her side, guiding her back to the meadow where they first met. There he watched as she made her way home.

It was not until she was back in her bedroom at the villa that Kara remembered the dream she'd had just before meeting the wolf today. *The wolf I've been calling a dog!*, she chided herself. Kara suppressed a cry of amazement as a shiver of recollection tickled her spine. In that dream there had been several tamed wolves and a cabin very similar to what that little shack must have been like before it was abandoned. *Or, did it burn down in some more sinister event than mere accidental neglect?*

Things are getting just too weird with coincidences! I'll have to ask Aunt Gina about that cottage. But no! That would mean giving away Rarjer's secret. Guess I'll just have to keep investigating on my own, she told herself, then realized she was thoroughly enjoying the mystery.

19

JOANNA : AFTERNOON DAY TWO

That same afternoon, while Mimi and Kara each pursued their explorations and adventures around the villa, Joanna sat between Giuseppe and Anthony on the grassy slope of the crater-park near Rome, watching a live performance on a stage set on the shore of the round lake.

Giuseppe had explained, as they walked back from the bistro to the park, that the play was a re-enactment of the rites of an ancient Cycle of Seasons, based on traditions lost in time. He hinted, but did not exactly say, these were the earliest traditions of her great-aunt Sophia's sect, the Stregheria.

Joanna attended the show feeling more excited by the presence of her two handsome male companions, than by the prospect of seeing the play. But, as she watched, she became entranced.

✳ ✳ ✳

A dark-skinned, diminutive figure danced before a small group of people seated about the terraced hillside overlooking the lake. She was dressed in a flowing garment that fell across one shoulder, baring one of her breasts, then cascaded down her back to cling lightly against her gracefully curved thighs. The fabric shimmered in the sunlight, creating undulating waves, like liquid gold, flashing in contra parallel to the swirling, turning, leaping movements of her body. Her bare feet slapped the paving stones in syncopation to the frame drum she beat by hand.

A resonant male voice narrated the performance over loudspeakers in the primeval setting of the ancient lake. The effect was haunting, even under a bright afternoon sky. The tale of long ago resounded about the hillside:

"In ages long before recorded history, a civilization bloomed and flowered, bore rich fruit and seeded itself from out of India, in the Indus Valley, called the Land of Sindh, bequeathed from a people called Dravidians, who had lived in that land from the time before time was known. These nomads worshiped a Goddess, Uma, and her consort, Aum, who were the forerunners of Shiva and Shakti, who are the Lord and Lady above all."

The dancer slowly collapsed onto the ground, bending low to the earth, so that her long black hair fell down about her like a shroud, and she drummed a faint heartbeat from beneath her veils and tresses for several minutes. Then she lay still and quiet as death.

The people watching held a collective breath.

Suddenly she leapt up from her fallen crouch with a wild cry, twirling faster and faster, spattering a red berry juice upon the watchers and the ground around her.

"That is supposed to symbolize menstrual blood," Sep whispered.

A chorus in the audience began chanting her name.

UMAUMAUMAUMAUMAUMA!

From within the dark cavern of a tent, another figure emerged.

He came from behind and caught her by the waist, lifting her in the air, where she spread her legs and revealed her yoni to the sky. Her partner, wearing only a loincloth on his tanned body, and a pair of antlers as a crown, set her down before him and they danced a mating ritual that ended with their feigning climax together.

AUMAUMAUMAUMAUMAUM!

The chorus cheered them on until he mimed shooting his seed onto the ground to mingle with the red berry drops of her blood.

"It's milk," whispered Sep "To represent his semen"

The drama's narrator continued, while a harp and flute ensemble played softly:

"This was the first fertility dance, a ritual for propagation of the crops, the people, and the gods. The horned god and his divine mate; the goddess and her consort; equal in power, yet distinct in each own function. He, the seed bearer and harvester; she the very matter from which life is formed.

"This was the first ritual, evolved from centuries of spontaneous worship. The dance. The drumming. The capture. The ecstasy. And then, inevitable death, followed by perpetual rebirth. This was the cycle, the dance, the rhythm of life as our earliest ancestor and ancestress marked it and gave thanks. So it is still, and will be ever and ever."

As the dancers and chorus exited into a tent alongside the stage, Joanna joined the audience in chanting and clapping, her own voice ringing clear as a bell, as she became transported into a time of ancient magic. AUMAUMAUMAUMAUMAUM! The dance was exquisitely choreographed. Joanna, having studied dance and music for years, felt drawn into the performance. Mesmerized.

Anthony broke into her thoughts. "Hope you aren't offended by the sex stuff here, little cousin."

Giuseppe added, "We don't want you to think we are trying to shock you, Jo. The sexual freedom is just a very significant part of the Old Religion because, after all, where would any of us be without it!" He laughed teasingly and waited for her to respond.

Jo considered teasing them along to give them the idea that she was shocked, just to see them squirm a bit. But then, such prudish sentiments were the farthest thing from her mind, so she was honest when she said. "Don't be silly! I have grown up with pop musicals like 'Hair' and 'JC Superstar' so the mix of sex and spiritual ecstasy is pretty familiar to me. I think this is terrific!"

The two young men gave her a joint hug, and Jo laughed heartily, feeling exhilarated. She felt as though she was living out her best fantasies in the company of these two good looking guys in this exotic setting. It felt almost as heavenly surreal as the dream from which she had wakened this morning.

Remembering the dream gave her a start. She felt a shiver up her spine, realizing how portentously that dream reflected this very performance. In each of them, the man had the form of a stag. She had assumed her dream-stag represented Sep, but now she looked at Anthony and a new thought occurred to her. *These two guys both sort of reflect 'horned gods' but Anthony seems more like the dignified and dangerous stag, while Giuseppe is the playful and mischievous goat.*

Such romantic notions were not at all foreign to Joanna, even though she pretended to dismiss her mother's mystical leanings. The story was not lost on Joanna either. She recognized immediately the familiar themes of matriarchal heritage which her mother had always woven into the bedtime stories and childhood fables told to them as children.

A sense of awe vied with chagrin, as Joanna thought how she had so casually dismissed her mother's tales as nonsense. *Now they take on a whole new importance beyond just the entertaining little tales I always thought they were.* She wanted to embrace the stories and claim that heritage for herself too! She felt deeply that she had even been that dancer, and much more.

Spontaneously taking a hand of each of her companions in one of hers, she beamed with happiness and they grinned with delight. They were bound in a chain of mutual admiration!

All too soon it was time to go home. But they made plans to return the following day for another 'adventure', as the two men teasingly told her. They would not reveal what they had planned, but insisted she would like it as much, if not more, than today's entertainment.

On the drive home Jo couldn't stop exclaiming over the magic she had experienced. Finally, when he let her off at the villa, she told Giuseppe about her impressions of him and Anthony as goat and stag, and he drove off laughing heartily, wiggling two fingers behind his head.

Only after he had gone did Joanna remember the little shrine in the courtyard, and that she could have asked him about it on their drive back home. *Oh well, there will be plenty of opportunity for questions later.*

20

EVENING TWO: A TOAST

The sun had set behind the hills and the evening breeze wafted warmly through the patio doors from the court-yard. An owl hooted from the orchard beyond and a wolf called from somewhere higher in the mountain. The family gathered around the big trestle table in the kitchen for a light dinner of minestrone soup, crusty bread, an assortment of cheese and fruit, plus wine.

Mario and Gina sat at the foot end, John and Barb at the head. Along one side, Joanna sat between Anthony and Giuseppe. Kara and Mimi sat on the opposite side, with an empty place set between them.

Toby tucked himself onto the bench at that spare place, just as if it was set for him. Kara tickled his ear and said "So you think you should be served like people, little cat?"

Mario laughed. "That empty plate is set for our unseen guest of honor, Sophia. Toby must be sitting in for her!"

"Why do you set a place for Sophia when she's dead?" asked Kara, feeling shocked at such a strange and seemingly irreverent way of dealing with death.

"And why not?" said Mimi, still irritated at her sister's inability to accept the magic of their ancestral villa. "It is just a nice way to honor her memory. I wish she could really be here with us though. I'd really love to meet her in person."

Giuseppe grinned at her. "You will have plenty of opportunity to get to know Sophie personally when you have lived here awhile. Her spirit is in everything."

Kara watched Joanna give him one of her toothpaste commercial smiles, and wondered how she could be enamored with such an odd fellow. Yet Kara had to admit that he was charming in a gentle impish way.

After they had finished eating, Mario spoke up. "Speaking of Sophia, I suggest we make a toast to her now." He raised his wine glass, saluting the 'empty' seat, where Toby placidly washed his face after eating scraps Mimi had fed him.

"Wait!" exclaimed Kara. "Mimi and I should be allowed to take part in this toast too. Dad? Won't you let us have some wine?" She was still miffed that he had forbid them to have wine with the grownups earlier.

"Of course they should join in the toast to Sophia, John," said Barbara. He assented with a grudging shrug, and Anthony quickly set out two more goblets, carefully pouring a half glass of red wine in each.

"Well then," said Mario, raising his goblet once again, and looking at each person in turn around the table, until his gaze came back to the empty place and stopped. "To you, dear Sophie. May you enjoy your sojourn with the Ancestors. We miss you here, but feel your spirit abiding with us, as always. Salute!"

"Salute!" chorused the others, and lifted their glasses toward the honored place.

Toby preened his whiskers.

Mimi coughed at her first sip of wine, and wrinkled her nose, but she remained intently focused on the toasting.

Anthony raised his glass. "To the Ancestors and our many spirit-relations abiding with us in the villa and among these hills. May they guide us in our celebration of the interment of our dearest Sophia's ashes this evening. Salute!"

"Salute!" they all chimed together. Anthony refilled glasses, except for the two young girls'. Kara noticed that her father's glass was empty, but that he had not joined in either of the toasts. He just sat sternly glaring at them all.

"We should talk about the burial plans, don't you think?" said Gina to Mario. He nodded for her to go ahead. Gina smiled brightly all around the table and winked at Mimi, whose cheeks were rosy with the flush of excitement, and probably from the two sips of wine. "First let me tell you about Sophie's peaceful departure from this earthly life. It was a truly lovely thing to see."

Kara glanced around the table as she listened to Gina recount the events of the afternoon when Sophia died, lying peacefully on her cot in the courtyard. Kara saw that everyone seemed fascinated except her father, who looked very uncomfortable. She sympathized with him. *This really does seem bizarre*, she thought. *It's almost as if they are happy that she is dead. Why isn't anyone crying?* Even her mother smiled dreamily at the tale aunt Gina was telling. *They all treat this as if it was a birthday party instead of a funeral.*

"I do so wish you all could have been with us," Gina ended. "Certainly Sophia had hoped you would be." She looked pointedly at Barbara, who appeared to flinch under her sister's gaze. "But the fates seem to have made other plans." Gina laughed softly, and Mario joined in. *It's as if they know a secret*, thought Kara.

"Poor Sophie!" exclaimed Giuseppe. "She tried so hard to make everything go as she planned, yet in the end, they would not let her have her way. And as she, herself, taught: It is not for us to question the designs of the gods."

"The goddess, in this case, more likely," chuckled Anthony.

Again, Kara saw Joanna flash that beatific smile at the two young men sitting by her. *She doesn't have a clue about what they are saying,* Kara thought. *She's just pretending to be interested. What an air head!*

"Are you saying she knew when she was going to die and made all the plans for it ahead of time?" asked Kara, feeling incredulous. "Like she actually even made plans to die on a specific day? That sounds really weird!"

John broke in. "I agree with Kara, it sounds very strange. Almost like, well, like suicide or something. Did she take some kind of poison?"

"John!" Barbara glared at him.

Kara bit her tongue. *Whoops! There they go again, the same old nasty arguments that they have at home. Why doesn't Dad learn to keep his thoughts to himself? Of course, I am the one who started it this time.*

"Not at all," Mario interjected. "Sophia was just highly attuned to her own psychic and spiritual rhythms. It is a basic premise of witch-wisdom that old people, like old animals, sense when they are going to die. It is no big deal for them. It is seen as a natural part of life, and not to be grieved overmuch."

He smiled at Kara. "The fortunate ones are those who can take the time to prepare themselves and others and bring full closure to the current life so they are ready to move on to the next." He shot a stern glance at John. "It is not so very different from the teachings of Jesus, although the Church has managed to overlay His wisdom with their fear-based dogma."

John looked about to argue, but Barbara put her hand on his arm. "Please, John. Not tonight. Let us have our ceremony in peace." She looked about to cry. He shrugged and gulped down the last of his wine.

Gina began again, "As I started out to tell you, tonight we will go to the oldest part of the villa. It is an Etruscan crypt that dates to around 800 BC._ a beautiful cave that has been built into the coastal cliffs just down the mountain from the house. It is believed that the great Roman queen, Tanaquill, is buried there, as well as her daughter, Tana, and several of our later ancestors. Over centuries, the remains of Rimini witches have been placed in that tomb, one generation next to another. It is our most sacred site."

Giuseppe took up the telling, "You will see paintings and hieroglyphic symbols on the walls that are astounding. The colors are as fresh as yesterday, though most were made centuries ago. Sophie added some of her own, as did others of your kinswomen through the years."

Kara thought Joanna's eyes were about to pop out of her head. *What an actress! She probably couldn't care less about the old paintings.* Kara was feeling particularly irked at her elder sister tonight, though they had hardly spoken to each other since they got here. Jo had been gallivanting in Rome with the two men, while she and Mimi had been acquainting themselves with this strange old house and its secrets. Kara shivered at the thought of all they had discovered so far. She was glad Jo had not been around to spoil their ventures.

Kara's attention was brought back to the conversation when Gina exclaimed loudly, "Oh! I almost forgot! Barb and I came across a dead owl in the Grove yesterday evening. It looked to have been strangled." She turned to Mimi, who was staring at her, horrified. "Don't be afraid, little one. The owl died for a good purpose after all, although I doubt those who did it had that in mind." The others also stared at Gina aghast.

"Who would have done such a thing?" asked Jo, taking part in the conversation for the first time.

"We can guess it would be some of the vigilantes who are preparing to make trouble for Friday night's Beltane celebrations." said Anthony. "But we are equally prepared for them."

The girls broke into chorus of questions: "Who? What? How?"

Giuseppe quickly interrupted. "No need to get into that now, Tony."

"No, I don't intend to. I just want to make sure everyone here understands that we do have enemies. And, tonight, we need to be vigilant as well, although I don't think those people know anything about the funeral plans." He looked around the table, a calm but stern expression on his face.

"Well, anyway. Back to the owl," said Mario, drawing attention away from the unanswered questions. . "We will bring the owl with us for Sophia's spirit companion. That, at least, solves one question for us. Seems it was one detail Sophie forgot to take care of, or at least until now." He raised an eyebrow at Gina.

Suddenly John pushed back his chair and stood up. "What rubbish!" He was flushed with rage. "I'm sorry, but all this talk of ghosts and animal spirit companions sounds completely blasphemous! I just can't go along with it!" He turned to leave. No one tried to stop him. He stood there, looking uncertain, expecting some argument.

"That's fine, John." Mario spoke in a level, but firm, voice. "It would be best if you stay away, since the sacred ceremonies should not be defiled by the presence of such judgmental disbelief." He looked at each of the girls with calm reassurance.

Anthony addressed them all. "It does not matter if you aren't totally convinced of the reality of magic, or if you don't understand the Strega spiritual faith. That is no discredit to Sophia's memory. But calling it rubbish and blasphemy is near to declaring yourself aligned with the Malandanti themselves."

At this point, Toby growled deeply, bared his teeth, and set his ears back. He was looking directly at John. Mimi said, "I think Toby means that this is making Sophia angry." Giuseppe smiled at her. "Your father has every right to disagree with our beliefs, but he must then refrain from attending our sacred places and ceremonies."

At this point John stomped out of the room and they heard him slam the front door. Barb began to get up and go after him, but Mario said, "Let him go, Barb. It is best for now. You can talk to him later."

The three girls looked at each other in shocked recognition. Kara thought: *We have seen this kind of thing at home for years. Maybe it's a good thing someone else gets to deal with it for a change.* Suddenly she felt ashamed of her father and sorry for her mother. *He doesn't need to be like that, she thought. None of these people are calling his religion evil or wrong. Why should he holler at them for their beliefs just because they are different from ours_ his,* she corrected herself.

21

A PROCESSION, A BURIAL, AND
A CEREMONY INTERRUPTED

Kara imagined they looked like a troop of medieval gypsies heading for a carnival in the woods. The night was bright with stars. The sea-breeze blew warmly, fluttering shawls and capes, tossing long curls and ruffling shorter locks on the celebrants.

At the head of the procession Mario, in huntsman's boots and fancy tooled leather pants and vest, carried a lighted torch to illuminate their path.

Giuseppe, in a green tunic over tights, blew a soft melody on a wooden flute, while Anthony, dressed in a knight's embroidered tabard, strummed syncopated notes on an old fashioned lyre. Joanna, wearing a flowing red silk cape, carried a frame drum that she tapped in rhythm to their tune.

From time to time Jo and Anthony would join their voices in a sweet paean to the goddess, and Kara was amazed that her sister knew such a thing. *Of course,* she reminded herself, *Jo's been involved in musical theater since she was a little kid.*

The music flowed out into the mountains above them, calling creatures of the woods to join the cheerful cortege. Mimi pranced delightedly among the celebrants, whirling and turning in the gauzy skirt and shawl given her by Gina. Toby frolicked at her heels, sporting a tiny clown's ruff with bells. Shaded wraiths and sparking fairies flickered about the trees, unnoticed.

Kara wore a filmy, flowing costume, similar to Mimi's, but she felt silly in it and not at all like dancing. She would much have preferred to wear her comfortable clothes, and she felt almost naked without her trusty backpack!

Gina and Barbara followed at the rear of the procession, wearing similar gauzy skirts and flowing silk capes as the girls, but theirs had embroidered symbols of birds, flowers, and animals sewn on them in elegant hand-stitchery. Gina carried a silver urn with Sophia's ashes, and Barbara carried a silver cask holding a few of Sophia's personal keepsakes to be buried with her.

Gina had told them that Sophia, herself, had created all their costumes to wear for her funeral celebration. This news caused Kara to feel even more uncomfortable, knowing that the old woman's hands had sewn them while preparing to die. *Creepy stuff,* she thought as she ambled along the trail. But, then chided herself. *Why am I so negative about this? Really, it is kind of exciting. Get with it girl, quit your skeptical analysis and join in with the others.*

They came to the edge of a stand of trees surrounding a pond in a meadow. The troupe came to a halt in a semi-circle, and quietly waited while Mario and Anthony went forward and gathered up the owl that they had wrapped in a linen shroud the night before. As they took it from the tree niche where they had secured it from scavengers, a single clap of thunder shook the woods and lightning flashed around the glade for a moment.

Kara nearly shrieked in surprise, but none of the others seemed disturbed at all. *Oh, sure,* she reminded herself with her usual familiar sarcasm, *this is a magic thing. Hang with it and don't be surprised. You can figure out the realities of it all later in calm daylight.* Nevertheless, her body tingled with anticipation mixed with dread.

The group reassembled and turned back from the Grove. Mario now carried the owl in one arm, holding his torch alight with the other. They made their way down a rough-hewn rocky set of steps that descended from the back of the villa to another level outcrop several hundred feet down the mountain.

Kara tried to keep close track of their location. *I might want to go back and see this again later,* she thought. *I have to admit, the place sure has a lot of neat secret stuff about it. It makes me feel like I'm in one of those old mystery stories I read as a kid.* An owl hooted mournfully nearby, and she wondered if it could be the mate to the poor dead one they carried with them. *Is it grieving too?*

Kara could smell a kind of perfumed musty odor as they moved down the mountain. The stone steps felt cool against the thin sandals she wore with her costume. They came to the square framed entrance of a cave. The wood door frame and threshold showed it wasn't just a natural cave.

Mario entered first and the others waited. His torch-light could be seen casting splashes of light against the wall, and it seemed to Kara there were actually some other people inside. *It must be much bigger than it looks from outside,* she thought.

But when she clambered in after the others, she saw that the walls were covered with brightly colored paintings of people and animals. The light from the torch-flame made them appear to be moving. *Or maybe not_ for some of them look very substantial, very real.* Kara could have sworn a guy in a mask with stag's antlers winked at her. She quickly looked away.

Gina removed two baked clay blocks from one wall of the rectangular chamber. Kara saw they had been decorated with a design of a woman riding a wolf. She thought it looked rather ridiculous, because, not only was the woman seated on the back of the wolf, she had a cat sitting on her head, and there was a bird on her shoulder. Kara nearly giggled at the comical image until she heard Gina explain that Sophia had painted this as a symbol of her own life.

Kara remembered the old journal and the pictures she'd seen in it of the wolf and bird. *Okay, that's maybe not so silly after all,* she remonstrated with herself.

"Sophie did enjoy a wry sense of humor, and she expressed it in many of her favorite paintings," Gina said, and smiled knowingly at Kara. Then Gina reached into a deep rock shelf revealed by the removed blocks and pulled out a scroll which she carefully unrolled.

"This is the 'telling' Sophia chose for us to hear at her burial." Gina glanced over the scrawled script for a moment, then looked up at the others. "It tells the story of Tanaquil, an Etruscan Queen and her grand-daughter Tana,

Gina nodded to Sep and Anthony, who then played a haunting Celtic tune, and Joanna joined in, tapping her frame-drum. Gina prayed, "Now attend us, spirits of the ancestors, as we recall early beginnings in honor of one who has lived many lives among you."

The story told of a peaceful, fun-loving and artistic folk in the seventh century BC, who were among the founders of Rome. They traced their lineage back to the first people to emigrate from the Far East, and Tanaquil's ancestry combined indigenous Latin stock with mysterious gypsy blood flowing with the gifts of healing magic. Tanaquil's direct foremothers included warrior Amazons from Anatolia and temple priestesses from Crete.

After decades of peace, their colony erupted in war. Tanaquil died in prison, but in time her grand-daughter, Tana, escaped to refuge in the wilderness and lived among a tribe of wolves. She became known for her powers of healing and found favor with the hill people. She is said to have founded the first Dianic settlement of women in the northern mountains of Italy.

As an old woman, Tana returned to the land of her birth. She and Tanaquil are said to be the first buried in this very chamber.

✳ ✳ ✳

While Gina read the brief legend from the scroll, each woman and girl imagined events in their own way, but seemingly without conscious direction. Kara saw Tana living with the wolves; Mimi saw her performing healings; Jo saw Tanaquil creating paintings in the crypt; and Barb envisioned them both in their struggles to retain, preserve and spread the sacred teachings.

No one thought to question the images that came to them so spontaneously, for it felt perfectly natural to receive revelations in the sanctified setting of this ancient crypt.

A thunderstorm had developed outside on the mountain. They could hear the wind lashing the waves against the beach far below, and angry clouds scudded across the sky like wolves chasing rabbits. A wolf howled outside the chamber door. It seemed to be very close by. Rain pelted the turf, and beat on surrounding trees. But inside the crypt a sense of peace surrounded the mourners, as if they stood apart in another world.

Suddenly the service was interrupted by the clattering of rocks falling down the mountain. Soon a drenched figure stumbled over the threshold into their midst.

Everyone jumped back. The men pulled out knives. Kara screamed. Then Mimi cried, "It's Daddy!"

The raven flew in after John and began angrily pecking at his back where he lay fallen on the ground. Kara screamed again and started to slap at the bird, for it did seem as if it wanted to kill her father. Strong arms pulled her away and Giuseppe's voice whispered "He won't be seriously hurt, but Melanthus must have seen something he didn't like. Maybe your dad followed us here to spy on the ceremony. He had been warned to stay away."

Kara settled down a bit, but she felt tossed between anger and fear and pity toward her dad.

Mario stepped over to John and helped him to his feet as he also lifted the bird off his back. It obediently flew to sit on a high ledge and watch. John raged and sputtered. His eyes bulged and he shouted so that his words echoed down deep into the bowels of the crypt. "What kind of deviltry is this? I just came down here to help bring you all back safely to the house. There is a hellish storm going on out there. Can't you see? Come with me girls, the others can stay and get drowned if they want."

He made as if to reach for Mimi's arm, wanting to pull her out of the chamber. Anthony stepped between them, and said. "The girls can choose for themselves if they wish to leave or stay. We have no fear of Nature's fury. It is the fury of men which we must guard against. Yours, at this moment, endangers us all. You must leave, John!" Anthony held his knife at his side and did not threaten John with it, but John chose to see otherwise.

"You dare to point a knife at me, you sonofabitch!" His fists clenched. Giuseppe and Mario stepped in and held John's arms. "Let go of me! I'm no thief or burglar come to rob your creepy gravesite. This is a demon's hideout for sure and I don't want my little girls dragged into your cultish spooky rituals." But he could not loose himself from their grip.

Barbara came over and faced him. She spoke in calm, soothing tones. "John. Come with me back to the house. The girls are safer here from the storm than anywhere else on the mountain, including the house. Gina will see that they get back home safely. Your rage brings fear and trouble into this holy place, and that is more dangerous for the girls than any storm." She gently tugged on his arm, and John meekly followed her, as if he had suddenly been drugged.

Kara and Mimi were holding hands. Kara felt protective of her baby sister, and realized it was not the strange rites, but their own father, from whom she wanted to protect her. Dad could be scary when he was mad, but she had never seen him direct that anger so personally before. For the second time this evening, she felt proud of her mother and ashamed of her father.

Gina lit a stick of incense and carried it around the chamber, chanting a psalm of purification. Then she said, "Let the negative energies be banished and let us conclude our burial rite for Sophia."

At this point, she beckoned to the men to bring the bird, and she picked up the urn. She nodded to Kara to pick up the little silver box that her mother had been holding. "Will you bring Sophia's keepsake chest, Kara, since your mother is not able to join us right now."

Kara hesitated, but decided she was not about to cause any more disruptions, and picked up the silver casket. It felt light. *Probably just has some jewelry and old love notes in it*, she counseled herself. *No need to feel creepy about it.*

When Gina took the box from her, Kara felt an unusual pang of grief. What's going on with me? It's not as if I should be missing the old lady, I never even saw Sophia in a picture. She suddenly wanted to know and found herself saying, "Aunt Gina, is it okay if I ask you a question?"

Gina nodded. "Go ahead, Kara. What is it that's troubling you?"

"N.. Nothing really, It's just that I feel so strange here. I don't even know what Sophia looked like, so it makes it hard for me to imagine her alive or dead. Could you tell us a little about her? I mean so we can get a clearer picture of her in our minds." She suddenly felt silly asking this. No one else seemed to need such explicit evidence of the old woman's actual life and death.

"Well, Kara, as a matter of fact I was just about to sing a short eulogy for Sophia. It describes a little bit about her. And we can

show you photos and tell you more stories in the days to come."
Kara nodded and stepped back by Mimi.

Gina chanted:

* * *

"Sophia. Her name itself hums with ephemeral tones-- Soh-
phee-aahhh, sounding celestial gongs through the ethers of
antiquity.

She has traveled over hallowed trails, sanctified by the
footprints of venerable sages from ages past. With ancestral
heritage that invokes Merlin and Medusa, her sorcery flashed
like fireworks, sparking showers of wit and wisdom along the
way.

Sophia has guided heretical pagan disciples on the treacher-
ous byways of shaman magic. She revealed mysteries passed
down from gypsy healers, the first true witches, the wise women
who wandered the original wilderness of Eden's fall.

Her work has always been to tend the balance between earth
and heaven, between woman and man, between body and spirit.

In her recent earthly life, Sophia had heavy-lidded deep
brown eyes that could snare hypocrites and torch their sanc-
timonious ravings in a heartbeat. Her sibilant voice mesmerized, and her sinuous movements tantalized all with whom she
came in touch. In flowing gowns and veils of sunset pastels, she
appeared to float among clouds on earth.

She was High Priestess of the oldest sect, one of the last
remaining Holy Heirodules of the Old Religion. She stood almost
alone against a growing tide of misogynist religious fervor, teaching the natural magic of the goddess to a few disciples from
around the world who came to her mystery school in these wind-
shorn hills on the western coast of Italy."

"And now we lay her to rest." Gina placed the objects into the rectangular opening. First the bird in its fairy-webbed shroud, then Sophia's box of memories, and finally the urn with her ashes. "Bless you dear aunt and priestess, our guide and teacher, our precious foster mother. You will be missed in your physical person, but welcomed always in your gracious spirit. And we do not bid goodbye, but only farewell until we meet again. Blessed be."

Now Kara saw the tears. There was not a dry eye in the chamber. Silently Gina replaced the painted clay blocks and Mario set them with mortar he had mixed earlier in the evening. The group quietly left the chamber, coming out into a calm night. An owl hooted twice and a wolf howled long and lonely. Then all was peaceful and they returned to the villa without speaking, each one pondering their own emotions.

22

KARA: SECOND NIGHT

Once again, when the family was retired for the night, Kara remained awake. She felt troubled by the conversations at the dinner table and by the events of Sophia's burial ceremony afterward. Questions tumbled around in her mind.

Why are the adults so seriously worried about some local rabble hunting the wild animals? That does not seem like such an unusual thing for folks in a rural community to do.

And dad's harping against Sophia's teachings is beginning to grate on my nerves. Why can't he just let it be? Now that I have looked around the place, I don't see anything so dangerous about these old traditions. In fact, I have to admit, I enjoyed the ceremony in the hidden crypt. What an amazing thing to be in that place where people_ our own ancestors!_ have been buried for over a thousand years!

I thought the story aunt Gina told about that ancient Queen was really interesting. I felt kind of excited to think of the grand-daughter who became a sort of wild-woman of the woods. It reminds me of the princess in a fairy tale of mom's that I used to pretend was me.

But the owl_ that's weird. Why would someone kill that beautiful bird? I was glad Aunt Gina gave it such a respectful burial with Sophia's urn of ashes. It almost seems as if the owl is a companion to Sophia on her way to heaven, or wherever she's gone.

Kara shook her ponytail. *Whew! There I go again, getting all spooked and fantastical. I'm getting as bad as Mimi. Get real girl!* She scolded herself. *It was just a ritual ceremony for the old lady. The bird gave it a kind of mystical touch, but it was just a dead bird, not some spirit ancestor.*

Kara's musings reminded her of the notebook and she dug it out of her backpack, turned on the little reading light at her bedside, and settled back to read some more.

She was fascinated by the interesting assortment of material covered by the author, *Cecelia, way back in the, what? Sixteen-hundreds?* The fact that the little book had survived intact for almost three hundred years seemed impossible to believe. She frequently found herself wondering if it wasn't a hoax. Like maybe Sophia wrote it herself, but from the perspective of her ancestor in the seventeenth century.

Oh well, whoever wrote it, and when, doesn't matter that much, I guess. It's still pretty fascinating reading, she thought, turning to a drawing of some potted flowers next to a wall with a cat lounging on its ledge. Kara chuckled at how much the cat in the picture did resemble Toby himself. *So that could have been drawn by Sophia, for sure.*

The next written portion was a memorial description of somebody's death. It was titled:

DEATH RITUAL OF A STREGHA WITCH-SHAMAN.

Kara began to read it with a bit of reluctance, expecting it to be gloomy and funereal. She was pleasantly surprised.

✳ ✳ ✳

The raven watched the old woman dying. It perched on a broken limb of the ancient oak tree where, for years, it had sat to view her comings and goings around the little shack in the woods.

This was a warm spring morning and the last of the snow-patch slowly dissolved into a puddle of clear water in the hollow below the garden. The old woman lay in the hammock that was stretched between porch-posts.

The posts, roof and walls of the porch were adorned with odd arrangements of hanging pots and baskets, containing seeds, stones and herbs-- all symbols of her life-work. A chip-munk scurried back and forth on the worn wooden steps, while an aged black cat lazily winked an amber eye from its sunny perch on the porch rail.

Four women attended, keeping vigil. One hummed sweetly in a low voice, another beat a gentle cadence on a frame drum, a third plucked chords on a guitar, and the forth blew grace notes on a flute.

A little girl crept over to the old woman and knelt beside the hammock. The crone placed her hand upon the child's head and murmured words of reassurance, to which the child looked up and beamed a smile through tear-brimmed eyes. The women continued their quiet serenade, and the old woman began to chant.

Her voice was strong and clear. She recited a familiar story, one she had repeated many times in her long life. The story was never-ending, yet it altered constantly in the telling. The fourth woman put aside her flute and scribbled down the old woman's words on sheets of parchment.

She told the story of Life. Of how each moment is woven as a thread in the tapestry of time, and each person leaves their colors on that pattern, which goes on forever. Generation after generation, the Weavers continue the task of making the tapestry, which carries the pattern of all Creation.

Now, the old woman reviewed the patterns of her own life's thread in the tapestry for the final time. In her mind, she saw how her colors wandered back and forth, sometimes a single strand, sometimes woven among many others, sometimes caught in a knotted tangle, sometimes gracefully intertwined. She had indeed lived many varied and interesting lifetimes. She anticipated a healing return to the spirit world, with which she kept constant communication in her earthly lives. She knew she had many friends waiting for her on the other side. Her dying was neither painful nor sad. It was a celebration.

At last, the day-long vigil drew to a close. Sunset arrived, and the old woman ended her chanted story. She closed her eyes and took a deep breath. As she once more opened her eyes, she looked up into the old oak tree where the raven waited. The eye of the raven met the gaze of the dying woman. In that moment a flash of recognition sparked between them. The old woman departed her body and flew up to join her sister-soul in the bird.

The raven's cry echoed exuberantly across the countryside, as it flew high into the clouds and disappeared over the mountains. A lone wolf howled a plaintive lament from the forest nearby.

✳ ✳ ✳

Kara sat stunned by this description of an old Strega woman's death. She read it again, to be sure. Yes, it was very much like what Aunt Gina had reported to them about the day that Sophia died. The whole thing had seemed surreal to her as she had listened to it at dinner.

But Gina's tale had drawn the usual cryptic remarks from Dad about satanic rituals, and he had been quickly silenced by both Mom and Uncle Mario. *I agreed with them on that score. It was rude of him to say those things, especially since we were just then making preparations to go and bury Sophia's ashes.*

But whose death is being described in the journal? Maybe the mother or grandmother of the journal's author, Cecelia? Whoever she was, she had a pretty smooth trip, Kara joked to herself. *But, in a raven? Yikes! Whose soul is the one that's been hanging around us waiting for, I wonder?*

Then she recalled how Mimi had relieved the tension at the dinner table by asking some innocent questions that made everyone but their father smile. Mimi had asked, "Were the fairies watching too?" and "When the raven flew away with her soul, did he leave some of the magic behind?" and "Will Sophia come back while we are still visiting here?"

Now, having read this description in the journal, Kara marveled at the wisdom of Mimi's questions. *How can my little imp sister know so much about magic? She seems to just naturally understand the stuff I've been reading about in this journal. She's probably one of those real 'old souls' that Mom mentions sometimes. Could I be one too? That's a weird thought. This story says that old woman had lived many lives, so does that mean we all have? Probably just certain people get to do that. Then who decides who can and who can't anyway?*

Joanna stirred in her bed on the other side of the room, murmuring in her sleep. Kara glanced over to be sure her sister was still asleep. *She's having some romantic dream no doubt. Jo certainly doesn't seem like a very old soul, else why would she be so stupid?* Kara and Jo had been rivals for her father's attention until Joanna abandoned him for her endless string of boyfriends. Kara unconsciously screwed her face in a scornful frown.

Nowadays, it seems like Jo is not even part of the family, she's so preoccupied with clothes and boys. Kara, herself, had yet to meet anyone she felt romantically attracted to, though she had her share of good friends and playmates who were boys. She shrugged and went back to the journal. Skipping over more drawings and tales, she flipped absentmindedly to the last entry in the book.

This was a scribbled list of names that seemed to have been added at some later time, and with a different handwriting from any of the others.

✳ ✳ ✳

THE RIMINI LINE OF WITCHES

1. <u>*Dianhea*</u>: *Circa 700 BCE*
2. <u>*Tanaquil*</u>, *fabled Etruscan Queen. Circa 600 BCE*
3. <u>*Tana*</u>: *Circa 500 BCE Legendary. grand-daughter of* <u>*Tanaquil*</u>.
4. <u>*Fariah*</u>: *Circa 30 AD Tana's lineage, husband Judaic lineage*
5. <u>*Sabrina*</u>: *Circa 30 AD, daughter of Fariah.*
6. <u>*Anasasia*</u>: *Circa 1250 AD descendant of Sylvia*
7. <u>*Aradia*</u>: *Circa 1300 AD Legendary "Beautiful Pilgrim" of Strega tradition in Italy. Her parentage is unknown.*
8. <u>*Karamena*</u>: *Circa 1350 AD daughter of Aradia*
9. <u>*Amelia*</u>: *Circa 1400 AD parentage unknown, raised by wolves Believed to be of the line of, Karamena.*
10. <u>*Maria:*</u> *Circa 1500 AD grand-daughter to Amelia,*
11. <u>*Cecelia*</u>: *Circa1650 AD first author of this journal. Marias daughter*
12. <u>*Iona*</u>: *Circa 1750 AD daughter of Cecelia. Sister of Sylvia*
13. <u>*Sylvia*</u>: *Circa 1750 AD Cecelia's daughter, Iona's sister*
14. <u>*Selena*</u>: *Circa 1800 AD Sylvia's daughter*
15. <u>*Juliet*</u>: *Circa 1800 AD Sylvia's daughter, Selena's sister, died at 13*
16. <u>*Sophia:*</u> *Circa 1850 AD Selena's daughter*
17. <u>*Diana:*</u> *Circa 1900 AD Selena's daughter, Sophia's sister.*
18. <u>*Gina:*</u> *Circa 1900 AD Diana's daughter*
19 <u>*Barbara*</u>: *Circa 1900 AD: Diana's daughter, Gina's sister*
20: *Barbara's three daughters:* <u>*Joanna, Kara, and Mimi.*</u>

✳ ✳ ✳

Kara's neck-hairs tingled. Seeing her own, and her sisters' names at the bottom of this list of witches was a shock. She stifled a little moan of anxiety, so as not to wake Joanna. She felt tempted to just put the old notebook back on the shelf where she found it and pretend she'd never seen it. *This is going too far*, she agonized. *It's okay to read about all these stories from ancient history; even okay to imagine these were real people who are distantly related to us. But it seems wrong to include us among them!*

This list was obviously added by Sophia, and fairly recently. Maybe it is her idea of a joke to play on us because we never got over here to meet her in person. But that's silly too. She wouldn't have any way of knowing I would find the thing and actually read it.

Of course, Mom and Gina would be next in the lineage, if you count only daughters. That's weird too, there is hardly any mention of the fathers or sons. Don't they count for anything in this stupid tradition?

Her ruminations stirred Kara's anger, but she wasn't certain whether it was from a sense of being tricked somehow or from pure disgust at letting herself believe in the mystery thing at all. *For sure, this is more than I want to deal with right now.*

But then a twinge of remorse tweaked her conscience. *I can't forget Rarjer and my promise to him!* Heaving a sigh, she resigned herself. *I guess I may be more involved in the mystery already than I want to be.*

As she was stuffing the journal, once again, into her backpack, she heard sounds coming from the floor below them.

Dad and Mom must be having another argument, or continuing the one from dinner and Sophia's ceremony. Jeez! When are they going to get over it and just let each other have their own thing.

Remembering her short conversation with her father that morning, Kara again felt torn apart by the many divergent beliefs and forces converging on her world. She shut off the light and fell sound asleep until morning. If she dreamed, she did not remember.

23

MIMI: SECOND NIGHT

Mimi, once again, sat in the small painted cave in the tunnel. She and Toby made their way back late in the night, after the others had all gone to bed. She'd had a moment of panic when, passing her parent's bedroom door, she heard their hushed voices. But they were intent on one of their arguments, and didn't hear her in the hallway.

Now she sat on the blanket from the cache of treasures left there by Sophia, lit the candle and examined the contents of the little pouch. She cupped the assortment of stones in her hand and pretended they were precious gems from a princess's ransom. The princess in her fantasy looked like one from the paintings on the walls of the crypt where they buried Sophia's remains earlier that evening.

Mimi was drawn out of her daydream at the sound of giggling. The fairy, Tinkle, joined them in the little cave, along with yet another wild friend. Mimi was stunned, but not frightened, to see the fairy ride in on the back of a small red fox.

"Hi everybody," chirped Tinkle. "Meet my friend, Reddy. He's been hunting in the high woods and says we need to be careful tonight. The vigilantes are already prowling the woods with their guns."

Now Mimi was alarmed. "What do you mean by 'the vigilantes'? And what are they doing at night in the woods with guns? Isn't it illegal to shoot game at night?"

"I don't know about that kind of thing," said Tinkle. "I only know they are bad people, and we stay away from them. Reddy says he will come and let us know if they are coming near, so we can leave in time." The little fox wiggled an ear at Toby, who merely looked bored and licked a paw. The fox yipped once to say goodbye, and ran back up the tunnel passage to the meadow.

It was the first time Mimi felt any fear in the company of her magical friends. She questioned Tinkle some more as they made their way down the tunnel to the grotto. Gradually she was reassured and allowed herself to trust in the magic. *After all, I know Sophia is watching over us too.*

When they reached the big cavern, they found Juliet already there, waiting to begin their next pool-a-vision episode.

Mimi had named the phenomenon 'pool-a-vision' as her private joke. None of the magic folk had any experience with television. Sophia's villa had no TV at all, which had been one small disappointment for Mimi, although she quickly forgot about it once her adventures began.

Now she decided to settle back with her friend to observe whatever Sophia wanted to transmit to her tonight. She would just have to trust in her companions to watch out for her safety.

Juliet swept her hand above the pool and flicked her wrist. The swirling water stilled. The two girls observed as an image appeared in the mirror-like surface. As before, Mimi heard, inside her mind, Sophia narrating the story.

✳ ✳ ✳

On a bluff overlooking the Ionian Sea, at the southeastern edge of the rock-hewn land of Greece, four wild creatures convened on a moonless night sometime around 1200 BCE.

The stag, the wolf, the lion and the bear were bound in a pact of secrecy. Although their kindred were traditional foes who survived by brutal competition over prey and territory within the barren mountains, these four had made a truce with each other. Each was the Alpha leader of his pack, herd, den, or pride. Each was King of his domain, and had sworn to protect and defend the tribe of humans newly settled in their land.

Their pact had been made as a favor to one young maiden of that small island community of refugees. It was she, who had declared their own dens, caves, and nests to be sacred. And as such, they were safe from the arrows, knives, and hatchets of the tribe's huntsmen.

Now that girl, Dianhea sat on a little stool in the courtyard of the temple grounds, milking a goat. "Stand still, Matilda, while I get this bowl filled," murmured the young girl to her restless nanny. "You know our friend, Dravid, needs your warm milk to get well."

With her mane of unruly reddish-brown curls tied back in a green kerchief, and her patchwork skirt hiked up above her skinny knees, the girl could easily be mistaken for the scullery maid of a wealthy land baron. She was, however, the crown princess of a royal family in exile

The nanny goat was not bothered by the four wild creatures stationed on the bluff above them. They often stood guard, like statues on the hill. And earlier this evening, Dianhea had sent the message for them to come.

Her family was among a small group of refugees who escaped a volcanic eruption and earthquake that had shattered their island home, on Crete. Having learned of the oncoming cataclysm, through the snake-prophecy of her grandmother, Sabrina, they had packed up their households along with treasure and sacred talisman in the holds of two of her father's great trading ships. Their gods had been with them, and the people gave thanks daily to animal messengers, through whom the gods spoke to them.

The gift of animal speech ran in Dianhea's blood from birth. The larger gifts of sight and prophecy did not appear in her until they were on their voyage to the Greek mainland. The fits first came upon her after she was accidentally bitten by one of the snakes being transported in a woven reed cage along with the ship's cargo. These snakes were sacred to the people as the primary sources of warning for earthquakes and other natural disasters. It had been Dianhea's task to feed and care for the snakes on the island, and now on the ship. It was a task she had always enjoyed.

However, because of the ship's rocking motion, the snakes were unusually restless on the sea journey. So, as she fed them the first evening at sea, one grazed her finger with its fang. She hardly noticed at the time, but a couple hours later, while sitting at the dinner table with her family, her eyes glazed over and she fell into a stupor. She began muttering gibberish, then called out in a voice that was low and harsh, (very unlike her own gentle tone) that pirates were lurking ahead to capture the ships. Because of her prophecy, they were prepared to escape when the pirates did take chase.

After that, Dianhea was given special quarters and was very carefully watched for further trance prophecies. For a while someone stayed at her side and wrote down every word she said. Some of the priests began to make plans for an oracular shrine where the rulers could come to the nine-year-old girl for advice. They imagined something profitable for the community, in the style of the famed Delphic Oracle, in Greece.

In the end, her grandmother, Sabrina, intervened to put a halt to the mercenary plans of the priests. Grandmother Sabrina was the matriarch priestess-queen, and held sway over all the upstart priests of the kingdom. Theirs was still a nature-based and goddess-blessed civilization, although the encroaching male-god worshipers had infiltrated the governing ranks in recent years.

Now Sabrina made them vow never to confine or restrict the freedom of her grand-daughter for their ritual purposes. Thus, when the ship found safe harbor, and settled, in one of the many hidden coves along the southern coast of the Peloponnesus, Dianhea was called upon to partake of the snake venom and join her grandmother in making spells for the community's protection. But she retained her freedom within the temple grounds and walls of the settlement.

She enjoyed her new role as acolyte priestess, for most of what came forth spoke positively of new growth, prosperity, and peace among the people. However, there was one warning that came through in all of Dianhea's trance-visions. It was in regard to the wild animals of the hills. They were not to be hunted or killed. They were to be honored and protected by all the community, and whoever broke this promise would bring certain disaster upon them all.

By means of her gift of animal speech, she created a pact with the predatory wolves and lions so that they did not attack the goats or other domesticated animals of the compound. In turn, she promised that the people of her tribe would not hunt the families of the wild ones. They lived in mutual peace for several years, each providing protection to the other.

But now that pact had been broken. A rogue farmer had shot a wolf and left its carcass stripped of its pelt. The wolf pack, in revenge, had come down from the hills, broke into the scoundrel's yard, and killed several of his sheep. Dravid had gone to the farmer to reason with him, and instead had been shot it the leg by the drunken fiend. This is why Dianhea had called her animal protectors together tonight.

* * *

Suddenly the pool-a-vision faded and the pool resumed its whirling and flowing. The voice in Mimi's head became silent, and the ghost-girl disappeared. Mimi heard Toby growl and saw that the little fox had returned. It yipped ferociously several times, then turned and ran up one of the other tunnels to the side from the one Mimi and her friends had used.

Tinkle landed on Mimi's shoulder. "Hurry. We have to leave right away. The hunters are in the meadow. We must take a different way out. Follow Reddy!"

Mimi jumped up, trying to get her bearings. Her mind was partly still in trance from the visions she'd been seeing. The fairy pinched her ear and tugged on her hair to get her attention.

At that moment Toby leaped, to the floor of the cavern, facing the entrance foyer. The little cat's fierce yowl sounded like he was a much larger wild animal. Then they all heard the beating of huge wings flapping down the tunnel. It was too late to follow the fox, for they dared not go out by the tunnel now.

Mimi looked about frantically for a place to hide. She saw no other exit but that through which they had arrived, and just then the talons and beak of a giant hawk appeared in the doorway. Mimi's heart pounded in her ears and she thought of diving into the pool and hiding underwater. But Tinkle's voice finally broke through her confusion, calling, "Follow me. Come right now. Hurry!"

The fairy flew into the cavern where the stream flowed out of the grotto into the mountain. Splashing into the brook, ignoring the stone path, Mimi ran along the length of the cavern. But she couldn't make headway in the shallow stream because her shoes filled with water. She stopped to pull them off and dropped one in her haste. She left it lying in the bottom of the stream and kept going. The cold water brought her back to a surer sense of reality.

She looked for Toby and called him. But he was still facing the entry in attack mode, his fur puffed straight out, his ears back, he was snarling viciously. Mimi gasped as she imagined him grown several times his normal size, transformed into a ferocious mountain lion.

She watched aghast as this feline apparition prepared to kill whatever was flying into the grotto. Her sweet little Toby cat, suddenly turned into something big and wild? What was going on? She shook her head, but before she could watch any longer, Tinkle landed on her shoulder again.

Somehow the fairy sprite managed to force Mimi down on her hands and knees, and she found herself crawling through the mouth of the canal. She dropped her other shoe in order to free her hands, then remembered she had put the lantern in one of the shelf-niches. She hesitated, considering whether to go back and get it. Once more, the exasperated fairy came and landed on her shoulder. "Don't go back there, dummy! Toby will guard us until we get away, but he can't hold on forever.

"Come! Now!" And, with another very sharp pinch of Mimi's ear, the fairy flew ahead into the water tunnel, its little wings throwing enough light for them to see their way. Mimi remembered the bag of tokens that hung on her neck, pulled it out from under her shirt, and gripped it tight.

A sense of comfort and courage flowed through her when she grasped the bag. She waded through the water and marveled how the stones did not hurt her bare feet. She found she could stand nearly straight up, except to duck under dripping stalactites from time to time. She followed the fairy with no idea where they were going. This is ever more befuddling than Alice in the rabbit hole, she joked to keep herself from crying.

After some unaccountable length of time, they came to a little door on one side of the canal. It was painted green and was about big enough for an average size adult to duck through. Tinkle stopped and hovered at the door, directing Mimi to open it. She tugged on the handle, but it refused to open.

"You aren't saying the right words," scolded Tinkle impatiently. "Say: 'nepo ta aidara"s gniddib'!"

"What? exclaimed Mimi in consternation. "What are you saying? Talk sense, you silly fairy!" In her excitement she forgot to be polite, and the fairy momentarily looked like it was about to desert her.

"Oh dear," said Mimi. "I'm just scared. Don't be mad at me. But I couldn't understand a word you said."

"Well, we have to go through the door backward," explained Tinkle resignedly, as if the fairy believed Mimi to have gone suddenly witless. "You say 'open at Aradia's bidding' to come in the magic doors, and you say it backward to get out." She frowned at Mimi's baffled look. "Nepo-ta-aidara's-gniddib.," the fairy pronounced slowly and loudly. "But you have to say it while you turn the knob. I can't do that."

"Nepo-at-aidara's-gidib?" said Mimi sarcastically. Nothing happened.

"You said it wrong!" screeched Tinkle, now fully convinced of Mimi's idiocy. "gniddib, not gidib,". the fairy corrected impatiently.

Sounds of a vicious battle could be heard coming from the grotto, echoing through the channel with enhanced volume. Both Mimi and Tinkle were terrified, and their little squabble served to help calm them.

"Okay," said Mimi, taking a deep breath. "I'll try again." She turned to the door with a determined huff. "Nepo-ta-dera's_ no, that's not right. Tell me again Tinkle. I can't seem to remember it." She looked frantically at the fairy, who was beating little fists against the door in desperation.

Tinkle repeated the words slowly and Mimi concentrated very hard. This time she said them clear and strong with all her attention focused on making that door open. "Nepo-ta-aidara's-gniddib!" And the door slid open smoothly and soundlessly, revealing yet another tunnel, similar to that which they had followed to the grotto.

Mimi stepped through backward, with Tinkle sitting on her shoulder. She closed the door behind them, and all the noise from the grotto faded away. Walking, this time upward on a slight incline, they soon began to see daylight seeping through crevices in the rock overhead.

On one side the tunnel opened onto yet another cave. It was not as big as the grotto, but big enough to hold several people or animals. The stench of freshly killed prey was strong. Then they heard a low growl from the back of the cave.

24

JOANNA: MORNING THREE

Joanna smiled happily. Having breakfast with Giuseppe and Anthony at another little café in Rome, she listened as the two young men discussed plans for the day's excursion. Sep had picked her up early this morning and they met Tony here as planned.

"Hey, Sep," said Anthony, "how about we take our fair companion to the Watchtower after a short tour of the real city?" He said this in a hushed voice, as if he was suggesting a clandestine tryst.

Giuseppe shrugged his shoulders and turned to Joanna. "It is an underground theater where they view films made to reveal teachings that are not given by the history books or preached in the churches. The stuff they show is interesting, but also heretical. Sometimes there are demonstrations and police busts. It could be a bit dangerous." He paused, grinned his mischievous Pan-like smile. "Do you feel ready for more indoctrination?"

Jo didn't hesitate. "I think I would love it!" She winked wickedly, adding, "Why should I worry when I have two strong brave men to escort me." She tugged at their hands. "C'mon, lead on, my heroes!"

They raced each other back to the convertible, laughing. Their conversation remained light and joking. But, driving into the heart of Rome, through narrow winding streets in the Trastevere district, Sep became quietly watchful. White-uniformed police directed traffic calmly from the center of chaotic intersections jammed with shouting pedestrians and honking cars.

Along the route, Anthony called Joanna's attention to points of interest, while Sep maneuvered through the maze of streets. Here was a corner where such and such rebellion occurred; here a building once housed a healing center abolished by the church; here a burned out shell of a temple bombed in the war. The sights Anthony called to her attention were not any of the typical tourist attractions, but esoteric reminders of ancient enemies still engaged in a battle for human rights.

They passed crumbling columned ruins interspersed by blocks of shiny steel and glass skyscrapers. Gradually, they wound their way through narrow alleyways, hidden behind shambling stone walls of the oldest part of the city where there was less traffic and a relative quiet. At last, Giuseppe pulled the car into a cobblestone alley behind a small run-down brick building housing a tiny book store. It was squeezed inconspicuously between other similar small shops facing a weed-grown lot with stalls of vendors selling vegetables, fruit, and other produce. A few people wandered through the open-air market and cars were parked haphazardly around the square.

Anthony hailed a man selling oranges and bananas. Another called to him from a stand piled high with tomatoes. They mimed carefree cheer, but Joanna sensed an undercurrent of intrigue, as if their greetings were meant more as signals or warnings, rather than simple friendly banter. *I'm probably just being melodramatic*, she thought to herself.

They entered the musty bookstore. Anthony exchanged furtive salutations with the proprietor, while Giuseppe idly rummaged among careless stacks of books. He selected one which he purchased and tucked into his jacket pocket. They left the bookstore and walked across the market square. Jo stayed between the two men and matched their casual pace, but she felt they were prepared to run at any moment. Jo found her senses oddly sharpened.

The smells and sounds of the marketplace came to her with unusual clarity, so that the general hubbub faded and she could distinguish specific voices, focus on particular activities, although she didn't know what she should be alert to see or hear.

Sep seemed especially on guard. Was he expecting trouble? The hairs on her neck felt tingly. Sep exchanged few words, but nodded acknowledgment to one or another person they passed. He kept one arm protectively around her waist as they made their way among the stalls, steering her away from, or toward, various paths. She could feel the tension in his body, like an animal prepared to spring. He still wore his mischievous grin when she glanced at him, however, which calmed her mounting anxiety.

On the far opposite street stood a large building resembling a church, but it had no religious symbols on its steeple. Instead, it bore a flag with a black silhouette of a large bird against a white circle in a green background. In large letters on the bell tower were painted the words "The Watchtower" in English, oddly enough. It was to this building they were headed. But, rather than climbing the steps to its wide front doors, Anthony led them around to a side door.

A man shouted to them just as they ducked inside a darkened vestibule. Joanna couldn't understand what the stranger said in Italian, but Giuseppe swore. "Damn! Where did that bastard come from? I thought I had us totally covered."

"Aw, don't worry about Carlo, old man," growled Anthony. "He doesn't know anything. He just likes to harass the Benendanti."

"I don't trust him. Wasn't he one of the guys you were going at it with in the bistro yesterday?"

"Yeah, but he's an outsider who just wants to feel like he fits in. Don't worry, I told those guys you and I had a double date, and they took it as a joke. He thinks we're coming in here for some so-called refreshments." Anthony said this sarcastically, insinuating something Joanna didn't understand at first.

Giuseppe snapped, "Oh great! Now they can finger us for drug charges as well as insurrection." He started to turn around and leave, but Anthony pulled him back. "Look, man. We're here among friends. Nobody's going to finger us. You're too damn paranoid and suspicious."

Joanna was afraid they would start fighting, but Giuseppe said, "I guess you're right. The creeps aren't likely to squeal on us, since it would just call attention to their own dealings." With an audible huff, he gave a Joanna a little squeeze and said, "Don't let our squabble scare you. Me and Anthony just have different ideas on who our friends are sometimes. In the end, we're on the same side of things and we will take care that nothing happens to you."

She wondered for a moment just what kind of danger she could be in, but decided to trust them and enjoy her adventure. She said, "I'm not scared. Like I said before, I feel well protected by the two of you. Now, where is this movie we're supposed to be seeing?"

Anthony slapped Giuseppe on the back, saying, "I knew she was game for a risk, old man. Let's get on down to the show." And he led the way down a flight of stairs into an underground room with heavy stone walls and no windows. The cellar was lit by an ornate Venetian glass chandelier hanging incongruously from the center of the bare ceiling giving an odd sort of formality to the otherwise decrepit cellar. A musty odor hung about the place, as if it had only recently been cleared of many decade's worth of accumulated trash.

Metal folding chairs sat in haphazard rows, facing a ger-rymandered bed sheet screen hung against the far wall of the ancient vault. About thirty people were seated in clusters, talking animatedly. In the back of the room, a long table held an assortment of film projectors and speakers and audio tape players. The fellow manning this equipment smiled broadly at Giuseppe and said, "Good to see you, Sep. It's been awhile since you've wandered into our den from yours." The two men shook hands and laughed companionably.

"We're just showing a friend from the States some of the local color," explained Sep. But he didn't introduce Joanna.

Meanwhile, Anthony set up three chairs for them at the front, on the end of the room farthest from the entry and near another side door. He waved to Sep and Jo, motioning them to sit there. Then he went to talk to a man and woman sitting at the center of the room, and soon returned with the couple in tow. "I want you to meet the director, producer, actress and screenwriter of this production, Joanna. They are a couple of Italy's hottest talents, but hardly anybody has heard of them."

The woman smiled warmly and the man laughed genially at his remark. Anthony continued his introduction. "Mia Felini is not only a brilliant playwright, but she is a fabulous screen-star. You will see her play several parts in this film. David Taviani is a master film maker, turned renegade. The production they have made on a minuscule budget strikes at the very heart of our resurgence against the power of patriarchal religious institutions."

Turning to the handsome couple, Anthony then added, "My cousin from the states, Joanna, also has the dancing and music in her blood."

They exchanged greetings. And, although they all spoke fluent English, Joanna found herself unsure of what to say. She felt awed by Anthony's flowery introduction, but understood it to be typical of the Latin gracious style to give effusive compliments.

"Have you performed on stage in the States?" asked Mia, in a whisper-soft voice. She smiled warmly, and Jo felt less awkward.

"Only a couple of bit parts in off-Broadway shows, professionally. But in school I have often been given lead vocal parts, and I love to do the dance numbers."

She felt a bit silly talking to a genuine professional as if she really had experience. Of course, she had been taking lessons and performing since she was only six or seven years old.

David leaned over and said, sotto voice, "If you stay in Italy, you could find work with our cinema or on the live stage. Of course, the pay is nothing like what you earn in the States," he added with a hearty laugh.

Joanna, who had never earned more than a few hundred dollars in the professional productions she'd worked in, laughed in return. "I don't think I ever would go into the arts for the money. It is the sheer joy of the work that I love." Again she felt silly speaking as if she had experience.

Mia wasn't laughing, however, when she responded, "The truly talented never seek fame and fortune, it simply comes as an added bonus or curse to some." Then she turned to David, "Joanna would be lovely in the part of Saluma, wouldn't she?" Again to Joanna, she explained, "It is the lead character in the film we are planning as a sequel to this one."

"Well," said David, "We are always looking for new talent. If you find yourself lingering in Italy, let us know. We can surely arrange an audition at least." Then, with nods and hand-shakes all around, Mia and David excused themselves to go back and sit in the front center, as the film was about to begin.

Joanna was left with her head spinning, full of new dreams. *My eighteenth birthday is in August,* she thought. *I am old enough to stay here and work with the theater even if the others go home. Wouldn't that be fantastic! Mom would be happy for me, but I'll have to convince daddy.*

It was hard to bring her attention to the black and white screenplay, but soon the drama caught her in its cryptic message. She hardly noticed that Giuseppe had placed himself facing the main entrance behind them, rather than the screen; and that Anthony seemed more occupied in observing who came and went than watching the film.

24

JOHN GOES TO ROME

John woke at the slam of the Ferrari's doors and the rev of its engine as it took off down the driveway with his eldest daughter and her newest boyfriend on their way to another sight-seeing jaunt in Rome. John recalled her telling the family about their plans at supper last night. *I still don't trust that smooth-talking Giuseppe, but the girl is too independent for me to control. Might as well try to tame a cheetah,* he grumbled to himself.

But he had to grin, too, because he was proud of Joanna's theatrical and musical accomplishments. He, himself, had once aspired to an operatic career. He shook his head at that long-ago ideal, and how far he had grown away from such romantic dreams.

He looked over at Barbara, now peacefully asleep next to him, and decided to get up and let her sleep off her anger from their late-night squabble. John felt a twinge of remorse at his tirades during dinner and later, in the crypt. But he quickly re-affirmed his righteous fury at the suggestion that his daughters should be allowed to learn the harebrained teachings of his wife's demented old aunt.

He quickly crept out of bed and took his clothes to the bathroom to change there after taking a shower. Truth be told, John wanted to avoid talking to Barb this morning at all. He didn't relish seeing the anger in her eyes again or hearing her silent dismissal of his fears. *Let her cool down with a day of shopping and visiting with her sister and their old friends down the coast in Salerno.*

Meanwhile, John planned to pay a visit to his cousin, Donnie Marini, at the Vatican Cultural Ministry. He'd spoken to the guy yesterday and they had arranged to meet for lunch. John decided to leave early, drive some back roads off the main autostrada, and take in a few sights along the way to Rome. It had been over twenty years since he'd seen the country and he wondered how much of the damage from the war could still be viewed. Seeing several bombed-out churches in the countryside had already fired his memories of the war years.

He reminisced on his two-hour drive to Rome. His family_ a staunchly Catholic clan, living on the island of Sicily in the 1920's_ was thoroughly of the 'old school' with boisterous men and dignified women who lived in large households full of relatives. Aunts and uncles, cousins and grandparents all congregated regularly at the Marini's generous table following Sunday mass. As a boy he listened attentively to the men discussing events of world and local politics, but he often searched within himself for answers to troubling questions of ethnic and religious rivalry.

His mother, who presided like a queen over the dinner table, would not allow political or religious argument there, and would bring forth topics related to theater or operatic events, or laughingly tease out debates about the latest literary works coming out of England and France. In this home, his Mama held sway. But, in the world of public life, she was a mere shadow behind his gigantic and aggressive father.

John learned a male-dominant view of the world, tempered with a profound, but suppressed, respect for the wisdom and gentler power of women. But among the relatives were a few with darker associations that would make pious religious dogma and heated political discourse seem simple minded.

Several in the family's ancestral tree had been high Church officials during the Medieval and Renaissance periods of the Catholic Church's Inquisition against Jews, Protestants, Gypsies, and so-called Witches. These ancestral relatives of John's family were held in high esteem by certain individuals of the twentieth century Marini clan. Moreover, some of these modern-day fanatics had secret ties to the powerful bosses of the underground movement_ the Sicilian Mafia. Some even held positions of high rank in both organizations, the religious and the mob.

He suspected his cousin, Donnie, was one such double-agent. John maintained a certain awe of these people in high places of power, even while disagreeing with much of their modus operandi. Although John's parents eschewed the rogue branch of the family, they nevertheless maintained loyal ties with the clan when they moved to America during Mussolini's rise to power in Italy.

John, himself, though an independent thinker on matters of political and nationalist ideals, never questioned the Church's stance regarding the absolute power of its male hierarchy. He dutifully made confession and accepted the word of those who claimed powers of intercession with God. He rarely gave his faith deeper thought, although he was a student and teacher of classical philosophy.

But he came to embrace a vehement belief in hell and a paralyzing fear of the Devil following several years of harrowing wartime encounters with the evils of humankind.

When the war ended and John came through virtually unscathed, he vowed to resist the family's pressure to enter the priesthood. He wanted to make himself a new life back in America, far from war-torn Italy.

As he drove, John let his mind wander over past memories to happier times. He recalled how, shortly after the war ended, he met Barbara. He had been completely charmed by her energy and vivacious wit. She soothed his troubled mind, and he learned to laugh again when they were together. Although John knew little of Barbara's family when they met, he sensed in her a spirit of freedom and adventure that he had rarely encountered among his own people. As lovers, they spoke only briefly of their religious upbringings, and neither was much concerned to learn how very different their backgrounds were. In fact, to John at that time, Barbara's pagan roots seemed romantic and vaguely challenging to his own dogmatic faith.

When they eloped to the United States, they each left behind much of who they had been in Italy. At least, so John chose to believe at the time. Through the years, while their daughters were born and grew, both John and Barbara worked as college professors; John in ancient Greek philosophy, Barb in music and the arts.

After a while John began to resent Barbara's assumption of total equality between them. He began to recall how his mother deferred to his father in matters of world affairs and religion. He tried to enforce a similar attitude in Barbara and the girls. When his efforts to assert his dominance failed miserably, John turned more and more to his Catholic religion, dragging the girls with him to church, even though Barbara refused to attend all but the most important services.

Moreover, John became painfully aware of the pagan themes in Barbara's artwork, poetry, and music. Soon her unique talents, which he had so admired, became great irritants to his need for absolute belief in the One Faith. He made remarks against her writing as being about superstitions and pagan deviltries, and he began to denounce her family traditions as satanic. What's more, he often made these hurtful comments when the girls were present, in a misguided attempt to persuade them to his views.

In time, John found he could barely suppress his nasty tirades, and he grew increasingly dour around home. It irked him terribly that Barbara and the girls continued their playful interchanges and fantasy games, despite his disapproval.

Pondering all this as he maneuvered the rental car through Rome's frenzied streets, his vitriolic resentments gained new resolve. He recalled how, over the years, when letters came from Gina or Sophia, he would hide them from Barbara. He felt some shame for this, but convinced himself it was for the family's good that they stay completely detached from the old ways.

When Barb bemoaned the lack of contact and wished aloud that they could make the trip back to Italy with the girls, John found reasonable excuses to put it off. His grandparents were dead and he had no pressing desire to return to his own roots. His fears of Sophia's evil influence over-rode any guilt he might have felt about manipulating Barbara in this way.

Now he found his way to the Vatican's business complex and turned in at the gate, giving the guard Donnie's name. The guard soon waved him into the parking area for visitors and John found his way to his cousin's office. He hadn't given much thought to just what he wanted from this man who had close contact with people in high places. *At least Donnie might fill me in on some of the weird subversive spiritual-political movements that I hear are springing up in Italy.*

A little later, after the two men had eaten a hearty lunch and were enjoying cigars with a liquor for desert, John broached the subject. "I do have some concerns that I thought you might be able to help me sort out, Donnie," he began. "It's about a school that Barbara's aunt had going here at her villa. The old lady died, and we are here to help put her estate in order. I'm not familiar with the legal and political ramifications of things in your country, and hoped you would be able to give me some advice."

Donnie sucked on his cigar thoughtfully. "Tell me more about this aunt of Barbara's and the estate you've inherited."

John hesitated a moment, unsure just what to disclose to this man who had ties to power in the city government and the church. He didn't want to make false accusations or arouse unnecessary questions about Barbara's family. He just wanted to find legal or political reasons to convince them to abandon the esoteric school.

He cleared his throat after a sip of cognac. "The villa is a very ancient structure, part of it going back to the fourteenth century and before." His cousin watched with mild amusement as John puffed on his cigar and blew a few smoke rings. "Sophia Rimini was a local shaman who taught a few acolytes in the Old Ways, as they call it. She died at the ripe age of 99, just last month. Barbara and her sister stand to inherit the estate."

His cousin took a rather large swallow of his drink and repressed a sputtered cough.

Oblivious to Donnie's sudden change in demeanor, John considered his own words carefully and continued, "My concerns are with local inheritance laws and the possibility of retaining the property as a center for the arts or a museum of antiquities. It has great potential, being located on a prime vista overlooking the sea, just above the little port of Terracina."

John noticed that Donnie's face looked flushed. He wondered if the guy had heart trouble or something. Donnie cleared his throat, and with a slightly reproving tone said, "The Rimini Witches. I've heard of that family for years. I had no idea your wife is related to them."

John swallowed and tried to sound noncommittal, "Well, it's not as if they are witches anymore, is it? The old lady taught herbalism, a perfectly respectable healing tool even in the twentieth century." He couldn't help but notice that he was parroting words Mario had said to him just a couple days ago. "Barb hasn't had anything to do with the family since we were married twenty years ago. Our interest now is in preserving the property as an historic site. Maybe make a little profit from tourism."

"Of course, John." Donnie quickly interjected, "I didn't mean anything except that the family was rather notorious in days past. I'm always interested in these enclaves of paganism that cling to our Christian country like little ticks on a dog's back."

This comment rankled John. Suddenly he felt protective toward Sophia. "I don't think their teachings are all that wrong-headed, Donnie. What I've known of the family, they are most respectful of human rights and work for environmental and animal causes." He blew another smoke ring. "Hardly seems seditious to me. Certainly nothing the power of the Vatican can't live with and control."

"You are right, to a degree, John," Donnie held to his point, "but the Strega movement is not as simple as that. That may be all your wife's aunt espoused, but there are others in the sect who seriously challenge the Church and the very Word of God." He was warming up to his subject when they were interrupted by the maitre'd.

"Scusi," the man bowed politely, then looked at Donnie. "I believe you are Mssr. Donald Marini?"

"I am. Have you a message for me?" said Donnie, sounding a bit irritated at the interruption.

"There is a phone call from the Vatican business offices. If you would like, I can bring you a phone to the table. Or, you can step into the reception parlor and take it on a private line there."

Donnie got up to follow the man, saying "I'll be right back John, and we'll continue this conversation. Whatever this is shouldn't take long."

He came back minutes later with a frown on his face. "Seems there is some trouble of the very kind I was about to tell you. I normally would let my assistants handle this, but perhaps this time I will make an appearance myself and you can join me. That will allow you to see what I am talking about."

John was baffled. *What am I getting myself into?* But his curiosity was aroused. "Sure" he said, "I would be interested to see what it is you are dealing with." Hesitating, he added, "but are you certain I will not be in your way or cause you unnecessary trouble?"

"Absolutely not, John." The Cultural Affairs Minister now grinned and slapped John on the back, leading him toward the door. "I think you may find this very interesting, indeed, even enjoyable."

25

MIMI MISSING

Sometime after Joanna and John had each left on their respective day-trips, Barbara burst into Kara's bedroom without knocking and shook her awake. "Kara! Mimi has disappeared! You've got to help me find her!" She grasped Kara's arm, trying to pull her out of bed.

Kara rubbed her eyes and stared at her mother. "How should I know where that little imp is? I've been sleeping." She pulled away from her mother's grasp. "Let go! That hurts!"

"Ohh! I'm sorry honey," Barb, her face flushed and tears welling in her eyes, sat on the edge of the bed and stroked Kara's arm. "I didn't mean to hurt you. It's just that I'm scared. When I went up to the loft to call her for breakfast, she was gone."

"Well, that isn't surprising," said Kara. "Mimi is so eager to explore our 'castle', as she calls it. Of course she isn't going to sleep in. She's probably out in the orchard talking to the trees." Kara began to climb out of bed. "Mimi is perfectly capable of taking care of herself. She's got a knack for always coming out on top of things, you know."

Kara's grin helped reassure Barb. She nodded and returned a shaky smile. She thought how her youngest daughter's innocent good nature often allowed her to walk through tricky situations and pass by danger without stirring things up. But now, she shook her head. "I've looked everywhere in the house and out in the orchard. There is simply no sign of Mimi. Her knapsack and lantern are gone too. So is Toby."

"Well then, you needn't worry. Toby is with her, and will see she doesn't get lost." Kara tossed her pony tail indifferently.

"Honey, I would just appreciate if you would go out and look for her. Maybe she is playing one of her little tricks on us. You are best at tracking and spotting her." Barb smiled at the memory of previous escapades their little prankster had pulled and how Kara caught her out. "Remember her hideaway in the rain culvert at home?"

"Yeah, I barely found her before rainstorms would have washed her out of there, or worse!"

Barb looked pleadingly at Kara. "Please at least walk up to the meadow and see if she's there. Gina is due to arrive shortly. We were going to make a drive down to Solerno, but we'll wait for you to get back with Mimi. If you don't find her real soon, come back here and we'll all go look for her." Barb frowned. "It's a good thing your father left early for his meeting in Rome. I don't want him to know about this. Not unless it turns out to be serious."

Kara shrugged. "I'll get dressed and go snoop around. But first, could you make me a sandwich or something to take along? I'm hungry."

Barbara went to the kitchen and prepared a sack of peanut butter sandwiches, some sliced cheese, cans of root beer, a bag of raisins, two apples, and some oatmeal cookies. She pictured Kara sharing these with Mimi when she found her, and that thought eased her mind.

When Kara set off in her well-worn hiking boots, cut-off shorts, and t-shirt, a windbreaker tied around her waist, and shouldering her ever-present backpack, Barbara reassured herself that everything was okay. It would be another of those innocent adventures they could laugh about later.

Nevertheless, she called to Kara, "Be careful yourself, sweetheart. And, by the way, don't tell your father anything about this. You know how upset he can get over nothing."

When Gina arrived a half hour later, the two women discussed the situation over a cup of coffee in the courtyard. They sat at a little ice-cream table by the far wall, opposite the fountain, set in the niche beneath the overhanging oak tree.

Anticipating the girls' return any moment, Barb's thoughts wandered to her own childhood in these mountains. "Gina, do you think Mimi might have found her way to one of our old hideouts? Would those caves still be accessible?"

"I haven't walked the wilds very much myself in the past few years." mused Gina. "But Sophie trekked in the woods regularly, right up until the day before she died. I'm sure she kept those secret places accessible for any who might need them. I wouldn't be surprised if Mimi finds her way to one, especially since she seems to have such a keen empathy for the animals."

This thought sent a shiver up Barbara's spine. "I had forgotten how many wild animals live around here! That isn't a very reassuring thought right now. Mimi is just a city kid, after all. What would she know about wolves or whatever else is out there? No matter how brave and attuned she may be."

Barb got up, nearly spilling her coffee. "The same goes for Kara! I shouldn't have sent her off alone! We had better go after her right now!"

"Hey! Slow down, honey," said Gina. "No point in rushing off without a plan. I really don't think they are in any danger from wild animals. It would be the Malandanti, if anything, that I would worry about. And they are not after little girls!" She said this with a small laugh, but Barb wasn't amused.

"I feel so confused," Barb said. She sat down again, but barely on the edge of her chair. "Things feel very spooky to me around here. I know, for you it is normal daily stuff, but I can't grasp the idea that people are really still witch-hunting and harassing pagan rituals."

Then another thought occurred to her and she gasped. "Uh, oh. What about Joanna? She and Giuseppe left about six this morning for another trip into Rome. They wouldn't be in danger would they?"

Gina shrugged. "I knew they were going since Sep has borrowed Mario's convertible again. As to danger, I don't know. It can pop up anywhere these days. But I wouldn't worry for Joanna. Sep knows very well how to handle trouble and take care of himself."

A furtive tone in Gina's voice made Barbara ask, "Tell me more about him would you? He's so charming he seems almost unreal."

Gina smiled. "He is a bit of a mystery man, for sure. Although he often came around to help Sophia, he moved away from the villa when he was only about thirteen. No one seems to know where he lives. He just pops up. Yet everyone knows him and almost everyone likes him. Except the authorities, of course."

A shadow fell across Gina's face. She looked up. The bird perched on the oak branch overhanging the garden wall. "Well, I do believe its Melanthus. Hi there old friend." Gina gave the bird a frank stare. "Are you eaves-dropping on our conversation, or have you come with some gossip of your own?"

Barbara felt an old premonition that always accompanied the arrival of a raven since she was a young child. Now Barbara met the bird's stare with a sense of urgency in her gut. "Do you know where my girls are?" She felt a bit silly and didn't really expect any response.

"Craaaack caw craaaack!" The raven flapped its wings and resettled on the branch, hopping a few feet closer to the table. It looked directly at them, turning its head as if to take in both their gazes. The women watched him intently, as if listening to what he had to say.

"Craack. Caaw." Then he flew off into the big old tree behind the house that they had called the 'magic tree' when they were kids. Many of her own childhood adventures had begun at that tree, Barbara recalled with a sudden rush of adrenalin.

"Do you think he wants us to follow him?" she asked Gina

"I don't see why we shouldn't go for a little walk up the old woods trail anyway," her sister replied. "We can meet the girls part way and walk back with them. I'm sure they will be coming along the trail anytime now." So the two women set off following the raven's caws.

26

KARA'S SEARCH

When her mother sent her to look for Mimi, Kara had set off directly for the meadow where she first met Rarjer. True to her instinct, she found the big wolf there. It seemed almost as if he knew she would come and was waiting for her.

At first she felt uncertain of his intentions, but when he crept up and quietly nudged his nose into her hand she knew she could trust him. She hadn't just imagined the incredible bond that seemed to have grown between them yesterday.

Kara sat down on the fallen log to gather her thoughts. Breathing deeply, taking in the scents of Nature around her, she felt momentarily reassured by the peaceful atmosphere. She could hear bees humming in the wild clover, birds chirping in treetop nests, and the gurgle of a small stream somewhere nearby. She tried to listen to the voice of Nature on the wind, but couldn't make out any answer for her quest.

Recalling her mission, Kara opened her backpack and took out a pair of dirty socks which she had confiscated from Mimi's bedroom. She held the rumpled objects out to the animal, saying,

"My little sister is lost and I need you to help me find her. Here is what she smells like."

The wolf nuzzled them thoughtfully, then bounced up on his haunches. "Do you know where Mimi is, my wild friend?" Kara laid her hand cautiously on the wolf's ruff, still unsure just how much human contact he would tolerate. She struggled with her doubts and fears. *Maybe we're just wasting time on a wild goose chase. Maybe Mimi is back at the house by now.* The wolf started off through the meadow a short way, then turned to look at her. *Or maybe she has gone somewhere worse.* She heaved a sigh of uncertainty.

Rarjer doubled back and loped over to the log. He lay down next to her, with his tongue lolling in a big grin. *He sure doesn't act like there is any urgent emergency,* thought Kara

Kara's doubts must have reached the wolf's consciousness, because he roused himself to push at her with his muzzle. Then he snuffled the log she was sitting on and scratched a bit of its bark. Then he pawed at Mimi's socks tucked in Kara's pants pocket which she took out again for him to sniff. He bounded two or three leaps away, turned and looked back and wagged his tail, beckoning her to follow.

He seems to be saying Mimi has passed this way. She decided to trust her own special guide from Nature. She pulled together her belongings and said, "Okay, big guy, lead on. I'll just trust you and Mother Nature, like Sophia's diary says."

She dug into her pack and took out a few raisins, scattering them around the log. "Thank you, spirits of the mountains, whoever you are," she murmured, glancing up into the trees.

Following a faintly trampled path across the meadow, Kara spotted several clusters of the fennel plant which she had read about in the notebook. She stopped to examine the wild herb, pinched off a leaf, and smelled its spicy fragrance. On an impulse, Kara pulled out her pocket knife and cut several twigs from the plant. Again, she took out some raisins and dropped them on the ground, giving silent thanks to the plant for its soothing balm.

Tucking the cuttings into her pack, she kept one twig in hand to sniff as she followed Rarjer into a thicket of snarled wood. The thicket hid a rocky escarpment with a cleft in its face. The wolf walked into this cleft, seeming to disappear into the rock. Kara watched him in surprise, and with a twinge of anxiety she followed, but stopped to pull a flashlight out of her backpack.

The recess appeared to be formed of giant boulders piled together, creating a snug passage into the mountain. Although daylight filtered into the horizontal cavity through crevices along its upper length, the tunnel grew dark farther along and sloped downward deeper into the earth. The wolf sniffed along the ground, plodding steadily into the recesses of the cavern.

Kara flicked her flashlight over walls of marbled limestone harboring patches of moss and fungi, beautifully colored like the gold and bronze and green shading of a snake's skin. The floor of the cavern was a shale surface that had apparently been worn smooth by the pads of animals and feet of humans over many years. A notion of walking in the footsteps of ancient ancestors came to Kara's mind.

She felt the urgency of her immediate quest dissipate. She momentarily forgot that her objective was to find her sister, not pursue the mystery of her forebears. She imagined herself living in the era of the first Rimini witches she'd read about, perhaps following a secret passageway to a gathering of their sect, or to escape from enemies. She shivered as she remembered that tomorrow would be the eve of one of their most sacred holy days, Beltane.

They came upon a lair, set off to one side of the tunnel, and Kara's flashlight beam fell upon a carved icon above the opening. It was an image of a woman riding on the back of a wolf and holding a cup in one hand.

To Kara, it seemed a peculiarly personal manifestation. *Here I am, following a tame wolf. Well, at least I'm not riding on its back, she joked. But who is the woman in this symbol? A goddess?*

Some ancestress of our family? It is sort of like the painting that Sophia had made in the crypt that we saw last night. She shivered, recalling how she'd imagined some of the older images to be alive and watching them. *There is definitely a weird sense of magic about all this, despite my logical explanations.*

When she shone her flashlight into the little cave, she was startled to see another group of brightly colored paintings. These, however, did not appear as realistic as those last night, nor did she see any of them wink at her. They were almost like children's drawings, fanciful and playful, and pretty in their primitive simplicity.

Rarjer, snuffling around in the little cave, picked up an object and brought it to Kara. His actions brought her back to their present search. In his mouth, the wolf held a snuffed candle. Kara felt the burned wick and found the charcoal still fresh_ evidence that someone had been here quite recently.

Kara's sense of urgency returned and she continued down the tunnel without examining any more of the small cave.

Winding down the gently sloping and spiraling tunnel, Rarjer abruptly skidded to a halt and growled deep in his chest. Kara felt a gust of cool air swirling up the passage and felt momentarily relieved at this sign of an exit ahead, for she'd begun to dread getting trapped in the mountain.

But very quickly her relief turned to fright when a huge bird with extremely long sharp talons flew up from the far end of the passage and swooped just above her head.

Kara screamed.

It turned in mid-flight and dove for the wolf

Rarjer stood primed to kill, his fangs barred and ears back.

Kara got ready to run, but which direction? She stood frozen, caught between the two combatants.

She tried to think how she could scare away the bird, but she could not make a sound. Her voice felt stuck in her throat. She could only stand stiffly and stare as the two wild creature battled each other.

The great hawk looked to be wounded, for its feathers were ruffled askew, and one talon hung limply. But the bird was fearsome nevertheless and perhaps, in its pain, saw her and her wolf as logical opponents.

Growling, snarling, screeching, spitting, the wolf and bird circled her and menaced each other, prepared to gore one another to death. Rarjer leapt, snapping off a jaw full of tail feathers. The bird aimed its vicious beak to gouge the wolf's eyes.

Kara shifted, trying to grab her backpack and throw it at the bird. But suddenly the raptor stopped in midair.

Hovering a moment, it glared at Kara. She felt her mouth form a scream, but it was drowned out by the hideous screeching of the bird as it turned and flew frantically up the passage they had just come down. It seemed to have been routed by some unseen foe.

Kara stood in shock, her legs and arms shaking from the release of tension. Her breath came in gasps. Rarjer also stood frozen in mid-crouch, looking dumbfounded.

Then the wolf looked at her and bounced up playfully, his paws on her shoulders. "Kah-Rah! Kah-Rah!" Mystified, Kara stared at her friend. She glanced up the tunnel to be sure the awful bird was really gone. Looking down at her hand, she realized she was still clutching the little twig of fennel like a miniature spear.

For a moment it seemed to glow with a pulsing light that formed the shape of a small spear. But instantly it returned to its normal greenish-brown twiggy shape.

The uncanny realization hit her. *Could it have been the protection plant that scared that hawk away?* She was incredulous. "The notebook says fennel is the weapon against Malandanti in the spirit world. Maybe it works in the real world too!" Laughing a bit nervously, she joined Rarjer in his little victory dance.

Pulling a few tiny petals from the plant's florets, she sprinkled them on the path. "Thank you spirits of the mountain for protecting us." Then they continued down the tunnel until they arrived at the entrance of the great grotto beneath.

The wolf stepped nonchalantly over the threshold, as if he were walking into his own familiar den. But Kara stood, her mouth agape. The high ceiling, dripping with stalactites, shimmered with light from its unseen source. The cascade of falls splashed into the pool and swirled into the stream that bisected the grotto. Stone seats, tables and an altar surrounded the pool. Somehow it all felt familiar.

I know this place, I have been here before.

Her rational mind instantly checked that thought. "It must be like something from a dream or a movie I've seen. I know I could not have actually been in here before. But it sure does seem familiar," she muttered to herself.

She found herself drawn to the altar by the waterfall and began looking around it, poking her hand between the piled stones of which it was formed. She seemed to be looking for something, and stopped.

"What the heck am I doing?" But she was compelled to continue to search. There was something here she was to retrieve. "What in the world gives me that notion? Am I totally nuts?" She shook her head, astonished by her own odd behavior.

Suddenly her groping hand touched something smooth and soft. Kara jerked away, thinking she'd disturbed a small critter asleep in its burrow. But when nothing stirred, she reached in again, tentatively exploring with her fingers. It was a bundle, wrapped in soft leather. She tugged at it gently to pull it forward, then grasped it. Her hand shook with unexplained anticipation as she examined the cylindrical package. Buckskin, tied securely with slender thongs. It was heavy for such a small package.

She sat down and carefully untied it, holding it across her knees as it opened to reveal a sharp-edged, but elaborately carved silver knife. No, not just a knife, she corrected herself. This blade was honed on both edges, and very sharply pointed. This was a dangerous weapon. But it was also a holy relic. She could just feel the power emanating from it when she grasped the handle.

Just then, Rarjer, who had been sniffing about the grotto, barked excitedly. Kara was brought back to the present emergency. She scolded herself for having forgotten about Mimi again. She carefully stowed the wrapped treasure in her backpack. Her heart was drumming hard. "What in the world is going on here?" She turned her attention back to the wolf.

Rarjer stood over a small figure lying motionless on the floor by the opening to the stream's canal. Kara ran to him and cried out in dismay. Toby lay in a heap, blood-spattered and barely breathing. Kara knelt down and gently stroked the cat's poor battered body, feeling for broken bones or wounds. Toby stirred slightly and purred, opening one eye in welcome.

Kara determined the cat was more exhausted than injured and carefully picked him up in her arms. He allowed her to wrap him in her nylon windbreaker in a kind of sling around her neck. Suddenly Kara realized her sister must have been in grave danger if she left her little companion alone and so badly hurt. Panic filled her mind and tears blurred her vision.

Overwhelmed, Kara sat down on one of the flat stone-seats and, cradling the cat, she wept.

27

JOANNA : AMAZING TALES

The movie was shot in vignettes, something like the little skit they had watched in the park. Here, however, voices intoned the story over a background of dirge-like organ music, reminiscent of a Catholic mass. The effect was eerie. The story followed general historical and biblical themes, yet the primary characters were women. (Several played by Mia, herself) And, always, the stories diverged quite sharply from traditional versions.

Jo watched now, completely entranced, drawn into the mystery as a hidden narrator intoned the tale.

Anu sat in the shade of a rocky outcrop in the desert foothills, her white caftan pulled around her like a shroud. A darkly wizened little woman, she gazed into a deep azure sky. Her eyes followed the flight of birds high over the horizon where desert met mountain range, and where Life now met Death.

Behind her was the cave that had been her sacred place of worship, love, peace, and in the past few years, her place of hiding and refuge. Gathered about her were some of her dearest companions: Enya, her faithful handmaiden, and Saru, Enya's partner and Anu's loyal bodyguard. They had both come with her from the old temple compound in the fallen city.

Harimtu, Anu's daughter by the old king, was now high priestess of the new temple in the resurrected city. Behind Harimtu, clinging shyly to her flowing skirts, was Anu's granddaughter, Enheduanna, 'virgin-born' in the sacred marriage of King Sargon and Harimtu, in her guise as the goddess Ishtar's representative in the seasonal fertility ritual.

A veritable menagerie of animal companions milled peacefully about the boundaries of the little compound of tents. Camels grazed solemnly without protest, as three small lion cubs gamboled around their feet. Farther away, but within leaping distance, a male and female lion lay beneath a scrub cedar, placidly yawning and preening themselves. In the branches of a tree sat a large black raven that had been tamed by Anu from the flock now circling the horizon.

All were gathered to observe the secret ceremony of Anu's passing to the Otherworld. She looked forward to reuniting with her loving life-partner and consort, who had died only last year in the battle of the temple against the usurpers.

Although the current King, Sargon, was still respectful of the old religion, his military commanders and priests were not. Therefore, Anu's people kept more and more to themselves, away from Ur, the large city. Gradually, they were dispersing farther to the northwest, into Anatolia, and to the south and west, into Canaan and Egypt. This emigration had been occurring for many decades, ever since invaders over-ran the land of the Indus, their peoples' original homeland.

Anu, as High Priestess of Ishtar, had kept vigil over the goddess' shrines, and with her large band of peasant followers, had succeeded in hiding and preserving their treasures from the ravaging armies. Despite the male-god's jealously violent attempts to obliterate their religion, the People of the Goddess maintained a degree of influence, even among some of the high and mighty rulers.

Anu's daughter, Harimtu, had succeeded her as High Priestess. But Harimtu has had to dance a fine line, creating a bridge between the new and old religions. This she has done admirably, and has won the confidence of the present king. The ancient ceremonies to consecrate and fertilize the land have been preserved and observed faithfully by this king because he understands that the people still demand it. He has taken part in the sacred marriage ceremony annually, and with evident pride and respect.

Harimtu's veiled dance, the horned crown, the multi-storied ziggurat temple, and the lions flanking the throne— these are some of the many symbols carried by Anu's people into the foreign lands to which they will migrate. Eventually, in coming years, Harimtu's daughter, Enheduanna, will be named High Priestess by her father, King Sargon. But then, at his death, a brother will take the throne and replace the goddess religion with that of the war-god.

Enheduanna will be forced to flee to the same refuge where her grandmother had, some thirty years earlier. Here, in her grief and rage, Enheduanna will compose a poem to Innana, which will live on and be recorded five thousand years later, as the first Sumerian writing by a named author.

In time, Enheduanna's daughter Kubatum will succeed her mother as High Priestess, and eventually become favored by the reigning king of Ur. In honor of their courtship Kubatum will write several songs and hymns that will survive to be copied into later holy texts.

Among the writings she leaves to posterity, is a poem honoring the sacred marriage of god and goddess, as King and Priestess. Its lines include the erotic phrases: "Lion, let me give you my caresses"; and "My sweet one, wash me with honey"; and other lines that will later be copied in a work that becomes known as the "Song of Songs".

Kubatum will pass the secret traditions faithfully to her own daughters, and they, in turn, will do the same for generations forward. Throughout following centuries, temple ceremonies and sacrifices will retain many aspects of the goddess religion because the people will not be forced to forego all their old ways. And so, consequently, the Goddess' worship will be overlain with war-god symbols and She will be called a 'warrior-priestess'.

Joanna caught the gist of the story quickly. Again, she recognized the Strega themes of matriarchal wisdom passed through generations of mothers to daughters. She wondered why these stories should be considered so revolutionary, since they simply told history from a female perspective. Joanna was fascinated by the filming style and the use of biblical quotes in such a feminist context. Mother would really enjoy this, she thought.

After a brief intermission, the film continued with the second reel. Joanna sat mesmerized, oblivious to her surroundings, caught up in the ancient historical dramas.

Where the People of the Goddess traveled, they took their treasured amulets and talismans with them. Wherever they settled, they drew on cave walls, chiseled into limestone cliffs, sculpted from local rock and carved out of bone, the figures and features and symbols of the Great Mother Goddess. No Father God could yet diminish Her divine power among the people.

Although priests attempted to do so, they were unable to make the people forget their goddess. Women passed their heritage on through their daughters, even as their sons and husbands went to war in the name of the almighty destroyer god who had first invaded their world with the foreign Aryan marauders from behind the Mother's mountain range in the great Himalayas.

Among those who left Sumer, fleeing Hittite invasions, were a small band of 'Habiru' (displaced persons) who migrated into Canaan. Abraham, (whose name means 'a wandering Aramean') took his wife, Sarai, there to begin the lines of legendary patriarchs and matriarchs of the Jews and Muslims.

But, unacknowledged in the later tales, Sarai was a priestess of the goddess Asherah (the Semitic Ishtar) and brought with her a retinue of holy women. Among them was Hagar, who was dark like the eldest race, the Dravidians of ancient Sindh in India (part of the old Indus civilization which became called 'Sin' in later biblical accounts.)

Hagar was a priestess of the horned god and lion goddess, Uma and Aum. She was a queen in captivity, her people having been assimilated into the warring tribes of conquerors, her religion supplanted by that of foreign gods. Yet, within her ran the true blood of the gypsy nomads, from the most ancient times.

Hagar was a wanderer at heart, so, when she was banished by Sarai, into the desert with her child, she felt liberated. It was not great trouble for Hagar to follow her goddess into yet another land_ Egypt.

About a century later, a several-times great grand-daughter of Hagar sat on the throne of Egypt. Hatshepsut began as queen to her brother, and then regent to her son. But eventually she took the title of Pharoah for her own, and ran Egypt's affairs without bloodshed for several decades.

During her reign, Hatshepsut constructed monuments that were to become centers of healing and sent trading expeditions to Africa and the Sinai desert, where she collected riches beyond measure.

Although she kept her personal beliefs to herself and honored the traditional gods of Egypt, Hatshepsut harbored a deep respect for ancient female wisdom traditions, and these, she quietly passed on to her own daughters and grand-daughters.

Through the passing of another century, the line of powerful mystery women continued. One pretty little girl with dark eyes, named Tiye, was born to the Chief Minister of Egypt, Yusef (called Joseph in later legend) and his red-haired wife, Tuya, another descendant of the ancient line of Indus people.

Tiye, because of her father's close ties to the throne, became bequeathed to the young pharoah, Amenhotep III, who dearly loved her. Tiye held a peaceful position of power behind the scenes throughout her husband's thirty-year reign. However, because she was not of the royal bloodline, it was decreed that none of her children could inherit the throne.

At this time, in the delta region of Egypt, a settlement of Abraham and Sarai's descendants lived in peace alongside the local native folk. Yusef was, himself, a refugee from Canaan some years earlier, and thus he was related to these people. He had risen to power in the pharaoh's court through his gifts of sight and wisdom which were his heritage through his great-great-grandmother, Sarai.

In the course of time, Tiye bore a son. Because there was an edict that her child should be killed, she conspired with her midwives to float the child down the Nile in a reed basket for a short distance to the settlement of Yusef's people in the delta. The child was rescued and raised in the One-God traditions of these people, and, when grown, returned to marry his half-sister, Nefertiti, and become a co-regent.

At this point, he changed his name to Akhenaten (servant of Aten, 'lord') and roused great political turmoil as he attempted to promulgate a single male-god religion upon the Egyptian people.

As an inheritor of the ancient wisdom of the Matriarch's, Tiye struggled to retain the feminine goddess traditions and pass them through her female lineage. Through the six daughters of her son and his queen Nefertite, she secretly succeeded in doing that.

These daughters, through marriages to chieftains of various tribes, carried the wisdom back to Canaan, Phoenicia, Syria, and Anatolia. As they interpreted the goddess' message, her name and legends became those of the great Egyptian goddess, Isis.

Now Joanna was shocked. *These stories really do challenge the church's official teachings, she thought. What if we had always been shown the magical powers of women in the Bible as well as the miracles performed by men?* Of course, thinking of her own father's anger at the subject of female leadership within established religion, she could imagine how the Church Fathers might even be more incensed at such so-called heresy.

What an amazing story! Even if only part of it is true, it really changes the picture of history. Religion really has been at the core of most of the world's big wars, that and power politics, of course. And aren't they the same thing in many ways? Joanna had studied a good bit of literature and was familiar with most classical works telling tales from Greek and Roman times. None of them even hinted at the undercurrent of female power that silently ran beneath men's affairs through all the world's history.

She glanced at Sep and Anthony. They both seemed preoccupied and rather nervous, she thought. But she brushed aside any worry about that and turned her attention back to the film, now rolling the third reel.

* * *

The great walls of Jericho, the oldest city in the world, crumbled at last in an earthquake that shook the land. Just then, Joshua and his armies in their wheeled chariots crossed the Jordan River. They watched the town fall. In later legend, it was told that the might of their war-god felled the walls as an affirmation of the Israelites 'claim' to that country. But, it was the Land, itself, in protest of the invaders to come, that gave up its best in order to deprive the greedy newcomers of the wealth of its peaceful peoples.

Miriamne, who was a poetess and priestess, composed a victory chant upon the successful invasion of Jerico. In it, she sang the praises of her father's escape from Egypt with the band of Habiru. But she danced in the fashion of her ancient matriarchal heritage, beating the frame drum and singing.

She was a woman of great psychic and prophetic powers who eventually drew her own band of loyal followers of the old religion. Re-establishing temples for the goddess, honoring ancient tribal animal totems, and training young women in the arts of women's wisdom, Miriamne split off from the warrior tribes of her husband and was eventually stoned to death by the Isrealite priests, as a witch.

In truth, the Israelites had no right, and were no more deserving than any other marauders of peaceful lands. They simply were more ruthless, crueler, and more spiteful than their victims. They immediately sacked what was left of the town and killed its citizens, or took them into slavery.

Among the slaves taken from Jericho, was a young woman named Jael. She was from a family of ancient matriarchal lineage, tutored in the arts of magic and intrigue. In captivity, she lived with other slaves, outcasts, and harlots who followed the Israelite armies as they ravaged and raided Palestine.

On a particular afternoon, Jael found herself alone in the women's tent as a battle raged nearby against the Canaanite general, Sisera. The Israelite armies were being commanded by a woman, Deborah, who was also one of the 'judges' then administering the hodge-podge of Hebrew tribes.

As Jael looked off into the distance where dust clouds indicated battle skirmishes, she saw a man limping and staggering across the sand dunes alone. She at first took him to be a messenger, for he was obviously in a hurry. But soon she saw he wore the paraphernalia of a high ranking officer of the Canaanites.

When he came within calling distance, she hailed him, realizing he was trying to escape from Deborah's army.

Although Jael had no fondness for the Hebrew war-lords, and she despised their war-god religion, she nevertheless admired the female warrior-judge-prophetess, Deborah, as a woman of power. In the manner of her foremothers throughout history, Jael knew how to make the best of her situation by adapting overtly to the ways of her captors, while covertly praying to the goddess Ishtar for strength to survive. Now, taking a cue from her woman's store of secrets, Jael invited the stranger into her tent to rest.

Being a man of lusty proclivities, Sisera considered her invitation, saw that no enemies pursued him here, and decided to take advantage of the woman's hospitality. She offered him 'milk and honey' (the milk of her breast and the honey of her vulva.) She spread her bed with scented herbs, whereby 'between her thighs he knelt, he fell, he lay', as the later teller of the tale phrased it.

Jael had seduced the fearsome warrior, Sisera. Then, when he was sated and asleep, she murdered him by driving a wooden stake through his skull. When the Isrealites returned victorious from battle, she called her leader to the tent and showed the body in her bed. Did her captors honor her as the heroine she was? Not likely, for they then perceived her capacity for potential vengeance against themselves as well and they feared her.

They banished her to the wilderness, as a witch. Thus, turned out from the tents to wander the desert alone, Jael found herself liberated_ not unlike her ancient ancestor Hagar.

Soon she found shelter in one of the numerous caves pockmarking the rocky hills around the Dead Sea. From here she traveled to find provisions and made new friends among the hill tribes. When she gave birth, she named her daughter Tamar, and taught her well in the ancient women's ways.

✴ ✴ ✴

The music faded and the lights came on. Joanna sat bemused by the possibilities that these stories presented. How had the church managed to lie to people for so long? She looked at Anthony, who gave her shoulders a squeeze. "I know, little cousin," he said warmly. "These stories leave your mind to spin, do they not?"

He laughed softly, "I remember the first time I started to think about what these stories really mean. It turned my world upside down, even though I was not brought up in the Church. The mainline stories are so deeply indoctrinated into the life of us westerners that we don't stop to question them." He shrugged. "I'd heard some of these tales from Sophia growing up, but they didn't hit home until I got out on my own and began to see how things work_ how men fear the power of women, so they manipulate even the records of history to keep women powerless."

Just then, Giuseppe, sitting off to the side, gave a low whistle. Anthony looked at Sep and caught his signal. Faster than she had time to realize what was happening, the two men shielded Joanna, one on each arm, and quietly hustled her out the side door into the alley.

They quickly made their way back to the car, but Anthony did not get in. He and Sep conferred in whispers for a few moments, then he came around to Joanna's side. "It was great to have you along," said Anthony, giving Joanna a quick peck on the cheek. "We'll be seeing more of each other soon. Remember to think about that offer from Mia and David. They were serious, you know."

Anthony waved them off as Sep put the car in gear and pulled out onto the street. Giuseppe saluted Anthony, "We'll be in touch. You let me know what goes down in there. Okay?"

"Will do. Take care now." Anthony ducked back into the bustling market square, heading toward the Watchtower building at a run. Joanna glimpsed a small crowd gathering in front of the building as Giuseppe swung the convertible into the maze of streets in the opposite direction.

28

JOANNA : MORE REVELATIONS

"What was that all about?" Joanna asked, feeling a bit perturbed at having been maneuvered and steered away from the theater so urgently by Sep and Tony.

Giuseppe drove through Rome's tangled streets without saying a word. He was frowning fiercely and seemed very upset or angry. Jo felt baffled by his sudden change of mood.

At last, as they emerged onto the autostrada away from the main city, he took a deep breath. "What was your father doing with the Vatican cops?" he demanded in a growl.

"What are you talking about?" Joanna, now felt defensive and angry herself.

Sep softened his tone. "I guess you would not have seen him. Sorry for snapping at you," he smiled apologetically. "I saw your dad standing at the back of the theater, watching the film with the 'Vatican's Vulture'. We call him that, I don't know his name. I just knew it meant the cops were about to make a bust, maybe arrest some of the group and question them about the underground film-makers."

"Whoa! Back up a little. Who is this Vatican vulture? And you say my father was with him?" She shook her head. "That's preposterous!"

"I don't know how he got there, but I'm certain it was your dad. I'm sure I recognized him. I'm as confused as you are about that!" Giuseppe reached over and squeezed her arm lightly. "I guess we'd best just get right back to the villa and hope he didn't see us there."

Joanna frowned as she recalled that her father had a cousin who worked at the Vatican somewhere. She decided not to tell Giuseppe this yet, it might only get him more riled up. But she shivered. *Could my father have been following us?* She knew he had not approved of her going with Sep to Rome and only allowed her to go because everyone else assured him it was okay. Jo had never given much credence to her father's tirades against the old female-god traditions her mother honored. Now she suddenly felt afraid for all of them.

Giuseppe and Joanna drove home in silence, each lost in their own thoughts. When they pulled into the driveway at the villa, Joanna said, "Thank you for a wonderful day, Sep. No matter what my father says or does, it will have been well worth it for me. I think you have helped me see a lot of things. Opened some questions that I have been ignoring and avoiding for years."

She suddenly remembered the artifacts she'd found in the courtyard yesterday. "Sep? Do you have time to come in for a minute? There is something I would like to show you."

"No problem. We got back earlier than I'd expected so I have extra time before I have to be at a meeting tonight."

Jo led the way into the courtyard. "What is that little house?" she asked him, pointing to the small structure in the corner.

"That's a kind of domestic shrine. It is called a 'Lare House' by Strega tradition." Sep laughed lightly, but looked fairly serious as he reached in to take out the silver goblet. "Sophia made prayers and offerings to the garden spirits and goddess of wild things here. It was a private and sacred ritual she did every morning." He looked pensive.

"I'm sorry, Sep, I didn't mean to waken your grief tonight, you have other things on your mind. But, something strange happened when I first found this little shrine. I thought it was a bird feeder at first, and went to examine it. There is this little bag behind the cup, and it fell out when I moved the goblet." She took it out now and held it for Giuseppe to see.

"That is called a Nanta bag. The witches carry them in their pocket or around their neck. They contain amulets for protection and power." He opened it and examined the stones and objects. Then he chuckled. "This one has been made for a reconciliation of opposites! It has talisman to bring love and peace between two people at odds with one another."

He looked at Joanna with that mischievous twinkle. "Perhaps she meant for you to find it! You could try wearing it for a while, just in case you want to talk to your dad or something!"

She was surprised he guessed that she was concerned about talking to her father. She also thought it was ironic that she should find the bag if it was meant to attract love. She didn't say any of this to Sep, but took the bag and hung it from its thong around her neck. It felt warm against her breast and looked attractive against her red silk shirt.

"Thank you Sep, I am beginning to feel like a real witch already!" A gentle sense of happiness washed over her, and she laughed delightedly.

Giuseppe grinned. "It gets exciting sometimes, but the Old Ways are well worth the struggle to keep them alive. This is exactly what Sophia would have wanted_ for you to become interested and involved with the struggle."

He reached into his pocket and took out a small book. "By the way, I bought this for you to read. It adds to the stories covered in the movie we saw today. I think you will enjoy it."

They kissed and hugged quickly, but enthusiastically and she walked him back to the car.

"Happy Beltane, to you my sweet," Sep added. "If things go well, I might come by to see you later tonight! But don't wait for me, I may get tied up." He laughed. "I'll be getting Mario's car back on time today! That will be a surprise to them, I'm sure. See you later." He wheeled the car around the drive, waving goodbye as Joanna blew him a kiss.

After Giuseppe drove away, Joanna went back into the house. None of the others had returned from their various excursions, so she decided to make use of the quiet time to reflect on her day's adventures. She sat on the bench in the courtyard, fondling the little pouch at her breast, and recalled what Giuseppe had said about it. He called it an amulet to help heal hurt and rebuild trust. She thought that could come in handy for all of her family's relationships, since feelings were so strained over the matter of Aunt Sophia's legacy.

Joanna shrugged off the worries about her family and turned her attention to the intriguing new ideas she was learning from Giuseppe and Anthony. She flipped through the book Sep had given her:

Soon she was engrossed in another of the strange alternative biblical tales.

✳ ✳ ✳

Of Histories Intertwined and Untold

Over the years, one branch of the Israelite tribes made its way into the hill country, separating from the rest with whom they were become estranged. In the ways of all large clans, sibling rivalry drove brothers apart to find small parcels of land in which each could 'rule' his own territory.

Judah arrived and pitched his tents in a meadow near a Canaanite village. Here he settled down to raise his herd of sheep, and looked for a wife for his eldest son from among the daughters of the local townsfolk.

Tamar was brought to the marriage bed, but Judah's eldest son was impotent. Then he was killed by local bandits and she was left a widow without children. In the way of the old laws, it was required that she be impregnated by her dead husband's brother. But this fellow may have been homosexual or pious because he wanted nothing to do with her. Consequently, he "spilled his seed on the ground" _meaning he masturbated to ejaculation_ in order to avoid conjugal sex.

For his trouble, he died of a mysterious fever. Suspicion fell on Tamar and she was sent back to her people. But by now, Tamar desperately wanted to bear a son who would give her an honored place at Judah's table. She was disgraced in the eyes of the Hebrew elite, and considered unmarriageable among her own Canaanite people because of her widowhood.

Shortly thereupon, Judah's own wife died of grief over the deaths of her two sons. The old patriarch was left alone and bereft. He made plans to travel back to his relatives and find a new wife. But at a crossroads he came upon a young woman 'harlot' who seduced him teasingly, lay with him tantalizingly, brought him to ecstasy, and tricked him into leaving his staff and his seal with her in payment.

He believed she was a temple prostitute rather than a common whore. And, indeed, he was right, for the woman was his daughter-in-law, Tamar, raised to be a priestess of the goddess Ishtar by her own mother. Judah had not recognized her because of the veils and makeup she wore, and also because he had never closely looked at her when she lived within his household as his son's wife.

In this seduction Tamar gambled on conceiving the long-awaited son. Her gamble paid off, but upon the news of her pregnancy, she was again brought up before the council of Jewish elders. Within her own Canaanite matriarchal traditions, her situation was honorable, for pregnancy was considered a blessing with or without a husband. But the Hebrew elders sought to burn her for adultery and witchcraft. They considered they held authority over her due to her marriage, despite the fact that they had cast her out.

She was brought before Judah, the patriarch, for judgment. Judah felt compassion for the young woman who had been his daughter-in-law, but he did not recognize her as the 'harlot at the crossroads'. Being a basically kind man, he felt torn between tradition and compassion.

When Tamar came before him, she laid a bundle at his feet, saying, "The father of my child is the man to whom these things belong." Opening the bundle, Judah saw his own walking stick and seal, realized who she was, and claimed the woman and her unborn child as his own

As it turned out, Tamar gave birth to twin boys, and the second born took claim to Judah's legacy in an oddly repeated theme in Jewish history. His posterity includes David, Solomon, and Jesus. Thus, Tamar, a Canaanite woman, through her own deliberate and daring action, became the great-great ancestress of two even greater kings and a martyred savior.

But, unrecorded in the accepted history, Tamar gave birth again, and this time to a daughter. In the tradition of her own heritage, she raised her daughter to honor the goddess and to be strong in facing whatever fate should befall her. At a young age, the little girl even danced at temple festivities to honor the Goddess.

As it turned out, that daughter, Sabrina, married a high-ranking man of the Philistine tribes, mortal enemies of the Israelites. Wars continued to rage about them and her husband was killed in battle. She was left alone with two young daughters, but having already betrayed her father's people by wedding a man of enemy tribes, she was banished by the elders and left to her own devices. By now both Tamar and Judah, her mother and father, had died.

Sabrina, with her children, her handmaidens, and selected eunuch guards, took passage on a ship sailing to Cyprus. There, they settled, to beget yet another line of the ancient 'wandering gypsy' goddess-worshiping heritage. These dark-haired, dark-eyed, intelligent, and athletic people gradually spread across the sea: northward into Asia Minor, settling around the shores of the Black Sea; westward to Crete and Mycenae; and eventually, by way of the Adriatic, into Italy, where their progeny founded the Etruscan civilization.

But some of Sabrina's line returned to Palestine, serving as temple priestesses in the great Temple in Jerusalem. One great, great grand-daughter was Mary Magdalena, favored disciple and lover and wife of the avatar, Jeshua, called Jesus.

Magdalena escaped from persecution with her daughter and another unborn child after the execution of her husband. They sailed, by way of Sicily and along the coast of Italy, to France in the protection of a brother-in-law and a wealthy friend.

That sacred lineage was preserved in secret throughout the centuries to come. Some of the line infiltrated royal houses in Italy as well as France, and descendants are found among the hill folk over all of Europe. The mystery has been preserved and the secrets never completely revealed, although many legends and myths have grown from them over the centuries.

* * *

Joanna set the book aside on the travertine bench and walked to the little shrine in the corner of the courtyard. She reverently took the silver goblet from its stand and peered into it, seeing herself reflected as before, but now she took time to watch more closely.

Indeed, the image in the cup seemed to gain a life of its own, for as Jo looked on, the woman in it turned away and ran to embrace another figure. The two merged and blended, becoming someone different_ a little girl who danced and twirled and clapped her hands in rhythm to an unheard music. Jo stood mesmerized, trying to imagine what this could mean. Then the image faded and her face was mirrored in the cup again.

My imagination must be running overtime, Joanna told herself. *It's just the memory of all these different stories I've been exposed to in the last few days. I could be hallucinating, but it doesn't matter because I do feel as if I have been reborn!*

She grinned and sat down again to think about the possibilities of working in the filming of these tales with her newfound friends. It would be like going back into a past life. *How strange, I never gave much credence to Mom's stories before, but now I see how thrilling they really are.*

Jo pondered more deeply. *Tamar was an actress when she seduced Judah. And she was a temple priestess who danced for the goddess. Both she and her daughter, Sabrina must have been extraordinarily independent and determined women to break free of the constraints of their cultural norms and go after what they wanted. Perhaps each of us sisters carry some their spirit in our present lives.*

She liked the idea and smiled to herself.

Joanna set the cup back in the shrine, picked up the book, and went into the kitchen to see what she could prepare for dinner for her mother, aunt and sisters. She could barely wait to tell them all about her exciting day.

29

FOUND

While Kara sat cradling Toby, Rarjer continued his search around the Grotto. He stopped at the edge of the stream, reached in with his paw, dug at something there, and finally fished out a small sneaker. He dropped the shoe at Kara's feet.

"Oh my god! It's one of Mimi's sneakers!" Kara wailed. "What could have happened to her?" She looked frantically around the big cavern and felt totally at a loss. Rarjer gave a short howl, directly into the canal tunnel, not mournful or longing, more like he was calling to someone, telling them he was here.

Kara rose, cradling the cat to her breast, and went hesitantly to where the wolf stood, next to the opening into the canal. Her heart pounding, she looked into the narrow passage where the shallow stream flowed out of the grotto. At first, she could see nothing unusual. Then she spied Mimi's other shoe a little way inside the opening. She set Toby down and reached into the water tunnel to grab the shoe. She began to crawl in farther, but found the tunnel quite low and narrow.

Calling Mimi's name brought only an echo of her own voice. *Did she escape, or was she kidnapped?* Kara's thoughts wavered between following the trail or going back for help. Her practical self counseled getting help, but her newly awakening mystical side urged her to follow on her own.

Thinking practically, she realized the huge wolf could not easily squeeze into the water canal, and she was not going anywhere without her guardian. She turned back to the grotto entrance and saw he was already waiting for her there. "So you figure we need to go back for help, too, big boy?"

But still Kara hesitated. Going back would mean revealing all the strange secrets she was discovering to the adults. She could imagine her father throwing a major conniption and doing something really awful, like calling in the police. She just couldn't risk harming her newfound magical world by bringing down such catastrophe. Not yet anyway. Not until she proved to herself whether it was imaginary or if this fantastic place really existed. She had a strong sense that Mimi was okay and protected by the magic, or whatever it was.

Part of Kara held to a belief that she was hallucinating because of anxiety over her sister. The bird was just an angry hawk, after all. Maybe they had disturbed it in its nest or something. And, although the wolf certainly was intelligent and helpful, it didn't necessarily mean he was magical, did it? And Toby had been hurt like any normal animal could be, by something bigger or stronger. But Kara couldn't reason herself out of the sense that magic was really happening here_ both the good and bad kind.

The wolf continued to stand, looking into the entrance foyer and back at Kara, obviously impatient with her stalling. She hung Toby's sling back over her breast, after tucking Mimi's shoes into her backpack, and hefting it onto her back. Loaded like a pack animal, she started toward the doorway, when Toby meowed and patted her cheek with his paw. "Are you telling me you agree with Rarjer? You think we should go get help, huh? Well, okay."

But then Kara noticed what she had missed while wiping the gore from the cat's face earlier. Small tufts of feathers clung to his claws and stuck in his teeth. She stopped to examine more closely. "Why Toby! You've been in battle with the big awful bird! You poor little cat. What a terribly unfair fight that must have been!" She gave him a little smooch on the top of his head, which he accepted with a little grunt of pleasure or disgust, Kara wasn't sure. *But if this little cat has the courage to face down a Malandanti hawk alone, I'm not going to give up looking for Mimi yet either.*

She was about to call the wolf back, when she realized he was heading toward a different tunnel from that which they'd come down. She hadn't noticed before, but there were actually two other tunnels, one from each side of the first one. "Well, I guess you aren't giving up yet either, my friend. I'm glad to see that. But wait a minute," she called to the wolf who was loping up the second tunnel.

Then she took the fennel sprig from her pocket and sprinkled petals along the entrance and around the little stone altar, as well as at the canal passage. "Thank you dear spirits of my ancestors and all good magical beings who live and travel through here. Please guide and help us find my little sister. And, please, let her be safe and unharmed."

Kara was amazed at herself. For the moment, she actually felt convinced that the spirits of Nature would hear and protect them. Then she took the dagger from its casing in her pack and gripped it in her right hand, while cradling Toby on her left side. "The fennel stalk is good, but this feels even better," she murmured to the cat.

Following the wolf through the second tunnel, Kara sensed that it veered off to the opposite direction from the first one. "Of course, it's pretty hard to calculate direction, much less tell the time of day down here in near pitch dark, she mused. I could fish my compass out of my pack, but that's pointless, we have to follow the tunnel, whatever way it's going," she kept up a whispered dialogue to the animals just to calm her own nerves. Her camper flashlight gave a good-sized beam that was easy to follow, but Kara worried that the batteries might wear out. "I can't remember when I changed them last. Probably not since the scout camp-out last year in upstate New York."

That brought her thoughts to her old friends in America. *What will they think of our adventures when we get back? If we ever get back. Maybe we will return changed into magicians. Or ghosts!* Kara joked to herself, her thoughts flipped from silly to mundane to morbid and fantastical. *But, seriously, how can I ever go back to that ordinary life after being through this?*

She wondered what time it was, and worried what her mother might be doing when she hadn't come back right away. *Maybe they have a search party out already.* That thought gave Kara a horrible feeling in the pit of her tummy. *They probably think we've both been attacked by wild boars or something.*

While Kara let her thoughts wander, she followed in Rarjer's steps without looking at things around them. She hadn't seen the little door they passed, and hadn't noticed that the tunnel was growing slightly lighter and wider. Now she was brought up short.

"Yip!" the wolf barked in a strange small voice. It was almost a whisper. He had stopped, and was sitting down across from a large cavern off to the right of the tunnel, which continued upward through the mountain.

Inside this cave, the most unbelievable scene was taking place.

Kara clutched Toby and the dagger and held her breath. She stifled an impulse to scream. She stood stock still, although every muscle and nerve in her body was trying to run right into the cave.

A mountain lion lay on its side, with its back to the entrance. At the lion's head, sat Mimi, also facing away from the entry. She was actually holding the big animal's head in her lap, stroking its ear, and murmuring quietly. On Mimi's shoulder, perched a small winged creature that didn't exactly look like a bird. Across from them sat a girl about Kara's age, who seemed to be holding fire in her hands without being burned. Above the group, on a protruding shelf of rock, sat the raven.

The group was so intent on the ministrations going on around the lion, that no one noticed their audience for several seconds. Suddenly the raven jerked its head and cawed. The girl with the fire disappeared into nothingness, while the winged creature flew from Mimi's shoulder into a high crevice. The lion slowly raised up on all fours, and turned to face them. It looked about to spring when Mimi laid her hand on its flank and spoke quietly.

"No Farah, these are my friends." But Mimi looked no less awestruck by the sight of Kara with the huge wolf at her side and a dagger gleaming in her hand. Kara set the dagger on the ground, to show the wildcat she meant it no harm.

Kara didn't need to tell Rarjer who this was, of course. He had apparently known where they were going all along. It seemed, moreover, that the wolf and lioness were acquaintances too. They both sat on their haunches and eyed one another from a short distance, but with no further menace.

Kara went to Mimi and hugged her, momentarily forgetting Toby, who got squeezed between them and gave a little yowl of protest. Mimi pulled back and cried, "Oh dear, dear Toby! I've been so worried for you. But I knew Farah did the fighting, and I thought you would be okay. Poor, poor Toby."

Kara untied her sling and gave the cat into Mimi's arms. The two girls said nothing to each other for a very long time. Mimi stroked and cooed to Toby, speaking silly words that Kara assumed were made-up baby-talk. The raven still sat on its perch, making no further comment. Kara took the opportunity to open her pack and replace the dagger in its casing. There were so many questions crowding her mind, as well as so much to tell Mimi, that it seemed impossible to even begin. She took a hint from Rarjer and Farah and waited quietly.

After about ten minutes, that seemed hours, Mimi said, "I think we had better get going. Mother is frantic, but she hasn't told daddy anything yet. She and Gina are searching for us. Melanthus says they are on their way to another secret tunnel entrance. We need to get to them before they try anything drastic."

Kara wondered how her sister knew this, and how she could remain so calm. *But, of course, that's like Mimi, she takes everything at face value.* Kara said, "I'm just bursting to tell you my story and hear yours, but you are right. We had better get going. We can talk later."

She took Mimi's shoes from her backpack and, while her sister put them on, Kara scattered fennel seeds in the cave's doorway and made another silent prayer of thanks. Mimi leaned over the lioness and said, "Thank you Farah, I will come back to visit you." Then she called out, "Tinkle? Won't you come down and say goodbye? My sister isn't going to hurt you, or her big friend either."

From up in the dome of the cave a small voice answered, "It not time for us to meet yet. I see you later. You must go. Follow the wolf."

So, with Rarjer leading the way, they trooped farther on up the tunnel, Mimi carrying Toby and Kara trailing, her mind swarming with unanswered questions and impossible tales. Very shortly Rarjer brought them into yet another large cavern.

This one appeared much more like a room that had been used by humans recently. There were actual stools and tables sitting around helter-skelter, and a stone fireplace at one end. The ashes were cold. It hadn't been used lately, but evidence showed it was not entirely abandoned either. Some jugs of water and several cups and saucers sat neatly on one table, as if set up for a meeting.

They spent no time exploring, but followed the wolf to a door at one side of the big room. This door opened onto what appeared to have been a storage closet. Shelves lined the walls and were piled with dust-encrusted bottles and jars. Cobwebs covered everything. Nothing in the closet had been disturbed for years.

Now, Rarjer stood at another door leading from the pantry closet, and barked. When Kara reached out to the knob, he snapped at her. She pulled her hand back in shock, having never seen him direct anything but gentleness toward her before. But she signaled Mimi and Toby to stand back as well, because, all at once, she realized where they were.

From the other side of the door could be heard a snuffling and scuffling of claws. Then a heavier step and an answering bark came directly from behind the door. Rarjer huffed and made gurgling sounds, followed by little yelps of encouragement. He seemed to be having a conversation and reassuring those on the other side. After a bit, he stepped back from the door and nodded to Kara, waiting.

Kara reached again for the door knob and turned it. The door opened into the closet, so at first she and Mimi couldn't see what was on the other side. She allowed Rarjer to enter first, then cautiously peeked around the door. As Kara guessed, they had come into the ramshackle cottage where the wolf and his family made their den.

But Kara now felt certain that it was also the cabin she'd glimpsed in her dream. A shiver traveled down her spine, but she refused to let herself get distracted by the mystical stuff right now. Behind her, Kara heard Mimi gasp in amazement. *Well, at least she is still capable of being surprised,* thought Kara with amusement. *So, now we have both discovered each other's secrets,* she realized.

The wolf bitch held her pups at bay in the other corner of the hollowed out cabin, while Rarjer entered with his friends. She was clearly not ready to join their camaraderie, but she allowed him to spend a bit of time nuzzling and wolf-talking with Mimi and Toby.

Then she growled a warning that sounded urgent.

Rarjer took her meaning instantly and made a bound for the front of the cabin. He moved through the broken down wall in slow stalking mode, ears back and tail low to the ground. Someone was coming up the trail from the woods.

The girls held back, not knowing whether to follow. The bitch and pups seemed to be waiting for them to go, however, so Kara beckoned Mimi to stay quiet behind her and they crept to an opening in the vines overgrowing the fallen side wall.

With a sudden intake of breath, Kara dashed through the thicket, running down the path to greet their mother and aunt. She had no idea what she would say to them but she needed to reassure them and keep them from seeing the wolf family. She was not sure why, but it seemed important to keep that secret from her mother.

Mimi followed close behind Kara, still carrying Toby. She immediately bounced about the women, creating a happy distraction. Kara realized she needn't worry about what to say because her little sister already had the women engrossed in her story. Kara was amazed at how easily Mimi lied, and she had to suppress a giggle when she heard the story of how Toby had gotten hurt and how Kara had found them by the little creek. Mimi made no mention of magical animals or fairies.

A raven cawed in the trees above. Kara turned to see Rarjer standing in the shadows watching them. She blew him a kiss and stopped briefly to drop a few raisins on the path.

30

TRACING THE MOTHER-LINES

Although she said nothing to Barbara, Gina had glimpsed the wolf standing in the shadows behind them. Mimi was so eagerly telling her tale of the cat's fight with a dog, that it was obvious she was making an attempt to divert their attention. Gina guessed this, but made no comment. She remembered her own encounters with the wild ones as a child, and how seriously secret those were. It was part of the magic of growing up around here. Moreover, few adults were trusted by the animals. Only Sophia and Heironymous, in Gina's memory. And, she suspected, maybe Giuseppe.

Mimi chattered, hugging Toby, who was looking increasingly fit as they walked along. *That girl has the healing touch*, thought Gina. Again she said nothing to Barbara. But Gina wondered just exactly how the cat did get hurt. It didn't seem likely to have been the wolf, unless the cat got into its lair by mistake. And that was hardly plausible, knowing how this particular cat had often visited around the wolves with Sophia in her wanderings.

Gina was aware how naive Barbara had become with regard to the woods magic. *To her it must seem like a fairy tale from childhood. But to me, it's still real because I've lived around it all my life. Like we said earlier, the girls are sure to bump into the magic on their own. I wonder_ what have they really seen today?*

They arrived at the meadow where Mimi's adventures had begun. Here Gina sat on the log and suggested they all rest awhile to enjoy the lovely afternoon. Kara brought out the lunch she still carried in her pack. They each ate a sandwich and drank a warm pop. They split the apples and oatmeal cookies between them, but the raisins were almost gone. "Guess I ate them," muttered Kara, without further comment.

Barbara, examining Toby, said, "He looks like he's been fighting with a bird. He has a feather stuck in his claws. Where exactly did you come across this dog, Mimi?"

Mimi stuck to her story. "It was a big black dog that just came out of the woods when we were walking along the stream. Maybe the feathers are from a nest that Toby played with earlier, that had fallen on the ground. There weren't any birds or eggs in it," she added.

Barbara turned to Kara. "And where did you find our mischief makers? Tell us about your search. I'm always amazed at how easily you seem to sniff Mimi out of hiding." She laughed and tweaked Mimi's curls.

"I, um, just followed that little stream." Kara stammered, "I think I heard her talking to Toby or something, so I guessed she was somewhere along there."

Diverting her mother's questions, Kara bent down and fumbled in her pack, looking for another pop. Suddenly the notebook fell out onto the ground. Kara began to grab for it, then stopped herself and just stared at it dumbstruck.

Gina picked up the tattered journal and turned it over reverently. She guessed immediately what the situation signaled, but needed to be sure. "This is Sophie's magic book! We've been looking for it and couldn't find it anywhere. Where did you find it, Kara?"

Kara looked at her aunt with dismay and guilt written all over her face. "It is okay dear," reassured Gina, "I am not angry with you, only surprised and happy to see the old journal is here and not really lost."

Kara grinned ruefully. "I just picked it off one of the shelves in the living room when we first came to the house. It looked interesting, so I took it to read when I had time. I meant to put it right back when I'd finished reading it." Then casually, as an afterthought, "How do you mean it was Sophia's magic book?"

"She always had it with her when she went anywhere, and she claimed that it contained information on anything that she needed to know. She just opened to a page and her answer would be there. She also said that it changed, depending on who read it, so that it has different information in it for different people."

Gina said all this matter-of-factly. She watched Kara's reaction and guessed the girl knew more than she let on already. "What's more, Sophia always maintained that the book chose who could read it. It finds its way to the person who is supposed to have it. So, I guess it is meant for you now, Kara." She held it out to her niece and watched a look of utter amazement cross Kara's features.

Taking the book back, Kara turned to a particular page. "For me, it has some stories about things that happened long ago. Also some information on healing herbs. And,..." Kara hesitated and looked at her mother, seemingly uncertain whether to say more. "th... there is a sort of list toward the back of the book. A list of names..." She plowed on, her curiosity apparently overcoming her anxiety. "I guess they are women from our ancestor line or something. Anyway, I wanted to ask you, Aunt Gina, who was Cecelia? It seems to have been written mostly by her. And, I guess I wondered about the other names too. Not much is said about any of them, just their names and the centuries they lived. It goes back a long way. It's really amazing." Kara chattered nervously, and seemed to be waiting for some reaction from her mother.

Barbara, leaning against a tree, looked to be off into her own memories. But she smiled and said, "Go on Gin, tell about the Rimini mother-lines. I'd like to hear those old tales again myself. I fear they've grown rusty in me after all these years, and the girls should know about their valiant foremothers."

She looked out to the sea, where the sun was gradually sliding toward the horizon. "It must be about three in the afternoon. We have plenty of time before we have to get back to the house for supper."

Mimi perked up at the suggestion of stories. "Please, Aunt Gina, I'd love to know more about the women who have lived here, around these woods, before us."

"Indeed, it was in these woods that many of them did live, my dear. In or about the woods, in little cabins, or sometimes even in caves. Their stories go back hundreds of years." Gina mused. "In relatively recent times, some built onto the stone hermitage and tower, which were the original buildings on the site of the villa. I'm not sure of all those names, and we don't have time for it all now anyway."

Gina stopped to consider, "I'll start with the line you just asked me about, Kara. Cecelia would have been your great-great-great-great-grandmother. I think that is about three or four greats!" Gina laughed, "Anyway, she lived around the middle of the seventeenth century, in the sixteen-hundreds. She had a very exciting life, indeed, but also a tragic one."

"Cecelia actually built and lived in the alpine cabin where we found you girls today. She chose to live out in the woods with Nature, rather than keep up the larger house at the villa. During her lifetime, the villa was kept by her eldest daughter, Iona, who was a very powerful witch as well." Gina stopped to think. "I'm not sure if I have all these dates and names straight. Let's see."

Kara turned to the page in the notebook with the list of names and handed it to her.

Gina glanced over the list. "Well, it looks like Sophie might have drawn this up fairly recently. And I see she made a couple of mistakes too! That's heartening to me, so I know I'm not the only one who gets confused by these many intertwined lives!" Turning the page, she looked up at Barbara. "She has us both in here, Babs, and the girls as well."

Barbara shrugged and grinned ruefully. "I suppose she never gave up hope that we might return to the fold! That's good to know, at least."

Gina resumed her tale. "At any rate, Cecelia did live in that cabin during some very dangerous times for women who were healers and taught the goddess traditions. She was admired and loved by many of the peasants who lived in the hills, and by the folk from villages nearby as well. But the authorities in the bigger towns, and especially in Rome, despised her and sought to arrest her for witchcraft."

"There are some amazing stories about how she escaped from them over and over again. We won't go into them right now, but maybe later." Gina realized she was not ready to tell the girls about the secret passages or the Grotto yet. *But, we will have to take them there soon, she reminded herself.*

"Eventually," Gina continued, "Cecelia was brought to trial by the church's Inquisitors, tried, and sentenced to die for witchcraft. She died in prison before they could execute her publicly."

"Her eldest daughter, Iona, managed to build closer ties with some high authorities, and evaded the inquisitors' clutches using both political savvy and magic. Iona lived to be over a hundred years old, and died peacefully much as Sophia did, surrounded by her close companions at the villa.

Iona's younger sister, Sabrina, moved to the cabin and carried on with their mother, Cecelia's, work, but she died tragically in a fire that destroyed the cabin and some precious artifacts many years later. Rumors said the fire had been purposely set by vigilantes, but that was never proven."

Gina laughed, and glanced at Barb. "The tales get awfully tangled, don't they? I keep wanting to go off on tangents, but I'll stick to this one story for now." She checked the Grimoire again, then continued.

"Iona's other sister, Sylvia, died fighting a resistance battle in the Crimean War alongside her husband. Her two daughters moved to live for a while with their aunt, Sabrina, at the cabin. One of these girls, Juliet, died tragically from wounds inflicted by a big hawk when she was only 13 years old."

Gina paused, because Mimi had made a little exclamation at this information. But when Gina looked at her, Mimi only murmured, "How very sad!"

Gina continued, "There is a mysterious story about that little girl. It was said that she remained as a ghost to assist and accompany her sister, Selena, who later grew up to become another well-loved witch. She founded the mystery school at the villa, which Sophia later continued. Selena lived to be very old and died peacefully at home attended by her loyal students and her two daughters."

"Selena was the mother of Sophia and our mother, Diana, who is your grandmother. Diana died in the sailing accident with our father, and that's when Barbara and I came to live with Aunt Sophia."

Gina stopped talking and stared off into the distance for several seconds. "Goodness! I haven't thought about all those wonderful women for a long time. There are so many, many adventurous stories and tragic tales connected to that list of women. I think I had better begin to write them down while I still remember, so they will be preserved for you girls to pass down to your daughters." She looked at Kara and Mimi, smiling wistfully.

Excitement sparked in Barbara's eyes as she said, "Gina, I would like to collaborate with you in that writing." She paused, chewed on her lip. "In fact, I think it could be a book of great interest to others as well as to our own kids. As you spoke, I was reminded of so much of that brave history that has never been known by most of the modern world. History has been so viciously overwritten to hide women's roles. I'm especially reminded of how several of our foremothers worked in underground resistance movements as healers and warriors through all the ages."

Gina smiled delightedly. "Oh! Babs that would be so much fun! You could draw illustrations for the book too. We could make it a sort of modern fairy tale, and I think it could even make money for the school. What a great idea!"

"What was the resistance movement?" piped in Mimi. "I'd like to hear more stories right now. Do we have time, Mom?"

Gina looked at Barbara, who said, "We should be getting home to make supper. Let's wait until tomorrow. It will be Beltane eve. We can celebrate then with more stories of the ancestors."

31

MIMI AND KARA: NIGHT THREE

When Kara and Mimi returned from the day's excursion with their mother and aunt, the sun was setting over the sea, casting the mountains around them in alpine glow. They found Joanna in the kitchen preparing dinner.

"What a surprise to find you back already,' said Barbara. "I thought you and Giuseppe would be out into the late hours tonight, celebrating in the big city."

"Oh, Mother, we had the most wonderful day," exclaimed Joanna, giving them each a quick hug. "We went to see the most amazing film production. You would have loved it. I'll ask Sep if we can take you someday soon. But we decided to come home early so we can get some rest. Sep has a meeting this evening." Joanna looked positively radiant, as she babbled on, "By the way, Aunt Gina, Anthony was with us too."

"You must have been at the underground cinema then," said Gina. Turning to Barbara, she said, "Those productions are part of the work Tony is involved in promoting. He sometimes performs in them as well. They are Avant-guard and very controversial." To Joanna, she said, "I can imagine you enjoyed them, being involved in theater yourself, Jo."

"I loved them," enthused Joanna, "and what is more exciting, I met the actress-writer, Mia Felini, and the film-maker David Taviani." She turned to Barbara. "Guess what mom, they have invited me to audition for a part in their next film. Do you think dad will let us stay for the summer?"

Barbara seemed taken aback by this sudden new turn in Joanna's attitude. She said, "Well, darling, you are the one who can charm him most easily when you put your mind to it. I would love to stay in Italy longer, but your dad and I don't exactly see eye to eye on the subject of the villa, as you may have noticed."

Kara, listening to Joanna's excited monologue, felt irritated at her sister's lack of interest in their day. *Seems she can only think about herself anymore,* thought Kara. She said, "Good of you to make us dinner, Jo. We've had some excitement too, in case you care to know." But she didn't really want to let her older sister in on the magic of their day, so she added, "Maybe we will tell you about it another time."

They sat down to a dinner of seafood salad with crispy bread dipped in olive oil, and fresh fruit. The women and girls ate quietly each deep in her own thoughts about the day's adventures. As soon as dinner was eaten and the dishes cleared and washed, Kara said, "I'm really beat. I'm going to go up and take a shower and get to bed."

Mimi, who had hardly spoken a word since they got home, said, "I'm coming up with you, Kara." She turned to her mother and aunt, "I think Toby is all okay now, but can I take a saucer of milk to him in my room?"

"Of course, go ahead," said Barbara. "Is he really okay do you think? Or might we need to take him to see a veterinarian tomorrow?"

Gina answered for Mimi. "He was almost completely recuperated by the time we came home, Barb. I think Mimi has the healer's touch for sure." and she ruffled the youngest sister's hair, adding, "You just take care not to wander off into any more trouble, okay?"

Mimi scampered up the stairs after Kara, calling over her shoulder, "Don't worry. I'm so tired after today I probably won't wake up for a week!"

But when they got to Kara and Jo's room, the girls stopped and looked at each other. "Are you thinking what I'm thinking?" asked Kara.

"I think we need to talk," answered Mimi in a whisper. "Come on up to the roof with me. They won't be checking on us now. Joanna will keep them occupied with her stuff for hours."

Kara first went into her room and retrieved her backpack and jacket. "Just want to be prepared," she said, in answer to Mimi's questioning look. "You never know when opportunity might call," and she winked at her sister, who grinned broadly in return.

Toby waited in Mimi's room and came to greet them, looking just fine. Mimi stopped to pet him. "We are going up to the roof to talk about things. Do you want to come along, or do you need to rest some more?" She set the saucer of milk on the floor.

Kara was amused and amazed at how the cat seemed to understand. Ignoring the milk, he bounded immediately for the door that opened onto the stairway to the roof and clawed it with one paw as if to say "Let's hurry up there right away."

Mimi grabbed her sweatshirt and her sneakers. "These are still wet, but they will be okay with the heavier socks I put on." With a laugh, she added, "I'm sure glad you brought them back from the grotto. It would have been hard to explain to mom and Aunt Gina what happened to my shoes if I'd still been barefoot when they found us." Both girls giggled at the thought as they climbed the stairway to the roof.

There, spreading her parka for them to sit on, Kara turned her camper flash lamp to low beam so they had a bit more light to see each other. Digging into her pack to make sure she'd remembered to take a set of fresh batteries, she said, "Well, speaking of your sneakers, maybe that's a good place to start. What happened to you in that big cave?"

So each took turns telling the other the tale of her day's adventure. After about an hour, they had pretty much covered everything. Kara still found the parts about the fairy and the ghost girl hard to believe in spite of seeing them with her own eyes in the lion's cave. But she didn't say so, knowing it would only upset Mimi. *No harm in pretending to believe in all the magic,* Kara told herself. *It's not as if I haven't seen plenty of weird stuff I can't explain otherwise.*

Toby, meanwhile, had kept lookout on the parapet. Now he made a soft whirring sound to get their attention. He stood hunched in a defense posture, looking down onto the driveway below. Kara immediately shut off the flashlight and crept to the edge. A car was pulling into the yard very slowly. "It's Dad," she whispered to Mimi. "Be quiet till he goes in."

Peeking over the parapet, Kara felt like a spy in a mystery thriller. She found herself feeling oddly suspicious of her father. *Wonder where he's been so late? He seems upset by something. Maybe he's seen a ghost,* she joked to herself. Soon she heard him open the door and call for Barbara. Then the front door slammed behind him.

Has he been sneaking around making trouble for our summer plans? This sudden suspicion of her dad, triggered a memory Kara had managed to suppress for several years. *Oh my god!* She frowned at the image in her mind: *Two bundles of letters hidden in her dad's desk drawer.* She swallowed back a moan of dread and pushed the unwelcome flash of memory away. *There is nothing I can do about it anyway. It would only hurt Mom if I said anything now. But I just know he can't be trusted with the secrets of the villa for sure. We will have to take extra care not to talk about things around him.*

"Maybe we should go to our beds now, in case he decides to check on us," Mimi said in a whisper, as if she was reading

Kara's mind. "But then come back so we can make plans for tomorrow. Leave a pile of blankets rolled up in your bed so it looks like you're in there," she suggested. Kara was impressed at her little sister's devious mind.

32

JOHN : RETURN FROM ROME

Earlier that evening, John drove down the coastal highway returning to the villa from Rome. After spending the day and evening with his cousin, his mind reeled from all he had seen and been told. In fact, things were starting to feel really bizarre and he questioned what he'd got himself involved in by going along on this bust of an underground cinema.

He drove cautiously along the unfamiliar autostrada. It seemed odd that there were almost no other cars on the road although it was only around 8 o'clock. He pulled over to a roadside rest for a night-time view of the sea. The evening was bright with stars in the west, since the moon had not yet risen above the mountains. The surf muttered to a rock-strewn beach below and the wind whispered in trees above, where a few early Beltane fires dotted the hills like mirrored stars. A wolf howled.

John momentarily sensed that he was re-living his life in a far distant past. He imagined that the night was enchanted, waiting for marvels and miracles. He made the habitual Catholic sign of the cross on his chest, to rid himself of such superstitious thoughts, and went back to the car.

Driving through a mountain tunnel, the car lights caught briefly on something flying alongside his car. It cast no shadow, but looked quite large, flying low to the ground. When John slowed down to see more clearly and avoid hitting it, the creature had disappeared entirely. Thinking he was just spooked after the films Donnie had shown him from the stash of confiscated materials, he crossed himself again and stepped up his speed. "Just an owl, probably hunting mice," he said aloud to himself.

He found the sound of his own voice helped to bring him back to reality. "I've got to think about what all this means to us. Barbara and the girls could be in some danger if the authorities connect Sophia's school with this underground movement. I wonder how much Mario knows about all of this? I'll give him a call when I get home."

John maneuvered the car onto an exit ramp, and prepared to pay the toll. At the toll booth, he was startled by another apparition. For a moment, the face of the woman taking his coins looked surreal: Her eyes held a haunted reddish gleam, and when she smiled, her teeth looked sharply pointed. John blinked, and saw an ordinary gray-haired woman. *Just a reflection against the glass cage*, he told himself.

Now on the local road leading to the small seaport town below the villa, John reviewed the films and stories he had been exposed to at Donnie's luxurious suite of offices. Sitting back in opulent comfort, drinking wine and smoking fancy cigars, they had viewed several of the underground films. They all depicted traditional Bible stories but with a different somewhat surprising twist. One even intimated a marriage between Jesus and Mary Magdalene, and her subsequent migration to Europe with their children.

Such stories were slightly upsetting to John's conservative Catholic upbringing, but nothing that he thought dangerous to the church. Yet, Donnie argued that such propaganda turns people against the authority of the church. "Makes them return to the Old Religion of the area, which taught reverence to nature and women, in equal portion to reverence to God." Donnie had explained. "Now, that would be unthinkable," he had added with particular vengeance.

Donnie had told John about militia surveillance missions, carried out in the mountain wilderness areas, in search of a group of local outlaw bandits who periodically harassed officials enforcing the heresy laws. Donnie had intimated that such a stakeout was likely to be carried out tonight in preparation for Beltane festivities tomorrow. As John left, his cousin had warned him, "Be careful. There may be hunters about the woods near your wife's aunt's place. Just keep your family inside tomorrow night, and you will be fine."

Now John wondered what Donnie had meant, and again found himself feeling surprisingly defensive for Sophia. The films he had seen seemed fairly innocuous to him. Sure, they portrayed biblical themes in altered ways. Women were centrally involved and had more power than traditional church dogma taught. *I don't see why that should be so upsetting.*

He had lived among strong women all his life. His own Italian mother had been no wilting violet. He grinned to recall her proud stance and strong voice commanding his father in their home. *Of course, she never spoke up to him in public. But that was the Sicilian custom. The men worshiped their women, but the women were sworn to loyalty and humble acceptance of the men's actions outside the home.* John had tried to enact that same clear discipline with his wife and daughters and had failed miserably. It was his main source of shame and resentment.

He drove through the coastal village with its painted stucco and terracotta buildings hugging the water's edge. Boats bobbed in the still harbor, anchored for the night. Wooded hills rose silently into a darkness studded by more Beltane fires of folks beginning to celebrate a night early. Lights blinked secretly behind shuttered windows. A shiver ran down John's spine.

He had the distinct feeling he was being watched. "No doubt local folk are watching me, since I'm the only thing moving in this town tonight," he tried to joke with himself. Soon he found the turnoff to the mountain road leading to Sophia's villa. As he began the winding climb, he continued his conversation with himself.

"Could be they even know who I am, and are just keeping tabs on the newcomers in the area. In these old fashioned places time seems to stand still. Anything new and different is a big event," he told himself.

He kept his eyes on the road, steering the hairpin curves carefully. The headlights bounced from wide-open vistas of the sea, to sudden densely closed stands of trees. Here and there a patch of field or meadow revealed a small cottage, or a poor farmstead, where peasants scraped a living from the spare and stingy land. *It's a tough life*, thought John, *yet the people seem quite content.*

Suddenly he slammed on his brakes to avoid hitting a huge deer that had come bounding from the woods. John held his breath, watching the big buck scramble up the slope into a dense forest of birch and pine.

His car engine had died with the sudden stop. Just as he was starting it, another movement caught his eye. Three men came out of the woods, with rifles held cocked. They wore military camouflage fatigues. John rolled down his window. "What's going on?" he asked the closest of the men.

"Best you get yourself on home," replied one of the gunmen gruffly. "It's not a night to be out on the mountain alone." The guy spoke in a clipped Italian tongue that John easily understood, despite his disuse of the language for the past twenty years.

John, thinking of Donnie's cryptic warning, felt curious to know more. "My family is visiting here from the States and staying nearby," he said, in his own somewhat rusty version of the native language. "I think I deserve some explanation of what is going on if my family is endangered. I insist you tell me what's happening."

"There have been reports of break-ins and looting around the area. Just keep your doors locked and you should be in no danger," answered another of the officers, who seemed more congenial than the first. Stay home tomorrow night for sure.

"Are there wild animals on the loose?" asked John. "What are you hunting?"

The first officer snorted, "Wild animals indeed!"

"No need to be rude to the fellow," said the second man. He came over to John's car. "There are always some wild creatures roaming these mountains, but they rarely bother people. Tonight, however, the reports include sightings of wolves a bit too close for comfort."

"Has anyone been hurt by them?" asked John.

"Not by the wolves, sir," said the polite officer, "but they are accompanied by some outlaws who are wanted by the police. They can be extremely dangerous."

The surly cop hefted his gun and nodded at John. "Better get moving now mister," he said. Then turning to his partners, he motioned toward the thicket saying, "That's the trail, but it's badly overgrown. Maybe we'd best follow this road up along the creek.

John pretended to fumble with his keys before starting the engine, so he could hear more of their conversation. They seemed to have forgotten he was still there because they began discussing their assignment. "The boss said we should just stake out their camp for now. We can't set a trap before we know where they will meet," said the third man. "We aren't supposed to shoot 'em. He wants them brought in for questioning is all."

"But he hasn't said we can't shoot the damn wolves," said the first man. "You wanting to wake the dead? You itching to see that old witch's curse set free again?" the third man countered,

"You're a fool, talking about killing the devil's wolves." The angry first man just snorted. "Well come on, Carlo, we can try for that deer anyway." he shouted to the officer who had been cordial.

Carlo beckoned for them to go on ahead. He came over to the car, "Is everything alright?" he asked John. "Having trouble with your car, are you?"

John thought it best to act the part of the ignorant American tourist. "Sometimes I get confused by these European models. I must have hit the ignition lock by mistake, but now I think it'll start okay," and he switched on the engine, put the car in first gear, and began pulling out onto the road. "Thanks for your warning, by the way," he said.

The militiaman named Carlo, motioned for him to wait a moment, and said quietly, "Are you the folks staying at the villa that belonged to Sophia?"

John was taken aback by the fellow's forthright question. "Well, yes, but how do you know about that?"

"Don't worry," he spoke softly so that his partners couldn't hear, "I knew her. A good woman. But the bandits we search for were also friends of hers. I can't say more, but you can contact me if you need anything. Don't call the police. Here," and he handed John a rather rumpled business card which John tucked into his jacket pocket.

"C'mon Carlo!" yelled his partner. "What are you doing? Giving the guy a lecture on our night life?" They laughed as they trudged off into the dark.

John drove on up the road, and passed the three men walking single file along the ditch. John waved, but only Carlo saluted back.

How odd, thought John. *Carlo seemed to be warning me not to talk to the authorities, but to get to him first. Is he trying to protect the so-called bandits? He insinuated as much when he implied he had been acquainted with Sophia in a friendly way and knew the bandits to also be friends of hers.* Intrigued, John pondered the possibilities as he continued up the winding road to the villa.

Keeping alert for more strange encounters, he talked aloud to calm himself again. "Must be a time for weird stuff. Beltane, they call this holiday. Some holy day in witch tradition. Like Halloween, only less scary." He crossed himself once again, peering into the darkness. His neck prickled with the sensation of being watched. "God! This road seems to go on forever." he muttered. "I don't remember it taking this long when we arrived. But, then, I wasn't so anxious to get to the place when we arrived."

Suddenly he felt a stab of fear. *What if something has happened while I was gone! I'll never forgive myself for leaving Barb and the girls alone in that damn spooky place.* He gunned the engine for a quarter of a mile further and, at last, turned up the driveway of the villa.

An owl swooped out of the forest, right over his car. A wolf howled, answered by another. They seemed to confirm his fears.

John's heart was pounding and he took a couple of deep breaths before getting out of the car. He crossed himself for the fourth or fifth time. "Beltane nonsense," he grumbled, as he cautiously made his way to the front door and let himself in. The door was not locked and he cursed himself again for having left the family alone. *What if those bandits have already come and accosted Barb and the girls!*

"Barb! I'm back!" he called, but heard no one answer. "Where is everybody?" He shouted louder, panicking. He was heading to the bedroom tower when the courtyard doors opened.

Joanna stood there in semi-darkness, a dreamy smile on her face. "Hi daddy," she said. "I've been waiting to talk to you. The rest have gone to bed already."

33

SEP AND RON: THIRD NIGHT

When Giuseppe returned the car to Mario, he learned that Anthony had just called from Rome asking Mario to come and bail him out of jail. "You know anything about this bust, Sep?" asked Mario. A twitch of his eyebrow suggested he guessed that the young man might.

Giuseppe hesitated only a moment. "I don't know what went down. But I was at the cinema with him when the Vatican cops showed up. We took Joanna to see David and Mia's new movie. We got her out of there before anything happened. Tony went back after we got away." for some reason, Sep didn't want to tell Mario that John was there with the cops.

"Anthony said they're on the wolf's trail again," added Mario. "Take care of yourself tomorrow night, kid. I'm sorry to miss the festivities, but we may need to stay at the villa with our visitors." He clapped the younger man around the shoulders as he took the convertible keys.

"Enough gas in this baby for another run into the city?"

"Just filled up before I brought 'er back, sir."

"I'll let you know what's up when I return." said Mario. And he drove off in a cloud of dust, down the winding road to the main highway.

Giuseppe shook his head and grinned his admiration for the older man. *Mario is still the hot-rod maniac he was when I worshiped him as a kid.* His thoughts flashed to a time when he would accompany Anthony and his dad to the race track where Mario was a champion driver. *Until the damn mob tried to get him into their pocket and he showed them not every guy will be bought. Mario is still my hero*, thought Giuseppe, a little sadly.

He climbed onto his motorcycle, kicked the throttle and revved the motor, then took off in his own cloud of dust, riding up the mountain road, away from the main highway. After about a mile, he veered off the road onto an old wagon track that scrabbled through a ravine and ended up on the bank of a shallow river, just downstream from a little hamlet.

Giuseppe parked his bike in a cluster of mountain bushes thick with sweet black berries. He looked around to make sure no one was nearby. Then he scrambled down the bank of the stream and ducked into a cave hidden under the roots of giant willow-woods. He lifted several rocks from a stack against the far wall of the cave, and removed a bundle wrapped in oilcloth. From the bundle, he extracted a turtle neck shirt, heavy riding pants, biker boots, a stocking cap, and a leather jacket. All were black in color and all looked well worn.

Giuseppe stripped down and changed into the riding gear. Then he stashed his casual jeans, tank top and tennis shoes in the plastic wrap and hid them in the stone cache. He drew a black mask from the pocket of his jacket and pulled it over his eyes. Finally, he pulled a small pistol from the inside pocket of the jacket, secured the safety and tucked it back in, with a tug on the pocket flap, to settle it easily under his left arm.

Checking the terrain on both sides of the river valley, he wheeled his bike back onto the wagon track and rode off through the woods. He entered the village just at sunset from the rear alleyway of the local parsonage. Most of the peasants would still be in their fields and vineyards finishing the day's work. The women would be inside cooking dinner. He kept in the shadows of the little mountain church, parking his bike in the lee of its rear entry.

There, he knocked three times and waited. Footsteps hurried through the slate-tiled passageway inside, and soon the door was opened just a crack. "Where the raven calls welcome," said a gruff voice on the other side of the door. "The raven calls today from home," answered Giuseppe.

The door was opened by a very large man in a cleric's collar, but wearing the pants and boots of a biker. "What's up man?" he asked, as he let Giuseppe inside. "I wasn't expecting you for a couple of hours yet." His voice boomed from deep in his chest, like boulders hitting canyon walls. Sep figured that was what made him such a good preacher to his little country flock. No one could tune him out!

"Hey, Ron! Glad to find you home." said Sep. He walked into the priest's study, whipping off his mask. "Looks like we've got trouble in the Trastevere district again. They've busted Anthony, for one. I don't know who else. His dad has gone to bail him out and I'll learn more when they get back." He pulled up a wooden chair, straddled it backward, and leaned his arms across the back.

The priest leaned against the wall, watching him. "So, why is this so urgent then?"

"Here's the real problem," continued Giuseppe. "The Marini family from the States are at the witch's villa, you know?" He checked to see his friend nod acknowledgment. "Well, turns out the father has connections to the Vatican big brass somehow. He showed up at the bust. We don't know how he knew to come there, or if he saw his daughter."

"Wait, wait! Slow down!" said Ron, taking a seat on a bench against the wall. "His daughter?"

"The oldest one, Joanna. I took her to see the sights and we ended up taking her to the film," said Giuseppe. He shifted in his chair, tilting it precariously. "She is pretty tuned-in to the mysteries, even though she doesn't know it yet. Anyway, me and Anthony thought she'd enjoy it. She did too. But we had no idea her old man was tailing us. Or if that is what he was doing." He stopped to reflect.

The priest calmly eyed his agitated young friend and waited for him to go on. "There was no sign of him earlier. I was on alert," Sep went on. "You know, I'm always the watcher. I never go anywhere without checking who or what might be on my tail. But this time I swear there was nothing to worry about."

"I believe you, man," said Ron, "but I still don't get the picture."

"Well, you see, Joanna's old man is dead set against the school. He has already had a go-around with Mario about it. And it seems that he must have connections with some Malandanti bigots at high heaven there. I think we need to do something to divert him so the Rimini women aren't put in danger."

The priest laughed heartily. "As if those women aren't capable of dealing for themselves when needed!" Then he scowled. "Hold on! But there is something I can clear up for you. I had forgotten about this over the years. It used to trouble Sophie and me a bit, but when nothing ever came from it, we let it go." The big man chuckled, deep throaty echoes in a cave. "The current honcho at Vatican Cultural Ministry is John's cousin."

"What?" Giuseppe sat up and let his chair crack against the tiles. "Does anyone else know that? Jeez, why didn't you warn me!"

"Don't go getting all paranoid, kid," Ron's voice was softened, but commanding. "Certainly does complicate the picture for you, but it doesn't mean the man's in cahoots with the Vulture. Could be he just happened to visit a relative and asked some questions."

"Yeah. Fat chance. The guy has been fighting against us keeping Sophie's school running, and now he has ammo for his cause from the bigwig liars. He's going to think I'm out to trick his daughter too." Sep put his head into his hands. "Damn! Why don't those creeps just get the hell out of our lives! Everywhere I turn, I gotta deal with them and their kind."

"The priest put his hand on Giuseppe's shoulder. "Hey, I said, don't go getting paranoid. We have the big night ahead of us tomorow, maybe it will give us opportunity to foil their tricks. Anyway, we have to be sure the family at the villa doesn't get caught in the crossfire. This is an age-old war, don't forget, and we've all been fighting it together for centuries."

Sep looked up at his friend and had to grin. "It's hard to remember that sometimes, especially when someone you care about is put in danger. I really like Joanna. She could be a great witch herself someday_ or at least a wonderful priestess."

"Oh? Is that all? Just a co-cultist, Sep, to your own priest-hood?" Ron's grin was knowing and a bit melancholy. "I sure wish Sophie was here with us now." Then he laughed again. "But tomorrow night we connect with those powers! We had better just go on with our Beltane gig and let the magic work its business."

Giuseppe wasn't ready to dismiss his concerns yet. "Mario said Anthony signaled to him that they're going to hunt tonight."

"Well, that's something we can fight. This other stuff doesn't concern us." said Ron.

"It's all connected." Giuseppe added bitterly with a shrug. "Those three girls are the next in Sophia's line. Each one of them has potential to learn the craft, and they'd all be good Strega. But their father is a superstitious religious nut. Believes in the devil." He added the last with a barked laugh.

"Perhaps we can give him a dose of his own superstition tomorrow," said his friend. And then they both laughed. "So, let's go see Mario and Anthony now."

34

BARBARA: THIRD NIGHT

Barbara lay in Sophia's big canopied bed, again unable to fall asleep. John snored, oblivious to her restless churning. Wide-eyed, Barb gazed about the room, seeing its familiar furnishings through a haze of moonbeams coming through tall mullioned windows. A slow shadow passed over the moon.

She slid quietly out of bed and tiptoed barefoot to the smaller sitting room, carefully over-stepping the shadow lines of window mullions in an old childhood superstition against breaking the walls of fairy's houses. She grinned at the thought, and snuggled into the worn overstuffed chair, breathing deeply of the familiar scent lingering in its cushions.

She pushed aside a filmy curtain and looked up at the moon hovering almost full, above wooded hills in a cloudless sky. Its beam fell on a small framed photograph propped on the table. Herself and Gina, with Sophia between them, arms linked, sitting on a fallen log, laughing. Barbara, age 7, wearing a white sailors hat, a couple of sizes too big, jauntily tipped over one eye. Gina, age 9, clutching a beaten up red tin box as if it held a king's ransom. A large bear-like shadow fell at their feet_ the shadow of he who snapped that photo.

The moonlight splashed her with retrospective regrets. Barbara was seventeen when she met John at a victory dance in Benevento, at the end of the war. She had worn a colorful medieval peasant costume with swirling skirts and had plaited her long unruly red curls into a French braid, which John had pulled playfully after they danced. She had woven a love charm and marriage spell into that braid, with the explicit purpose of captivating a man to take her away from increasingly restrictive duties as a witch's protégé.

Now, she recalled their romantic escapades ruefully, knowing how deeply she had hurt Aunt Sophia and others by eloping with him to America.

Except in her artwork and poetry, once married, Barbara had suppressed her occult gifts and ignored the surges of supernatural insights, extrasensory perceptions, and mystical transmissions that occasionally arose in her with each season's turnings.

She surreptitiously made blessing charms for her daughters when they were little, and occasionally, in private, lit candles to give thanks for good tidings, or to cast protective spells against trouble. Any such activities she took special care to hide from John, however, for he grew increasingly suspicious and resentful of her mystical heritage.

Now that she was back in the center of power_ the source of all she had run from_ Barbara felt torn in two. The magic of her childhood called to her from every stone and twig, while John's bitter resentment of that heritage gnawed holes in her heart. Barbara leaned back in the moonlight, watching the silhouettes of trees dance. Soon she closed her eyes and dreamed.

Across a group of individuals gathered in a large circle a serene dark-eyed woman, draped in a swirling blue robe, catches Sophia's

eye and nods in acknowledgment. Sophia goes over and speaks to her:

"Magdalena, I greet and honor you. You were my first mentor in the goddess mysteries during a lifetime twenty centuries past. I owe you deep gratitude."

"You are blessed among us, dear Sophia," returns the beatific being who sits within a halo of moon-splashed radiance. "We were neither of us so wise when we joined life-threads in that age so long ago. Ours was indeed a fateful meeting in which we both taught and learned from each other."

"How strange that the little band of refugees from Rome's persecutions could have been the nucleus for two thousand years of misinterpreted and misdirected spiritual forces." Sophia muses.

Magdalena nods. "But they were there from the start-- the Malandanti-- ready to intervene with their malicious messages of guilt, shame, and greed. We were too naive then. We were mortal and afraid for our own lives. We forgot the blessings of eternal light, even while we lived to preserve that very message."

"The minds of humankind have become badly disconnected. The design was no doubt flawed from the start, with a purpose toward learning difficult lessons, but it seems rather than gaining in tolerance, compassion, and open-mindedness, people have grown only more narrow, petty and mean." Continues Sophia. We can't only blame the Malandanti, for a good portion of fault lies in our own misdirected actions."

"The secret is in allowing ourselves to accept the inevitable, rather than rationalize the mysterious to make it fit our mundane concept of reality. The greater purpose continues to be served, even as we make our mistakes and stumble through difficulties.," advises Magdalena.

"Will you join me in transmitting our early tale to my progeny on the planetary plane?" queries Sophia. I earnestly desire that they learn to see the grand view; that they remember their heritage and trust in the mysteries."

"Let us remember together," murmurs Magdalena, with a nod of her head.

"Faria was a poor fisherman's wife in southern Italy in the first century of the current era of western history on earth. Poor and simple though she was, Faria harbored an eminent blood-line. She was thrice great-grand-daughter to Cyna, Amazon warrior princess from the northern Balkan mountains who came to fight alongside the last Etruscan forces against the growing might of Rome around 200 BCE.

Cyna, in her turn, was directly descended from the great 7th century BCE Etruscan Mystic-Queen, Tanaquil through her gypsy daughter, Tana, legendary founder of the first settlement of Stregheria, Dianic Witches of Italy.

Of course, Tanaquil, herself, descended from the fabled and revered goddess, Dianhea, who was said to have been the first of the gypsies from the East to arrive in Italy from Crete in 1470 BCE when the Minoan island civilization was destroyed in an earthquake and volcano.

Moreover, Faria was married to Jezuah, whose heritage descended to the lineage of the Hebrew line of David through the Canaanite woman, Tamar of Judah. His direct ancestors also migrated to the Italian peninsula about the time of the Babylonian diaspora.

Yet, despite the rich history in their combined lineages, Faria and Jezuah lived a simple existence and neither much thought nor cared about their illustrious ancestors. Neither gave much credence to any religious creed, nor did they attend temple or synagogue. Theirs was a simple faith in the grace of Nature and the good will of their own human spirits. Their young children, a girl and a boy, ran freely in the wooded mountains with animal companions trained by their mother to guard them. The whole family worked hard to bring in the fish and to plant and harvest the meager crops of grain and fruit they ate and sold at market.

When a small group of ragged pilgrims chanced upon their humble homestead in the hills of the south-western coast of

Italy, they welcomed them and took them in with gracious hospitality. The visitors had sailed a refugee craft from the eastern shores of the Mediterranean, from a land besieged by Roman occupation and cruel governance.

A bedraggled young woman, with a newborn babe and a little girl of around three years of age, was their spokesperson. An older man was in charge of their voyage, and seemed a very capable seaman. Yet, their little boat had run aground on the beach and he was beset with frustration and rage at himself.

As things turned out, the meeting was predestined, for his sails drew them to meet the fisher couple in Italy before they were to resume their voyage farther west to France and Spain. Thus, the seeds of their story were planted in the fertile soil of a rich pagan tradition where it could evolve unpolluted by opposition forces

Their story was of the woman's husband. He had been an Avatar, a sacred teacher and healer in the Nature and goddess traditions in the land of Palestine. But he had been sentenced to die, for the crime of heresy, by Rome's favorite method of punishment: crucifixion. He, himself, secretly escaped to study, and eventually die a natural death, in the original holy land of India. But his family could not travel with him, and were forced to disperse to the opposite shores of the sea in order to preserve his lineage in secret.

It was a tale that needed to be preserved, yet hidden. The tale was already being falsified and perverted to serve the purposes of a scheming and greedy priesthood. In centuries to come these perverse teachings would all but destroy the Avatar's positive message of peaceful coexistence with their deceptive threats and promises. It would be left to a clandestine and cryptic cadre of loyal followers to preserve the true mystery.

Thus, after camping in Faria and Jezuah's woods and sharing meals for about a month, the refugee group embarked again for the western lands. This is when the daughter of the fisher-couple left with the strangers to serve as a companion handmaiden to the young mother, Magdalena.

It was a sad parting, but the mystery had stolen thirteen-year-old Sylvia's heart. She chose to follow in the adventurous path taken by her ancestors, and ventured into strange lands to plant more seeds of secret sacred healing.

Magdalena finished the retrospective saying, *"Your spirit, Sophia, resided in that young girl, and it has traveled with you through time as a desire for adventure. More recently the spark that prompts desire for journeys to new lands kindled in the niece who fled home for romantic adventure, but who has now come home to her heart. We give her the message that courage grows with adversity, and redemption for past failings comes mainly from within one's own soul."*

When Barbara woke, it was with a renewed sense of purpose and power. The dream was merely a retrospective of long-dead legends, but it awoke in Barb a new perspective on her differences with John. Or, more exactly, on their respective distrust of each other's spiritual foundations. She was also heartened by seeing dear Sophia in conversation with other beloved souls.

Somewhere, in the far reaches of history, those spiritual foundations had merged. They were not so very different at their core. Both held love, peace, and forgiveness as central tenets. Both understood the miraculous to be a natural part of life. Both honored the mystery of divine wisdom. Perhaps she could find a way to help him see this.

Filled with her revived hope, Barbara gracefully unfolded herself from the chair, stretched like a cat, and smoothed the wrinkles out of her sheer cotton nightgown. She shook her hair loose from its bedtime braid, letting the curls tumble down her back and shoulders.

Then she lit four candles in a candelabra on the side table, chanting softly: "One for air, one for fire, one for water, and one for earth. What I call here, let it harm none, but bring my own renewed powers to birth. As I will, so mote it be."

Feeling a little shaky, she faced the window and raised her arms to the moon. All her attention focused on that mighty orb, as she drew the power down to herself. After some minutes, she turned to pick up the photo and cradled it in her hands. A single tear fell on the glass. She raised her face and spoke to the moon.

"Let my memories awake for my own healing. Let me be strong enough to accept myself for who I truly am_ a daughter of the goddess. Show me how to stand up to all adversaries, especially my own doubts and my husband's recriminations. Most of all, dear goddess, help me do my part to keep the Circle unbroken. Blessed Be. Thank you, dearest Mother."

Just as she finished her prayer she heard a rustle and a grumble. She whirled to face the door. John stood there, hair awry, pajamas rumpled, and wearing the devil's own wrath on his face. Barb stood calmly and waited for him to speak.

"Talking to the moon, are you?" he said, gruffly. He barked a cough and blinked sleep-fogged eyes. His eyebrows twitched like two mangy caterpillars sparring. His breath stank, and he farted as he lumbered into the room. He plopped into the big chair and spread himself all over it with clumsy disrespect.

She watched him, her mouth curved in a half-smile. *The guy just takes over wherever he is, she thought.* She waited to see what else was coming. *Funny, I don't feel my usual fear of him at all. No heart palpitations, no knotted stomach, I'm not even holding my breath.* Standing two feet away from him, she held the picture to her breast and rested her other hand casually on her hip. She felt ready to take him on.

"Guess it's time we have that little talk you have been avoiding since we got to this god-forsaken place," John said, glaring at Barbara from the depths of Sophia's old armchair.

"I have been avoiding you because I don't want a fight in this sacred place. You may think it is god-forsaken, but that is because you are unwilling to see, feel, or hear the evidence of holy magic." Barb spoke softly, calmly. She watched his eyebrows madly twitching and stifled an urge to giggle. "Our fight is not about Sophia's gracious villa or about her mystery school. It is about your refusal to allow for different ways of seeking and honoring the divine."

She felt an urge to reach out, touch him, calm his fury. He seemed like a wounded bull, sacrificed to his own superstitions. "We are of two very different worlds, you and I." She sat down by a writing table across the room from him, waiting, watching him build up his rage.

"You can sure as hell say that again!" John's voice rasped with venom even as he spoke in a whisper, evidently trying not to wake the household at three in the morning. "Where I come from, there is only one God and He has warned us against people like, (he hesitated,) your ancestors."

"Like me, you mean," said Barbara looking unflinchingly into his eyes. "And like Sophia. And like Gina." She saw his jaw clench, the veins pulsed at his temples. She thought she might as well throw it all at him. She drew a deep breath and added, "Like our daughters. Kara, Mimi, and Jo each have the Gift, whether you want them to be witches or not."

John shot out of the chair, his hands clenched at his sides. "How the hell can you say that? What makes you think those girls are tainted with the devil's lust, just because you are their mother!" Spittle formed at the sides of his mouth.

"Your voice is rising, John," she said reasonably. "You will wake up all of them in a minute."

"I don't give a damn!" but he dropped his voice to a hoarse whisper. "Jo just likes the magic of the theater. She doesn't give a rat's ass about religion of any form." He paced the tiny room as he talked. Barbara moved her chair closer to the desk so he wouldn't trip on her legs. He raged on.

"Mimi is too young to understand any of this garbage," John turned and shook his finger in Barb's face. "But I want her out of here as soon as possible. She could get hooked on the magic crap just because she's an imaginative child and vulnerable to your sister's fantastic tales."

"The tales of the Strega are no more fantastic than those of your own tradition, John," she interjected quietly. "In fact, many of the stories derive from the same sources, only they are given different interpretations."

John ignored her comments and continued his diatribe. "Kara, thank God, certainly has no witchery in her. She's got a sensible head. In fact, I'm not worried that she'd get caught in this net of evil because she basically agrees with me. This place is crawling with deviltry."

He frowned, as if remembering something that puzzled him, then he shrugged and sat down again. His bluster seemed spent for the moment.

"Deviltry to you, John. Healing magic to me." Barbara got up from the desk and set the picture back in its place on the table. John scanned it briefly but said nothing. "I have decided to stay here for the summer months," she added, "you may go back to the States whenever you wish." She carefully pinched out the flame of each candle. Then she turned her back on him and went to bed, leaving him to brood in the moonlight.

35

MAKING PLANS, THIRD NIGHT

Giuseppe and Heironymous cruised at a leisurely rumble over the short trail between the Parish to Mario and Gina's casa. They rode their bikes at low throttle, not speaking, alert to any signs of vigilante activity.

Suddenly Sep pulled up short behind a stand of pines at a sharp curve of the road. Ron halted beside him and they listened, shutting off their engines. Soon they heard muted voices and several pair of footsteps getting louder, coming toward them from a bit ahead around the curve. They pulled their bikes under some thick brush, then moved out closer to the road and squatted down to wait.

Shortly four men rounded the curve, walking abreast, carrying rifles. Two of them were arguing.

"I could have got that big buck if you hadn't been so damn clumsy-footed, Carlo" They spoke the local patois of Italian sprinkled with broken English slang.

"No need to get all stressed out man, the buck is no longer that important. Now that we know where they will be celebrating, we have a better chance to get The Fox and his pals tomorrow night," replied the one called Carlo.

As the group came nearer, Ron stepped out to meet them.

Giuseppe stayed back, hidden in the undergrowth. It would be better for him to remain unseen, but he kept his revolver cocked and ready in case Ron needed back-up.

"Ho there!" Ron imitated their local dialect naturally. "What brings you guys out tonight?" Ron spoke in a jovial tone, like the good natured priest the local folk knew him to be.

"We might ask the same of you, Reverend," said Carlo politely. They all seemed a bit edgy, caught off guard.

"And what's with the riding gear? Where's your bike," demanded another man, who seemed more belligerent.

Ron laughed. "I left my bike back in the woods when I heard you coming. Never know who might be out and about and I didn't want to run anyone down! I'm just on my way to visit some members of my parish. We are preparing a quiet church service for May Eve. Just want to keep those folks out of the woods and away from the revelry as much as possible."

"Oh, yeah. Well we were out for similar preparations. Just checking some places to watch tomorrow. The High Ministry is pretty serious about stopping that deviltry this year." That was a third fellow talking. The forth one merely nodded his agreement, saying nothing. He seemed nervous in the presence of the priest.

Ron said, "Well you guys just watch out for yourselves, okay? We don't need unnecessary violence or bloodshed over this. After all, it is just one night of a year and pretty harmless at that. Could be wiser to just let the pagans have their parties and all will be peaceful."

He stroked his beard. "I wonder why our esteemed Cultural Minister is so intent on causing disruption in the area this year," he cocked an eyebrow at the men. "You guys have any idea about that?"

"We aren't privileged to know The Vulture's purposes or reasons. I'd think you would have his ear more than us," said the belligerent one. "We're just foot soldiers," and they all laughed without humor.

"But we do have our suspicions," said Carlo, the more civil of the fellows. "There is a family of Americans visiting at the Villa of the old witch, Sophia." He coughed, "you do know she died a few days ago, don't you?"

Ron only nodded and then said, "But how should that involve the Church and Beltane, and what does this family have to do with it?"

"Well, rumor has it there is some family connection between the Culture Minister and them. We think he wants to scare them back to the US so he can close the witch's school and grab the property for the Church."

Heironymous listened with interest, but only said, "Well thanks for the information. I haven't had occasion to meet the family yet."

"Well, we gotta be on our way. Nice talking to you, Reverend," said Carlo, with a salute. The group took leave and Ron walked back a ways into the woods pretending to go pick up his bike. When the men were sufficiently far from there, he returned to Sep and they continued on their way to Mario's.

"That's an interesting theory they have," said Ron. "I wonder how they know about the family connection."

"I'll bet its Carlo. He's the one who gave you the info. He plays both sides of the game, you know." Sep glanced at Ron to see if he knew this.

Ron looked surprised. "So he has connections with Tony's troupe too?"

"Probably. He's in pretty tight with the Stegerhia's pagan militia group for sure. He can be helpful, but you gotta watch him."

Ron chuckled at that. "Well, we both know something about what it's like to play that game!"

When they arrived at Mario's the Ferrari was parked in the drive. They left their bikes on the side and entered the house without knocking. They found Mario and Anthony deep in conversation at the kitchen table. Both glanced up when they heard the other two come in.

"Glad to see you men," said Mario. "I was about to try calling the parish."

"We would have been here sooner but ran into Carlo and his buddies on the road," said Sep. "Ron had an interesting talk with them. I stayed out of sight."

"Carlo!" said Mario. He looked at Tony. "Isn't he the one you were talking with in the jail?"

"Yeah, Dad. We all know Carlo. He's a snitch, has connections on both sides. That's why I dropped him the info. I hoped he'd use it to give the vigilantes an idea for tomorrow night. I'm trying to set something up."

Giuseppe watched the interchange between Tony and his dad. "Would you mind clueing us in on what you are talking about?"

Anthony explained, "Carlo was with the group that got busted at the Watchtower."

"Yeah, I remember we saw him there." Sep frowned. "But what's this about you giving him information?"

"Well, here's the shtick," Tony stopped to take a swig of beer, then offered bottles to both Sep and Ron who gladly accepted. He went on, "see, I've been thinking that we need to set up some kind of diversion tomorrow night to pull the vigilantes away from both the villa, where the family could be in danger, and the Grove, where the animals will be and where the Special Ones will manifest"

He cocked an eyebrow at Sep and Ron. They both nodded and gestured for Tony to go on.

"Well, I figured the troupe could celebrate at the wolves den, since the wolf family should be at the Grove's festivities. We could ambush the Wizard and his soldiers there."

"Sounds like a risky plan," said Ron, "but it could work. Sep and I should be able to join you before things heat up too much."

"And we could make sure to have Rarjer keep his family away until the dust settles," said Sep, " although the wolves might lend us some good support too," he mused.

Ron looked at Tony and laughed. "Good thinking, kid! You saw an opportunity and made use of it." He thumped Anthony on the back.

They all drank their beers, each in his own thoughts for a moment. Then Ron looked at Mario with a grin and a wink.

"So we have a double agent in the mix again. We both know something about that game too, don't we? Do you remember all the intrigue we lived through during the War, Mario?"

Mario chuckled. "And you have never yet outgrown that habit, Ron. You are still playing the double role as priest and loyal Stregheria member."

Sep broke into their reverie. "I've been in that spot too, and I don't ever relish going back. I'm still evading both the vigilantes and the Mafia for my drug patrolling years!" He ran a hand through his short-cropped hair. "Wonder if I'll ever live through it to be free again." Then he grinned. "But the "special talents" Sophia gave us are a big help, right Ron?"

His big friend nodded agreement, then turned to Tony. "By the way, I think your plan is in motion. One of the things we heard from the boys on the road is that they believe they know where you will be and are setting up to go there tomorrow."

"It was Carlo who we heard say that before Ron went out to meet them," added Giuseppe.

Mario broke in. "Good! Then it looks like we're set for tomorrow night. Gina and I will stay behind and go visit with the family at the villa, just in case any action comes that way."

"Best we all get some rest now, tomorrow will be a long day." Ron patted Sep on the shoulder and they left, riding back to the parish where Sep would stay the night. All remained quiet and the men each dreamed of battles won and enemies vanquished.

36

A BREAKFAST MEETING

Early the next morning, before Barb or the girls were up, John called his cousin Donnie and made plans to meet for breakfast. He had been brooding all night since the argument with Barb. He kept thinking of the remarks Donnie had made the day before about the Rimini Witches. What he heard made him feel anxious, but also somewhat defensive. He wanted to know more.

They met at a small bistro in the village on the coast just below the Villa. After the waitress brought them their coffee, John opened the conversation saying, "Donnie, your comment the other day regarding my wife's aunt and the Stregheria beliefs left me a bit confused. Have you had occasion to meet Sophia Rimini?"

He waited while the waitress set their plates of omelets, fruit, and garlic bread on the table. Donnie looked taken aback by his question.

Donnie signaled the waitress to bring them a carafe of wine. Then he looked at John a moment and cleared his throat. "I expected you to ask what I'd learned about the possibilities of your idea for a museum at the villa. Are you giving up on that?"

John suspected his cousin might be stalling for some reason, pulling him off track. "No but I've had time to talk to others and got some good information to go on. Of course, I'm still interested in what you may have on the question."

"Well, I did give it some thought and checked with my attorneys. They said it could be done quite easily, but might be better if it came through higher official channels rather than privately by yourselves." He stopped to take a few bites of his omelet and sipped some wine.

John ate too, but watched his cousin more closely. *Was the guy avoiding the question? He does look uncomfortable, guilty maybe? What's going on?* He asked, "You mean like through someone in the local government or the Church?" *It would be like the power-mongers to want the place and profits for their own coffers*, he thought. He sipped some wine and waited for Donnie's answer.

"Well yes, the Church could certainly back a museum of antiquities, and you would be richly paid_ all of your wife's family, I mean." He did not meet John's eye, but kept nervously shoving food around on his plate.

The guy definitely looks shifty, thought John, *I wouldn't want Barb's family history drawn into the greedy and dangerous manipulations of this country's power-mongers. I got away from all that long ago.* But he said, "I'll give it some thought, Donnie. Sounds like a feasible plan."

After another few minutes eating in silence, John said, "But tell me what you think you know about Sophia and her traditions."

When Donnie didn't answer, John continued, "Why are you so convinced they are against the Church? My understanding is that they hold much the same values and do not interfere in other's choices of religion." He ate a few grapes and waited. Again that furtive look flashed in his cousin's eyes.

But then Donnie laughed and said, "Oh I don't mean to infer anything sinister about the old woman, although I did have occasion to meet Sophia once or twice regarding a pagan fair her school was involved with at that theater and market square you and I visited yesterday. This was a few years back. She was quite the feisty old lady, I must say!" He chuckled again, and went on, "Nothing much came of that occasion, but I have good reasons to be wary of those pagan cults all over the country. Especially the ones here in Tuscany and nearby districts as they are some of the most entrenched."

He stopped to pour himself another glass of wine. John accepted one as well and waited for his cousin to say more.

"You see, during the war those people were closely involved with underground rescue movements, hiding enemies of Mousiolini and the Church within their ancient mountain properties. I, myself, got involved with attempts to root them out, and we met with some very bizarre forms of resistance indeed!" His eyebrows shot up like a pair of startled crows.

"Oh? Like what?" asked John.

"You would never believe some of the tales I could tell you of unearthly goings-on, but on one occasion, for example, I was personally attacked by a pair of wolves." He looked at John for a reaction. John only munched more grapes, listening with interest.

Donnie became more agitated as he continued his tale. "These were no ordinary wolves of the woods, you understand, but animals tamed and taught to attack at a signal. I nearly lost my eyesight and was torn up pretty badly in that attack. Another of my associates was killed and ripped apart by the beasts. It was gruesome."

Donnie shook his head to rid the memory, and John did feel shocked. "But how do you know they were set on you by the witches? There were plenty of wild rebels and country folk living in the hills back then."

"As I said, we had been watching the pagan enclaves for some time before the war. And that was only one of many barbaric incidents that happened back then. It has been quiet for the last couple decades, but none of those witches were ever apprehended. At the time, we were ready to re-instigate the old witch hunts, but the War brought an end to those plans."

John thought his cousin's tale sounded preposterous, but he couldn't help feeling a shiver of fear, given the current intrigues he had heard of in just the last three days.

"Well, Donnie, I appreciate you explaining all that to me. And I'll keep your suggestion for the villa in mind. You'll probably need to get back to your office now. Thanks for taking the time for me today." He held out his hand to his cousin.

They shook hands and Donnie got up to leave while John paid the waitress. On the way out the door Donnie said, "One more thing John, you might heed my warning and keep your family close to home tonight. These Beltane revels can still get pretty devilishly bizarre sometimes."

With that, each man went to his own vehicle and drove away in opposite directions. John pondered all he'd heard with mixed feelings. He felt disgust at Donnie's greedy efforts to manipulate him for the Villa, yet his remarks about the weird dangers of Beltane and his story of a personal vendetta toward the pagan Stregheria frightened him.

One thing for certain, he told himself, *I am getting my girls out of here as fast as I can. We can turn the whole villa and its affairs over to Gina and Mario. They are better able to deal with the locals than we are, and, if she insists, Barb could stay here for the summer but I'll go home with the two younger girls at least!*

As soon as he got back to the house, he placed a couple of phone calls.

37

PICNIC INTERRUPTED

This is the big day! thought Kara, happily stretching and climbing out of bed. *I wonder what new surprises are in store for us now?* Barb and the girls had all slept late, tired from their excursions and adventures of yesterday. Now wearing tee-shirt and jeans, Kara climbed the stairs barefoot and carried her sneakers to avoid making noise. She found Mimi also up and getting dressed.

"Hi Mimi! I thought we could go up to the top of the tower and review our stories from yesterday. So much is happening so fast, I feel a bit overwhelmed."

"Sure, sis," Mimi grinned wickedly. "So the magic is finally getting through to you after all?"

Once they had settled on blankets on the roof tower, Kara answered. "I have to admit that much of what goes on around here does not seem to have a rational explanation. But I'm still skeptical of 'magic' as you call it." She tossed her pony tail impatiently, then bit on her thumbnail, deep in thought.

"But you do believe the animals are magic, don't you?" Mimi raised her eyebrows questioningly.

"Well, I do believe they are very unusual and smart, and that they have very definite abilities to communicate with humans_ or at least with some of us." She studied her little sister for a moment. "You especially Mimi. You clearly seem to understand and communicate with them in some very mysterious way."

"Well, Kara, that *is* magic. I *know* it, and I don't question." Mimi again frowned at Kara. "If you could make yourself really believe the magic around you instead of always doubting and second-guessing, then you could feel what I do. It is wonderful!"

"Oh, Honey," Kara sighed, "yes, I do envy you there, and sometimes I feel very close to just letting go and believing_ but my mind just isn't ready to let go of the questions and rational explanations." She looked around the stone ramparts. "No fairy this morning? And where is your little buddy, Toby?"

"I don't know. He was gone when I got up. He probably does have a life of his own somewhere that doesn't involve us humans all the time." Mimi laughed with good humor.

"She seems so confident and at ease with it all," thought Kara, *"I really should take some lessons from my baby sister!"*

They made a quick review of events from the last couple days, and both girls filled the other in on some details they had not yet shared, but still, they each held back a few secrets.

Recalling her earlier memory flash of her mother's letters hidden in her dad's desk, Kara said "Oh, Mim, I think we should be especially careful not to give away any of our secrets around Dad. I heard them fighting again last night after we went to bed. He sounded even more crazy-mad than he does sometimes when we're at home."

"I heard them too, and I am already being very careful." Mimi sounded sad. "I sure wish he could see how wonderful the magic is. It would probably help him and Mom get along better."

" I think the folks are planning to keep around home tonight and not go to any of the festivities," added Kara.

"Well, I sure wish we could go to see some. Even the animals are looking forward to the fun." Mimi sighed with longing.

Kara gave this some serious thought. "Maybe we can figure a way to sneak out for a while. Do you think Toby could help us?"

Mimi smiled brightly. "Good thinking, Kara! I can ask Toby to show us where to go. I'm sure he would want us to get in on some of the fun."

When they came downstairs they found Jo and their mother already sharing stories from the day before. Jo was excitedly telling Barb again about meeting the actress and director at the films. "You would love those films, Mom. They are full of the kinds of stories you used to tell us, only these stories are actually re-interpretations of some well- known Bible stories, only with a very different slant." She got up to set out a platter of fruit, but kept talking. "Oh, I forgot to mention that when dad got home I met him and told him about the invitation to stay and study with the actors group. He wasn't very impressed, but I am determined not to let him stop me as long as you will back me up, Mom." She gave Barb a quick hug.

Kara was amused at how Jo could go on and on without taking a breath. *What an airhead! All she thinks about is herself.* Kara still held resentment at Jo's apparent disinterest in hers and Mimi's adventures.

Barb looked up as the two girls entered. "Oh good! I'm glad you two sleepy heads are here." Barb got up and placed plates of toast, butter and jelly, and glasses of orange juice before all of them, then sat down and joined them. "Gina will be coming over in a bit and we are going to have a picnic in the orchard today, so don't stuff yourselves too much now."

"Sounds like fun", said Mimi. "Maybe aunt Gina can tell us more stories."

At that moment, Gina entered the kitchen. "I am ready to do just that, Mimi! She smiled warmly, "and we would like to hear a few of your tales from the last few days too!"

Mimi glanced at Kara, who gave a little shrug. "I suppose we could tell them a bit about the magical animals, right Mimi?" and she winked to show she didn't intend to give away any of their real secrets.

Soon the two women and Jo were toting the picnic baskets Gina had brought. They contained enough sandwiches, cookies, tea and pop to feed a small army. Kara carried her ever-present back-pack, and Mimi ran ahead skipping and singing.

When she got to the big oak tree on the way to the orchard, Mimi gave it a friendly pat and sat to wait for the others to catch up.

Barb glanced at Gina. "Looks like Mimi has discovered our old 'magic tree'," she whispered. The two women were walking together a few paces behind the girls. They saw Kara look with surprise at Mimi, as Mimi laughed teasingly.

The group followed a rambling path under gnarled olive trees and around more weathered grapevines. The trees showed budding leaves, but the vines still looked shriveled and dead. Kara explained to Mimi that they would come back to life later in the summer and ripen in the fall.

"See," exclaimed Mimi thoughtfully, "even the plants come back to life after death."

Kara was amazed at that allusion to reincarnation, one of the big mysteries she had been reading about in the Grimoire. "You are pretty smart to see that connection, Mim, I hadn't thought much about it myself."

They came at last to a neat clearing at the far side of the orchard. It perched on the edge of a small outcrop with a view to the water below. A picnic table was set under a carefully pruned arbor, covered by a climbing hibiscus that twined among more grape vines. The flowers were in bud and had lovely green leaves providing some cool shade on an already warm day.

The group settled around the table and began unpacking snacks and drinks. Mimi looked at Gina. "Do you know a story about a girl named Juliet from long ago?"

Gina turned in wide-eyed surprise and glanced at Barb. "Where have you heard about her, Mimi? She must have lived back in the seventeen or eighteen hundreds, if it is the girl I'm thinking of. She was our grandmother Selena's sister who died tragically at a young age_ right, Barb?"

Barb said, "yes, I do recall that story now you mention it. But, Mimi, is this the person you asked about? Where did you hear of her?"

Mimi sucked in her cheeks and thought quickly. "I found a book up in the tower room and it had her name on the cover, that's all." She glanced at Kara, who smiled with a questioning look back at her.

Mimi knew she had not told Kara about the "pool-a-vision" yet. She hoped her sister would let her get by with the little lie.

Gina went ahead and launched into some tales about the ancestral line again as everyone listened raptly. Jo intervened a few times making references to some of the biblical accounts of women in the films who had similar tales of persecution or betrayal by the Church and other authorities in the far distant past.

Amelia lived in the fourteen-hundreds, during the early part of the period known as the Italian Renaissance. Although history books describe that as some sort of idyllic time, it was far from ideal in reality. Just within the previous century, the Black Plague had killed nearly a third of Italy's population. Amelia's grandmother, whose name was Karamena, had been a notorious war-witch, who was later credited with working to help end that terrible epidemic.

Amelia's own parents died of the disease, however, when Amelia was but a tiny babe, and she was left with no one to care for her. Consequently, the legend is that she was actually raised in the wilderness by wolves, who taught her all the tricks of foraging and fending for herself.

In any case, by the time she was thirteen years old, Amelia knew every back street and alley-way intersecting the seven hills of the great city of Rome. She knew intimately every tavern, bath-house and brothel around the red light district. She recognized all the shopkeeper's stalls in the central market and made daily rounds of those through whom she conducted her own business on the side.

But, she made her home outside the city in the wooded hills on the other side of the Tiber, in the singular company of a primitive pack of wolves. The wolves were her family, for she had never known any other. The great alpha bitch whelped her along with her litters of pups. The huge male pack leader accepted her as one of his own, protecting and rescuing her from harmful human encounters throughout her early years. As she dared make forays into the company of city folk, the wolves kept close watch from the hills overlooking the city wall. While they never ventured to follow her through the gates, they remained instinctively attuned to her whereabouts, as she did to theirs.

By the time Amelia was fifteen years old, she was on her way to becoming Rome's most popular courtesan. By age seventeen, she ran her own brothel. By nineteen, she married the city's most powerful senator and was the mistress of one castle, three fabulous town houses, and the country villa that we now own.

She rescued our villa from demolition by government authorities into whose hands it had fallen during the chaotic Middle Ages. It was Amelia who made most of the additions to the hermitage and retrofitted the tower structure that had been built by our previous ancestors. Amelia designed the grounds of our villa and laid out some secret tunnels connecting it to certain other places in the area.

✳ ✳ ✳

At this information, Kara and Mimi exchanged a knowing glance, but said nothing to interrupt Gina's story, and Gina continued:

* * *

At around thirty years of age, Amelia had become the mother of several daughters (some say six, other say three, and I have forgotten most of their names.) and she was the High Priestess of a secret sect called Stregheria: our Nature and goddess traditions that had been handed down through generations of pagan peasants in private, under the very nose of the patriarchal church.

During these years, Amelia was accompanied, wherever she went, by two or three mastiffs the size and bearing of feral wolves. They were, in fact, actually wolf pups she adopted from her old family pack and bred with domestic stock to become guard dogs. They were animals known to all the city's inhabitants as sacred, to be respected and feared. When one of them was found shot by local militia, it started a guerilla war between Paganini and church vigilantes that goes on to this very day.

As an old woman, Amelia departed the city, leaving behind all her wealth and riches. She went to live in the wilderness with her animal friends and made her residence in a hidden cavern set into the hills overlooking the sea. She died at over one hundred years of age and was revered as a goddess by local pagans after her death.

Amelia left our villa to one daughter, Margaret, who followed in her mother's footsteps as a renowned healer-witch and ran a kind of home and temple compound for orphaned girls during years of French invasions and war in Italy. Margaret became a much sought-after midwife at a time when patriarchal medicine was killing more mothers and babies than it was successfully birthing.

Margaret's own daughter, Maria, was a warrior-priestess during the height of the vile Inquisition period. This would have been around the mid-fifteen-hundreds. She had the tunnels reinforced, and added other hiding places for those escaping the vigilantes of that period. Maria, herself, was ultimately burned as a witch. (And that is a gruesome tale I will leave for another time.)

Maria's youngest daughter, Sabrina, carried on her mother's work. But, given the harassing from church authorities, she closed the school and left the villa to her elder sisters to maintain. They kept it open for refugees from the ongoing persecutions and warring factions all over Europe. But they lived as respected citizens of Rome, themselves, working to cover up the secrets of their sacred lineage so future generations forgot the family was of fey blood.

It was an exciting and dangerous time to be living. Sabrina was an artist and journeyed to Florence, where she met and married a kind and generous man. Both worked as artisans: he sculpted and she created gold jewelry. They made a good living and raised two daughters, Iona and Cecelia. But tragedy befell them when Sabrina's husband was called off to war and was killed in the line of duty. That is when Sabrina took her daughters back to her ancient home territory in Abruzzi, built herself an alpine cabin higher in the mountain behind the villa, and had another tunnel constructed from it to join those from the villa. In these tunnels and caves, the sisters and their followers often took refuge during raids and battles and even during some earthquakes.

Kara and Mimi looked as if they were bursting with questions but they didn't ask about the tunnels and Grotto, as Gina had expected they might. Gina wondered briefly why they weren't begging to be shown those secret places immediately.

While the women and girls were entranced in listening to the ancient legends, Toby quietly ambled into the arbor and came to sit by Mimi. She cuddled him, bending down to give him bit of cheese.

Kara watched Mimi with the cat and wished she had Rarjer there to cuddle too. Under the table she felt Mimi pat her knee. *How sweet, my little sister is so sympathetic,* thought Kara. But then she felt Mimi poke her harder, which made Kara look down and see a black raven's feather in her sister's hand. Mimi had apparently taken it from Toby's jaws when she petted him. Kara took the feather, throwing another questioning glance at her sister.

Is this some kind of message or warning? wondered Kara. But then she laughed at herself for the 'magical thinking'. *Why would a cat bring a message from a bird? How silly!*

Then suddenly their peaceful gathering was interrupted by someone crashing clumsily through the orchard vines from the direction of the house. Soon John burst upon them unannounced and uninvited. They all stared at him in in various states of surprise and anger.

Barb spoke first, angrily "What are you doing so rudely interrupting our picnic?" Then a bit softer, teasing him, she said "Were you feeling left out?"

He glared at her, ignoring the others with no apology. "I came to tell you I have booked us a flight home for the day after tomorrow. I do not intend to let our family stay here and get sucked into all the devilish intrigue and nonsense any longer!" He glanced around the table and was met with wide-eyed stares of shock and rage.

Mimi, tears spilling down her cheeks, said "Daddy! How could you? We are learning so many wonderful things and having such a great time!"

Barb put her arm around Mimi's shoulder and gave her a squeeze of reassurance. "John, let me remind you that I already said I will not leave until matters at the villa are settled."

Kara seethed with astonished rage and disbelief that her father could be so insensitive and oblivious to their feelings. She realized now, for the first time, that she was not at all ready to leave Italy. She felt cheated by her father. She only said, "That is so unfair! You didn't even ask us."

Toby came and rubbed against Kara's leg. As she scratched his ear she remembered the feather. *Was that some kind of warning the raven gave them? Were the animals trying to keep them here too?* Somehow such thoughts no longer seemed so strange to her.

Jo, meanwhile, had remained serenely quiet watching their father's expression turn from controlling dominance to some level of contrition. Kara knew Jo planned to stay and study with the theater group here, whether their father approved or not.

But now Jo only said, "Daddy, maybe this isn't the place to talk about it. Come back with me to the house. I have something to show you." She put her arm through his and he meekly turned and left with her. "We can talk more after supper." Kara heard Jo assure him as they walked away.

38

A MAGICAL MEETING

Kara was enraged by her father's overbearing plan to make them leave before they were ready. As soon as he had gone with Jo, Kara left the table and ran up the woodland path without a word to anyone. She ran blindly, tears fogging her sight, stumbling over rocks and branches. She fell to her knees and just sat on the ground, crying tears of rage. Finally she calmed herself and shook her pony tail fiercely. "What is wrong with me? I'm acting like a baby!"

Mimi, who had also cried at their dad's news, quietly came up beside her and sat on a nearby boulder. "It's okay Kara," she said, reaching out to stroke her sister's shoulder. "I think we are all mad at Daddy_ Mom is too."

Toby licked Kara's hand. She still held the raven feather. Kara felt comforted, although this was a very awkward situation for her. She saw herself as the usually 'stable' sister in the role of 'protector' to her little sister.

"Thanks, Mimi, I'm glad you and Toby followed me." She hesitated. "But I'm hoping to find Rarjer. Do you think Toby might keep him away?"

"Oh, Kara! I think all our animal friends know each other and understand. Remember, Rarjer helped you find Toby and bring him to me in Farah's cave when he got hurt by the big bird.

Kara laughed out loud at the recollection. She was amazed by all the mystical events that had occurred to them in the short period of yesterday afternoon. She got up from the ground, brushed off her jeans, and gave Mimi a hug.

They set off for the overlook meadow where Kara had first encountered the wolf. Rarjer was waiting for them, his tongue lolling in a big wolf grin. When he saw them top the rise, he ran to Kara, who hugged him, while Mimi and Toby stood by and watched.

"R'caw! R'caw!"

Kara jumped back and looked around anxiously, her heart pummeling her ribs.

The Raven was perched on a branch right above them. Upon seeing the bird, Kara sighed, "This must be the same bird I keep seeing wherever I go. I suppose he's one of Sophia's tamed magic animals too, huh?"

Mimi grinned broadly and nodded. Toby put his whiskers forward in amusement at Kara's agitation over the bird. But Rarjer came to sit right beneath its branch, looking up with his head cocked to one side as if asking a question. He wasn't grinning or growling. He only peered intently at the Raven and made a quiet bark as if to ask "What is it? What do you want to show us?"

Kara looked again at the feather and wondered, *is this supposed to be a message of some kind? From who?*

The raven dropped down in front of the wolf and gave a light peck to Rarjer's front paw. Then he waddled to Toby and did the same, and hopped to Mimi and pecked her foot. All three of them simply observed the bird while Kara stepped back, still apprehensive.

The bird cawed three times more and took flight, landing in another tree a few paces away, it turned and cawed again. Then it flew away in a direction leading back down the mountain behind the villa.

Rarjer loped down a rugged trail in the same direction and looked back at the others, indicating they should follow. Toby leapt and scampered easily after the wolf.

Kara picked up her back pack from where it had fallen, but she stood rooted to the spot, unsure of what to do.

Mimi, starting after the animals, called over her shoulder. "Come on, Kara. We have to follow them!"

But Kara still waited a moment, feeling a bit stunned by the communication she had witnessed between the three animals. "Why do I keep being surprised by these things?" she scolded herself aloud. "I should be used to the 'magic animals by now!"

Shaking her pony tail in exasperation with herself, she took off at a faster pace to catch up with Mimi, who was confidently picking her way down a nearly invisible trail. Occasionally Toby or Rarjer would stop to wait for them while the other one raced ahead to follow the bird.

A few minutes later they came to stone steps leading to the Etruscan crypt where they had buried Sophia's remains two days earlier. "Oh! I had been thinking of coming here after the picnic, but forgot when dad broke in on us," said Kara, a bit out of breath from their erratic run down the woodland path.

"Looks like the animals remembered anyway," Mimi said, stroking Toby's ears and grinning at Kara.

Rarjer nudged Kara and she bent to hug him, but he quickly headed toward the crypt with a nod to tell her to follow. Entering the dimly lit cavern, the animals and girls all hushed in reverence to the spirits there. Kara felt a shiver of anticipation and had the momentary thought, *Someone else is here already!* But she saw no one.

"Hello there!" said Mimi. She didn't sound surprised at all. Kara looked behind herself and all around the crypt, but failed to see who her sister was addressing. She stopped herself from asking, and kept still. Words from the Grimoire came to her spontaneously: *The Magic is always with us, we need but trust and believe that we can use it for the good of all.*

Kara took several deep breaths and closed her eyes a moment. Laying her hand on Rarjer's soft back, she felt the reassurance of his guarding presence. *Thank you spirits of my ancestors,* she silently prayed. *Help me to see and hear without judging or doubting this moment.*

When she opened her eyes she saw another young girl holding hands with Mimi. They were smiling at each other as if they had been friends for years. Mimi turned to Kara, "This is my friend Juliet. Can you see her? She and Tinkle are here to show us things."

Kara bit her tongue to keep from crying out in surprise, for she could see, not only the girl, but the fairy sitting on Mimi's should too. In a shaky voice she said, "Yes! I see them both, Mimi." She calmed herself and addressed the apparitions. "I'm happy to meet you, Juliet_ and you too, little fairy."

"Hmph! Well, it's about time you learned to believe in us," scolded the fairy, "Sophia is very happy to hear this too."

Kara refrained from asking for further explanation of this enigmatic comment, acknowledging that some very special energy inhabited this cave.

"What did you want to show us, Tinkle?" asked Mimi.

But just then they were interrupted by the raven who flew in carrying some objects in its beak. The bird hopped first to Mimi and dropped one, then to Kara and dropped the other. The girls each stopped and picked up what lay at her feet.

"It's the little magic bag from the first cave Tinkle showed me," said Mimi. She examined it a moment and looked up at the fairy. "But I thought it was just for visiting the big cave. Are we going there now?"

"You are s'posed to wear it to all the magic places, silly. No, we aren't going there yet, but you might want it for later and you should be wearing it here now." The fairy sounded annoyed at Mimi's questioning.

"Oh. Okay." Mimi hung the deerskin bag on her neck, and looked up at the raven. "Thank you Mister Raven."

Kara picked up and examined an identical bag, recognizing it as that which she had found in the Grotto with the magic dagger. *I must have dropped it when we found Mimi's shoes.*

The fairy, scolding again, said "His name is Melanthus, not Mister Raven."

Kara was amused at the fairy's impatience with her ignorant human charges. Yet she felt encouraged and calmed by Mimi's easy attitude around their unusual new friends. Yet now Kara had to clear her throat before speaking for she suddenly felt unusually shy.

"Well, I want to apologize to all of you for being so slow to accept that you and the magic are for real. Tinkle, I thank you for helping Mimi, and I am very happy to meet you Juliet. Aunt Gina told us a little about you." She wondered why the girl, ghost that she might be, did not speak.

The fairy answered her thought: "Juliet can't speak, but she can hear and is glad to see you too. She can show you things in your minds."

Then Kara turned to the raven, who was perched on the ledge of the cave. "Melanthus, I am sorry that I have been so rude to you. I didn't mean to insult you. I see now that you are a very special Messenger and protector of Aunt Sophia's villa."

The bird made a little bow toward her and made a soft sound like an amused chuckle.

While Kara made her apologies Toby, with the help of Rarjer and the fairy, pulled a small rectangular box from a niche in the wall of the cave. The fairy instructed Mimi to open it and told each of the girls to remove three objects from inside.

Kneeling, Kara gingerly reached in and felt several egg-sized stones, each with one flat side. She took one and lay it down in front of her. Then Mimi did the same and they repeated this twice more so they both had three stones. Following Tinkle's instructions they took turns holding one of their stones, palm over the flat surface, eyes closed.

Kara saw an image of a wolf with the first stone; a mountain lion on the second one; a raven on the third. With each one she heard in her mind the voice of Juliet telling the spiritual role of each animal: *intelligence, loyalty, guardianship respectively.*

Then Mimi did hers: a cat, *cunning_* a fox, *trickster_* a serpent, *sight.* Mimi inhaled sharply on the last one and looked startled at Juliet who only smiled reassuringly. Kara was amazed that she had been able to 'see' and 'hear' what was given to Mimi as well as that of her own talismans.

"You need to know each other's animal totems," explained Tinkle with uncharacteristic patience, "because sometimes they can bring you messages from or about each other."

Kara and Mimi looked at each other wide-eyed. "You mean we will be having more adventures?" asked Mimi with delight.

Kara sighed and said with a smile, "I feel overwhelmed already with all the amazing things I have seen and learned in the last couple of days! I'm not sure I can take in much more."

"Oh you will be fine, young priestess, don't worry. You have lots of friends watching out for you, but just be sure you don't let yourself start doubting again." Tinkle shook a tiny forefinger at her, but the ghost girl smiled and the fairy giggled happily too.

Tucking their amulets under their t-shirts, Kara and Mimi began to put the stones away, preparing to return to the house. But just then a small red fox darted into the cave and yipped urgently at the fairy. Mimi exclaimed, "Oh! It's Reddy!"

Tinkle flew to Kara's shoulder and whispered for her to take out the raven feather. Kara obeyed without a word and watched another drama unfold.

All at once, Rarjer raised his hackles, growling; Toby put his ears back, hissing; Juliet faded into the wall; and Melanthus ruffed his feathers, croaking loudly. Mimi screamed.

The biggest rat Kara had ever seen crept through the door, with fangs exposed, aiming directly toward her. But she didn't even feel surprised when she found the raven feather had transformed into a spear, for at the same time she grew remarkably calm and focused.

She prepared to stab the rodent. But before she had time to aim, a large snake slithered from under a stone slab in the crypt. They all watched in various states of shock, horror, fury, and amazed fascination. The snake calmly opened its huge jaws and proceeded to swallow the vile rat alive and whole.

Mimi was shaking and nearly in tears. Juliet reappeared, putting her hand into Mimi's, calming her. She even stayed calm when the snake came and curled up right at her feet. "Well, now we have each met our totem animals," she said to Kara. "But you were so brave, all ready to stab that awful rat. Where ever did you get that spear?"

Kara held out her hand in which she now merely grasped the raven's feather again. "I will tell you that secret later, honey. We really must get back to the house now."

Kara's smile seemed to light the cave as she looked at each of its occupants, including the snake, and said, "I don't think I could ever doubt the magic again. And I am ever so glad to know we have so many wonderful friends to guide us."

Rarjer bounced up, paws on her shoulders, "Ka Rah!" She ruffed his ears. The fairy giggled, Juliet smiled serenely, and Mimi hugged them both. The raven cawed softly and flew out the door. Toby snuffled the snake, who looped itself in a figure eight between their legs before slithering back under the rock.

"Oh my! What fun this is," said Mimi.

Again she was reprimanded by Tinkle. "Don't think it is all just a game! You are supposed to be learning how to be good witches." And with a final tweak of Mimi's ear, she said, "go now. We will meet again later."

Mimi and Kara climbed back up the path to the house, each lost in her own thoughts.

39

BELTANE BEGINS

I n the early evening on Beltane Night, two motorcycles
cruised south along the ancient Apennine roadway, where
once Caesar's Roman troops marched. The Harleys chugged
along at half throttle, their riders absorbed in the grandeur of
a crimson sun setting over the azure sea, gilding the mountains
around them with its glow. The biker's shadows rode beside
them over rock and rill, through brush and bramble, growing
longer and darker mile by mile. Gradually night overtook them,
with its star-shadowed silence like a panther on the prowl, and
they arrived at their destination.

Killing the engines and walking their bikes down a ragged
embankment, Giuseppe and his priest friend stowed the
machines in an overgrown hedge out of sight. Then they clambered back to the road and walked about half a mile to the ruin
of an ancient Greek temple built on the ridge of a cliff overlooking the sea. Here they lit a fire in a cauldron set upon the
cracked marble slabs of the temple's crumbling veranda.

Giuseppe and his companion hunkered on opposite sides of the fire, mutely gazing into its flames. Soon they heard the calls of others coming to join them. An owl hooted, and a raven cawed. The howl of a wolf was answered by another.

A bobcat sprang from a thicket, landing softly to sit watching the fire. It was followed by a mountain lion, pacing slowly across the meadow to lie silently at the smaller cat's side. Two wolves appeared, their eyes aglow with firelight, and lay down, one beside each of the two men who were in deep trance. The owl hooted again from a perch in the temple's shattered frieze, and the raven watched from a nearby oak tree. Finally, from beyond the moon-dark mountain ridge, a stately stag, with a rack of antlers broader than the raven's tree, took his place in the circle around the fire.

Still sitting in trance, the voice of the priest carried forth as wind in the hallowed hills chanting:

We call upon you in loyalty and honor, Goddess of the Moon. Come to our counsel, come to our aid, come and guide your people in this hour of shifting patterns.

Giuseppe took up the plainsong in tones of a rising sea-tide.

God of the forest and mountains, we humbly call forth your power to help us withstand and overcome those who strive to tame your wild glory. Come to our counsel, come to our aid, come and guide your people in this hour of shifting patterns.

Their chants reverberated through the hills and valleys, echoing across rivers and through forests like a tumultuous wind. The tempest reached into hidden caves and tunnels, calling forth yet more of Nature's guardians, until the little temple on the hill was thronged by creatures of the night, both terrestrial and supernatural, visible and invisible. The coterie watched in silence, as a transformation occurred.

Where had been two men, now sat two ethereal visitors. The priest transmuted the form of an ageless woman with haunting eyes in an equine face of utterly serene countenance. Dark-skinned and robed in gossamer veils, she sat surrounded by spirits of the mountains. Her presence encompassed the night, where hundreds of small bonfires gradually blinked awake all around the mountainside, like stars fallen to earth.

Giuseppe, metamorphosed, became the horned god of the forest. He wore the curled horns of a mountain goat, wreathed in ripening grapevines. His mischievous grin warned of trickery, while bestowing mirth upon their mission. He stood up, reaching muscular arms toward the ancient beauty sitting across from him, and the two danced into the night with their motley band riding the wake of their luminous trail. Soon all that was left on the temple hill were the ashes of a vagabond's campfire, and a single raven's feather.

40

BELTANE MAGIC

After eating a light supper with the family, Mimi and Kara slipped quietly back to their respective rooms. But when Kara got to her room she heard voices downstairs and crept closer to listen. Dad and Joanna were deep in conversation. Mother had gone down to join them.

Kara quickly rumpled the blankets on her bed into a sort of human form and shoved a crumpled brown bag against the pillow so just a bit of it peeked out to look like her head. In dim light the effect was pretty convincing. *It'll have to do,* she thought.

She returned to Mimi's room where a similar dummy already lay in her sister's bedding. "Just hope no one tries to kiss us goodnight!" joked Mimi. They both laughed.

Back on the roof, someone was waiting for them.

Kara stifled a scream. She was still shocked when she could actually see the fairy, despite their earlier encounter in the crypt.

Mimi looked surprised for only an instant. "Tinkle!" she exclaimed with a delighted laugh. "I was hoping you would come." She went over to the fairy who was sitting on the ledge of the parapet and realized someone else was there too. "Oh! Excuse me, Melanthus," Mimi said, "I didn't see you 'cuz you're so black in the dark."

"Draack caw kraaack," croaked the big bird, and hopped back and forth a couple of times.

"We camed to take you to someone," said the fairy. "Sophia sended us and said for you to hurry." The fairy flew down to sit on Mimi, s shoulder, but she eyed Kara warily. "I guess her meaned both of you," Tinkle added in a grudging murmur. She also seemed uncertain of Kara in spite of their earlier meeting.

"Tinkle, you know you don't have to be afraid of my sister Kara, she is one of us now, even though she used to be an unbeliever." Mimi winked at Kara.

Kara took a deep breath and tried to let go of her discomfort at really seeing and hearing the magic creatures. The raven, of course, was ordinary enough, except for his unusual size. But a fairy? Kara was surprised that she was not yet prepared to accept, since she had felt so sure this afternoon.

She swallowed, "I, I'm pleased to see you, Tinkle. A_ a_ and you too, Melanthus *At least it's not the ghost,* she joked with herself.

"Kara could make us go away," whispered Tinkle into Mimi's ear. "She still doesn't want to believe in us."

Mimi looked surprised, and turned to Kara. "Is Tinkle right? Don't you want to believe in the magic people even after what happened this afternoon? If not, maybe you shouldn't come along, because you could frighten them away. They only show themselves to people who totally believe. I guess because of what happened in the crypt, Tinkle is showing herself to you now."

Kara felt hurt. Then she realized the fairy was right. She was withholding complete acceptance of the magic. She recalled reading in the journal how magic would not work if you didn't totally allow yourself to believe. *'Suspend disbelief' was the way Cecelia wrote it.*

Kara took another deep breath and willed herself to set aside her doubts once and for all. After a moment she said, "I'm truly sorry if I offended you, Little Tinkle. You are right, I was not really ready to let myself believe in you at first. But now I am. I see you and hear you and know you are my sister's friend. How can I possibly not believe you are real?" And she smiled, holding out her hand, palm up.

Then Kara turned to the raven, who was perched on the ledge of the parapet. "Melanthus, I am really very happy to know you watch over us and protect Aunt Sophia's villa."

The bird merely cocked his head and snapped his beak at a bug on the wall.

The fairy sniffed, "Well, that's more better. Just be sure you don't betray us to the unbelievers." She was not ready to accept Kara's offer of friendship yet, however, and stayed close to Mimi as they sat down to plot how best to get out of the house unseen.

Toby had been observing the interactions, and now he stepped into the middle of the group to get their attention. The cat looked directly at each of the two girls, and then turned deliberately toward the stairway, tail held up authoritatively, indicating they should follow him.

Mimi said, "I bet he knows a way for us to go out. Let's follow him." She jumped up, grabbed Kara's lantern, and headed for the stairs. Kara followed without objection, shouldering her backpack and carrying their jackets.

Tinkle fluttered ahead of them close on Toby's tail. Melanthus flew off into the woods with a cackle. Somewhere nearby a wolf called.

Toby led them back down the turret stairs, past the doorway into Mimi's bedroom, and along a short corridor that was full of storage boxes. It turned out that the closet actually led into a hallway behind the wall, and shortly they came to a long, steep stairway leading down between the walls.

Kara was delighted to find this secret passage in the outside wall of the tower. It was very narrow, only about three feet wide. Built of heavy stone and mortar on both sides, it had not been used for some time. Dust lay thick on every step, and heavy cobwebs had to be brushed aside at each turn. Narrow slotted openings, every ten steps or so, let in air and brief glimpses of the villa's surroundings. Kara wondered why she hadn't noticed these openings from outside, but realized they would simply appear as dark shadows, there being no light behind them in the hidden stairway. It added to the mystery of the place and, once again, Kara was transported into some long-past age.

Which of our ancestors built this tower as a fortress? It is clearly meant to be both for hiding and for defense of the tower. She had the sense of hurrying to a secret rendezvous, or to a clandestine gathering in a time of great calamity or danger. There was the sense of an urgent need to escape, or to lead others to safety here. These images and feelings passed through Kara's mind, as if she were re-living another lifetime when this tower and its inhabitants had been involved in dangerous and important goings on.

They kept going down and down. They passed a landing and a doorway that stood at the ground level. Faint voices could be heard on the other side, and Kara realized this door must open into the living room. But she could not recall seeing one there, and she guessed it must be hidden behind the bookcases.

Beyond the landing, the stairway took a 90 degree turn to the left, and they continued on down farther into the bowels of the ancient structure, until they came to a final door. Here, Toby stood on his hind legs and pawed at its old fashioned latch. Mimi held the flashlight, as Kara tried the door. The latch gave easily in her hand, but the heavy door creaked loudly on rusted hinges as she shoved it aside. Kara held her breath, fearing those in the living room might hear, but if they did, they did not bother to investigate.

Kara peered around the door and nearly fainted.

Right in front of them, on an old wine keg, sat the faun. It was the same horned figure she knew from statues and drawings she'd seen many times in the last few days. But this one was alive and grinning at her. And, for once, it wore a short tunic to cover its nakedness. It spoke.

"Hello Kara and Mimi. I've been waiting for you girls," said the Horned God. "It is Beltane, my dears, and tonight is a night of dancing and celebration. I have been waiting to take you to see the woodland festivities." He hopped down from his perch, and held out a hand. "Won't you come with me for an hour or so? I promise to bring you back safe and sound. No one will even know you are gone."

His smile was so disarming and his voice so warmly reassuring that Kara could not help but drop her initial revulsion toward this grotesque creature. A god, she seriously doubted, but she was willing to suspend her disbelief for a while and go along for the adventure. *After all, today certainly seems to be a day for mystery and magic.*

She turned to look for Mimi, and saw that her sister had already accepted the outstretched hand of their strange escort. The fairy, Tinkle, perched happily on the fellow's left horn. Toby pranced alongside, with his tail in the air as if he were on parade for a king_ or a god. Kara had no choice but to go along.

She followed the little group, and quietly observed the ancient stone-walled cellar with interest. She recalled reading that this part of the villa was built very long ago as a hermitage for one of the early Rimini witches. She could not recall the woman's name. An old fireplace hearth sat in the center of the nearly square room. Its chimney had fallen or burned down long ago. But someone had recently used it as a cooking area, for there was a little camping gas stove set into it. *How odd*, thought Kara.

Cobwebs hung like veils over another stairwell on the other side of the room and all the casks in its vicinity were moldy with age. Yet, the area they walked through now was perfectly clean, except for a little dry dust. It was as if this part of the cellar was still being used, while the other side was completely neglected. *Avoided, maybe.*

There is something distinctly weird about this house, and it isn't just about fairies and statues that come alive. Kara's attention was taken back to the present by the voice of the faun.

"I'm going to have to blindfold you two girls for a short distance now," said their horned escort. "Don't be afraid. It's just that where I'm taking you is a secret place that can't be revealed to most people. I can't risk letting you know how to find it just yet, although someday you may learn the secret. When we get there, I'll take your blindfolds off."

Kara felt a stab of foreboding and prepared to resist the blindfold. But she watched him gently tie a fine black silk scarf over Mimi's eyes. *It is all a delightful game to her,* thought Kara. *I'd better not go spoiling it yet. I'll let old horny tie one on me, since I can always take it off later.* She shifted her backpack so he could reach around to tie the scarf. Then she felt him take her hand and a shock of excitement vibrated from his fingers through her whole body. *Well,* she thought, *getting touched by a magical being must naturally feel pretty shocking.* She clung to his hand and followed blindly into the unknown.

Probably not so unknown, Kara reasoned to herself. *He's leading us into a secret tunnel, and I bet we will end up in the big cavern.* She was reminded of the Malandanti hawk that attacked them when she made the trip yesterday with Rarjer. *Sure hope that bird and its ilk aren't lurking around now,* she thought. It occurred to Kara that she might tell the horned god about their earlier trip, but she kept quiet and observant as they walked along.

She noticed there had been a soft scraping sound when some door or other object and been moved. Then they had entered what felt very much like the tunnels of their earlier escapade. The floor and walls felt dry and cool to the touch. Occasional gusts of night air could be smelt and felt, *so this tunnel must have other openings leading outside,* she reasoned. After a relatively short distance, they turned into a narrow rocky passage with rough dirt floor and walls. Then they emerged into the open air and stopped.

Their blindfolds were removed and they found themselves, not in the Grotto, but in a circular copse of trees surrounding a small pond. Around the circumference of the pond a motley group of individuals danced and frolicked to a jig-like music being played on pipes and flutes by various of their members, while others clapped their hands or barked, stamped, hooted, and snorted to keep rhythm. A fire burned in a large pit at one end of the pond. Some big boulders were piled to one side of the Grove, forming a sort of dais for a pair of throne-like rocks in the center of the arrangement.

Several fairies and other woodland people stood in attendance to someone sitting on one of these. Tinkle gave a squeak of delight and flew to join that group, calling back to them as she went, "It's the queen! Come meet our queen!"

The Horned God led them to the creature on the throne. Bowing gracefully, he said, "We have arrived with the guests of honor, your Majesty."

Kara and Mimi stood speechless before a hauntingly beautiful woman wearing nothing but a transparent shawl that shimmered with rainbow hues. Her skin was the color of dark maple syrup and as smoothly glossy. She wore lots of sparkling jewelry strung about her ears and her neck, waist, wrists, and ankles. The jewelry wove a silvery web over her body. Her dark brown eyes were like deep pools sparked with stars. Her smile shone like a full moon upon her attendants. All around her, wild animals of every size and kind lounged in perfect peace.

"Welcome to Beltane, sweet ones. It is a long time since we have been honored by the presence of human children." Her voice was deep and rich, like warm cocoa. She reached her hands toward them in a sign of blessing saying, "Please feel at ease and join the celebration as you will. Our night is short, but it is full of love and joy."

Kara recalled a similar blessing somewhere in Cecelia's journal. She suddenly had the impulse to ask, "Who are you?"

"It is a long time since anyone has thought to ask my name." The queen's delighted laugh rang around the Grove like a chiming cymbal. All the celebrants stopped to listen. "I am She Who Watches over you, earth-child. And I am She Who Mediates between your world and the Other. I am known by many names, but always I am the Moon Goddess, the Queen of the Fairies and Witches. Your own family has known me as the goddess Diana-Aradia."

Kara drew a breath in recognition. "I am honored in your Presence, dear goddess. Thank you for your blessing." The words came naturally and Kara wondered how she knew to speak so easily with a goddess and fairy queen? Most amazingly, Kara found she harbored none of her usual cynical doubts or misgivings. Standing in the luminous aura of the queen's blessing, Kara felt tears spring to her eyes. This meeting recalled in her a terrible sense of loss. It was as if she had got lost in some long ago time and just now found her way home.

A wet object nudged into Kara's hand. She looked down to see Rarjer gazing up at her with a big wolf-grin on his face. With a little squeal of delight, she knelt to hug her friend. "Rarjer! How did you get here?" Then she laughed, "But of course you would be with the queen of fairies and witches. You are pure magic yourself." She looked lovingly into his eyes.

He barked, "Ka-Rah! Ka-Rah!" And then he pranced off to another group and back again. She took the invitation to follow him and found herself in the midst of a very unusual throng. A great horned owl and a raven sat together on one branch of a tree overlooking the group. A golden mountain lioness sat amicably next to a bobcat; a couple of raccoons shared the remains of a walnut; a pair of rabbits rather nervously tended several young bunnies playing among flowers; a doe and her fawn stood serenely nearby, accompanied by a giant stag with a huge rack of antlers; a small black bear rolled playfully with a red fox. And. in the middle of this group sat Rarjer's golden mate. Their four pups ran in and out, playing tag with a pair of chipmunks.

Kara couldn't believe her ears. The animals were talking with each other. This unlikely group was having a conversation in words that she could actually understand. They were sharing stories, recalling legends from some far distant time.

Kara looked around for her sister and saw Mimi on the other side of the Grove in a similar gathering with Toby at her side. That group was made up mostly of fairies and elves and other ethereal beings. They also seemed to be telling each other stories. Kara guessed she must be dreaming, but she decided to go ahead and enjoy whatever it was and ask questions later.

This is the story the animals told:

✳ ✳ ✳

In a time long ago, the exiled princess, Dianhea and her brother, Dravid lived in the islands of the setting sun, across the smaller water on the other side of our mountains.

This young pair had befriended the animals of the land and were guarded by them, in turn. Their grandmother, Sabrina, was an ancient and revered priestess of the Moon Goddess, and Dianhea had inherited magical powers and knowledge from her.

But it came to pass that after their grandmother's death, the priests of their kingdom plotted to imprison Dianhea and exploit her prophetic gifts for their own devious ends. Dravid learned of the plot, and the two young people convened their animal protectors.

The stag, the lion, the bear and the wolf gathered together, with the raven and owl, on the mountain top. The wild ones told the human brother and sister of a land over the water to the west which was yet relatively free of civilization's greed and corruption. The animals knew, from telepathic communications with their own kind living there, that it was a land richer in forest and green growth than their own barren hill country. They told of higher mountains and clearer streams, and kinder climes.

Dianhea and Dravid determined to make their way across the sea to this new land. But they could not go alone. They needed a few loyal and brave comrades. Yet, they could not trust anyone in their home compound, which had grown into a large fortified town awash with intrigue and brigands.

Moreover, the ancient goddess' wisdom had become badly corrupted through an insidious redefining in terms that glorified the villainous male gods and defiled the goddess.

Again, the animals came to their aid. They knew of certain peasants and vagabond gypsies in the mountains who were sympathetic to the goddess. Dianhea and Dravid traveled to where a gypsy gathering was being held in the high hidden mountain valleys of Greece.

There they met several others eager to escape to the new land with them. The band of about thirty people, all accompanied by loyal animal companions, sailed in a fleet of small boats, west across the Ionian Sea.

These were the first of our ancient magic folk to settle in this land.

When the story ended, Kara looked around her again. The Horned God sat on a stone throne next to the Moon Goddess. The two were deep in intimate conversation while the celebrants sang and danced around them. It was like a scene from a Disney movie, Kara thought. *Only these creatures are real.*

Suddenly the festivities were interrupted by a great commotion.

A deer charged through the woods and fell bleeding by the pond. It was immediately surrounded by fairies who set to work washing and binding its wounds with fairy silk.

The Horned God strode over to the wounded buck and asked, "What news, Ganymede? Who shot you?"

"Beware! Beware!" gasped the deer. "The hunters have set a trap. Do not return to your stream-side dens, for they await your coming." He stopped to take a drink of water from a leaf-cup held to his lips by Mimi. She stroked his head and murmured unintelligible sounds that seemed to soothe him greatly.

Thank you, little goddess," he addressed her. She merely nodded and smiled warmly as she continued the healing ministrations for another few minutes.

Kara stood in awe at her youngest sister's power with animals. She noted also that Mimi made nothing of being addressed as a goddess. *Maybe she really is a goddess incarnate,* mused Kara only half-jokingly. *Sometimes I think of her as other than human-- but I see an imp, not a deity!*

When the wounded deer stood up and bowed to Mimi, paying her homage for healing him so quickly, she accepted graciously, as if it was something she did every day.

Kara went to Mimi's side and gave her a hug. "You really are a miracle worker, sweetie," she said.

Mimi giggled, then said, "I just know where the animal hurts and I go there to give it love. It's nothing different than you or mom do when I'm sick."

Kara thought there was more to it than that, but she didn't argue the point. The horned god came and put an arm around each of them. "It's time to take you home" he said. "It has been a great pleasure for us to share Beltane with you. You have both brought healing energy to our world. Now the queen has a final message for you, before I put the blindfolds back on."

They stood before the woodland throne and bowed to the Moon Goddess, Queen of Fairies and Witches. Kara had a fleeting image of a similar circle of ethereal beings watching them from someplace far away.

"Go in great peace and love, my little ones," said the queen. "You will remember some of tonight's revelries, but the details must remain shadowed, for there are those in your world who would try to purge the knowledge of magic from you, should they guess what you know." She smiled upon them reassuringly. "But we will meet again. Until then, do as you will, but harm none, and above all, remember I am always watching over you. You may call upon me at any time."

Walking blindfolded again, back through the tunnel to the villa's wine cellar, Kara again made mental note of sounds and smells along the way, and she counted the number of steps they took. Something told her this passage would come in handy sometime. She had no idea whether for herself or for others, and why. *My imagination is working overtime*, she chided herself.

Meanwhile, Mimi chatted with the horned god and asked him, "Do you have a name I can call you by, if I need to reach you?"

He chuckled mischievously, "You won't need to call me. I'll be keeping an eye on you also, just like the queen. Only I'll be right here on earth." He thought a bit, then said with a laugh, "But you can call me Faunus, if you like."

When their blindfolds were removed, Kara and Mimi turned to thank their horned escort, but he had vanished without a word.

Toby led them back up to the roof from the cellar. There they saw only the full moon rising over the mountain. A wolf howled and an owl hooted to greet the moon.

The clock downstairs struck nine as they came back inside. Their parents were having a heated discussion, and no one heard when Kara and Mimi finally went to bed.

41

CONVERSATIONS

The grandfather clock in the entrance hall was chiming eight, and John and Joanna were still heavily into their discussion. They met in the living room to talk after supper, as they'd planned earlier. Jo had given him the booklet to read when they came away from the picnic.

Barbara had come down to join them and to lend her support as Jo declared her intentions to stay and study in Italy. As anticipated, John continued to resist and rail against the 'wicked ways' of Strega, but it seemed to her that he was weakening, at least regarding their eldest daughter's plans.

Now Barb excused herself, saying "You two will have to work this out between you. I'm supportive of Joanna's plan to work with the theater group here, but I feel too angry at you, John, to be of much use in this discussion. Your judgment of the Old Ways is simply not fair. It leaves me enraged. Your cousin at the Vatican doesn't know what he's talking about."

She turned to go upstairs, then added, "You and I will have our own discussion when the two of you are finished. I know we can't resolve all these things in one night, but it is time we get our real feelings out into the open."

She bent to kiss Joanna on the forehead. "Hang in there honey. What you are asking for is not wrong, no matter what your father's cousin says about devil worship and heretical conspiracies." She threw John a challenging glance. "I'll be waiting up for you."

John raised an eyebrow. "Guess I'd better be prepared for a long night. I think I'll pour me a drink first. Do you want me to bring you one?"

"No thanks. I want to keep my head clear for this discussion," replied Barbara, with a mirthless chuckle.

Barbara had been thinking long and hard about her heritage since this afternoon when she listened to her sister retell the old stories. Now, as she sat in Sophie's Morris chair, waiting for John to come upstairs she continued her thoughts.

Too much of that inherent female power has been undermined by women's own submission to men. Men like John, who hold thoughtless obedience to misogynist religious propaganda. It is time I take a stand on the matter of spiritual direction in my daughter's lives. Long past time, if I am to be completely honest with myself.

∗ ∗ ∗

Downstairs, Joanna sat on the chintz-covered sofa, her legs tucked up under her. She turned a defiant gaze on her father, sitting across from her in a matching lounge chair. She took a breath to steady her nerves, and said, "Have you taken time to read the little booklet I gave you?"

John nodded and said grudgingly, "Well, yeah. I skimmed it on my walk before supper."

"The book is full of interesting history, Dad. It was written about twenty years ago by a guy named Heironymous." She spoke with a new-found self-confidence, and realized she was not at all afraid of her father's bluster. "I was hoping it would help you see the other side of things more clearly."

John looked a bit taken off guard, and he hesitated a moment before taking the book from his jacket pocket to glance at the title page. Then in a louder voice he said, "But no one will convince me that goddess worship, devil's play, and nature orgies are sacred rites equal in power to that of the church." He frowned and cleared his throat as he casually flipped the pages of the book, then tucked it back into his pocket.

"According to that book," said Joanna, "a whole lot of what the church does for its religious rites and ceremonies is borrowed directly from the old traditions and what you call devil's play." She laughed congenially. "Go ahead and read it more carefully, Dad. I promise you will be entertained anyway, and I'm sure you won't be struck dead by God for looking at the stuff."

She waited for his angry retort, but he sat quietly looking at her for a long minute.

"You remind me so much of your mother, when we first met." He shook his head. "It's that intrepid self-confident spirit that gets to me. I have to admit that my religion doesn't give me the happy confidence in life that all of you seem to feel naturally. Perhaps it is time I took a serious look at what the Strega believe."

He grinned ruefully at his eldest daughter, coughed, and said, "You will be glad to know I did read your little booklet carefully, and nothing in it seemed all that strange. Thanks. It at least may help me cope with your mother's anger more gently."

She rose and gave him a hug. "I love you daddy," she said. "Don't worry, we aren't all going to the devil like your cousin prophesies." She tousled his thinning hair. "You'd better go talk with Mom now. I'm going to bed."

The little bag of amulets snuggled warmly between her breasts and she was reminded to give a little prayer of thanks to Sophia's spirit friends. *Seems there really is a power of reconciliation in this thing*, she thought.

On an impulse, she knocked quietly on the door to her parent's bedroom suite. When her mother opened the door, Jo handed her the little pouch and said, "Good luck." Then she went up to bed.

* * *

John sat thinking for several minutes. Then he poured himself a scotch, taking it and the book with him to the bedroom. Barb waited there, sitting in the overstuffed Morris chair with a fringed shawl around her shoulders. She fondled the little bag of amulets that hung on her neck.

Another serene and determined woman, thought John. *I'm nuts to think I can resist all this beautiful female energy.* The thought brought a sense of frustration combined with a certain resigned relief. *It is really beyond my power to control them.* He sighed and sat down in a wing-backed chair opposite his wife.

"Well Barb," he said, looking harried. "Let's have at it. Joanna will do whatever she decides to do. I realize I can't control her. But I am still determined that my family will not regress to living in the dark ages as gypsies and witches. This school thing is much too dangerous. I learned today how seriously the church is fighting your traditions. I don't want you or the little girls subjected to that kind of harassment." He stopped to take a sip of his drink and swirled the ice cubes so they clinked in the glass.

Barbara said, "And I have come to exactly the opposite resolve. I believe it is our deepest duty, as the last of Sophia's lineage, to carry on her work regardless what opposition we might encounter from the established power brokers of society. I am ashamed of myself for having hidden from it for so long. The girls should have been introduced to their spiritual heritage long before this." Stopping to take a breath, she glanced warily at John.

He looked away. He couldn't bring himself to meet her gaze.

She went on, "I feel Sophia must be very upset with me, and I don't blame her." She wiped a tear that threatened to spill down her cheek. "Sophia never harmed a soul; in fact, she brought great love and peace into the lives of everyone who knew her." She blew her nose and waited.

In a gentler tone than usual, John said, "I was reminded of that yesterday. I met someone who knew Sophia and he seemed to hold her in high esteem, despite his own affiliation with the church and government."

"Oh? Who was that? Your cousin?" inquired Barb.

"No not Donnie." John frowned, remembering his cousin's damning remarks against the Strega traditions. "It was one of several local militia I happened across on the road coming home last night." John savored a sip of his scotch. "Seems they were on a stake-out for some rebel group that convenes in the mountains on Beltane. Earlier, Donnie had warned me about a hunt that might be going on around this area."

"Well! For goodness sake," said Barbara, shaking her head. "Who would be out, making trouble, on the goddess' holy night?"

"I don't know about that," replied John, "but what my cousin said got me worried. I was surprised to find I felt protective toward your aunt and her school. Don sounded pretty hostile when he spoke of the Rimini family legend. Almost like he still upholds those barbaric laws of the Middle Ages' Inquisition."

He saw Barb visibly shiver. "Oh Goddess!" she swore softly, "Could the witch hunts still be happening?" She turned to the phone on the table beside her. "I would like Gina and Mario's input. Do you mind if I call them?"

"Go ahead. It's getting late, but this feels important. I wanted to talk to Mario about several things I heard today anyway. See if they can come over for a nightcap."

✳ ✳ ✳

About half an hour later, Mario and Sylvia arrived. The clock was striking 10:00. "It's Beltane, alright," said Mario removing his jacket and helping Gina off with hers. "We counted about thirty bonfires dotting the hills between our place and here."

"Yeah, I saw some of them when I went for a walk a couple hours ago," said John. "This is a major holiday for the local pagans, is it?" He tried to act nonchalant but his palms were sweating. *I feel damned nervous,* he thought. *Hope we don't end up in some kind of fight over all this goofiness.*

"Anthony tells me the local covens are partying more than usual tonight in defiance of the new ordinance against the rites of spring," Gina explained. She looked pointedly at him. "Could be the reason for the hunt you were warned about, John."

They made their way to the kitchen where Gina put a pot of water on the stove to heat up. They sat around the trestle table and sipped their drinks. Mario got up and lit a fire in the big stone hearth. "This way we can take part in the festivities without getting caught in the crossfire," he joked.

But John couldn't bring himself to laugh. "Are the local militia serious about hunting down these people who worship on the pagan festival night? Don't you have these celebrations many times a year? Why is this one so troubling to the authorities?" He got up and paced the room. He felt agitated, confused. He pulled up a chair, but sat a bit apart from the rest.

"Anthony believes the mob has gotten involved somehow," said Gina.

Barbara threw a glance at John. "Why would the Mafia be interested in pagan ceremonies?"

"Could be related to drugs," answered Mario. He also looked at John for some reaction.

"Do you mean the drug lords are infiltrating the paganini?" John asked. "Seems like a pretty unlikely scheme to me." He noticed the others watching him and cried, "Don't look at me like I should know. Just because some of my relatives are hooked up with Sicilian gangs around Naples doesn't mean I have inside information. My dad and mother bowed out of it in the thirties. We don't have anything to do with the outlaw arm of the family." He was feeling unusually defensive.

"But you did meet with your cousin at the Vatican today, according to Anthony," said Mario.

John was startled. "How did your kid know that?"

"He was at the bust that you witnessed with your cousin. He asked me why you would be there. I couldn't give him an answer." Mario looked pointedly at John. His face showed no emotion.

John felt caught, although he knew he had no reason to feel guilty. "Wow! A regular lawyer's interrogation here." He tried to make light of the situation. "I just met Don for lunch. He got a call about the bust, and he invited me to come along because I'd asked him about rumors I've heard about the underground movement here." He realized he was sweating, and it wasn't just heat from the fireplace.

"Well," said Mario, "then you saw something of what the church is so outraged about now."

"Donnie took me back to his office, and we watched several of the confiscated films." John cleared his throat. "I have to admit to being shocked by some of them. They go pretty drastically against a lot of church tradition" He looked at the three of them. They all watched him intently, but no one looked accusing. He softened his tone. "Frankly, I couldn't see anything that bad_ certainly nothing dangerous_ in any of it." He stopped to reflect.

Gina got up and poured them all a cappuccino.

John continued, "It seemed to me the main point of the films was to show women as more important and influential in biblical history than most church doctrine will admit." He grinned amicably at the group who were still intently watching him. "Now, we all know women hold the real power in the world anyway! I, for one, have no control over the four women in my household." John laughed at their surprised expressions, but realized he was surprising himself as well.

He took the little book Joanna had given him out of his shirt pocket. "Joanna is on a mission to convert me, I believe. She gave me this little propaganda pamphlet to read." He held it out for their inspection.

Mario took it and turned it over. He read the title out loud. "Of Histories Entwined." Then he chuckled and winked at Gina. "Hey! The author is a priest, John. We know this fellow."

He handed the booklet to Gina, who glanced at it and grinned. She handed it to Barb.

"Oh my goodness!" exclaimed Barb. "Is this *our* Heironymous?"

When Gina nodded, Barb said to John, "He is the man we rescued from his downed plane during the war. He became a very close friend of Sophia and all of us. I remember him being a kind of magician, a mage is what Sophie called him, isn't it?" She looked puzzled. "But I had the idea he had died or moved away some time ago."

"Yes, and no." Gina said, "He still comes around once in a while, though he keeps a low profile around the school. He has a parish in a little hamlet up the mountain from here."

Barb said, "That seems amazing to me. I remember him as a kind of wild pagan fellow. I can't imagine him converting, much less going into the priesthood."

"He chose it as a means to understand the opposition better; and to be in a position to influence local authorities against the renewed witch-craze," answered Gina with a shrug.

Gina supplied this information as if it was of little importance, but John felt a twinge of anger again. *What kind of priest would write a pamphlet condoning witchcraft?*

Mario turned the conversation back to the immediate. "So, John, are you warming up a bit to the idea of continuing the school here?"

John frowned. "Not at all. In fact, if anything, all the strange events of the past couple days have only convinced me that I should get my kids out of here sooner than planned. I've got the plane tickets for the day after tomorrow. If Joanna wants to stay, I guess that's her prerogative since she is nearly eighteen. But the younger ones need to be kept innocent of it as much as possible. It may not be evil witchcraft, but it is dangerous nevertheless, because of the church's opposition." He had raised his voice again, prepared to argue with them all.

Gina glanced at Barbara, then said, "The girls may already have discovered the mysteries on their own, John. It's not the kind of thing you can plan or direct or avoid. It just happens, and most easily to kids. If even you, who are so adamantly closed to it, had a couple of surreal experiences, you can be sure the magic has touched them too." She said this in a quiet, calm voice.

John felt disconcerted. His little girls? "Sure, they can make mysteries out of anything with their bright imaginations," he countered, "but that doesn't mean they would already be into the devil's work you all call magic! Be reasonable!" He was pacing and clenching his fists.

Barbara said, "Please, John. Sit down and relax. It's nothing to get so riled up about." She put her hand on his arm.

He sat down, frowned at his wife.

She continued in a quiet voice, "When we were in the woods yesterday afternoon, Toby hurt his paw. We observed Mimi do some pretty intuitive healing work on the cat. It is just her natural gift, John. Nothing we need to fear or try to suppress."

John felt perplexed, but he wasn't ready to give in just yet. "What about Kara? That girl is not likely to get sucked into this magical nonsense. She's much too sensible."

Gina cleared her throat and glanced at Barbara, who nodded for her to go on. "It seems Kara has come across an old Grimoire written by one of the Rimini witches a few hundred years ago."

John shrugged as if to say, 'so what?'

.Gina continued, "It has been considered a kind of numi-nous work. Claimed to present itself exclusively to the person intended to use it. Sophia carried it everywhere, but after she died we couldn't find it anywhere." She looked at John, who was now starring fixedly out the window. She went on, "Kara found it right after you all got here."

Barbara took up the tale, "Anyway, Kara has been reading the journal and has become interested in learning more of the old Strega legends. She didn't seem nearly as skeptical as she often is, although she is full of questions."

"Damn!" John swore. He was up and pacing again. "Things are moving much too fast. We barely get here and the weird-ness begins. It sure does seem like some kind of deviltry to me."

Mario watched John's face contorted with rage. *The guy could really be a problem for us,* he thought. *But I don't think he is as convinced of the evil as he makes out. Too bad we can't show him where the real 'evil' lies. But there's nothing we can do with just arguing about it.*

"Stop calling it deviltry, John," cried Barbara. "The magic of Strega is nothing evil. It is no different than a lot of the stuff your church teaches, only it shows that miracles are part of nature and that women, as well as men, can have access to the sacred and supernatural."

John raised his hand to stop Barbara from arguing. "No, hear me out," he said. "I've been giving it some thought. I'm still against us promoting a school of witchcraft, or esoteric studies, as you call it. But, I might consider turning this villa and all it contains into a museum and archive of Strega history. It does seem a shame to let this huge collection of ancient artifacts and the library of antique books get broken up in auction. We'd reg-ister the place as a historical monument of some sort, and create a tourist attraction."

He looked at Mario. "You'd know about the legal angles to accomplish that?"

When none of the others said anything, John went on, "We can pay someone to live here and take care of things. It should at least cover its own upkeep. That way we get the church off our back and still keep the property in the family." He stopped, looked at them as if he had just said something brilliant.

The guy is totally insensitive to how insulting this is to us, thought Mario, prepared to argue.

But Gina gestured for him to let it be, so he just sat back and observed. At last, after several moments of silence, Barbara said, "Well, at least it would allow us to stay and work on the place for the summer."

Mario was impressed. *It's a good ploy_ keep him here working on his museum idea and meanwhile we'll get things in order for the school. Better take it slow. This is more of a concession on John's part than we had hoped for, actually.*

Mario spoke up, "The red tape in this government can get pretty tangled, but I imagine it could be done. I agree with Barbara, we can get to work organizing things through the summer. Cleaning up the place and so forth. By fall we may be able to clear the legal hurdles." He looked John in the eye. "It's not a bad idea, old man. I appreciate your sensitivity to the family heritage. I know you have good reason to mistrust it all, having grown up in the opposing tradition."

John appeared reassured for the moment. "Well, thanks for listening to me." Then, gazing out into the dark woods, he said, "But we still haven't dealt with the hunting threats. Is there anything we should be concerned about here? Are the authorities likely to mark the villa for their investigations?"

Just then the phone rang, startling them all. "Who could be calling here at this time of the night?" said John as he got up to answer it. "Hello? Who? Oh yeah?" He listened. He looked stunned. "What do you mean? Explain yourself!" John shouted into the receiver. He waited for a moment, then slammed it down.

John turned to the group by the fireplace. His face was blanched. "I think it was the vigilante who stopped and talked to me. The one called Carlo, who said he'd known Sophia. He seemed to be warning us that we are in danger, or at least that something may be happening here that could be dangerous. He said we should go somewhere else for the night."

"What the hell could he mean?" swore Mario. "Maybe they think the banditi are hiding out at the villa? Have you checked the tunnel lately, Gina?" He turned toward the hallway prepared to go down the stairs to the wine cellar.

Gina and Barb got up to follow him. But John shouted, "Stop! Where the hell are you going? Don't you think we should just get the girls and get out of here? We could stay at your place for the night, couldn't we?"

They all stopped and looked at each other. "Maybe John is right, Mario," said Gina. "If they are using the tunnels, there's not much we can do about it now. It would probably be best to take the warning and go now. We can check on the tunnels tomorrow."

The phone rang again. Mario grabbed it, "Hello? Who is this?" He was shouting.

"Dad? Is that you? What are you doing there at this time of night?" It was Anthony on the other end of the line. "I was calling to warn John and Barbara that some of the banditi may be hiding out around the villa, and maybe they could spend the night at your place."

Mario laughed. "You are a mind-reader, Tony. That is just what we were about to do."

Then he spoke in a whisper, so the others didn't hear. Barbara had already gone to wake up the girls and John had gone into the front room. "What's going down, Son? Is it Sep? Should I stay here and keep an eye out for him?"

"I'm not sure, Dad. I just know the big guns are out. We're setting up a stakeout at the wolf's den that Sep sometimes uses. If he's on the lam, I figured he may use the tunnels and that's why I called to warn Uncle John." Anthony paused "We've got people out ready to warn Sep. I'm going to the den with a few of the actors to set up a distraction. With covens celebrating Beltane all over the mountain, they won't know us from any of the revelers."

Mario could picture the acting troop in their bizarre costumes. Yes, they would blend into the night's festivities just fine. "Okay, kid. You take care."

Mario felt worried, but he knew Anthony could take care of himself. The same for Giuseppe. But nevertheless, someone could get hurt. He decided to send the others away and stay at the villa to keep watch. If truth be told, Mario relished the idea of a good skirmish with the so-called authorities. It had been awhile since he was out on the front lines, in the trenches, of this age-old war. Nowadays he did his fighting in the courtroom.

Mario's thoughts were interrupted by a cry from upstairs. Barbara came flying down the steps. "The girls are all gone! All three of them left blanket dummies in their beds to fool us. I checked the roof too. They aren't there!"

As she said this, she ran for the doorway to the wine cellar.

42

EVIL INTRUDES

The Horned God, Faunus, transported himself instantly back to the Grove after taking the girls home. Ganymede, the deer that had been wounded, was now back on his feet and telling the others of a pending attack by the Malandanti.

"Yes," said the deer, "it was human hunters that shot me, but they are accompanied by one of the Evil Ones_ a hawk, recently wounded itself in a failed attack against the young witches in the grotto. I think they have widened their hunt to include our new young friends as well as our regular protectors."

The moon goddess, Diana, sat on her stone throne listening with a deep frown on her face. She beckoned to Faunus and said, "That hawk is the Wizard's messenger. Seems they are trying to scare the newcomers away from the villa. Away from us and Sophia's legacy, more exactly."

Faunus asked, "Did you say earlier that they are planning an attack at the wolf's den, Ganymede?"

"Yes, that's what I heard them discussing when I was tailing them. But then one of them spied me and got off a shot before I realized what had happened. Sorry," he bowed his head, "it was terribly clumsy of me."

"Don't blame yourself Gany," said the Moon Goddess. "You did well to bring us the news. But no doubt they will be able to follow your tracks here soon enough. We'd best be on our way now."

Most of the other animals had already left for the safety of their nests and dens. The fairies hid quietly among trees listening, but not taking part in the conversation.

Then Tinklebell flew down to Faunus' shoulder and whispered in his ear. "The evil ones are here now. You must leave immediately!" Then the fairy fluttered off and became invisible.

Faunus looked around in time to see the great hawk swoop down from the sky and land on one of the wolf pups. The little wolf screamed as the hawk grabbed its leg and began pulling it into the air. The mother wolf instantly leapt high and caught her baby in her jaws, pulling it free from the bird.

But as she bent to tend to her child, a shot rang out from between the trees, ripping into her side, and the mother wolf fell bleeding to the ground.

Rarjer had, by now, attacked the big bird and the two were locked in deadly combat. Two men in camouflage fatigues dashed out of the woods into the melee. A couple of wolf pups sat whimpering at their fallen mother's belly. One of the men hit them with the butt of his rifle, and they fell limp. The second man was taking aim at Rarjer when he was startled by a voice from the other side of the Grove.

"Hold it right there or you're dead."

The fairy gods Faunus and Diana had been invisible to the hunters when they entered the clearing. But now, clearly visible in black riding gear and masked, Giuseppe and Heironymous stood by the rock cairn, pistols cocked and aimed. Sep pointed at the gunmen, while the priest had a bead on the hawk attacking Rarjer.

"Call off your bird or we shoot it," shouted Giuseppe.

Someone unseen whistled from in the woods. The bird hesitated a moment, during which time Rarjer got a good bite of its tail feathers, and then it soared back into the trees. The two vigilante backed off slowly, eyeing the two men in black masks. They seemed unsure of themselves, evidently unprepared for a stand-off here without backup forces. When Rarjer snarled and crouched to spring at them, they turned tail and ran into the woods.

Rarjer was bleeding a little from one eye, but otherwise seemed fine. He immediately went to his mate and began sniffing and whining around her.

But Giuseppe called to the big wolf, "Rarjer, we need to go after them. The goddess will look after your family while you are away. Your mate will be alright." He said this, not knowing whether it was true, but they needed the wolf's help in tracking the hunters.

"Guess we surprised them," said the priest. "Wonder what made them take off so fast though? They could easily have taken us on in a fight. The numbers were even." He shook his head. "Doesn't make sense that they would send the bird to attack a puppy."

"I think the bird got out of control. Looks as if it's been humiliated by the wolf recently. That Malandanti has its own agenda that its humans don't know about." Sep laughed.

"Sophia always said you can't really control the wild ones. They rule in a world beyond human perceptions or reason."

The priest laughed too. "She was always right when it came to the animals." He looked wistful. "I sure do miss her. And right now we need her help in healing these animals. How in hell are we going to do it all, Sep?"

"I wouldn't worry, old man," answered Giuseppe. "The goddess always looks after her own. And that includes us, remember?" He clapped his friend on the shoulder, "C'mon now. We've got work to do."

Then Giuseppe went over to the wolves, knelt down to feel the female's pulse and noted that her life was ebbing, but still holding on. The puppies, he couldn't be so sure of, but he guessed they would make it. He ruffled Rarjer's neck and ears affectionately. "They'll be alright, good buddy. The goddess will take care of them. We've got our job cut out for us, and you will have your chance for revenge. He got up and the big wolf followed, looking back only once at his wounded mate and whelps.

Rarjer noticed, for the first time, that one of the pups was missing. But it would have to fend for itself until he could come back for it later. He howled once, long and sad. Then he took off at a trot after his human comrades.

Sep and Heironymous, dressed all in black and masked, were nearly invisible among the moon-shadows of the deep night woods. But Rarjer's wolf-sight had no trouble following them. In his silver streaked black coat, he created only a wavering shadow himself. The three of them sprinted swiftly through the forest, over gullies, and across mountain streams. They ran on in silence, moving as easily as mist over water. Nothing hampered their progress. It was as if the mountains ran with them, clearing their path.

On their way, they passed close enough to the villa for Rarjer to make a quick side trip and call out to his friend Kara. Howling her name, "Kah-rah" several times, he waited until her face appeared at the window. Then he turned back onto the trail of his companions.

They continued along hidden tracks until they reached the little travertine temple ruins, glowing with a cool ambiance under the moon's watchful eye. Several people waited there, among them, Carlo, the vigilante who had warned John earlier. He was out of uniform and changed into the same black night-riding gear as the others. Sep felt mistrustful of the fellow, but could do nothing but stay alert at this point.

Carlo was accompanied by about a dozen other men and women from the mountain villages. They were all members of the Paganini, celebrants of Beltane earlier in the evening, but now part of a people's army standing against civil authorities who were attempting to squelch their beloved festival customs.

"What's come down?" asked the priest of Carlo.

"The Wizard himself, for one," answered the double agent. "I've been out with a patrol, but got myself excused for family business about an hour ago." Carlo threw a glance toward Giuseppe. "I think my pals were on the track of your wolves. They shot a buck in the woods by the stream. That's when I decided to get out of there."

"You say the Vulture is out on this Patrol?"

"Not with the group I was with, but nearby. He had his hawk with him, and looked prepared to raise some hell," answered Carlo. "He's all riled up about something. Like he's got a bee up his ass. You have any idea what's bit him recently, Sep?"

"If I did, I probably wouldn't tell you, Carlo," Giuseppe answered, but with a grin on his face. "Who knows who you might go talking to, eh?"

They all laughed, knowing that Carlo played all sides pretty much for himself. But they also knew his deeper loyalties lay with the underground movement. He held a useful position for their purposes, even when there was a risk of his crossing them up at times. Sep knew about that position, he'd held it himself with the mob in past years.

Tonight was definitely one of those times, thought Giuseppe to himself. He guessed that the bug biting Donnie may have had to do with their earlier brief encounter at the underground cinema. And, Sep reminded himself, there is his link to the villa, through Barbara's husband. Sep suddenly felt afraid for the Marini family.

If the Vatican's Vulture wanted them out of there he would very likely play the 'spook' card first, believing the Americans to be too naïve about witch traditions not to get frightened away. But if the scare tactics did not work Sep feared the worst, for he knew these religious fanatics could be as ruthless as the mob.

43

SISTERS UNITED

Kara woke with a start. Someone had called her name. She sat up and looked at Joanna, but she still slept undisturbed in the other bed.

"Kah-rah!" The voice came from outside. She got out of bed, tiptoed to the open west window and peered down. The wooded hills were deep in shadows, but the moon shone brightly on the path by the magic tree. And there, under the huge old oak, Kara saw a phantom-like figure. The moon, shining on silver fur, made it fade and reappear in ghostly light, its eyes glinted red, staring straight at her. "Kah-rah!" it howled once again, then turned and disappeared into the darkness.

Kara's heart leapt to her throat. She forgot to remain quiet as she scrambled into her jeans and sweatshirt and grabbed her backpack to run upstairs and get Mimi.

Joanna awoke to Kara's clatter and sat up in bed. "What are you doing? Where are you going, Kara?" She whispered. "It must be almost midnight."

Kara was too upset to think of a good lie. She told Joanna the truth. "It's my wolf-friend, Rarjer. He's calling for my help. Something has happened. The magic people might be in trouble! I've got to go out right now!" She dashed for the door.

"Wait a minute," Joanna's urgent whisper, "Be quite for god's sake, or you'll have the whole household up here." She threw off her covers and slid out of bed, climbing into her sweats and tennis shoes as she talked. "I'm coming with you. I want to help."

Kara stopped at the door and stared at her older sister. "What?" Kara's mind whirled. Jo would get in the way. "Jo, you don't know what we've seen today. I can't take time to tell you, but you won't believe it anyway. I can't let you come along! Just don't worry about us." Kara felt desperate to get going. She felt caught. She babbled. "And don't tell Mom and Dad anything. Or, better yet, you can cover for us. Tell them we went on a moonlight hike to the crypt or something."

"No, I'm coming along. I've seen some pretty amazing things myself the last couple of days with Giuseppe. I promise I won't get in your way." Joanna was bunching up blankets in their beds to form sleeping dummies. "I used this trick in New York when I snuck out late at night with friends," she told Kara with a chuckle.

Kara shrugged and gave her sister a goofy grin. "Okay. But don't say I didn't warn you."

They climbed the tower stairs to the loft and found their little sister dressed and ready to go. Her bed also displayed dummy lumps, and Toby stood alert at the door to the secret stairs, his tail twitching with excitement.

"I was just coming down to get you," said Mimi to Kara. "Melanthus woke us to come out." Then she saw Joanna. "Oh! Jo. I didn't know you would want to come too." Mimi frowned at her oldest sister.

"It's alright, Sugar," said Joanna. "I won't interfere, but some things happened to me today too, and if the magic people are in danger, I want to help."

Mimi and Kara looked at each other with raised eyebrows. Kara said, "Well, we don't have time to tell each other our stories now. I guess if you really believe in the magic it will be okay. What do you think, Mimi?"

"Tinkle said if you don't believe in them you will make them go away. Then we won't be any help at all," she looked askance at Joanna, then shrugged. "But there isn't time to argue. Come on." Mimi made a dash for the door where the cat waited to lead them into the perils of the late Beltane night.

Joanna wasn't sure what had prompted her to buy into the girls' urgent mission. Very likely it was merely Mimi's overactive imagination and Kara's insatiable curiosity combining to create some fantasy adventure. But, after her own introduction to the mysteries of Strega history, and seeing the mysterious face in the goblet, Joanna felt prepared to believe almost anything.

More than that, she felt a deep desire to join the fight to preserve the ancient mysteries. Whatever was happening with Kara's animal friends could be related to the cause that Giuseppe and Anthony were involved in protecting. Joanna felt certain she was meant to go along. She assumed the role of an Amazon warrior-queen in her imagination.

The three girls tiptoed down a dim cobwebbed stairwell, following Toby. Joanna bit her tongue to hold back exclamations of surprise at the hidden passage in the tower wall. It was obvious that her sisters had been here before and knew where they were going. When they came to a rough wooden door, Kara pushed it open and it creaked loudly. They heard voices upstairs in the kitchen, and the clock was chiming 11:30. All three girls held their breath, but no one stirred upstairs. They entered the wine cellar. A single dusty bulb hung from the ceiling casting shadows of cobwebs over a hodge-podge of shelves and old wine bottles.

Kara looked purposefully toward one wall of shelving and went to examine it. "I'm pretty sure this is the spot where Faunus led us in and out of the tunnel." She laid her hand on one rack that was slightly askew and tried to pull it aside. It didn't budge.

"I'm sure this is the place," she murmured to Mimi. "How do you suppose it opens up?"

Joanna wanted to ask who Faunus was, and what they were talking about. But she determined to simply stand by and watch. Questions could come later. She would maintain the discipline of a cool, controlled Amazon queen.

Mimi stood very still. Her eyes were shut and she wore an expression of deep concentration for a few minutes. Then she said in a husky whisper: "Nepo ta aidara's gniddib!" She opened her eyes and seemed nearly in tears when nothing happened.

Kara and Joanna exchanged glances of quizzical amusement, but neither said a word. Had their little sister lost her senses? What nonsense was she muttering?

"Oh!" exclaimed Mimi, and her eyes opened wide with apparent realization. "Tinkle said it backward to get out of the tunnel. You are supposed to say it forward to get inside. She beamed a smile at her sisters, and turned back to the wine shelves.

"Open at Aradia's bidding!" commanded Mimi to the wall. The wine racks slowly slid back to reveal a tunnel opening. Kara looked at Mimi in astonishment. Joanna stood breathless with surprise. But Mimi motioned for them to hurry and they all trooped through the opening silently, with Toby in the lead. They turned to see the wine rack slide back into place on its own.

The tunnel was in total darkness, but Kara quickly took her girl- scout lantern out of her back pack and they could see that the tunnel walls were chiseled carefully into the granite of the mountain. The floor was finely ground sand and shale. Their shoes crunched softly as they walked.

"If someone is here, they will surely hear us coming," said Kara in a stage whisper. She stopped and dug into her pack again, pulling out several twigs of a dried weed. "It's fennel," she explained, passing one to each of the girls and keeping one for herself. "Hold these in front of you if anything happens," she said, demonstrating by grasping the little twig like a sword or shield. "It's a powerful protection herb, according to Aunt Sophia's journal."

She bent to tie one sprig of the aromatic flower onto Toby's collar. Mimi and Jo sniffed theirs appreciatively and tucked them into their waistbands.

Very quickly, Toby led them directly to a crevice in the rock through which could be seen a glade in the moonlight and a shimmering pond at its center. They crept single file through the narrow opening. Mimi went first, after Toby. Joanna was at the rear.

Mimi stepped into the Grove and stopped dead still. Then she ran forward with a cry of anguish. As Kara followed into the open glade, she, too, cried out in horror and ran to the edge of the pond to join Mimi, who was bending over a wolf's carcass.

Joanna held back and let her sisters tend to the situation for now. She gazed about the Grove with awe. It held an ambiance that Jo's theatrical instincts immediately knew to be enchanted. The trees stood in a nearly perfect circle with the mirror-like pond at the center and a cairn of rocks at one side in the shape of a pair of high backed seats. *Like thrones for the Queen and King of Faerie in 'A Midsummer Night's Dream,'* thought Jo.

The glade put her in mind of the little amphitheater she had attended in the park yesterday with Sep and Tony. She smiled at the recollection. There was no one in sight except the wounded wolf and three small wolf pups, who lay at its feet, unmoving. Kara and Mimi were urgently examining the animals.

As Jo stepped forward to help them, she noticed a slight movement in the bushes next to the stone cairn. She knelt down and pushed the shrubbery aside. There another wolf pup huddled alone, shivering in terror. Joanna held her hand to its nose and gradually it allowed her to stroke its ear. She stayed crouched by the scared little one and watched her sisters tend its siblings.

44

GATHERING FORCES

While the group of black-clad night riders discussed plans for the coming stake-out, Giuseppe sat down on the chipped marble staircase and leaned against one of the temple's ancient Doric columns. Rarjer leaned against his leg, while Sep absent-mindedly scratched the wolf's head.

Together, they watched the moon shine its beam across the sea. A raven landed in a tree nearby. "News, Melanthus?" asked Sep, in a stage whisper. The bird cocked its head, listening to the discussion.

Giuseppe reflected on his situation. He was definitely falling in love with Joanna. But could he afford to bring a woman into his unruly life? Reveal his secrets to her? Even if she was a Strega witch of the great Rimini clan?

It had been many years since he'd lived among civilized folk. Although Giuseppe kept company with a good many town-people, he had lived alone in the wilderness since he was about thirteen.

His childhood had been happily spent around Sophia's villa with a passel of other foster kids orphaned in the war. He had never known his own parents, but always thought of Sophia as his mother. She may have known who his parents were, but she never told him. Possibly because he never asked. As a little kid, he pretended that Heironymous was his father, but the mage would never admit to having any women friends other than Sophia.

And, why was he compelled to live in secret among the wolves? In his teen years he had played the double agent like Carlo is doing now. Only Sep had played with the really bad guys. He had been an informer for the mob on drug raids. Hanging out with narcs and druggies, he'd sent a lot of them away by setting them up with the cops. His personal connection with the Stregheria made him a natural enemy of the church officials, and he had worked from the start with the underground movement as well. When he tried to turn straight, the Mafioso naturally turned on him, and he could hardly get protection from the crooked government or the corrupt church.

So, he went underground. Literally. He now lived in the caves and hidden tunnels where he had played at Robin Hood games as a little kid. It was not a bad life, since he was blessed with animal speech as well as the rather weird ability to metamorphose and also to turn invisible at will. These talents had been there from the beginning, but it was Sophia and Heironymous who taught him the Strega magic and helped him learn to discipline the transformations for good use.

His underground hideouts were comfortably temperate most of the year. When weather turned inclement, Sep kept a place in Sophia's cellar. She'd known, of course but never spoke of it even with him in private. Heironymous was the only other person he'd told.

Now, Giuseppe's reverie was interrupted by the priest, who came to sit by him. "They want to stake out the villa," said his friend. "Carlo says the Vulture is aiming to put a scare into his cousin's family. Plans to come over there with 'evidence' of devil worship at Beltane festivities. What that is, Carlo says, he doesn't know."

Giuseppe frowned, thought a minute, then he said, "Maybe Donnie's plan is to use me as his proof."

"That occurred to me too, Sep," said Heironymous. "Think we should tag along with them, or stick with our own agenda?"

"If the group plans to accost Donnie with proof of his deviltry, it could mean a fight. Could be dangerous for the family there," mused Sep. "But my being with them wouldn't help anything. I'd just be playing into the Vulture's hands."

Too bad we didn't kill that bird of his when we had the chance," muttered the priest. "There's the real proof of deviltry, and it's him, not us."

"But maybe we can trap him yet," said Giuseppe. "Let's go to the den like we planned. If we can surprise Donnie there, maybe we can prevent a fight at the villa."

Without saying anything to the group gathered at the front of the temple, Giuseppe, with Heironymous and Rarjer, quietly exited around the rear. They picked up their motorcycles in the ditch where they'd left them, and headed in the opposite direction from the villa. The raven remained perched on the tree, listening to the group debate plans.

They rode into the hills above the villa, following a dry streambed. Soon they came to a trickling spring that fed water into another stream. They followed its course southeast a short distance until they came to a gully where the stream entered an underground tunnel. Here they, once again, ditched their motorcycles behind an overgrown bramble of vines and entered the water tunnel, wading in the shallow stream.

Rarjer followed easily behind them, loping through the water and occasionally stopping to snap at a fish or frog. They hadn't eaten anything for hours and he was hungry. But a hungry wolf is the best fighting wolf, so he chose to leave the small prey alone for now.

They followed the stream, feeling their way along the tunnel's walls in the dark. Both of the men, like the wolf, had good night vision trained from years of wandering the wilderness. Their boots made sloshing sounds through the tunnel and would scare away any other creatures that might be holing up in the ledges and ridges. Eventually they arrived at a wider place in the tunnel, where Giuseppe groped along the wall to his left until he found a small door.

The priest spoke strange words, and the little door swung open at their touch. From the water tunnel, they entered another tunnel which they then followed upward for a short distance. All three crept quickly and silently along the familiar corridor. They entered the lion's cave and found Farah dozing. The lioness woke and rose to her feet, but made no threatening moves. She seemed to have been expecting them.

Giuseppe bowed to her. "Good greetings, your Highness," he said without irony. "Will you come with us on this mission? We can use your assistance to beat the Vulture and his hawk."

The lioness twitched an ear. She turned toward the back of her cave, where she gingerly picked up a stone-like object and brought it to the priest, who took it carefully from her mouth and examined it. It was a hand grenade, still intact. *Possibly left here so long from the war? Or perhaps dropped somewhere more recently by careless enemies?* "Do you know where this came from, Farah?" queried the priest. She waved her tail in a loop twice, then purposefully paced to walk up the tunnel. They followed along.

The wolf and the lioness kept a respectful distance from each other, but neither was inclined to cause trouble. They were both old friends of Sophia and knew these men to be her friends as well. The animals sensed the gravity of their mission and made sure not to defile it with old territorial grievances long settled between them.

At last, they arrived at their destination_ another cavern in the maze of secret tunnels. This one, a large comfortable room-like space. They stopped to rest here for a moment. The priest examined the hand grenade and determined that it was still functional. He tucked it firmly into his belt with practiced confidence. Both men checked their revolvers to be sure all chambers were loaded, then set the safety locks and tucked them into their underarm holsters. The lioness nonchalantly licked her paw, while the wolf watched the door at the front of the chamber in alert anticipation.

45

A RESCUE

Kara had screamed in fear that Rarjer was killed. But when she reached Mimi, who was cradling the animal's head in her arms, Kara was relieved to see it was not Rarjer. Then, her relief turned to sorrow when she recognized his mate. The beautiful golden-coated mother wolf lay with blood oozing from a deep gash in her side over which Mimi now held one hand and chanted incantations.

Rarjer was nowhere in sight and that disturbed Kara even more. Surely he would have stayed with his dying mate, unless someone forced him away. Kara wanted to run through the woods calling for him, but she soon realized that would be foolish. If he was in danger it would hardly help to have her hollering like a banshee. Possibly he was on the trail of the killers. She remembered the stand-off between the great wolf and the Malandanti hawk in the tunnel the other day. *That's it, of course,* she told herself. *He was probably on their trail when he called to me at the window.*

Kara turned her attention to the three pups scattered at the feet of their mother. Two were still breathing, but unconscious, with no external wounds. Evidently they had been knocked out by blows to their heads. The third pup lay bleeding from one leg, but still conscious. He opened one eye and growled when Kara reached toward him. "You brave little guy," she murmured, holding her hand by his nose until he sniffed that she meant no harm. "Looks like you tried to defend your mom."

Kara took a red scarf from her bag and a branch of fennel. These she held toward the pup who sniffed them and looked at her as if to give permission to do what she could. She gently pushed the torn leg close against his body, made a splint of the fennel branch, and bound it all together tightly with the scarf.

Meanwhile, Mimi continued ministering to the mother wolf, who had begun to regain consciousness. "I think I can save her, but I wish we could get them to the Grotto," said Mimi. "She tells me the Malandanti are being chased by Rarjer and the others, but they could still come back here."

Kara took no time to wonder about Mimi's ability to converse so naturally with the wild animal. Instead, her mind raced to find solutions. *'The others' must mean someone went with Rarjer. Maybe Faunus and his moon goddess queen. Where could they have gone?* She would rather follow and help her friends fight the evil ones, but how could she leave Mimi alone?

Then she remembered that Joanna was with them. She turned to see her older sister sitting near the cairn thrones with a fourth wolf pup in her lap. Joanna was holding an object, examining it closely. "Look at this, Kara," she said with a puzzled expression. She held up a wreath of grapevine. "It almost looks like the kind of crown worn by that little horned statue, doesn't it? And there is actually some hair caught up in it."

Kara felt impatient with this digression. Yet, she understood immediately what it was. She said, "The horned god, Faunus. He was here earlier. Must have dropped it in the battle or whatever happened after we left." At Joanna's amazed look, she added, "It will have to wait, Jo. We can tell you all about it after this emergency is over. Please help us figure this out now."

Joanna tucked the green man's vine into her jeans along with the bunch of fennel. Picking up the puppy, she tied her baggy sweatshirt into a hammock in front and he curled up there.

Kara recalled how she'd done a similar thing with Toby earlier. Kara continued, "We need to get the mother wolf and pups moved to a safe place. We can tie the little ones into slings around our necks like you just did," she nodded at Jo. "But what can we use to carry the big female?"

Jo came to the group by the pond and looked on silently for several moments. The golden wolf's gaze followed her suspiciously until Kara appeared next to her. Then the wolf seemed to decide Jo could be trusted and closed its eyes again.

Joanna walked carefully around the pond, until she spotted a sturdy tree limb fallen to the ground. She hauled the long hunk of wood to the others and explained her idea. "Hunters, in olden times, carried game hanging by their feet. I've seen pictures. If we cushion her paws against the branch, and tie a sling under her, we can carry it between us with the third person in the middle to make sure she doesn't fall off or get jostled."

"That's great Jo!" exclaimed Mimi, who immediately began setting the log in place by her patient.

Kara was surprised by her elder sister's interaction. *I never thought she had it in her,* she grudgingly admitted to herself. "Quick thinking, Sis," she said, flipping her pony tail, "I think it will work."

At that point, Toby, who had been nosing around the Grove, came to Kara with something in his mouth. It was a filmy piece of cloth, the color of moonbeams. "This looks like a piece of the moon goddess' veil," she said.

In unison, Mimi and Kara turned their faces up to where the moon hung like a beacon above the trees. "She always watches over us and we can call on her at any time," chanted Mimi. Its beam fell directly on the opening into the tunnel from which they'd come.

"Of course," exclaimed Kara. "This tunnel must lead to the grotto just like the one from the cottage in the woods does. They are both places built by Aradia's progeny during the centuries of witch hunts. They used the tunnels for escape and the grotto is a sacred, safe hideout." Then she clapped her hand over her mouth, staring at Joanna. She'd forgotten these were secrets never to be given out to unbelievers.

"I haven't any idea what you are talking about, Kara," said Jo. "But it looks like you've been learning secrets about our ancestors just like I have. Don't worry, I won't give them away."

"We have no choice but to trust you now," said Kara. She grinned and gave a flip of her pony tail again. "I'm really glad to have you with us, Jo."

They set to work tying socks, scarves, and tee-shirts into various parts of the stretcher for the mother wolf. Joanna added the two still unconscious pups to the hammock of her sweatshirt where the unwounded one now cuddled warmly. They bound the fourth pup over the mother's stomach, where it might feel less mistrustful of the whole business.

When they had the animals in position, Toby bounded for the rock opening and into the tunnel in the direction that led away from the villa. Kara picked up the front end of the pole, and Joanna took the rear. Mimi walked in the middle holding the wolf so she wouldn't bounce or feel stretched too much. They made slow headway.

"Remember to keep your fennel branches handy," said Kara, as memory of the hawk came to her mind.

46

A STAKE-OUT

G iuseppe motioned to Heironymous and the wolf and lioness to stay back while he went to the door at the front
of the cavern. He cautiously slid aside the panel, which moved
silently on a hidden track. He entered a smaller room, snuck
up to yet another door, and listened. All was quiet. Too quiet.
There was not even the usual scratching of night insects and
rodents.

He slipped a hunting knife into the door jamb, opened it a
crack without letting the latch fall. He was at first appalled by
what he saw, then amused and relieved.

Moonlight poured into the roofless enclosure illuminating
a grotesque scene. Anthony stood there, his back to the pantry
door. With him was a troop of actors from the underground
movement. They were dressed in costumes of mythological
characters from a theatrical Beltane production. Arranged in
bizarre poses were gargoyles, harpies, trolls, dragons, and a
Minotaur.

Sep slid the door latch back in place and returned to his waiting crew in the adjoining cavern room. He described what he'd seen with wry humor.

"This menagerie is enough to scare the wits out of the devil himself," he chuckled. "And they are all armed, not only with the standard knives, daggers and pistols, but I saw spears, hatchets, slingshots, as well as a fire hose, and an old cannon lined up at the entrance of the cabin."

At this image, Heironymous grinned broadly. Then he sobered. "But what can we do now?" said the priest, nodding toward the two wild animals with them. "Our companions aren't likely to get the joke. They're more likely to attack what will look to them like more Malandanti than they've ever seen in their worst nightmares."

"I know," said Giuseppe. "But if all goes right, the presence of this bizarre army will serve to confuse the hawk in the same way, and its master too!" He grinned and said, "I'll go in alone and join them now. I'll get the troop to move outside of the cabin first thing. You stay hidden in the pantry until you hear the Vulture's gang arrive, then just come out with the animals, fighting."

"It will be everyone on his own, but we can watch out for each other," said Heironymous. "Good luck, son. Goddess be with you."

The two men embraced briefly. Giuseppe stroked the wolf on its muzzle and nodded to the lioness. "You two stay with Heironymous, and Goddess be with you all."

Then he went back into the pantry, closed the panel, and opened the door to the cabin carefully. He slipped into the back of the cabin, shut the pantry door firmly behind him, and no one heard him come in.

"A fine bunch of warriors you make," he said. "Don't you know enough to watch your backs?" He laughed at Anthony's surprised stare, and took off his own mask for a minute to reveal his identity to his friend.

Anthony was disguised as a satyr, and carried a longbow, with which he was a crack shot. He had it aimed at Sep, but at too close range to be any real threat.

"Good goddess, Man," exclaimed Anthony. "You could have given me a heart attack. I nearly was ready to shoot you." But he laughed with Sep at the trick he'd played on them. "How did you get here so soon?"

"Explanations later, Kid," said Sep as he reapplied his mask and adjusted his gun. "You having a party here, or is this a serious stake-out? I'd suggest you position yourselves outside, a bit farther from the den. We don't need to trash this place any more than it already is."

He moved toward the open front of the cabin and they trooped after him, creating an amazing and hair-raising parade of characters. The last of them, a big dragon, flapped and flipped its way out of the cabin snorting pyrotechnical flames.

They arranged themselves about the cabin yard, and upward on the rocky ledges, where they had full view and aim at whatever came through the woods.

Giuseppe stood behind some bushes on a granite outcrop, at about the center of the yard, where he could keep an eye on everything. He made himself invisible so as not to draw attention to himself since he was the vigilante's prime target.

Anthony took a position in the limbs of a big oak, camouflaged by his makeup to blend in with the greenery. It was a good place from which to fire his arrows. Sep knew he had probably fixed them with the numbing poison and admired his friend for cleverness.

Sep considered their situation and looked forward to the fight to come. *This should be a great show*, he thought. *Too bad we can't be filming it for David and Mia's Theater Company.*

The thought brought his mind to Joanna and his stomach gave a lurch of anxiety recalling how she and her family might be in danger. *We've got to stop the vigilantes here, so they don't get to the villa and harm those good people.* Giuseppe cursed again, wishing he had killed that vicious enchanted hawk earlier and put a stop to the evil that was on the prowl. He pulled his gun out of its holster and cocked it, ready to fire.

Looking around him, Sep regarded the Minotaur loading a slingshot and one of the harpies warming up her javelin-throwing arm. Up in the branches of a cedar tree, he saw another of the harpies stringing a bow and arrow. Off to his right, hidden in the lee of an old tool shed, a big troll brandished a fearsome battle axe, and his partner troll was hooking up the fire hose to the water pump. He noticed that two gargoyles had pulled the old cannon into position behind a crumbling stone wall, and were loading it with shot aimed into the woods. Sep wondered whether the thing would actually fire. *It looks imposing anyway,* he chuckled.

The cannon suddenly burst forth with a terrible noise and a brilliant array of fireworks! "Wow!" *those guys really know how to put on a show.* Then he saw what they were shooting at.

A great hawk flew out from the woods, screeching and baring talons the size of small sabers. Behind the hawk, an army of about two dozen men in camouflage fatigues marched in military formation through the trees.

Following them, was a fellow in a tall black pointed hat, wearing long flowing robes and wielding a tall staff_ The Wizard, himself.

"Hey Sep," Anthony intoned from the tree behind him, "Looks like we've raised an authentic old fashioned spirit battle of Benandanti versus Malandanti." They laughed together, but both knew they were in for a real battle as well.

Within seconds the fight began.

47

DECISIONS AND SECRETS

Meanwhile, back at the villa, Mario and Gina stood together by the fireplace in the kitchen where they had been visiting with John and Barb over cappuccinos. Barb had just discovered the girls were all gone missing.

John was already grabbing for the telephone and Barb was racing headlong for the cellar steps.

Mario reasoned that without the girls, there was no point in moving the family from the villa to their house for the night as earlier planned. If some kind of demonstration was going to happen here, he wanted to be around to see it. He did not feel especially alarmed at the girls' disappearance, but knew Barbara and John might make things worse by taking rash actions.

Gina came to his aid. "Barb!" she called. "Don't go rushing down to the cellar without a flashlight and other preparations. No one has used it for years, and the place is probably a rat trap." She calmly walked after Barbara and laid her hand on her sister's shoulder.

Barb turned to face her, staring wild-eyed. "But what if the girls have gotten trapped in the tunnel? They won't know how to get out if they did happen to find a way into it. And if the banditti are using it for a hideout?" She ran her fingers through her hair, holding her temples with both hands. "Oh goddess! I don't know what to do!"

"Calm down, Hon," said Gina soothingly. "You know they've faced some kind of challenges already and come through perfectly safe. Your girls are smart, and they've already tapped into the mysteries enough on their own to understand the essentials." She hugged Barb reassuringly. "Besides, we can assume they're all together. The three of them will help each other. No point in our getting involved without good reason." She chuckled softly, "Remember how we hated it when any adults poked into our adventures with the magic people?"

Barbara looked at her sister more calmly. "That all seems so unreal to me anymore, Gina," she said. "I'm having a hard time retrieving my belief in the magic world. I've been trying to let myself open to it again, but I think the years away have dulled my sense for the mystical." She shook her head and hugged Gina in return. "Thanks for stopping me. But I would like to go down there and just see_ whatever. It might help me regain my own faith."

Then she looked toward the living room where Mario and John were having an earnest discussion. "But, on second thought, you are probably right. It would only strengthen John's resistance if we revealed the tunnels to him."

"Maybe the two of us can sneak down there later on, just to look around," said Gina. "But right now we'll be of more help if we stay here to reassure John. Mario seems to be having a hard time calming your husband." The two women walked back to the living room arm in arm.

"How can you just stand around chatting about old times when our daughters are in danger?" bellowed John when he saw the women enter looking totally unruffled. He was holding the telephone receiver, but Mario had his hand over the hook, preventing its use.

"What danger, John?" questioned Barbara, assuming a casual air, far from her real feelings. "They've just gone for a moonlight hike to Sophia's crypt. They wanted to do a Beltane ceremony for her in private. I'd forgotten they told us this earlier today." Barbara made up the lie with not even a twinge of conscience. She felt a wicked pride and delight. *I've gotten pretty good at covering up for myself and the girls over the years,* she thought.

Gina picked up the tale. "That's right, John. There is really no danger to them there. We know the vigilante are too superstitiously fearful of the dead to go near the burial cave."

"If these vigilantes come and make trouble here, it is better if the girls aren't around to see. They are safer where they are." Barb walked to John and gently took the phone out of his hand, laying it back in its cradle.

John was about to argue, but Barbara took him by the arm and led him to the sofa. "Let's talk it over. What is it we're expecting exactly?" She looked at her sister's husband. "Mario, tell us what Anthony had to say when he phoned a bit ago."

Mario cleared his throat. He paused to think. "Tony said the action was likely to be at another place a couple miles from here, actually. It would probably be an attempt to arrest some of the Beltane celebrants up in a sacred meadow. But he wanted to warn you in case Giuseppe was among those being pursued." He looked at Gina, who nodded assent for him to disclose more.

But John interrupted. "What the hell does that kid have to do with the villa anyway?"

Gina explained, "He lived here as a child, brought up by Sophia. He often came here to stay when he was between jobs as a caretaker for various people's properties."

Mario continued, "He's had some run-ins with authorities over the years. Largely because of his connection with Strega, but also because he once worked undercover in the drug scene. He made some pretty dangerous enemies back then. Now Sep makes use of the villa as a refuge when any of them are after him."

Barb interjected, "This place has lots of nooks and crannies where someone can easily sneak away unseen." She brightened up a bit and said, "In fact, it is just as possible that the girls are exploring some of those hidden niches!" She looked at Gina for confirmation. "Wasn't there a secret stairway in the tower too?"

"Yes," answered Gina. "And I believe there was a bookcase in this room that pushed aside to reveal a door into that stairwell." They all looked at the bank of books on the north wall. None of them could discern just where such an outlet might be, if it was there at all.

"That's it!" exclaimed Mario. "We can make use of one or two of the secret passages to foil the interlopers if they show up here." He noted John's expression of complete disbelief. Mario laughed and went on, "This house has been designed with espionage in mind. You see, over the years the Strega have periodically been persecuted by the church and government authorities. So, the Rimini clan, beginning with the first to build her little hut on this property back in the fourteenth century, each included some safety features such as double walls, trap doors, and hidden stairwells in the portions of the house they built. Over the centuries, many of the secret gimmicks have been forgotten and fell to ruin from disuse. But others are still viable."

Gina and Barb glanced at each other, then said in unison, "Why don't we give John a little tour?" They jumped up eagerly and, like girls cajoling a recalcitrant boyfriend, tugged on John's arms to get him to come along.

Soon everyone was laughing as John allowed himself to be cajoled and begrudgingly said, "Well, if you can't beat 'em you gotta join 'em I guess." and he, too, laughed. "Lead on, my fair witches!"

Mario hung back a moment to make sure the main door was locked. He looked once at the phone, thinking he might need to contact one of his colleagues at work if things really heated up.

But he decided to play along with the game at hand. He checked inside his jacket to make sure his own police revolver was in place. Although he seldom wore it away from the job, tonight he had decided to pack it on an impulse when he and Gina came to the villa. It was a weird night in any case, being Beltane. Magic was in the air. So was trouble

48

TO THE GROTTO

The mother wolf hung limply from the pole. Mimi resolutely balanced the makeshift sling that bore the burden of the animal's deadweight and that of her wounded pup. The girls walked slowly, careful not to make unnecessary noise on the scrim floor of the tunnel. Kara's lantern at the front end of the pole cast eerie shadows. Each kept to her own thoughts. Toby sauntered ahead nonchalantly, lending them confidence in their mission.

Joanna held the rear end of the pole firmly propped over her right shoulder and steadied the three wolf pups, cradled in her sweatshirt, with her left hand. By nature, her fanciful imagination quickly adjusted to the incredible situation. She found herself playing the role of an Amazon warrior as she had envisioned it when first starting out from the villa. But Joanna was awed by the courage and ingenuity her younger sisters had shown in the emergency. She felt proud of them and honored to be allowed into their living drama.

Since early childhood, Joanna habitually saw life as the proverbial stage upon which individuals played their chosen roles. Now she marveled at the astonishing family epic in which all three sisters found themselves starring. *We are part of a living legend*, she thought, with a shiver. She felt thrilled at the idea, as fanciful as it might seem to others.

An exclamation from Mimi brought Joanna's attention back to the immediate moment. A spectral light shown around them in the tunnel. It floated about them, wraithlike, wavering from an opening just ahead of where they had stopped. Mimi spoke softly.

"We are bringing our hurt wolf friend and her puppies. Please let us pass safely. We mean no harm to anyone here."

Kara glanced back toward Joanna with a puzzled wrinkle of her forehead. Joanna shrugged her shoulders to show she was equally in the dark. But neither one said anything as they continued to observe their little sister's odd behavior.

The ghostly light coalesced into a wavering oblong shape at Mimi's side. "Oh, I'm so glad it is you," said Mimi laughing with relief. "These are my sisters. Kara up front, and Joanna behind. You know you are safe with them. Is it okay if we bring the wolf and pups into your grotto?" She continued to explain, "They have been attacked by the big bird that came here yesterday. But the bird is not following us now. Kara's wolf-friend Rarjer is going to kill it." Mimi said this as if she was certain. She added, "This mother wolf is his mate."

The ghost drifted to the big wolf and looked into its face with great sadness. Then she gently stroked the unconscious animal's muzzle and forehead. The wolf opened its eyes and looked at the ghost, then closed them again with a soft moan.

Kara had turned off her lantern when the apparition arrived, but neither she nor Joanna were able to actually see the ghost girl. To them, the tunnel shown in a soft luminous light without shadows, but they could not see who Mimi was addressing. By now both had accepted that their kid sister held strong supernatural powers and so they kept their questions to themselves.

Kara again thought of the stories in the Grimoire and wondered if Mimi harbored one of those powerful spirits. She was also reminded how the magic people addressed Mimi as a goddess in the Grove. She shivered a little at such unearthly imaginings.

Joanna held no reservations against mystical ideas, however, and had already decided that all three of them must have been alive during important events of the past and were together now for some significant purpose. She liked the idea of having once been a queen, and had immediately identified with certain of the characters in the theater and film productions she'd seen with Giuseppe.

Mimi didn't wonder about the mysteries at all. She simply accepted them as natural. For this reason, she drew the trust of the ghosts and fairies, as well as the animals. Now she said to her sisters, "We can go ahead into the grotto. But be careful not to disturb anything. It is the home of some of the magic people."

They resumed their cautious procession with the wolf's stretcher. Soon they came to the anteroom of the grotto with its confluence of three tunnels. They stopped there and listened. No sounds carried down from any of the passages, and they determined that nothing had followed them.

Mimi directed them to take the wolf to the area of the scrying pool and altar. She instinctively felt that healing magic lay in this waterfall's aura. They lay the pole-sling gently down on the cool stones behind the altar and untied the wolf and pup. The animal heaved a sigh and moaned again, giving a small jerking kick with her hind legs, but she did not rise.

The little pup with the torn leg held tight to its mother's belly and they did not disturb it. Joanna undid her sweatshirt and gently lifted out the two pups who had not yet regained consciousness. She set them near the mother's belly, but not so close as to bother her wound. The bleeding had slowed, but not yet stopped.

The mute ghost assisted Mimi in ministering to the wounded animals, but she remained invisible to Kara and Joanna. Mimi scooped water from the pool over the wounds, while the ghost girl dabbed at them with a poultice made from the silk of butterfly cocoons.

Joanna, still cradling the single unharmed pup, looked around the grotto in amazement. "I wonder if this is the actual place told about in some of the tales." She said this quietly, to herself.

Kara overheard and said, "Have you heard those stories too, Jo? I am certain this is the grotto where some of the Rimini witches from ages past hid out during times of persecutions." She watched Joanna for acknowledgement, then added, "It is pretty awesome, isn't it, to think our ancestors have used these tunnels and caves for centuries, and here we are, following in their footsteps."

"Or maybe we were here ourselves in the past," answered Joanna. "I had such a strong sense of identifying with a couple of the women's stories Gina told us at the picnic. And, now, I got the distinct feeling that I have actually been here, in this place, before." Now she looked at Kara for a reaction and was pleased to see that her sister's typical skepticism was nowhere in evidence.

Instead, Kara said, "I've had exactly the same feeling. And even though it seems bizarre, I'm beginning to believe that all of us have the spirits of our ancestors in us. But I don't know if it's good to try to figure out whose spirit exactly. Somewhere in the journal it says the spirit will reveal itself only if it has a need for you to know. Otherwise we should just live our own lives knowing we are guided by an ancient soul."

"That sounds sensible," mused Joanna, "But I must admit I get awful curious about who I've been and when I've lived in the past."

Just then, Mimi interrupted their conversation. "Would you two be quiet for a minute? I'm trying to hear what Sophia is telling me."

49

SECRETS REVEALED

At the villa, Mario led the others into one of the rooms that
Mimi and Toby had explored when they first arrived.
"This was Sophia's studio, she was quite an accomplished artist
in the style of representational fantasy and mythology"

They all stared at the painting that stood partially draped in
the corner. Dimmed moonlight shown through sooty skylights,
made the picture seem supernaturally eerie, as if the figure with
the raised Athame was about to strike the horned figure in front
of it. "Damned evil looking painting," said John with a hollow
laugh. The others ignored his rudeness.

Mario flipped on a light. Gina walked to one corner of the
room and tugged on an ancient bell-pull. A single chime rang
softly, and a set of heavy green velour draperies, dusty from disuse, gradually rolled aside to reveal a wide partition between two
tall mullioned windows. The window openings were unusually
deep, with nearly three feet of stuco'd concrete block protruding into the room, and another foot or so outward beyond the
window pane.

Gina pulled a metal lever at the side of one of the windows and the partition creaked open. She hooked her fingers into the crack and pulled. The hidden door opened onto a vestibule about four feet deep and six feet wide, big enough to hide an adult person or several youngsters.

Some pillows and blankets were tucked in a corner and there was a bench that could serve as bed or table. There was a little shelf that held a pitcher for water, a bowl and candlestick. Under the shelf stood a rather fancy porcelain commode. And against that leaned a raggedy teddy bear wearing a dirty white sailors hat over its ears.

"I remember now!" Barbara smiled joyfully, going over to the tiny room. "We used to play house in this little alcove while Sophia worked on her paintings. It never occurred to me then that it may have been designed for the more sinister purpose of hiding refugees."

Then her eye fell on the teddy bear with its silly hat and she squealed with delight as she reached down to pick it up. Cradling the teddy to her breast, she quietly took the hat and placed it on her head, then looked up at Gina with tears in her eyes. "It still fits. Maybe it will help me regain my trust."

Gina put her arm around Barbara's shoulders. "It was never really lost, only misplaced. It has been waiting for you to come back all these years." She meant both the hat and Barbara's trust in the magic of her upbringing.

At the back wall of the alcove was a heavy wood door with one small window that looked out onto an overgrown vine climbing the outside of the Tower. "This was the old front entrance into the house before other sections were added in later centuries," explained Gina.

John stuck his head into the small room, ducking to avoid the low ceiling. "Must have been designed for midgets," he joked as he bumped his head.

"Let's go up to the attic," suggested Mario.

They all trooped back to the hallway and followed Gina into the music room. Here, over the stage platform by the side wall, Gina held her arm up to the ceiling and, seemingly by magic, a stair-ladder slowly dropped from a trap door. It was activated by a thin wire traversing the room at about six feet up.

"Wow!" said John laughing at Gina. "Good thing you entered before me, Shorty. I would have tripped that thing with my head. Could have been decapitated right here." Then as they all stared up into the gaping hole to which the ladder led, he said, "Well, I'm game, let's go look." He placed his foot on the ladder. It groaned under his weight. He stopped and looked at Mario. "Are you sure the ladder will hold me? Or are you guys trying to get rid of me here?" He joked casually, but seemed uneasy.

Mario said, "I'll go first. Although I'm a good deal lighter than you, JM, I'll test the old ladder to be sure. If I fall, I won't sue you." He reached the top without incident and clambered into the attic, calling down, "You'd better bring a flashlight or candle, Gina."

"I'm way ahead of you on that," said Gina. "I've got two flashlights and a battery lantern here with me." She handed up the lantern to Mario.

John and Barb watched their interaction and each felt a stab of envy at the comfort the other couple seemed to have with each other. It seemed a long time since Barb and John were able to cooperate on anything without getting into an argument.

Gina scampered lightly up the ladder, calling "Come on you guys. This is a very special hideout."

Barb, wearing her newfound hat, quickly made the climb with John close behind her. Again the ladder groaned in its hinges, but it held firmly. John hoisted himself onto the attic floor with a grunt. "Sorry. I'm a bit out of shape," he said. Then he looked around and exclaimed, "Good lord! It's a regular ballroom!"

Here the ceiling rose at a steep pitch of about twenty feet above them. The attic room was about 35 feet long and 20 feet wide. Three levered skylight windows were set into each slope and a tall set of French doors opened onto a balcony at one end of the room. The full moon shone brightly through one side of skylights. There was no furniture. But there was a raised ledge running along each side of the room at sitting height. The whole area was surprisingly clean of cobwebs or other debris.

"This was the site of many Witches' masked balls during the years that Sophia ran the school," said Gina. "It's a terrific space to decorate for Samhain or Winter Solstice. A bit warm during the summer, though."

They each beamed a lantern or flashlight around the room. In one corner the light moved over a tall standing mirror draped in a black cloth. A bit of the cloth had blown aside, so that they caught a brief glimpse of their own faces, peering wide-eyed out at them. The women laughed delightedly.

"Remember the ball before your graduation, Barb?"

"Oh my," answered Barbara. "It's a long time since I've thought of that. We had such a wonderful time dancing on the balcony where it seemed we were literally dancing into the sky." She stopped to reflect. "Heironymous was with us then. He brought total magic into everything he did. I wish we could see him again. Do you ever hear from him?"

Gina nodded, but didn't answer. She walked to the French doors and tugged them open. A cool evening breeze wafted into the closed space, freshening the rather stale air. She was about to step out onto the balcony when Mario stopped her.

"Wait, Gina. Let me escort you." He held out his arms and they whirled together into the night as if they were dancing a moonlight waltz. John looked at Barbara. She smiled and tucked her hand into the crook of his elbow as they promenaded onto the balcony.

For a few minutes both couples enjoyed a special inti-macy as they stood looking out from the high balcony across a moon-shadowed expanse of woods to the sea where the goddess Luna lay her shimmering trail into infinity.

John bent down and kissed Barbara gently on the forehead as she leaned against his shoulder. She looked up with a bemused smile. "I had forgotten too," he said, "how special the magic can be."

Barbara didn't say anything, but she took it as a signal that he was definitely softening. *I just hope nothing too drastic happens to throw him into his superstitious funk again,* she worried. She leaned up and kissed him on the lips and they held each other close for a minute.

Mario whispered. "Quiet everyone. Listen."

They stood still, harking to the night sounds.

An owl hooted three times.

The howl of a wolf, not too far distant, gave a plaintive cry, repeated over and over again and lingering on the wind. It made John shiver, and Mario suddenly felt inexplicably sad. Barbara and Gina drew close to each other and held hands.

50

A SHORT BATTLE

Back at the ruined cabin farther up the mountain, the battle was underway. Gunshots rang out from several directions, water spewed from the fire hose, fireballs shot out from the cannon, arrows whizzed through the air, javelins flew, slingshots twanged, and hatchets chopped.

Soon blood was flowing everywhere, men were howling in pain, others were cursing as they tried to bring down the motley army of monsters. The vigilantes found themselves in arm to arm combat, rolling in the bloody dirt and grappling with flimsy layers of fabric and crepe paper, while the occupants of those costumes neatly removed themselves and turned knives, clubs, and swords against their attackers.

The Wizard looked on in dismay. He raised his staff and hollered at his troops to take positions. But only a few heard him, and fewer were able to obey his command.

One soldier aimed his gun at Heironymous. He was viciously attacked by a mountain lioness, who made short work of the guy and immediately turned to strike at the wizard. The hawk then swooped on the lioness, and they engaged in battle, thus sparing the wizard. But one of the soldiers fired a shot that hit Anthony in the shoulder. That soldier found himself in arm to jaw combat with a ravenous wolf and lost both the battle and his arm. The wolf then turned to help the lion bring down the hawk.

The Wizard raised his staff. From it protruded a razor sharp blade that was now aimed at the wolf. But as he prepared to stab Rarjer, a pistol shot rang from the cabin and the Wizard fell to the ground howling in pain. A second shot took down the last of the standing soldiers, while the lioness and wolf worked over the dying and mutilated hawk.

Then everything was quiet. The priest went and stood over the wizard. "Beltane greetings, Minister Donnie Marini. Hope we haven't spoiled your party too badly." Heironymous grinned down at the prostrate Wizard.

The 'Vatican's Vulture' twisted around and stared up at the priest from where he lay in the dirt. His right arm dangled awkwardly. "Heironymous!" he croaked. "I thought you were on our side."

The priest laughed. "A Benandanti Strega never switches sides. Unlike some others I've known at the church." He took the wizard's staff and examined the blade. "Nasty little gadget you've got here, Wiz. You won't mind if I borrow it for a while?"

Donnie turned ghostly white, expecting his staff to be used against himself by the man who once was his pupil in the seminary. But of course, Heironymous had no such intention. He merely wished to confiscate the object as an 'exhibit of proof' for later.

Gradually, the acting troop gathered itself together, counting heads, congratulating each other and comparing battle wounds. Apparently none other than Anthony had sustained a serious wound, and his turned out to be relatively minor as well. The bullet had just grazed his shoulder. They staunched the bleeding and soon he was joking and sharing stories with the others.

No one noticed, at first, when the wolf began to howl.

When they did, they saw the wolf and the mountain lion standing over a crumpled figure. Although he'd been protected by his invisibility, Giuseppe had been caught in the crossfire as he tried to direct the fighting. He now lay dying at the feet of his animal companions.

The wolf howled and howled and howled as the moon veiled its face behind a dark cloud.

51

IN THE GROTTO

In the grotto, Kara and Joanna looked at each other wide-eyed, and then at their little sister who was now rocking back and forth in a trance as she continued automatically bathing the female wolf's wounds.

With her eyes closed, Mimi began to speak. But it was not her usual voice that her sisters heard. She spoke with a deep husky voice, like an old woman who spoke rather formally.

"Great tragedy has befallen our friends," she began. "We must hold tight to our newfound knowledge and believe completely in the magic to which we have been introduced." Mimi stopped talking and listened, then she nodded and continued, "This was not the plan. We were to have received our lessons over many weeks and months, gradually and easily, so that we could naturally accept the wisdom to which we have been born."

She stopped again and listened a moment, frowning. "But evil ones are attempting to prevent the good magic from spreading into the world. The Malandanti are attacking Benandanti forces in the forest around the wolf's den. Someone dear to us has been mortally wounded." Mimi choked back a sob. "It's Faunus, the Horned God!"

Kara cried out in horror, "I've got to go back there! I had a feeling I should go and help Rarjer. I just knew something was very wrong." Tears were streaming down her cheeks as she looked frantically about for her back pack. She found it where she'd dropped it against a stone seat, and began pulling it over her shoulder.

"Wait a minute," said Joanna. "What do you think you can do alone against evil spirits?" She put out a hand to stop Kara from running back up the tunnel that led to the cottage. Kara pushed her aside, but stopped at the sound of Mimi's chanting voice.

"Do not rush unthinking into danger!" The 'old woman' voice coming from Mimi held immense power. Kara stayed to listen.

"It is essential that we take and use the magic that channels through us, even though we may not understand what or why." Mimi cleared her throat. "It is Sophia who speaks through me here, in an urgent need to help us fight the newly reorganized enemies of Strega. We are to listen to the inner voice and follow its direction. We must not act rashly or unthinkingly. The magic folk are with us, and will show us what to do."

Mimi opened her eyes and blinked. Her hand on the wolf's wounded body clenched in anger. "We must not let them scare us," she said in her own voice. "We have to be strong to help." But then her face wrinkled into tears. "Poor dear Faunus," she sobbed.

Tinkle had been assisting Mimi and the ghost girl in healing the wolf and pups, unseen by Kara and Joanna. Now the fairy made herself visible to them. She appeared, perched on the rim of the pond below the cascading waterfall.

At first, the girls took no notice of her presence for their attention was caught up in the message sent through Mimi from their dead great-aunt. Kara fought against her old feelings of skepticism, while Jo struggled to grasp this newly disclosed evidence of reincarnation.

Mimi simply emptied her mind of any such critical analysis or doubts and concentrated again on bringing healing energy to the wounded. She was rewarded by seeing one of the puppies regain consciousness and crawl to its mother's teat. The she-wolf seemed much more alert, and the wounded puppy was dozing peacefully at her neck.

All three girls turned in surprised unison toward the fairy when it spoke. "Come over here and sit by the water," said Tinkle. "There is a story that Sophia wants you to see." At Kara's hesitance, she added, "Don't back away. It will be a short story, but it will help you know what to do."

Mimi looked from the fairy to her sisters. "Can you both see Tinkle and hear her? I think she means we should go and watch another pool-a-vision, like they showed me yesterday."

Kara and Jo just stared at the fairy, their mouths agape.

Tinkle fluttered her wings and rearranged herself on the pool's rim. She shook her little finger at them and said, "You can stare all you want to, I know you won't hurt me anyway. But you'd better get over it, 'cuz Sophia has really important things to show you and there isn't that much time." She huffed a tiny puff of fairy dust at them and turned to face the pool.

She waved her hands over the water like Juliet had done for Mimi previously, and the whirling surface stilled to a mirror-smooth reflection. Curiosity and a sense of immediacy aroused the two older girls, so that Kara and Jo crept quietly to sit by Mimi at the pool's edge, saying no more.

The vision appeared, drawing all of their attention. They each felt personally pulled into the scene, as if they were actually there in person, and each heard the voice of Sophia narrating the story in her mind. Because they had all experienced lucid dreams and manifestations of the arcane in various forms during the past few days, they now were able to take in this surreal phenomenon without undue questions.

✳ ✳ ✳

A stag stood majestically on a bluff, his antlers branching like the limbs of an ancient oak. Below, in the valley, the river branched as well, into several smaller streams that flowed around and through the mountains, eventually rejoining their courses to empty, at last, into the great sea beyond. A full moon lit the landscape, creating silver etchings against barren rocks in dirt-poor fields.

The big buck lifted his muzzle to the sea breeze and snuffled its salted breath. He angled an ear downwind to catch the voices of those pursuing him, then he flicked his tail twice, and disappeared into the forested mountain slope. Behind him the pounding of hoofs continued relentlessly, getting closer and louder.

Farther up the mountain, a tall, tawny-complexioned woman waited quietly at the edge of another span of woods that camouflaged her in its shadows. A moss-green hunter's tunic draped over her left shoulder, leaving her right arm and shoulder exposed. At her back hung a quiver of arrows, and she held a longbow ready to fire. At her hip hung a curved sword in its leather sheath, and around her waist was a wide belt decorated with gemstones.

Gemstones, likewise, sparkled from a gold torque around her neck and on leather bands at her wrists. Her bare legs were encased in knee-high doeskin boots laced with leather thongs.

She sat bare-back upon a great white stallion who wore gems on his halter to match hers. From under a jaunty green peaked cap, her short auburn hair caught the gentle breeze and fluttered, as did the hairs on the backs of the two magnificent wolves flanking her.

Suddenly a giant stag charged across the open meadow and into the cover of woods to their left. Her animal companions stayed silently alert and quivering with tension at her side. She smiled and relaxed for a moment, relieved to see that the great buck would escape.

Now she tensed, cocking her bow and arrow, her piercing gaze directed upon the rock-paved path leading out of the trees across the meadow. Soon they heard the clatter of hooves and four horsemen came at a fast gallop straight toward her and her companions.

She let fly with the first arrow and the lead rider fell to the ground. His horse turned in confusion and ran back along the road. She notched two more arrows in time to hit the next two riders in the exposed area at their throats. Three Roman soldiers lay dead on the ground. Horses milled about in confusion. The wolves took after the fourth soldier who had retreated into the woods.

The woman cautiously moved forward to search the bodies, taking weapons and whatever coins were in their purses. She knew the local militia could use these. She waited while her wolves captured and dragged the fourth man back to the meadow. His arms and one leg were bleeding, but he struggled when she strapped him to one of the rider-less horses. She quickly muffled him to stop his cursing. Then she gathered the reins of the remaining horse and turned to take her captive and booty back to the camp.

At their campsite by the river, she was greeted by the Etruscan leader. "Welcome back Amazon Queen Cyna! I am so grateful that you have come to lend your skills in our war against the Romans."

✳ ✳ ✳

Gradually the images faded, leaving the girls to watch the pool resume its swirling and splashing. They sat in silence for some second, each taking from the story some insight or inspiration for herself. Kara shook her pony tail and frowned. "I don't really see how this helps us."

"We probably won't understand until we need to," said Mimi wisely. She turned back to tend her wolf patients.

Joanna looked awestruck when she spoke. "I have been pretending to be an Amazon warrior woman since we left the house. It just helped me stay calm, but maybe this vision says we have their spirits in us."

Kara shrugged. "It hardly matters, does it? That doesn't tell us how we can help Faunus."

Joanna spoke up. "Sep told me that Faunus always dies at harvest time and is reborn in the spring. It's part of the ancient mysteries of Nature being celebrated now. It's too soon for him to die."

She said this to comfort her sisters, but she needed to comfort herself too. Although she had not met the mystical horned green-man god, she felt a strong connection to him. She pulled the little wreath-crown she'd found in the Grove from her pocket and held it to her heart. "Dear goddess, help him revive and return to us, for it is not yet the season for his death." Joanna found herself praying, although she had never been the least bit religious in her life.

"But we've got to do something," Kara's voice broke as she interrupted Jo's reverie. She squared her shoulders and, once again, turned to go back up the tunnel. "The fennel stalks work as protection against the Malandanti spirits. I know, because the big hawk nearly attacked me and Rarjer yesterday, but it flew away as soon as it saw the fennel I was holding." She pulled a stalk from her pocket and motioned to the others to take theirs out too.

Toby, during all this time, had been quietly licking the one wolf pup who was still unconscious. Now the cat jumped up on the altar stone and growled. He sprang from the stone onto the ledge above the entry, puffed up and hissing viciously.

Then they all heard the shuffling sounds in the tunnel, coming down from the direction of the mountain cabin.

52

ON THE BALCONY

John and Barbara stood with Mario and Gina on the hidden balcony of the secret attic-ballroom. They listened to occasional rustlings within the sudden eerie stillness of the night.

This balcony was situated facing toward the backside of the villa, and sat high on a gabled peak of the main house. Behind it rose the top two stories of the tower, with its crenellated rampart. Below, was the courtyard with its walled garden, the orchard beyond, and the woodland path with its magic tree. The balcony's parapet was crenellated, like the tower's, and thus virtually hid anyone on the balcony from anyone on the ground.

The balcony, while blending almost invisibly into the structure of the multi-partitioned stucco building, afforded a clear view in three directions. The sea glimmered far to the right, wafting its aquatic scent on a southerly breeze. Directly ahead spread a patchwork of fragrant hills and valleys, blanketed in wild flowers and vineyard crops interwoven by a network of mountain streams and rivers. To the left, loomed dense woods rising up the mountain under which, unseen, wound the tunnels to the grotto. Beltane fires flickered from scattered points among the trees and hills.

The tunnels, Grotto, and Grove, of course, could not be seen from the villa. But the song of their ethereal magic created a vibrating chord within anyone attuned to its haunting music.

On the balcony, three of its four human occupants were well attuned. John, alone, was oblivious to that sublime rhythm. A fifth individual, the raven, Melanthus, was himself part of the tune.

The bird had just landed on the parapet, and Mario said in a low murmur, "Melanthus. What do you wish of us? Who is coming?"

The bird's presence made John distinctly uneasy. *How can my perfectly sane brother-in-law talk to a bird as if it has real knowledge of human affairs?*

The bird cocked its head to one side and eyed Mario directly. "Crk" it clucked softly, as if it knew to keep hushed. Then it hopped down to the floor and waddled into the attic-ballroom. Mario followed, but signaled the others to stay where they were.

The raven awkwardly made its way to the ladder opening and looked down, then up at Mario. "CAWRK." It said in a scolding voice. "CAWRK!" Then it tugged with its beak at the ladder's guy-wire and the whole contraption raised up and closed shut.

Mario followed the bird back to the balcony. "It seems he's telling us to stay put up here," Mario whispered to the others. "We'd better turn off our lights too," he suggested. But only Mario's own lantern was still lit, in fact. He turned it off.

They all stood leaning into the night, trying to catch and make meaning of muffled sounds coming from behind the house.

The moon shown eerily on the wooded hills below so that they could barely glimpse the ghostly figures who moved down there, slipping between the trees. Mario adjusted his revolver in its holster under his jacket.

John, still struggling with incredulity, nevertheless kept his doubts to himself for now because he, too, began to perceive mist-like figures floating through the woods and felt an uncanny wind blowing through trees that stood perfectly still. He shivered and held Barbara's hand a bit tighter. She gave his a squeeze of reassurance. Her face was bathed in a moonlit glow reminiscent to John of the woman in the painting on Sophia's easel.

Then they heard voices that carried up from the orchard. "Looks like no one's here tonight," said one. "The lights are all off."

"More like they're all sleeping, as any sane people would be at one in the morning," answered another.

"Did Carlo say to wait in the woods or by the garden gate?"

"In the woods, stupid. He doesn't want us disturbing anyone unless the Wizard actually shows up. Then we are supposed to get into the courtyard and set up a howl."

"Well, we'd better settle in and shut up then," said a third voice.

"You two jokers talk loud enough to wake the dead, and we don't need more of that tonight." Someone laughed. Then all was quiet in the orchard again.

John struggled to contain his rage. "Shouldn't we get down there and check on those guys? What are we doing here, watching some kind of fantasy show instead of going after those goons?" His voice began rising to its normal booming volume.

Barbara placed a finger gently over his mouth, "Shhh. John, keep your voice down. We don't know that anything is happening yet."

He pushed her hand away, but lowered his voice. "I'm not going to stand around helplessly and watch a bunch of goons trash my property." He headed into the ballroom prepared to lower the ladder.

Mario rushed forward and grabbed his arm. "Wait a minute, John," he said in a hoarse whisper. "I know you feel exasperated. I'm feeling exactly the same way, but there must be a good reason that we've been warned to stay put for now. You've got to trust us. The raven really knows."

John turned, ready to fight off Mario. "That's pure rubbish! It's exactly the kind of foolishness that makes me hate your witch traditions. Talking to birds, for god's sake! Use your good common sense, Man!" John held his fists clenched, threatening.

Suddenly Melanthus flew directly onto his shoulder and pecked once at his right ear. John batted at the bird, which only clung on harder. It made no sound other than an occasional ruffle of feathers as it settled itself on him.

"Looks like the bird likes you, John," laughed Barbara. But she quickly stifled her laughter, seeing the rage in her husband's face. "Please Dear," she said, "Don't try to force your way here. Whether you choose to believe it or not, there is magic afoot tonight, and we need to observe closely in order to play our parts effectively. If we do that, everything will work out just fine."

Mario interjected, "She's right old man. We're not in charge right now and any way we try to intervene might only make matters worse. We'll go down there when the time is right." He put a hand on John's shoulder to reassure him.

"Get this damn bird off my neck, anyway," growled John.

Mario stroked the raven's back gently, "You heard him Melanthus, let go. You've made your point."

"Crk," it said, and hopped down to waddle back to the balcony.

53

CONVERGENCE

When they heard the sounds from the tunnel, Kara and Joanna positioned themselves inside the grotto entrance, prepared to fight. They both held the fennel stalks before them at arm's length, legs spread and ready to take a stand against whatever was coming.

The unearthly atmosphere of the moment transformed the two young women's spirits into those of their warrior ancestors from ancient Amazon tribes. Both of them had suddenly acquired extra height and strength. They both wore the features of terrible raging barbarian fighting women. The fennel stalks transmuted to become sharp tipped spears in their hands.

Joanna had a moment to reflect on the fact that she was actually living the role she'd fantasized earlier. Glancing at Kara, she thought, *perhaps we are incarnating the spirits of Amazon warrior queens, like Tana, whose story aunt Gina told us at Sophia's funeral rite and the woman we just saw in the pool*. But she had no more time to ponder this insight.

The sounds in the tunnel grew closer. They were coming from the direction of the left passage, the one that led to the wolf's cottage den. Groans and soft mumbling could be heard. Then a male voice said, "Be careful with that shoulder of yours, it's still bleeding."

Another male voice answered, "I'll be fine. We've got to get *him* settled quickly though. His pulse is going down fast. I hope the fairy healers haven't got scared away by our noise."

When Anthony and a strange man in black arrived in the vestibule, carrying a limp Giuseppe between them, everyone stood frozen in this bizarre tableau for several seconds. The men, seeing the girls in their warrior guises, were taken aback. Then Anthony recognized his cousins through their astral transfiguration. "What the hell are you doing?" growled Anthony.

Joanna quickly forgot about the two men when she saw the unconscious figure carried between them. "Oh my god! It's Sep!" She ran forward to help the men carry him into the grotto.

"Where is the Horned God, Faunus?" demanded Kara, furiously. "We were told he has been killed. Did you just leave him to the Malandanti?"

Kara followed, raving, as the others carried Giuseppe to the healing pool and laid him down gently.

Mimi, who had instinctively gone back behind the altar to protect the wounded animals, now came forward to help with the unconscious man. As she did so, she spoke sharply to Kara, "Don't be a dolt, Kara! Can't you figure out that Giuseppe was being Faunus tonight in the Grove?"

Kara felt foolish and chastised. But she was still upset and could not let go of the terrible sense of danger and urgency she was feeling. She didn't respond to Mimi's reprimand.

Joanna immediately stripped away Sep's shirt and began washing his wound with water scooped from the pool. She imitated what she had observed Mimi doing with the wolf and murmured soothing sounds into his ear. Giuseppe moaned softly, but did not open his eyes.

"What's happened?" demanded Kara of the two men now standing aside to watch as Joanna and Mimi performed the instinctive and powerful healing ritual. In a voice that broke with hysteria, Kara said, "Where is Rarjer? Has he been hurt too?"

"Calm down, young woman," said the strange man in the black mask. "I believe your wolf friend is guarding the entry." He nodded toward the door. Kara rushed there and found Rarjer standing with his hackles raised, facing the tunnel they'd just come down. Kara curbed her impulse to hug him. She wisely deduced he was in no mood to cuddle.

On the other side of the entry, a tawny golden lioness hunkered, ready to spring at anybody coming down the ramp. Kara stifled her shock, and nodded recognition to Farah, glad for the presence of another fierce fighter.

With Giuseppe being cared for, Anthony and his comrade turned to leave. Coming out into the vestibule, the man in black ignored Kara and spoke to the animals: "You stay and meet them. Then bring them along to us. You know where we're going. It shouldn't be too hard to convince them to come along now," he said with a bitter laugh.

Then looking at Kara, he said, "Just leave the fighting to the animals, young woman. You can lend moral support but keep out of the way and, if you like, come after us to the villa. There should be some interesting action up there before long."

Anthony stopped before heading up the tunnel that led to the villa. "I should introduce you two," he said, looking at Kara. "This is a dear friend of the family and an old friend of Sophia's, Heironymous."

The big man waited a moment for Kara to speak but saw she was still too upset. "You must be Kara. I have observed your courage already. I know you will be a great help to us." And then the two men hurried up the tunnel.

The wolf and the lioness stood their ground watching as the men disappeared from view. Then they turned back to watch the opposite tunnel. Kara could sense the tension in the alert bodies of the two wild animals. She seemed to have regained her composure again as well, and felt the surge of power return to her body. She'd been so focused on fighting, that she'd forgotten to thank the men for bringing Giuseppe to the Grotto.

She turned her attention to the immediate situation.

She checked on her sisters and saw they were still intently focused on the injured 'man-god' as she now thought of him. She looked for the cat, and saw that he was still sitting guard on the high ledge over the doorway. She saluted a silent thank you to the brave little cat and was amused to see him flick one ear in acknowledgment, as if to say "Don't worry. I'll take care of things in here."

Kara went back out and stood quietly between Rarjer and Farah. As more rustling and scraping sounds echoed down the passage, the uninjured fourth wolf pup came and stood, unnoticed, beside his father, ready to join in the battle to come.

54

KARA'S TEST

Kara stood at attention holding her fennel stalk in front of her as if it were a holy relic to ward off vampires. In her other hand, she gripped the sacred knife poised for combat. She could feel her muscles tense with unnatural power and sensed herself somehow grown bigger, bolder. Her heart pounded, sending vibrations through her body that seemed to shake the very walls of the Grotto antechamber.

The wolf at her right side, and the lioness at her left, stood statue-still, not a muscle twitching to betray their fighting tension. A miniature version of the great silver wolf shivered at his father's right side, but the pup was equally ready to engage the enemy that they could hear now advancing down the tunnel.

The smell arrived first. A stench of burned flesh, bloody feathers, drenched fur and enraged ectoplasm wafted down the tunnel, making Kara's skin crawl. Whatever was coming toward them was not entirely of this world.

Kara recalled a change-spell from Sophia's journal, and sent a prayer to the goddess for help in using it now. She conjured an image of Celtic witches fighting battles against the Roman armies during the first century. Kara had read how those women, called Velada, used spells of enchantment against their enemies. But this image brought none of the change that had come over her and Jo earlier.

At last the pool-a-vision came back to her mind and she realized Cyna, the Amazon warrior princess, must be one of their foremothers. She called on that spirit and felt the change come over her instantly.

When the spirit of Kara's ancestress entered her consciousness Kara felt fierce courage and cold fury overtake her usually stoic nature. Her ponytail whipped back in a sudden gust of witch-wind. Her eyes flared with an interior fire and she saw the scene before her with superhuman sight.

The fennel stalk transformed into a spear that she hefted to her right shoulder with practiced ease. In her left hand she grasped Sophia's sacred knife with expertise. Kara felt the power of its piercing sharpness and knew she aimed to kill.

She thought of Joanna and Mimi, tending their patients inside the Grotto chamber. Glancing behind her, Kara saw that an impenetrable veil had been drawn over the entry, hiding the sanctuary. She was on her own. She drew courage from her animal companions as the din emerging from the tunnel's passage grew to an overwhelming uproar.

First a pair of hyenas loped drunkenly into view, slobbering and baring bloody fangs. Rarjer charged at them, snarling. He made short work of bringing those cowardly devils to their knees. The stench of their vomit was toxic, but the puppy peed on it and the poisonous odor was instantly neutralized.

Next arrived a deranged creature of the skies. Kara barely recognized the once grand hawk that had attacked her a couple days ago. It now resembled a robot pasted over with feathers. Indeed, the bird must have been killed, and its master had revived it in this disgusting and demonic fashion. It squawked and snapped menacingly at the little wolf pup, who yipped and snarled with equal menace. The big wolf merely knocked the ugly thing over with one paw and then snapped its head off in his jaws. Kara felt a great relief to have the bird destroyed.

A rather impressive black bear ambled into view, but its dazed expression revealed it to be under a spell that had gone completely wrong. Its huge maw gaped ferociously, but the big bruin's roar came out as a pitiable whine for help. The lioness paced to the bear's side and nuzzled its ear. The magnificent spell-struck animal shook itself back to sensibility and turned to face its bedeviled captor.

This is all so preposterous, thought Kara. *I must be dreaming the entire thing.* But the magic knife in her hand throbbed strongly, warning her to stay focused. *Put aside doubts. Believe the impossible. Don't scare away the magic.*

Then the Wizard himself marched into view, a great drumming reverberated with every footstep. The powerful master rattled the walls, followed by a cadre of about half a dozen soldiers in ridiculous old fashioned battle armor. In his flowing black robe with stars pasted in its lining and his tall pointed hat decorated with cosmic symbols, the guy presented such a hackneyed stereotype of wizardry that Kara nearly laughed out loud. But the evil that glinted from beady eyes under bushy black brows looked terrible enough.

Kara aimed her spear directly at the wizard's heart. He raised his staff and pointed it at hers. Sparks flew between their weapons, although neither one landed a physical blow. Kara's arm burned with witch-heat as she held her position against the wizard. She met his glaring hate-filled stare with one of serene self-assurance. She never let her gaze falter as pandemonium broke around her. She held the Wizard with her concentrated will, turning his own evil power back on him.

Men in armor battled against ripping claws and snapping jaws. In too-close quarters to use their guns, they pulled out knives and hatchets and began thrashing and stabbing blindly, maiming each other rather than the animals. Their armor hindered their vision and dexterity, while it gave the animals purchase through the network of mail on their torsos. Soldiers, howling in agony, crawled to escape through the tunnel from which they'd come, only to be forced back into the melee by their evil wizard master. Eventually some escaped through the middle tunnel, although Kara's forces prevented any from gaining access to the villa's tunnel. The wolf engaged violently with another pair of hyenas, yet they seemed to have lost spirit for the fight and soon capitulated, turning instead upon the soldiers, and chasing them up the tunnel as they fled.

Kara kept her focus on the Wizard, but she remained aware of everything going on around her. She seemed to have gained a second set of eyes, seeing the whole thing from above as well as below. But she did not stop to wonder at this new miracle either.

The wizard's power was ebbing, but was not yet depleted. Kara's grip on her spear tightened and she redoubled her efforts to maintain serenity and faith in the power of white magic. She could not allow her conscious mind to question what was happening. She drew a veil across her thoughts as the spirits had drawn one over the Grotto entrance, thus shielding herself more effectively from the Wizard's assault.

Still, she needed to make a great effort to deflect the evil. She could feel fragments of malevolence nipping at her spirit. She forced herself to think kind thoughts and feel compassion for her enemy as Cecilia's journal had instructed. This was the hardest part, for Kara's naturally willful spirit bristled at the very idea of forgiving such a monster.

Neither Kara nor her opponent uttered a sound. Kara tried to read into his mind, but was blocked by the raging venom that spewed within his brain. Her arm began to tremble with the fatigue of holding the spear aimed straight. But she willed herself to maintain her position and focus.

Suddenly a shot rang out and the little wolf pup fell dead at her feet. Kara's concentration broke. She knelt by the fallen pup and wept. Her energy was completely depleted, the sense of witch-power totally gone. She tried to take the puppy to her sisters in the grotto, but found the entrance still veiled.

For that brief moment, she forgot to hold her power directed at the Wizard. When she remembered, she feared it was too late. She expected to be killed at any second. Yet, although she retained a fierce determination to fight to the finish, Kara felt oddly ready to die.

She made a final plea to the Goddess to protect her sisters and her animal companions. Still in the trance state, Kara understood that the ability to face death willingly was also from the Amazon warrior spirit, in whom the readiness to give her own life for her cause was her ultimate source of power.

Kara picked up her spear and turned, expecting to face the Wizard's malevolent force once again.

But the shot must have unnerved the Wizard as well, for he had turned and fled up the tunnel. Rarjer, Farah, and even two or three hyenas took off in rabid pursuit.

Soon a great snarling and roaring echoed down the tunnel and a torturous scream pierced the air followed by agonized moaning. Kara heard a crash, then silence, then the sound of something heavy being dragged back down the tunnel.

Kara laid the little dead wolf pup's carcass near where she recalled the entry of the grotto to be, although it was still hidden from sight. She stood up as Rarjer and Farah emerged from the tunnel dragging the Wizard, who was now unconscious. The other animals had retreated to the wilderness, having had their senses restored from the enchantment.

Rarjer deposited the Wizard in a heap. Then he turned to his son and snuffled the lifeless youngster. He looked up at Kara, who had tears pouring down her cheeks, and he came to her, placing his muzzle in her hand. She knelt and hugged his neck, while the lioness stood guard over their captive.

55

KARA'S INITIATION

The bullet had been meant for Kara, for there was a deep dent in the wall near where she had been standing. It had ricocheted and hit the puppy instead. He was a martyr to her victory. She thought, *I will take him as my mascot when I have my initiation ceremony*, and then wondered where such an idea had come from.

Clasping Sophia's magic dagger to her breast, Kara redirected her thoughts to the task at hand. They must get the Wizard to the villa, for that had clearly been Anthony and his mysterious companion's intent. *What was that big guy's name again? Sounded vaguely familiar, someone mother and Aunt Gina had mentioned.* She pushed the questions out of her mind, forcing herself to stay in the moment.

She fought off the exhaustion that threatened to consume her and turned to look at the Wizard. Seeing him lying there, slack-jawed and stupefied, helped her realize just what an enormous amount of energy she must have sustained for the last *how long had it been? Hours? No, just minutes!* It actually felt as if time stopped during the stand-off. She shook her pony tail and brought her attention back to the moment.

Rarjer lifted his muzzle and gave a single mournful howl for the dead puppy. Then, together with the lioness's ready assistance, they set about dragging the insensible Wizard up the tunnel to the villa.

At the last minute, Kara went back and picked up the wired-together remains of the hawk, stuffed them into the Wizard's smelly hat, and carried the whole mess before her at arm's length.

Hauling the unconscious man was awkward, but they didn't have to go very far after all. They passed by the exit into the Grove, and soon came to another narrow opening out of the tunnel on the opposite side. With Rarjer pulling and Farah pushing the deadweight of Wizard between them, they managed to get the guy out.

Kara followed, uncertain of where they were and what they were to do next. But the animals seemed to understand what to do, so she put aside her doubts and put her trust in the magic of the night.

They emerged into a ravine between two hills. Kara saw the back side of the villa just above them, silhouetted in the moonlight. *I think we are out of sight, unless someone is on the roof of the turret looking down?* She peered up there intensely but saw no movement. "What now?" she asked aloud, addressing the animals.

"Welcome, young woman," said a vaguely familiar deep voice from behind some trees. "We've been watching for you from the tower." The big masked man in black stepped into the clearing, followed by Cousin Anthony.

They looked down at the unconscious and bedraggled Wizard and laughed heartily. "Good work Rarjer and Farah," said Anthony.

"Kar-rah!" barked the wolf, and stood behind Kara on his hind legs with his paws resting on her shoulders.

She laughed then too, and said, "I believe he is trying to give me credit, but all I did was stand in one place and watch." She had not meant to belittle her part in the capture, but she suddenly felt shy and a bit embarrassed around the strange man.

"Well, I would guess you stood with some extra power behind you, my dear," spoke the masked giant with a hint of admiration. "This guy is full of nasty tricks and would have quickly put a spell on you if that were really all you did. I could see the witch power in you when we met, otherwise I would never have left you there alone with the animals to face this devil."

Kara decided to trust the men. *After all, these are Sophia's people.* So she acknowledged some responsibility, "Actually I did have a very strange experience. I had the feeling that someone else's energy was in me. I don't mean just supporting me, but more like I actually became that other person for a while."

She saw that both men listened intently without any sign of mockery, so she continued. "I had this fennel stalk that I was holding in my hand_ she stopped, feeling a bit foolish. But then she felt an urgent desire to share her tale more completely. Talking about it helped make it more real, more okay. "I read in Sophia's_ she checked herself again. *Don't disclose all your secrets, she reminded herself.* "Anyway, I'd read how that plant was used for certain protective charms, and I had just picked some of it earlier. But the weird thing is how the fennel turned into a spear in my hand and I felt myself grow taller and stronger. I pictured a warrior princess from one of the stories we were shown and pretended I was her so I could feel more courageous. Then I made myself think peaceful and compassionate thoughts toward the Wizard."

She stopped to consider, "You know, like shamanic codes in Sophia's books tell you?" She saw both men seemed to understand what she was saying, so she felt encouraged to continue. "His staff sent strong zaps of evil energy toward me, but somehow my spear turned them back on him. But I think a few did get through to me, because I felt nudges of hatred that I had to push away."

She reached down and stroked Rarjer's muzzle. "The animals really were the ones who caught him though. I just helped hold him in place while they dealt with the enchanted beasts and the poor soldiers all tangled up in their silly armor." *It really is a relief to tell someone about my adventure.* She grinned at the two men. Then she remembered the wolf puppy and laid a hand on Rarjer's ruff. "But one of our wolf babies was killed in the fight. He had come out to help and we didn't notice until it was too late to send him back." She fought to keep her emotions in control as tears threatened to well up again.

"You were extremely brave, young woman," said Heironymous. "I would guess that you have the spirit of several of our warrior priestess ancestors working through you." He harrumphed and rather awkwardly patted her on the shoulder. "Your little wolf pup will be honored in his next life too. You may even meet him again, as he passes through."

Kara wondered what he meant by that, but pushed the question aside. She had another issue to deal with first. She said, "I know you are being polite, but would you please not call me 'young woman'? My name is Kara."

The man laughed. "And my name is Heironymous, my friends call me Ron. I am most pleased to make your acquaintance, Priestess Kara."

She began to object again, but Anthony interrupted. "The title is deserved, Kara, for you have clearly studied and passed the initial tests for priestess-hood. Sophia intended for us to give you instructions over the summer, but it seems you have managed the lessons on your own, with the help of magic, of course. Were Sophia here, she would be initiating you herself." Kara could only wonder at this, so she didn't make any more objections.

Glancing at the Wizard lying in a heap, Anthony said to his companion, "We had better get this guy to the show now. I saw some of the night riders lurking at the back of the villa when we were on the rampart. But he's not going to make an entrance on his own now, so what do you suggest we do with him?"

Heironymous looked up at the tower, contemplating. "As you know, when Sep and I saw Carlo with the banditos earlier, we told him we would be watching from the tower after we finished at the cabin. But we hadn't planned on having caught the guy, and only expected to be prepared to surprise him when he came to the villa." Ron paused to think. "So what if we take him up there by the hidden stair? If we just plop him down before the banditti, they might tear him to pieces right there. From the tower, we can make it look like he's still got some spirit left. We can make of him a puppet in truth."

The two men laughed at this mockery of Donnie's position in the church as a puppet of the gangsters. "But of course, what we really want is to expose him as a charlatan practitioner of black magic. Too bad we don't have that creepy bird to use as a prop anymore."

Kara spoke up, "I have the bird right here, or at least what's left of it." Picking up the Wizard's hat with the remains of the bird in it, she held it out to Heironymous. "But, how come you know your way around the villa so well?"

"What?" Heironymous started at the sound of her voice, having momentarily forgot she was listening. "Uh, well yes," he stammered. He took the hat and looked at the broken mess inside. "Thank you, maybe we can still make use of this critter." he mumbled, handing the whole business to Anthony.

Then in answer to Kara's question, he said, "I've been around here for quite some time, Kara. In fact I have lived with Sophia in the villa at times and we have explored quite a few of the secret passages through the years, particularly when we were helping refugees from Nazi persecution." He smiled ruefully at Anthony. "Maybe even you weren't aware of that bit of our history, huh Son?"

Anthony looked nonplused. "Nothing you folks have done can surprise me anymore. You are all our heroes and heroines, you know." He put his arm around the big man's shoulders. "Are you prepared to be exposed again though? You have managed to keep yourself anonymous for quite a while now. This bruha is likely to blow your cover."

"Yeah, I know," grumped the big man. "But I'll be relieved to be myself again. This priest disguise is starting to get old." He looked at Kara. "Your mom will be surprised to see me alive. I believe Sophia led people to think I'd died after the war. It was her contribution to my undercover operation." He chuckled. "Of course Gina, Mario, Anthony, Giuseppe and Sophia kept in touch with me regularly."

"Well enough history lesson for now," said Anthony. "The tower ramparts? Let's get going!"

Heironymous turned to Kara. "It would be most helpful if you and your animal friends stand guard down here. Signal us with a whistle if anything looks suspicious. We can hear you from the tower." He handed her a small bone whistle and squeezed her shoulder warmly. "Just take care not to get into the middle of any standoff. Hide in the tunnels if things get rough down here. This ravine is pretty much out of the way, but you never know. We don't want anything to happen to our newfound priestess."

Anthony added, "If it looks like trouble, I think you should get back to your sisters in the grotto. We will all find our way there after the dust settles anyway." He grinned at her.

"Thanks for all your help." And with a quick hug, he turned and joined Heironymous in carting the Wizard toward the cellar and its hidden stairs to the tower roof.

56

MESSAGES

Gina had waited on the balcony while the others struggled to convince John not to rush downstairs. Now she came into the ballroom and said, "I think I heard something up on the tower rampart, but I can't see up there from here."

The raven, sitting on the balcony ledge, careened its head upward, then spread its wings and took off for the tower. A few moments later, it returned with something in its beak.

Gina took it gingerly from the bird and turned it over in her hand. "Oh!" she exclaimed, still keeping her voice hushed, "It looks like one of Anthony's peace medals. What could this mean? Do you think Tony could be up in the tower with his group of actors?" She held out the object to Mario.

He examined it. "It's the medal from last year's awards. But Tony wasn't the only one to get one of these." He frowned in concentration. "Of course, who else would know how to get up there unseen? And the bird would hardly take something from a stranger. Maybe we'd better send something back as a signal that we know he's there." Mario began digging through his pockets.

"A note would be helpful, maybe," said Gina. "I happened to bring my purse along." She shrugged embarrassedly at Mario's grin. "Weird woman thing, I guess. Never leave without it." She took her small strap bag off her shoulder and began rummaging through it.

"Here's a pad of paper and a pencil. What shall I write?"

"Better keep it brief and simple. Don't give away too much until we're sure it's him." Mario pulled at his ear, "How about something like 'having a ball on the balcony' and sign it G&M. He'd know."

Gina quickly scribbled the note and folded it into a small square. She began to hand it to the raven, then stopped and said, "Should I send up the note pad and pencil too?"

"Good idea, if Melanthus can handle it."

Gina tore off several sheets of the small notepad and wrapped them around the pencil with her note. She held it out and the raven took a firm hold with his beak and flew off instantly.

Mario chuckled. "Our very own messenger raven."

Barbara and John had continued their argument in the ballroom. Now they returned to the balcony. John still looked sullen, but less angry. Barbara said, "Is anything happening?"

"Seems we've got some visitors up in the tower," answered Mario. "Melanthus is carrying messages for us. We think it is Anthony, but we don't know who else."

"What?" John looked startled. "How the hell did he get up there? All the doors were locked, I checked before we started our tour of the house."

Mario exchanged glances with the two women.

"Oh, I get it," said John. "More secret passages." He shrugged as if to say 'I give up.'

Mario grinned and Gina laughed softly. Barbara said, "Now you're catching on," and smiled warmly at John. "We have only begun to explore all the secrets this house holds."

"I'm not at all convinced that I want to know any more of those secrets," replied John with a scowl.

He paused, remembered suddenly that he had no idea where his daughters were at the moment. "Godamighty! I just hope the girls aren't anywhere near here. It's probably a good thing if they went on their excursion to the crypt where they should be safe. Just hope they stay away until whatever this nonsense is blows over." He looked anxiously in every direction from the balcony. "So, what now?" he asked, and glared at all three of them.

"We just wait," answered Gina. Then she extended her hand as Melanthus flew back onto the parapet, landing next to her. She accepted a little rolled paper from his beak. The pencil was included too. "This will give us some answers," she said as she began to unroll the note.

She read it to herself first, smiling and frowning in turns at Anthony's hurried scrawl. Then she passed the note to Mario, who read it aloud to the others, still keeping his voice low.

"Once upon a time," the note began, "a wicked Wizard held a high position in the kingdom. A prince and a very good old friend laid a trap to force the evil one to reveal himself as the source of much wickedness in the land." Mario glanced up at John and Barb's puzzled expressions.

"It's signed 'A.N.Tonini', that's Tony alright. It's a secret signature we invented during the early police raids on the mime troop." He handed the note back to Gina.

"Fairy tales!" exclaimed John disgustedly. "You people are living in lala land here." The others ignored his ranting and puzzled over the cryptic note.

"Should we send another asking for clarification?" asked Barb.

"That seems useless. If he could be clear, he would be. I suspect I know who he means by the Wizard," said Mario, "and the good friend is probably Sep." He looked at Gina for ideas.

"We could just ask what he wants us to do. Our questions will be cleared up later." she suggested sensibly. When Mario nodded assent, she wrote another note, saying "The king and queen stayed in seclusion awaiting word of the princesses. But they were eager to help the prince in his mission."

Melanthus took considerably longer to return from this trip to the tower. When he did, he held a larger object folded into the paper. Gina again accepted the delivery, but when she opened it she handed it directly to Mario without further examination. She looked frightened.

It was a key. The key ring showed the face of a fox. The note read: "The prince's brother has been wounded, and is being tended by the three princesses in their magic cave."

Mario wasn't sure how to explain this to the other couple. He recognized the key for Giuseppe's motorcycle. The 'magic cave' obviously referred to the grotto. But he didn't want to disclose this, the deepest of Rimini secrets, to John, a total unbeliever.

The first rule of the old craft was complete confidentiality and loyalty to the clan's private magic. It was certainly not time to open those ancient mysteries to such judgmental eyes. *If the mysteries even allowed themselves to be opened,* he reflected. *Most likely any attempt at disclosure would be met by severe repercussion to those breaking the trust.* The Strega's rules were eminently fair, but equally stringent in doling penalties to violators.

Mario's mind raced over different options. He decided a lie and a diversion were in order. He showed them the key and said, "It's Tony's motorcycle key. He wants me to bring the bike around from the back of the garage and have it ready for him. If you want to come down with me, John, you can. We can go check on the visitors down there now too."

He gave Gina a hug and kiss on the cheek. As he did so, he tucked the last note into her hand without letting the others see it. "You gals had best stay up here in case there are more messages or some action to witness." He pocketed the key to Giuseppe's motorcycle.

"Melanthus will keep us informed," said Gina to her husband. Barb nodded assent to the plan. Then Mario opened the stairs and climbed down. John, rather shakily, descended after him. Mario hitched his gun in its holster and walked purposefully to the front room. There he stopped to check the time. It was three-ten in the morning. Mario had left one flashlight and the lantern with the women, but John still held the other flashlight. Mario took himself a pocket flashlight and handed John a small handgun from a console by the front door.

John looked at the gun in surprise. "What are you expecting out there?" he asked with a catch in his voice.

"Not expecting anything. Just want to be prepared for the unexpected," said Mario. "You know how to use that thing?"

"Sure. It's been awhile, but I was an officer in the war," answered John as he checked the barrel for bullets, closed it and set the lock. He shoved the gun into one jacket pocket, the flashlight into the other, and said, "Let's go see what's out there."

John headed for the front door and unlocked it, but Mario stopped him from going out that way. Instead, he led him back to Sophia's studio alcove and pushed open the big door that had once been the house's main entrance. Now it was overgrown with vines and he had to lean hard against it to make an opening large enough for them to go through.

John, ducking his head at the low archway, squeezed himself out after Mario. They exited into a tangle of vines and evergreen bushes. Keeping close to the wall of the house, they snuck along it to the adjoining garden wall and a narrow opening that led into the backside of the courtyard.

John held back, hunkering down behind Mario. He peered into the moonlit spaces, his eyes slowly adjusting to the shadowed darkness. He imagined he saw movement and pulled out his revolver with a shaking hand. The faun statue grinned at him from its perch in the middle of the courtyard as if it enjoyed watching John's discomfort.

57

INTO THE TUNNELS

G ina stayed on the balcony alone and read the note Mario
  had tucked into her hand. She knew what she had to do,
but she wasn't sure how to break the news to Barb.

Just then Barb came onto the balcony from the ballroom
after watching the men climb down the ladder. "What news in
this last note?" she asked cheerfully.

Gina handed the little paper to her and Barb read it quickly.
She looked deeply puzzled and said, "What do you make of this
Gina? It seems to say that Tony knows of the girls' whereabouts?"

"That's what I make of it," said Gina, keeping her voice calm
and cheery despite the anxiety she felt. "I think it implies they
have found our old secret Grotto."

"Well," Barbara sighed in relief, "If that's where they are, we
can feel pretty sure they are safe. Right? But who do you think
is wounded?"

"Barb," said Gina with some humor, "do you feel up to
another adventure tonight? I'm thinking I want to go find out
what is going on and be with the girls. They are certainly safest

there if trouble starts here, but they might come back too soon. I just thought I'd make a quick trip down the tunnel from the cellar. You don't have to come along if you'd rather stay and keep an eye on things here."

"Don't be silly," said Barb. "Of course I want to go with you to the Grotto. Now that my memories have been reawakened, I'm eager to explore that wonderful hideout again." She glanced toward the courtyard, "With the men checking on things down there, there is nothing I can do here. They'll be okay. Just some Beltane antics, no doubt."

Gina decided not to remind her sister that everything about the tunnels and grotto was not necessarily safe. "Okay, let's go," she said and turned for the ballroom without looking back into the courtyard.

The two women clambered down the ladder and raised it into position. They had the flashlight and lantern with them, and Gina still carried her purse. Barb grabbed a couple of sweaters from a hook by the kitchen door. They were both wearing their sneakers and comfortable slacks from their afternoon hike in the woods.

Gina opened the door to the wine cellar and they crept down the long-disused stone stairway, Gina leading the way, brushing thick cobwebs from before her. "No one has come this way in years I bet. Wonder why Sophia didn't use the cellar for anything."

Barb was holding her breath, trying not to touch the webs covering every surface. She shivered with a mix of revulsion and excitement. The stairway brought back a memory:

In her memory, she and Gina followed their aunt Sophia down these very steps. They all carried lit candles that sent light bouncing down the walls and created huge shadows of their heads in silhouette. They had been moving to the grotto for safety during the bombing raids of World War Two. They carried candles because the electricity had been turned off for the air raid, and they wanted to save the batteries of their flashlights for use later.

In the cellar, they met Heironymous, who then accompanied them through the tunnel and into the grotto. They had lived down there, in that magic place, for days at a time. Among several other families who joined them there, were Mario and his folks.

Periodically Sophia and others of the adults would make forays up to the villa and neighboring places for supplies and to learn news. Heironymous, whose plane had been shot down in the mountains above the villa a few months earlier, stayed recovering from his wounds in the grotto. He spent most of his time entertaining the children with magic tricks.

This was a very special memory for Barb. She had been a young teenager about Kara's age at the time, and she had been enchanted with the Mage's knowledge of the ancient mysteries and his stories of their ancestors. She realized now that it was through Heironymous, even more than Sophia that she had become interested in the tales and inspired to illustrate them in her painting and writing.

Gina interrupted Barb's reverie as they came to the bottom of the staircase among dusty kegs and bottles. "Looks like someone has been down here pretty recently, after all," said Gina, holding her lantern toward the other side of the square stone-walled room.

Scanning the large area that was clear of cobwebs, they noted the camp stove set up for use in the old hearth. They inspected shelves and saw boxes and bags of personal articles tucked here and there; clothing, boots and shoes, cans of food and jugs of water, shaving paraphernalia, a small mirror.

In a far corner stood a modern camper's latrine. In another corner a bed roll and sleeping bags were stashed. There was even a collection of books neatly stacked on one shelf, which Gina briefly scrutinized_ a mix of history, art, literature, and technical stuff on electronics. There was an herbal medical guide and a tattered copy of a Stregheria meditation book written by Heironymous.

"Someone lives down here," said Gina at last. They looked at each other in amazement. "This must be where Giuseppe hides out."

"Do you suppose Sophia knew?" asked Barb.

"No doubt she would have," said Gina. "He spent a lot of time helping her the last few years. No doubt she helped him when he needed to hide out. That's probably why the stairway was never used."

"But how did he get in and out?" wondered Barbara, looking around for another entrance. Her eye fell on the creaky wooden door in the south wall. She walked to it and pulled it open. "Here is that hidden stairway that goes to the tower roof," she said.

"Shush!" warned Gina, "That's where Anthony is right now, remember? We'd better get on out of here. We don't want to cause them trouble, whatever they're doing up there." Gina went to the north wall where the wine racks stood mostly empty and murmured the secret words. One of the racks slid aside and revealed the opening to the tunnel.

Barb gave a startled cry, seeing the magic performed by her sister. Here was another part of their childhood that she had dismissed as mere fantasy in later years. Now she remonstrated, "How foolish I've been to let myself forget all this amazing stuff! Gina, how will I ever make it up to you and Sophia for turning my back on you all these years?"

"Don't talk about that now," said Gina. "Come along. This is why we came down here, remember? We'd better get going in case Tony and his friends need to use the tunnel."

She entered the tunnel, turned her lantern to a low beam, and pulled Barbara in after her. Then she made a blessing motion toward the house as the partition closed behind them. She dug into her purse and took out two stems of fennel, one of which she handed to Barb. When her sister looked surprised, Gina said, "I never leave home without it!" She grinned and beckoned Barb to follow her.

They walked quickly through the tunnel, noting scuff marks that proved others had traveled there recently. They came to a crevice that opened out behind the villa and stopped to peruse some deep scrapings that indicated something heavy had been pulled through there. Barb picked up a crumpled hawk's feather and tucked it into her pocket. But they chose not to investigate this situation any further now.

Continuing down the passage at a fast walk, they both were deep in thought, and didn't speak. Gina mentally prepared for finding the girls in serious trouble, perhaps tending a severely wounded Giuseppe. *Of course,* she recalled, *Mimi had already demonstrated considerable healing skills and Kara certainly was clever enough to devise splints and bandages. But, drat it,* she swore to herself, *I should have thought to bring along medications.* Gina chastised herself for not preparing better for an emergency.

Barbara was lost in memories of happy times in the Grotto. She recalled the ceremonies Sophia led them in, and the fun of camping out in the magic cave, as they called it. Another memory tickled at the corner of her mind too. Something about invisible beings who could only be seen by the children and Sophia. And Heironymous. *We were too young to realize the tragedy and danger of our situation. To us it was all a magical adventure.* She smiled thinking that now her daughters could enjoy that magic too.

Gina's sixth sense was alert for any signs of the magic folk. She'd had no direct contact with the fairies since childhood, but she knew they still habited these underground spaces unhampered by modern life. Sophia had sometimes spoken of seeing them in her wanderings about the woods too. Now, Gina sent a prayer to her deceased aunt to help her be receptive to the secret Being's if they needed to connect with her.

Twirling the fennel branch she held, Gina silently called to the invisible ones and the fairies, reassuring them that she and Barb meant them no harm, but wanted their help if such were needed. Suddenly a shimmering light shown about them in the tunnel.

Barb stood behind Gina, gazing in wonder as rainbow hued waves danced across the walls and over their heads. A subtle spicy scent filled the air and the gentlest breeze stroked their faces. A soft chorus of piping, humming, buzzing, drumming, laughing tones accompanied the spectacle.

Gina was drawn into the music. The sounds felt as if they were coming from within her head, yet also from far away. After a few minutes she said in a voice not quite her natural one, "We are allowed to enter the grotto, but must not interfere with what we find there."

She looked at Barbara, seeing her through a haze. "The magic is already underway. If you harbor any doubts of its reality, you must not come any farther. Your unbelief would cause the magic to leave and that would open the way for the evil ones to enter."

Barb hardly recognized her gentle sister. Gina suddenly appeared fierce. Her dark hair was wreathed in a golden halo and although she still wore her casual clothing, she was veiled in a gossamer robe. She held the stance and gestures of a priestess, commanding vows from an acolyte. The fennel branch in her hand had become a witch's Athame. Barb felt awed and very frightened.

"Maybe you'd better go ahead without me," said Barb in a small voice. "I, I don't know what I believe anymore. I'm afraid of the magic." She looked about to cry in her frustration. "I guess I don't belong here anymore." Tears spilled down her cheeks.

"Please forgive me," she pleaded. "I don't want to interfere in the magic. I want to believe, but I'm not sure I can overcome all the years of denial. It's been too long and this is all happening too fast." She turned and fled back up the tunnel sobbing.

Gina, still in the aura of fairy-spell, called out, "Don't run away. This is a chance to test your faith. You know we want you here with us."

But Barb did not turn back and Gina did not go after her.

58

IN THE COURTYARD

Mario crept along the darkest edge of the courtyard, his gun cocked. A shadow by the gate had an unusual shape to it, but it did not move. Something in the tree branches over-hanging the wall glittered with reflected moonlight. *The eye of a night creature? The reflection of a knife or gun?* Mario watched closely. It blinked or flashed. Once. Twice. Once again. Then it disappeared. *A signal?*

Mario stood stone still. A movement caught the corner of his eye and he spun to face it. Just the wind rustling the leaves of the acanthus vine on the wall. *Except there was no wind tonight.*

Mario spoke. "Alright. Whoever you are, show yourself. We've got you covered." *The words sounded so trite. Why am I acting like a cop in a B-grade movie?*

Mario felt foolish as he waited for a response that was slow in coming. He saw that John had his gun cocked too, and felt slightly less the fool. "You see sumthn?" asked John in a low growl. "I think there's someone behind the fountain."

Mario took a step toward the vine that had moved. "In here too," he said as he reached to pull back a branch.

"Jeez, Mister Pozzuoli, don't shoot!" said a frightened voice in the shrubbery. The man who stepped out was dressed all in black and carrying only a stick, but Mario saw the hilt of a knife protruding from the top of the guy's boot. He looked vaguely familiar.

"Who are you, and what are you doing here?" demanded Mario in his best trial lawyer's voice. "Tell your pals to show themselves too. Now."

Two more men in black stepped out from behind the fountain, and one jumped down from the oak tree. They moved with quiet assurance, catlike, unperturbed. These three wore masks so Mario didn't recognize them at all. He waved them toward the garden wall with his pistol. They obliged and stood together quietly. One glanced up toward the tower.

Mario didn't take his own eyes off his captives. "Give me the story," he said. "What's going on here?"

John remained by the back wall, his gun pointed toward the four men, and scanned the courtyard for others still in hiding. Some shuffling sounds came from the other side of the wall, in the orchard. John strode to the gate and shined his flashlight into the trees. Two figures hightailing into the woods stopped abruptly at John's voice. "Halt or I'll shoot."

They turned to face him. More black masks and riding gear. "Get on in here with your buddies," commanded John, authoritatively brandishing his gun. It was a small women's handgun, and he was aware of looking a bit silly. But the two men came inside the courtyard willingly enough. They both sent a glance up to the tower as they joined the others.

"Is this all of you?" asked Mario. Their silence suggested there were more. "Well, give us the scoop. I'm aware that you are members of the Benandanti Banditos. I'm on your side, so you don't have to be afraid of arrest here. We just need to know what you're up to, hanging around this man's property." He nodded toward John, who stood to his right, still scanning and listening, hawk-like. John's large size and commanding military attitude added credence to Mario's warning.

At last one of the masked men spoke. But before he began, he again shot a glance toward the top of the tower. John followed his gaze, but saw nothing more than the saw-toothed outline of the crenellated parapet against a moonlit sky. He wondered what Anthony was doing up there, and imagined he saw a gargoyle-like shape duck behind the wall. He dismissed it as a cloud's shadow. *But it was a cloudless night.*

"We tried to give you warning to leave, Mister Marini," said the spokesman of the group. John recognized the voice of Carlo, but chose not to acknowledge him. Carlo coughed and continued, "It's been rumored that the Wizard was planning to pull some tricks here tonight, as a way to scare you and your family away from the villa." Again he looked toward the tower.

This time Mario looked up there too. He knew Anthony was there with others, but wondered what these fellows were watching for. A signal of some kind, no doubt. *But a signal for what? And from whom?*

All was quiet throughout the house. Mario stole a glance at the secret balcony too. He was glad to see that Barb and Gina were staying out of sight.

John cleared his throat and said, "What the devil are you people up to anyway? Is this a weird Beltane ritual or something? All night we've been besieged by bizarre events and cryptic warnings." He looked directly at Carlo. "I think you'd better clue us in, because I'm not leaving until I get answers and see this bedevilment done with."

"You'll find out soon enough, Mister Marini," answered Carlo. He kept watching the tower.

John brandished his gun. "I want some answers now, Carlo." As he spoke, a flare shot up from the top of the tower. In its glare, the tower shown bright as day.

Three figures stood at the edge of the parapet.

59

A BATTLE OF MAGICS

A nthony and Heironymous had a bit of a tussle to get the unconscious Wizard up to the tower by the secret stairway. The man wasn't overly large, but his robes added bulk to his deadweight. Carrying him between them, Tony and the priest maneuvered through the wine cellar as quietly as possible, hoping no one upstairs heard and came to investigate.

Tony had expected his parents to take John and Barb to their house for the night, except that finding the girls in the Grotto made him realize their parents could be out looking for them now. *That would only add confusion to the chaos,* he thought.

They struggled up the narrow staircase, bumping the limp Wizard's head against the wall a few times. They stopped to make sure they weren't detected by anyone inside the house. Finally they made it to the roof of the tower without incident and dumped their burden unceremoniously on the floor.

The Wizard began to come around. He moaned and twisted on the slate floor where they had dumped him. He opened his eyes, blinking in the light of the moon, and gazed dazedly at the two men standing over him. "Wha ?" he sputtered, coughing and struggling to rise.

"Don't bother to get up," said Heironymous, placing a booted foot against the Wizard's chest to push him back down. "We'll let you know when it's time for you to play your part."

"Whuda hell," the Wizard said, struggling harder against his captor's weight. "Lemmeup! Where's my bird?" he looked about him frantically. "Get me my bird!" his voice raised to a squeaky pitch in his frantic fury.

Anthony laughed. "Your bird's been dismantled," said Tony, "but we saved a few pieces for you." He pulled some feathers and a mangled wire wing from inside the Wizard's hat. "You could try to reconstruct him again if you'd like." said Tony, tossing the mess beside the man lying face up on the floor.

The Wizard grabbed for the feathers and hugged them to his breast, moaning again to himself and writhing on the ground. Suddenly he went silent and still, staring wide-eyed toward the northern parapet.

The raven had alighted. It eyed the group menacingly before it flew off into the trees beyond the orchard.

Anthony shrugged and returned his attention to the Wizard, who was still staring open-mouthed at the spot where the bird had taken off.

A small winged dragon perched in the raven's place.

Heironymous laughed and reached forth with a fennel wand drawn from his jacket, waved it toward the little creature and made it disappear. "Woops," said the Mage, "I didn't mean to bring him up here just yet."

Anthony stared at him. "What was that? I thought you'd given up conjuring magical creatures when you took to wearing the priestly collar."

"Just needed to see if I could still do it, I guess," answered Heironymous with a chuckle. "Cute little bugger though, wasn't he? I think we can use him here in a little while. Just wait." He winked wickedly at the Wizard.

"Well," said Tony with a sigh, "We came up here to put on a show, I guess. You're the ringmaster, so tell me, what now?"

"Looks like we'll just have ourselves a real old-fashioned spirit battle. May the best specter win," chuckled Heironymous, throwing another piece of broken wiring down to the Wizard, who was furiously focused on his wrecked bird-contraption. "Old Wizzie here will see to that, you can be sure. He's not about to give up without one more skirmish between his hawk and our dove."

"I don't get it," said Tony. "Why is this so important to the old coot? He's got all the power he needs in his position at the Vatican. Why keep dabbling in the Black Arts?"

"It's his wizardly pride," said the Mage, Heironymous. "Always has wanted to acquire the Rimini magic for himself. Ironically, he never realized that his avowed enemies were related to him by marriage. The world works in strange ways, doesn't it.?"

The Wizard fiddled with the feathers and wire in his lap. Shortly he stood up, holding before him a re-contrived version of his mangled bird.

"Good work, Donnie, my old theology instructor," said Heironymous. "You have proven yourself a master at deviltry, just as your church's witch-hating minions taught." The Mage thumped the Wizard's back. "You are Satan's true son, as they say."

The Wizard said nothing, but looked balefully at Heironymous.

Tony and the Mage gathered the weakened Wizard between them to stand at the parapet. Heironymous made a few healing gestures to help restore some of the Wizard's power. Just enough to provoke a believable demonstration of his evil intent, but not enough to overturn his captors.

"Let the show begin," said the Mage. With a flick of his wand, the dragon specter returned to his side, spewing match-sized flicks of flame. "Dragon's blood lives. May the Hawk be downed and its master exposed," chanted Heironymous. "Let the battle engage!"

The Wizard shook with rage as he let his flying contraption loose and watched the Mage's little dragon bring it down in flames within seconds. He ranted curses to color the air around them purple. But the little dragon merely flew back to perch and sat bowing arrogantly next to the laughing Mage.

Suddenly the Wizard pulled himself up to full height and stuck out his arms, causing the two men holding him to fall back for a second. The robes around him formed wings. He leapt to the parapet ledge and prepared to push off, but Tony and Heironymous each grabbed at his arms and legs, trying to pull him away from the edge. In his weakened state, they believed the Wizard could never conjure strength for a true flight. He would fall and kill himself. They didn't want that. They needed him alive to prove his evil doing. Otherwise the authorities could turn the whole thing against them claiming the Benandanti had bewitched their minister.

Rather than take that chance, Heironymous the Mage released his spell on the Wizard and allowed the man's full strength to return. *Better he get away than we trap ourselves in his demise*, thought the wise man. To Tony he just said, "Might as well let him fly. Maybe he'll give himself away without our help."

As they released their hold on him, the Wizard took off from the tower in a swooping glide, heading across the orchard to the trees beyond, where he would disappear into the night and foil all their hard-won effort. It had been a good plan and everything had seemed to fall into place. *Where did I go wrong?* Worried the Mage, as he watched the Wizard fly away.

Melanthus, the raven, reappeared on the parapet at that moment, taking a perch next to the little dragon. "Craaack, Caw, Craack" said the bird and hopped to Heironymous' shoulder, then down his arm. It began pecking at something on the Mage's belt.

Heironymous looked down and saw the grenade given him by the lioness in her cave. He'd forgotten about it. He grabbed the grenade, sighted on the trajectory of the Wizard's flight, pulled the pin with his teeth and lobbed it in a high curving arc to land on target where the evil one flew. It exploded in a very satisfactory discharge, bursting woodland debris into the Wizard's flight path. The detonation caused momentary confusion in which the evil one seemed about to stall for a dive. Then he turned in midair, heading blindly back toward the villa.

60

BARBARA'S TEST

B arbara turned away from Gina and ran back through the tunnel toward the villa. Anguish tore her heart as she fought against doubts solidified by years of denial and struggled to regain her childhood faith.

The vile accusations made by churches and governments against witchcraft, the centuries of secrecy and dwindling faith among the pagan peoples, the seductive power of modern civilization and its materialistic philosophies had all worked to turn Barbara away from the truth of her upbringing. For so long she had lived in denial, pretending to her husband and family that the stories of her early years were merely fantasy.

Yet, she had continued to tell the tales, for she'd insisted on keeping the legend alive for her daughters regardless of her husband's disapproval. Now the girls were caught up in the magic, despite her negligence in teaching them correctly. Yet she, herself, felt closed off from the mystery.

Blinded by her tears, she ran stumbling through the tunnel until she bumped into something soft, but firm. She screamed and skidded to a stop, her body vibrating with fright. She aimed her flashlight downward.

Toby, the cat, blocked her way.

With a sob of relief, she bent to scratch the cat's ears. "Where did you come from, kitty? I thought you would be with my girls down in the grotto."

Toby rubbed against Barb's leg and she felt comforted. "I'm very glad for your company," she said, wiping at her tears and looking around. She realized she might be trapped. "I don't know where I'm going, Toby. I don't know the secret words to open the door back into the house. Will you show me how to get home?"

The cat arched its back and stretched. Taking only a few paces forward, it stopped at a gap in the tunnel wall. Barb came over and peered into the opening that led to a circular stand of trees with a small pond in the center.

"This opens into the Grove!" She took a few tentative steps into the narrow passage. The cat sidled between her legs, running on ahead. It stopped and looked back as if to say, "Come on, I know where we are."

Barb decided to trust the cat, although she was aware of long-repressed memories tugging at her. *Why do I get a chill here?* She thought to herself. *Seems there was something about this place that scared me as a kid.*

She entered the Grove on tiptoe. All was still. The moon, reflecting in the circular pond, glimmered invitingly. Barbara crept to the edge of the water and gazed into the pool's depths.

An image appeared that took her breath.

Aunt Sophia, herself, smiled up at her from the mirror of moonlight. She wore a crown of flowers and looked as she had when the girls first came to live with her over thirty years ago. Barbara recalled that Sophia always wore a wreath of flowers when she danced at the summer festivals.

Memories washed over her of the shy dread she'd felt toward the magic folk as a child. Gina had held no such fears and quickly joined in the frolic. When the animals talked and the fairies danced and the great horned god and the moon goddess sat on their thrones, Barb would watch transfixed, but seldom dared to join her sister in the merry making.

Something held me back from accepting the mystery. Yet, Sophia always assured me that I needn't follow along with the ritual celebrations if I didn't wish to. Sophia said the goddess never forced or commanded fealty.

Now, although Sophia's image in the pool did not speak, it conveyed a strong message in memory of her love for Barbara and Gina and of her assurance that her love would never die. Barbara suddenly knew herself to be forgiven, and she wept in the hush of that mystery.

"Thank you dear goddess," she whispered into the night.

She walked to the cairn of rocks at the glade's edge. Pulling herself up on to one of the stone seats, she sat and looked about her. She breathed deeply and felt truly at peace for the first time in years.

Her thoughts turned to her troubled marriage and she suddenly wanted to share this feeling of contentment with her tormented husband. She desperately wanted to help him accept the mystery and feel its healing forgiveness.

Toby leapt over the rocks and perched himself on the other throne seat next to her. She met his gaze. Amber eyes glittering moonbeams, he spoke and she heard him unquestioningly.

"If you want to help John learn to believe in the magic," said the orange tabby, "you will need to bring him here for healing. Evil has entered the villa gate, but is being banished by great forces of good. Your husband is still unable to distinguish the good from the evil. He is in great danger of selecting the wrong course and bringing tragedy down on himself and all of us."

The little cat spoke with the voice of a whispering wind, but Barbara was able to hear him clearly. *How is this possible?* She asked herself. *Does it mean my own magic has come back to me? Will I be able to join with the others now in the healing work? Oh how I hope so! I must let myself believe and accept this miracle without ever doubting again!*

The cat turned his gaze to the moon. Barbara took in his cryptic message thoughtfully. She said, "What must I do?"

"Learn to believe in yourself first," said the cat. "Use the magic you were born with. Create beauty from within your soul. Dance to the music of your own spirit." At her doubtful glance, he added, "Your inner magic will captivate him as it always has."

Toby stared intensely at Barbara, and as he did so, she felt a glowing start from deep in her core. A warmth suffused her and she saw herself reflected in his eyes. She was transfigured. Her face shone with inspired beauty. She radiated joy and laughter, sorrow and weeping, anger and grief and deep sexual desire. Her passionate feelings intermingled to manifest as an irresistible erotic magnetism.

She began to shy away, started to turn aside and flee from this terrible power, this fearsome responsibility. But the cat laid a paw on her shoulder and licked the tears from her cheeks.

When she opened her eyes toward his again, she found herself looking into the face of a handsome horned man, wearing a crown of leaves and carrying a flute. He held out his hand, and she took it and together they danced around the magic Grove to the song of his piping.

With Pan, Barbara became the goddess Shakti and remembered again how to sing and dance, how to create beauty from her vivid imagination, and how to love. Time moved out of time. They were observed by the fairies of the Grove and blessed by the moon.

But the magical moment was interrupted by a great crashing and explosion from the direction of the villa. They stopped dancing in mid-step, clung to each other briefly, and then became Barbara, the woman and Toby, the cat once again.

The cat put his ears back and hunched himself.

But Barbara remained goddess-empowered, fueled by her renewed faith. She listened to the noise echoing through the woods and discovered she still had the fennel stalk Gina had given her. She watched in amazement as it became a sharp knife in her hand.

She gripped the weapon and headed into the woods, running toward the villa. Toby ran ahead, showing her the way.

61

PYROTECHNIQUES

John and the group of men in the courtyard stared up at the tower where lightning-like flames lit up three figures. The one in the center wore a tall pointed hat and billowing robes. On his right stood another figure dressed in black like the banditti, but he was the biggest man John had ever seen. He looked like a giant. On the left stood a tall fellow wearing ordinary jeans and t-shirt, but his red hear blew about his head like the flames of a torch.

More flares burst and eerie screeching sounds whistled through the skies like bombs falling in war. The figure in the center held a large cumbersome object before him in both hands, evidently preparing to drop it onto those below. The object squirmed and flashed electrical sparks from outspread bat's wings.

John stood astounded and terrified at the spectacle. *Am I losing my mind? None of this can really be happening,* one part of his mind told him. Another part of his mind said *it's the very kind of thing I've always imagined witches to do* and he crossed himself against the evil. Yet, still another portion of John's consciousness realized that *whatever these banditti are up to, it is not they who are evil. Something evil is out there. These guys are fighting it.*

John stood frozen to the spot as fireworks burst around them. It was like a Mardi Gras festival gone amok. The whole courtyard was aglow in the light of small flares. John blinked. He had to be seeing things. The lights were coming from the wings of very tiny individuals. *People, not bugs. Fairies? "No way,"* said John's rational mind.

Someone laid a hand on John's shoulder and he flinched, expecting a confrontation. But it was Mario who said, "We better just sit back and watch now, John. This thing is way out of our hands."

"Well, that's an understatement if I ever heard one," said John, with a sneer. "Can you tell me what's going on? Is it a Beltane bruha of some sort or what?"

"Best I can make out is that there was a plot to scare you and your family away from Italy, but it has been diverted by the banditti. I have no idea exactly what and how." answered Mario in a whisper. "The good guys have the upper hand here, anyhow, and the only Malandanti in sight is the fellow up there standing between Tony and..."

Their conversation was interrupted as the men around them all began a rhythmic chanting and hooting. They sounded like a cross between wild cats in rut and a pack of hyenas on the prowl. John said, "It seems the whole world has gone crazy." He sat back in a crouch against the courtyard wall. He intended to watch the show as Mario had suggested, but also to keep an eye on those weirdoes on the tower. *One of them might be Mario's son, but that doesn't make him any less crazy than the rest of them,* thought John.

At this moment the guy in the pointed hat let loose the contraption he'd been hanging onto. It zoomed off toward the woods above the trees in a shower of sparks, with a roaring hiss. Then, fast on the flying gizmo's tail came another surreal creature. This one looked like a dragon from the marquee of a Chinese fun house at the carnival. It had a snake-like body with razor-back spine, alligator-like legs with claws back and front, a spear-tipped tail, bat wings, a long snout shooting flames through its nostrils, and eyes that blazed like rubies.

The two uncanny creatures turned upon each other to engage a battle in the sky. But it lasted only seconds. The dragon quickly got the upper hand of the mechanized bird which simply exploded and fell apart on contact. Another explosion could be heard where the thing hit the earth. The dragon flew back and perched on the tower next to the giant. It sat there bowing and blowing multi-colored spangles toward the moon.

The men on the ground raised a cheer.

John began to feel irritated at the pyro-technics. "Just a bunch of smoke and mirrors," he muttered, "Like a two-bit carnival show." But his sneer died in his throat at the next episode.

Up on the tower another sort of battle had started. The guy in the robes was struggling against the others. He seemed to be trying to fly off the parapet himself, or jump. It seemed the other two were trying to prevent him from killing himself, or escaping. John couldn't guess.

He watched, dumbstruck, as the fellow tore himself loose of his captors, spread his cloak into bat-wings, took a literal flying leap, and sailed above the trees. But another blast went off just where the madman seemed about to descend. Debris flew from the trees, striking the guy in the face and disorienting him. The air-born man turned around in mid-flight, aiming for the sea off to the west, but he lost buoyancy just as he came above the courtyard.

He crashed to the ground in a fizzle of spent magic, landing square in the fountain at the feet of the grinning faun.

Several of the banditti surrounded the fountain, their weapons at hand. John followed them to observe the bedraggled and drenched Wizard being fished out of the water. Gasping and sputtering, the guy swore a streak of curses unfit even the crudest of street fighters. He waved his arms, making vows to call down Satan's minions upon the entire world.

John had never seen such wretchedness, even in his worst witch nightmares. *Who the hell is this vile creep anyway?* He wondered, and was given his answer almost immediately.

Mario, who had been standing back to let the others handle the Wizard, now stepped forward. He put his arm across John's shoulders. "You had better be prepared for a shock, old man." said Mario. "This is the one responsible for setting the edicts against us. I believe you know him in his more honorable role as the Vatican's Minister of Cultural Affairs."

Mario's words didn't register with John immediately. But then the man in the soggy pointed hat turned his face toward him. The baleful grin he bestowed on John made his spine crawl.

And then recognition registered.

"Donnie?" said John with a gasp. "Is that really you?"

"Known better to us as the Vatican's Vulture," said Carlo, laughing bitterly and tightening his hold on Donnie's arm.

62

PRIESTESS KARA

After Anthony and Heironymous left them to wait and keep watch in the ravine, Kara laid a hand gently on Rarjer's back and they walked together into the copse of trees. Kara sat down on a stump and the wolf lay down at her feet. The lioness made herself a comfortable perch on a large boulder at the edge of the ravine.

The raven came to sit on a tree branch near Kara. She looked up at the bird and addressed him respectfully, saying "Your presence here is a great source of comfort to me, Melanthus. I thank you."

Only the night-sounds of the mountain came to them for the next hour or so and Kara reflected in amazed wonder on all that had just happened.

But she reminded herself that she must not doubt, for clearly she was involved in some enchanted and mysterious events far beyond her understanding. *I must continue to believe in the magic without question for now. I can look for the answers to my questions later.*

Her reverie was interrupted by a sudden commotion at the rear of the villa, by the courtyard gate. Shouting, whistling, and a great explosion erupted.

The wolf and lion immediately struck out through the woods to come from behind at whatever was taking place. Melanthus cawed at her twice and flew along with them.

Ignoring Anthony's advice to go to the grotto, Kara followed her wild animal companions at a racer's pace. She caught up to them in the woods behind the orchard. They were inspecting a smoldering log and newly scattered debris from an explosion.

Kara stood between them, puzzling over the strange sight, but since nothing seemed to be seriously damaged, she turned her attention toward the cacophony of voices in the courtyard.

She leaned down between the two animals and spoke to them. "We are going in there, okay? You stay by me and don't make trouble unless I tell you to."

Then she pulled out her fennel stalk and the sacred dagger. She closed her eyes and conjured the image of the warrior priestess, sending a prayer again to the goddess.

She looked up at the full moon that still rode high above the villa's rooftops and breathed deeply of the mountain air. Her backpack became a quiver full of arrows and she saw the fennel stalk become a strongly fashioned bow in her hand. She felt herself metamorphose the warrior queen's height and strength. She felt the ancestral spirit infuse her own.

They walked in line, keeping a measured pace. The raven flew down and perched securely on Kara's shoulder, lending his strength to that of the others.

Waiting and watching a few minutes longer, Kara and her companions then stepped out of the orchard, through the gate, and into the courtyard.

63

JOHN'S REVELATIONS

John stood speechless while Mario watched sympathetically. "I wouldn't have wanted you to find out this way, John," Mario said, "but I guess it was the Wizard's own plan to bedevil you enough that you would be scared back to the States." Mario grasped John's shoulder and said, "I'll bet he never intended for you to discover his true identity, however."

The wet Wizard said nothing. He just glared at them both.

But the show was not over. A trumpet blast from the tower called everyone's attention. The big fellow standing there extended his arm toward the orchard beyond the gate. The group in the courtyard turned to the gate in unison, anticipating another astonishing spectacle. They were not to be disappointed.

John and Mario turned toward the gate and saw a mythic vision emerge from the woods.

The tall slender woman paced serenely between two elegant animals-- a wolf and a lion. The entire group in the courtyard, including the wicked Wizard, stood awestruck as the trio strode purposefully in through the open gate.

On the tower parapet, Heironymous and Tony watched Kara and the animals enter the courtyard. They saw the glimmering light envelope the trio, and knew their young priestess was protected by higher beings. The Mage knew she was channeling the spirit of a warrior priestess from her family lineage. To Anthony, she appeared as the Huntress Goddess, the Lady of the Beasts.

Those down in the courtyard bowed to her, saying, "Welcome Diana-Artemis, Guardian of the Wilds. Let the power of your weapons banish evil from our midst." It was an ancient pagan ritual prayer, customarily given on Beltane and other holy festival days. Tonight, to the group at the villa, it was more than mere ritual.

Everyone in the courtyard stood entranced by the apparition of a maiden warrior goddess flanked by a huge silver wolf on her left, and on her right, a majestic golden lioness. She carried a silver bow with a quiver of arrows over her shoulder, and a finely honed silver dagger hung from a loop on her belt. She wore a short doeskin tunic and knee-high moccasins. Her hair was pulled back and plaited with wildflowers.

The moon cast a shimmering aura around the three figures.

For a few moments everything was quiet. Then John's mind registered the reality of who stood before them. "It's Kara! What kind of witchery is this?" Looking madly around him, he hollered, "Get those beasts away from my little girl!"

Pulling his gun, he aimed at the lion and shot.

The shot rang loud in the stillness of the courtyard. The lioness jerked back with a roar. Kara instinctively pulled a fennel stick from her pocket and held it before her. This time it became a lethal sword, flashing sparks of lightning.

Without taking her eyes off the group of men standing before her, Kara reached out to touch the wounded lioness' shoulder. A trickle of blood oozed down from her right ear. The bullet had grazed the right side of Farah's head.

Now provoked, the wildcat was primed to attack, and snarling viciously. Rarjer stepped to the side of the lioness, and she calmed somewhat, allowed the wolf to lick her wound.

Kara faced her audience. She saw her father with gun still raised to fire again. "If you dare to shoot again, I will not hesitate to use this blade against you." Kara spoke in a stern, deadly serious voice. "If anyone causes harm to these animals, I will personally take vengeance against your very soul."

John lowered the gun, looking stunned at his daughter's words.

Kara's human consciousness was shocked at the words that came from her mouth too, for she had never dared speak to her father in such defiant tones. Although she was very willing to defend her animal companions, the powerful rage she felt at this moment was not entirely her own. Another spirit inhabited her now, just as when she'd fought the Wizard in the tunnel.

And here he was again, the miserable fiend. The warrior priestess, Kara, sneered at him. "Just what do you think you are doing here in this sacred place, you vile scum." She felt great satisfaction to see he was afraid of her. She reveled in this new sense of power.

Kara became aware of fluttering points of light all around the courtyard. The fairies! A whole army of them seemed to have gathered to lend her their magic. Kara smiled. *I have truly become a believer, she thought in amazement. Not only do they no longer fear me, but they have come to my aid. Than you, goddess,* she prayed, *please guide me now.*

Kara hefted her silver bow, notched an arrow, and aimed at the Wizard's heart. Several men in black stood around the evil one, holding him from escaping. He looked as if he would run at the first chance, but then she noted a subtle change take over his features. He glanced from her father to her and back again.

The Wizard spoke in a quavering voice, directing his remarks to Kara's father. "So, John, I'm glad you are here to witness the terrible witchery taking place. See how they have bewitched your own daughter. And look at what they have tried to make of me. Go ahead and shoot the beast. It will help break the spell." He looked pleadingly at John, as if the two of them were allied against the rest.

John was tempted. This was his cousin Donnie, with whom he'd had lunch and learned of the debauched underground movement. His nephew was part of that movement. Mario seemed to side with the outlaws as well. The edict against Beltane revelries seemed to make more sense to John, now that he'd witnessed what he thought was its method. He began to nod assent to his cousin, but something hit him just above his right eye and his attention was distracted.

"Ouch!" Bringing his hand to his face, he bent to pick up the shiny object. It was just a shiny mica pebble. "Who threw this?" John bawled in agitation. No one answered. He pocketed the little missile with a shrug. A trickle of blood ran down his temple.

Others in the group could see the flickering lights, and some even saw tiny creatures with wings flitting in and among them. Most felt calmed by a fluttering breeze that seemed to whisper "Be still, it is going to be okay."

But John saw and felt none of this faerie magic. He only saw his daughter standing between two normally dangerous wild animals in total confidence and ease. He saw his cousin, whom he barely knew, dressed in absurd robes and pointed hat, wielding a rather limp wand. Things had gotten far too goofy for him to figure out.

Ignoring the Wizard's continued pleading, he sat down on the bench by the faun statue and buried his face in his hands.

64

VIEW FROM THE RAMPART

B arbara and the cat raced up to the front of the mansion. The porch light was on, but otherwise the house was dark. The noise seemed to be coming from the back, in the courtyard. Barb climbed the portico steps and opened the front door cautiously. Toby slipped inside and she followed, quietly shutting the door behind them.

It took a moment for her eyes to adjust. Through the glass patio doors she could vaguely discern movement in the moon-shadowed courtyard, but she could not make out what was going on.

Rather than walk directly into the melee, she took the bedroom stairs up to the tower rampart, where she could get a bird's eye view. She'd got all the way to Mimi's bedroom loft before she recalled that Anthony and some friends had been up on the rampart earlier. Were they still there, or had they gone to join the action below?

Barb didn't hesitate, for she still embodied the charisma and determination of the goddess from her transformation in the

Grove. She opened the door leading to the roof and bounded up the stairs. Barb made the top ahead of the cat, who collided into her legs as she came to an abrupt halt.

Four figures were silhouetted at the parapet in the glare of flares going off below. Two of them were men and the other two looked like birds. *Probably Melanthus and a friend,* she thought. The two men turned at hearing her enter. They came toward her and she held her knife ready to defend herself. Then she recognized Tony and tucked her knife into her belt.

"Anthony?" she said, "It's just me, Aunt Barb. Don't worry, I'm not here to cause trouble. I just wanted to see what is going on down there." Tony stood quiet and looked up at the big man beside him. Both seemed stunned. "Tony, what's wrong? Tell me what's going on, please!"

Then she looked at the other man and gasped.

Barb and the two men stared at each other, mouths agape, for several seconds. The men saw another goddess apparition before them. Barb saw a man she had believed was dead.

The cat jumped up on the parapet with the raven and the dragon, both of whom seemed totally unperturbed. Toby nodded a rather condescending cat-greeting to them, and all three creatures turned their attention back to the activity going on below.

Barb broke the silence. "Heironymous! Is it really you? Oh how I've longed to see you again and talk to you these last couple of days!" She took a step forward and he came to her with his arms outstretched.

The giant-sized man picked her up and hugged her as if she were a long lost child. Then he set her down and said, "Barbara, we waited for you to come back all these years. Sophia must be very happy to see you here now at last!" He laughed, then in seriousness said "But clearly you have made connection with the mystery yourself. Though your own beauty shines through the disguise, you are another vision of goddess-power, just as your daughter is at this moment, down there in the garden."

At these words, Barb recalled her purpose and went quickly to look down into the courtyard. Her hand flew to her mouth at the sight of Kara and the wild animals facing off the group of men. At first she wasn't able to make out who was who among them.

Anthony and Heironymous came and stood on either side of her. Then a shot was fired and Barb recognized the man with the gun as her husband. She wanted to shout to him to stop, but the Mage gave her shoulder a squeeze, warning her not to call out.

Barb watched open-mouthed, as Kara stood up for the animals against John's ranting. She felt tremendous pride in her daughter and knew then, that Kara, for one, was definitely safe in the goddess' protection. She breathed a silent prayer of thanks.

From the tower parapet Barbara watched the drama escalate.

A man in a tall pointed hat was waving his arms angrily. His shouting was garbled and those watching from the tower could only make out a few words. "Curse you Witch!... may Satan rape you!... beget abominations!_ Devil's spawn!" and other phrases familiar to those having knowledge of the infamous church doctrine of the thirteenth century, called the 'Witches Hammer' written, some say, by the Devil, himself.

Barbara looked at her companions and whispered "Who is that vile man?"

Heironymous chuckled.

Anthony answered her. "You will be shocked to learn he is John's own cousin, the cultural minister of the Vatican." Tony stopped to glean Barb's reaction. Seeing that she seemed only mildly surprised, he continued. "He is, in fact, a practicing Wizard of black magic, though not a very good one. His duplicity extends in many directions, for he is also a minion of the mafia, serving as their watchdog in the church."

Barbara exclaimed, "That creepy little man? He holds all that power?" She looked amused as well as baffled.

"So he believes," laughed Heironymous. "I've had considerable close dealings with him over the years, and have come to know how fearful and weak his so-called power is." Sobered, the Mage said, "Yet, those with less knowledge of the magic arts can be easily fooled. So he has managed to turn many against the Strega over the years, for he hates and fears the good magic of witchcraft above all."

"My goodness" exclaimed Barbara. "To think he is actually related to my husband. I always knew John's family was anti-Strega, but I'd never guessed my husband came from such evil stock."

"It was this guy who set the edict against Beltane this year," added Tony.

Barb silently contemplated her own potential role as she beheld the continuing drama below them. *I see now that my marriage to John may have had a deeper purpose than we could ever have imagined. Sophia,* she recalled now, *once intimated to me that I might have a signal part in overcoming evil forces through my marriage.*

Although Sophia had been saddened at our moving to the States, she had never openly objected to my relationship to someone from a family with mob connections. It had surprised me a bit at the time, but I never bothered to ask Sophia what she knew. Now it begins to be clearer, but I still didn't see what action I can take.

Suddenly a commotion grew around the group at the fountain. Barb saw that John was sitting on a bench somewhat removed from the others and didn't see the Wizard leap at Kara and the animals.

The Wizard held a flaming torch in his right hand and brandished it in the face of the wolf, who backed up, growling. Then the evil man grabbed for Kara, who again held her sword and brought its sharp blade down in a flash, cutting through his wrist so that he fell back crying out, and dropped the dagger he'd been aiming at her.

Carlo quickly picked it up and threw it to Mario.

John, brought to his senses by the vicious attack on his daughter, now grabbed the Wizard and wrestled him to the ground. But the Wizard still held the torch in his good hand. He slammed the burning stick into John's abdomen, causing sparks to burn John's jacket. John did not release the Wizard, however, and as they continued to struggle, the Wizard's robes caught on fire, flaring quickly, and engulfing the pair in a ball of flame.

Barb, watching from the tower, screamed in fright and Heironymous gripped her arm to keep her from running down to help rescue her husband. "It will be alright," the Mage assured her. She saw Mario and Carlo grab the ball of flame and throw the two fighting men into the fountain, where the flames were doused, but not their rage.

At this point, Heironymous made a gesture with his arms and a single bolt of blue lightning flashed from the tower, spearing the combatants in a trance. They made a grotesque sculpture, frozen in their violent hate.

The little dragon flew down from the parapet and disengaged them with its claws. John stumbled away in a daze, and Kara went to him where he fell down next to the faun statue.

The lioness and Rarjer stood over the dazed Wizard, while the dragon sat on his head, holding him in the water. Putrid steam rose from the ashes of his still simmering robe, and black smoke swirled up from his now un-pointed hat. The Wizard, himself, sat mute and immobile, blood streaming from his slashed wrist.

Now Barb followed Anthony and Heironymous as they made their way rapidly downstairs, and ran together through the sliding doors into the courtyard.

✳ ✳ ✳

Kara, seeing her mother, cried out in her normal voice, "Mom! Thank goddess you are here. Dad is pretty badly hurt."

Barb hurried to her daughter's side and examined her husband. He was lying unconscious. Kara had stripped away the burned jacket and his chest was beginning to fester. "We've got to get him cooled off," said Barbara with a calmness that surprised them both. "Don't try to move him."

Running to the kitchen, she gathered a large bowl of ice from the freezer and several towels. They packed the ice in towels bound to his chest and arms. Then Barbara said to Kara, "We've got to get him to the Grove. I can heal him there."

Kara looked at her mother in amazement, and saw the light of power that shone about her. Now Kara realized that Barb, too, had connected with the goddess' magic. "Can't we take him to the Grotto?" Kara asked. "Mimi and others are there doing healing on Giuseppe already."

"Not yet, dear." Barb said. "He is not ready for that. We can't let the Grotto be contaminated by his unbelief. Maybe someday we can show him that magic place, but now is not the time. The Grove can absorb his negativity without becoming defiled." She explained all this to her daughter, even as she herself came to the understanding. They looked at each other in shared delight, in spite of their fear for John.

A deep voice at Barbara's side said, "So the Rimini magic goes on. It is Sophia's greatest reward to see you both come into the Circle."

Barb looked up to the giant man in black and smiled, saying, "Kara, I want you to meet my dear old friend, Heironymous. He was the hero in many of the fairy tales I made up for you girls when you were little." She grinned at her daughter. "He is a true magician. You haven't seen anything until you see Heironymous the Mage perform his magic."

Kara grinned back at her mother. "We have already met, Mom, but I look forward to hearing more of your stories from years past."

Then Heironymous helped them carry John to the Grove. It didn't take long. Rarjer and the lioness followed on their heels down through the ravine and across the tunnel to the sacred meadow.

Meanwhile, Mario and Anthony, with Carlo and his men, arranged for the arrest and imprisonment of Donnie, the Wizard, the Vatican's Vulture.

65

TRANSFORMATIONS

Meanwhile, as the drama was unfolding at the villa, Gina had arrived at the Grotto transformed into her priestess persona, and surveyed the situation there. Her first act was to reinforce the fairy-shield that held strangers and unbelievers out of the sacred space.

However, she knew that should the evil force make its way back, a greater form of protection would be needed. She located a hidden cache of supplies in a niche of the grotto wall and prepared a decoction from fennel and other herbs, mixed with water from the sacred pool.

The decoction would provide both an antidote against the effects of evil Malandanti, and a drug to paralyze their forces. She pulverized the mixture with a mortar and pestle and spoke words of enchantment over each of the Grottos' occupants as she anointed them, one by one, with the salve.

The grotto had always been known for its healing energy. Some believed the waters of the cascade, its pool and stream derived from an otherworldly source. Whatever its source, it was pure clean water, uncontaminated by the pollutants affecting most streams and lakes in the modern world.

The healing power of the Grotto, however, came from more than the water. It must be attributed as much to the fairies who inhabited the place, and to its many Otherworld visitors. The grotto had been preserved as a Rimini clan secret haven for over a thousand years. Few others today knew of its existence, which certainly helped keep it safe from the corruption of human affairs. *Another reason not to make the Villa a public tourist venue as John advocated,* Gina mused.

Gina thought about these matters as she moved among the group, administering the protection charm. She realized that the situation they were in presented a perilous threat to the inviolability of this sacred refuge. *If events taking place at the villa should go wrong, the entire magic world will be in jeopardy.*

✳ ✳ ✳

A short while later Toby returned to the grotto where he found Gina transformed and administering magic protective potions to all the occupants.

The cat observed a private interchange between Mimi and the ghost girl, Juliet. They hugged each other and, about their feet, a puppy romped_ a ghost puppy. Toby put his whiskers forward in a pleased cat-smile. *So now lonely Juliet has her own companion. The goddess surely does always look after her own,* he thought.

Toby could see the love flowering between Joanna and Giuseppe *Their love will heal our goat-god friend, and, once again, Life will be renewed in its perpetual cycle.*

In this way Toby pondered those things his ancient spirit knows to be true, and he recounted the events through the Goddess' timeless wisdom, for the cat was well acquainted with Her mystical forms.

The ancient tales told that a sacred cat named Bast was Diana's constant companion and familiar. And that same spirit now inhabits Toby's soul. He knows Diana-Aradia-Shakti, Goddess of the Moon, primary goddess of witches and fairies, can take any of several forms, depending on the need and the occasion.

Toby mused upon the evening's events. *This holy and terrible night She has appeared in the courtyard, as Kara, the warrior-huntress; in the Grove as Barbara, the muse-lover; and here, in the grotto, as Gina, the shaman-healer.*

Those who metamorphose to embody Diana's forms carry within themselves the seeds of her power, which can reincarnate through their spirit when called or when circumstances dictate. She comes bidden in ceremony, but unbidden in times of urgency. During the displacement, her carriers remain conscious and can reason from their human perspective as well.

To her devotees, Diana-Aradia's divine light glows through her corporeal emissary. To unbelievers, her manifestation rouses terror, if they see her at all. Mostly they feel the feral force of her eminence.

Now, the strength of divine protection suffuses the Grotto, bathing its inhabitants and their surroundings in a wash of healing love.

Toby knows that, although danger and tragedy do still lurk nearby, these good folks are provided safety here.

66

HERITAGE OF HEALING MAGIC

Kara stood quietly by the rock-face leading back into the tunnel from the Grove. She watched her mother tending to her father's burns and knew their love for each other was a powerful magic that would heal more than his physical wounds.

Heironymous lit a small bonfire nearby and set up a cauldron with water from the pond to boil. He prepared herbal ointments and salves for John's burns, and a decoction similar to the one Gina brewed in the grotto for repelling evil.

Kara could see some of the magic folk busily fanning the flames and others spinning the fairy webbing over John's body.

Melanthus, the raven, surveyed it all from a branch overhead.

Kara sent a prayer to the goddess that her father would finally overcome his foolish superstitions and learn to trust in the mysteries surrounding the natural world. *Maybe someday he could even believe in the good magic folk.*

That thought lifted Kara's spirit so that she smiled and hummed happily to herself as she trotted after the wolf and the lioness, back through the tunnel to the Grotto. She arrived at the alcove confluence of the three tunnels, and looked about for evidence of the battle she'd just fought there a few hours earlier. The area had been cleaned up to its original pristine condition. Even the puppy's little carcass was taken away. But the veil of protection still hid the entrance.

"The fairies have been busy," said Kara to her companions. "Now let's see if we can find our way through their clever barricade."

She took out another branch of fennel from her pack, which she had somehow managed to keep strapped to her back through the entire escapade. "Oh Boy!" she laughed. "This thing is going to grow right on to me someday if I'm not careful. I'll be like a kind of backward kangaroo!"

She understood that the backpack had transformed with her during the magic events, so that it served as the carrier for her bow and arrows. She looked down at her grubby jeans, t-shirt, and sneakers and laughed out loud to imagine her ordinary daily attire altered to become an Amazon goddess' hunting costume.

Then, with the fennel in her hand, she drew a circle around herself and the animals. She prayed, "Bless this place Diana-Aradia, and keep us all in your gracious care. Let us enter your haven now in peace and love" She made up the words which came to her naturally without question.

Immediately the grotto entrance appeared before them and they walked in together, Kara, flanked by Rarjer the wolf and Farah the lioness. There she found her aunt, Gina, with Joanna and Mimi, tending Giuseppe's wounds. She saw fairies helping them, like those she'd just left behind in the Grove with her mother and Heironymous.

Behind the waterfall she glimpsed the furry tails of the mother wolf and her three remaining cubs. Rarjer immediately loped over to them and began a vigorous nuzzling and woofing.

"Good greetings, our Warrior Priestess, Kara!" called Gina. "What news do you bring us from the villa?" Her tone and manner were so natural that Kara could not feel surprised at the title. They were, after all, still operating in magic place and time.

"The news is good, Priestess Diana-Gina," answered Kara in an equally familiar and comfortable manner. She realized these words and actions to be a regular part of the rituals of the healing craft of Strega. *How odd it is that I automatically know and understand them,* she mused again to herself. Gina merely smiled acknowledgment of their mutual understanding.

Kara relayed the events of the past few hours at the villa, ending with a description of her mother and Heironymous with her father in the Grove. At this last, she finally drew a reaction from Gina. "Your mother is doing healing with the Mage? I feared she had abandoned hope of regaining her magic connections when she couldn't let herself come with me into the Grotto." Gina's face warmed in a look of tender compassion. "Thank Goddess something wakened her."

Kara said, "She had the same glow about her that you do, Aunt Gina. And, I think she looked happier than I have ever seen her, even while she was so worried about Daddy.

Giuseppe stirred and opened his eyes. He struggled to sit up with the help of Joanna, and sat, leaning against her shoulder. He grinned crookedly and said, "So the priest has blown his cover after all."

Joanna asked, "The priest? What does he have to do with this Beltane witch stuff? "

"That priest is our dear friend Heironymous, whom you've heard us talk about often," explained Gina. "It was his wish not to be known by you folks for a while until you'd become more familiar with the villa and our traditions. He has been living nearby in a mountain hamlet, functioning as the priest of their small church for years. The local folk know him as a kindly priest and healer."

Joanna, wide-eyed, said, "A priest? Disguised as a mage? or, whatever. How could he pull that off?"

"He even attended the seminary and officially made his ordination," chuckled Giuseppe. "But, of course, he was never converted. It is only that the teachings of the church, at their core, are no different from ours. Jesus, after all, was of the Mage lines Himself."

"Yes, of course," said Gina nodding. "It is told as part of our own shamanic histories how the Magdalene brought their children through Italy and into France at the beginning of the current era, two thousand years ago. One of our first foremothers, in fact, was a handmaiden to the Magdalene."

Joanna nodded. "I guess I shouldn't be surprised given the tales I saw at the show with Sep and Tony. I also read a little book written by your friend, Heironymous. In it he hints at that legend."

Gina looked up at Kara, who stood fascinated by this exchange. Gina said, "Kara, you will be interested to know that our own Sophia was incarnating that handmaiden's spirit in this lifetime."

Kara sat down cross-legged next to the group and heaved a sigh. "Aunt Gina, this is the part of the mystery that seems hardest for me to get. I keep running into this past-life idea, but it just seems so astounding to think that we keep living over and over again in new bodies."

Mimi had been quietly watching the wolf family reunite and listening to the conversation going on around her. Now she spoke for the first time. "It feels perfectly right to me, Kara. I've always known there was more in me than just who I am as Mimi in this life. How could I know some of the things I do if I hadn't learned them somewhere before I was born?"

Kara, as usual, was impressed by the depth of her little sister's wisdom. "I guess you're right, Mim honey," she said. "But still, it seems kind of surreal to me. Do those other spirits or souls run our lives then? Don't we have choice or control over our own destiny?"

"Sure we have," answered Mimi with a giggle. "But why would you want to choose something against the wishes of magic? It's the best way to live anyway."

Here Joanna joined in, "I've always easily identified with other women's histories and imagined that I might have been that other person in a past life. It wasn't exactly a spiritual understanding for me until Sep and Anthony introduced me to the Strega heritage mysteries. I just always thought it was part of being an actress, the ability to step into another person's or character's shoes." She looked at Sep. "Now I know we are not only reincarnating our ancestors, but that we can even incarnate the deities themselves if need be."

"How do you mean that, Jo? Kara asked, with a shiver.

"Well, look at Gina," interrupted Mimi, "She's being the goddess right now, don't you see? And you, yourself, Kara," their little sister went on, "You turned into some warrior goddess tonight right before all our eyes when you went out to fight the monster Wizard."

She looked each of them in the eye. "I know I can be a goddess too. But right now I'm happy being part Juliet and part just me, Mimi."

Giuseppe coughed and sighed. "It can take a lot out of you sometimes. Bringing down the gods and goddesses, incarnating other forms, it's not always fun and games." He lay again with his head in Joanna's lap and she resumed stroking his forehead where the wreath and horns still left a faint impression.

Kara thought of the horned god and moon goddess and realization finally dawned. "That was you, Sep! In the Grove, I mean, with the Moon Goddess. You *were* Faunus, weren't you?" She stopped and thought. "Mimi did say that, but I just thought she meant you were wearing a disguise."

Although he didn't answer, she knew it was true. Again, Kara shivered. "I'm really going to have to work on this piece for a while. It has been a lot just accepting the fairies and talking animals! For me, it's quite a leap, even if you-all find it perfectly natural." She tossed her pony tail. " I mean, I don't have doubts that magic is real anymore, but some things are so strange I have trouble even imagining how they can happen." The lioness was comfortably lounging behind her with Toby the tabby sitting nonchalantly at the big cat's side.

Kara went on because she felt a little defensive. "Like, how is it that little Toby can morph into big Farah? And the big man, Mage, Priest, whatever, how can he become the Moon Goddess?"

No one answered and Kara felt embarrassed. "Yeah, I know. Magic does not discriminate, and it is not meant to be explained or understood. We are just supposed to accept it." Kara sighed. "But sometimes that is so hard to do."

67

KARA REMEMBERS

While the girls were discussing their beliefs and questions about their magical heritage, Rarjer paced to Kara's side and nuzzled her neck. She laughed and turned to give him a hug. "Of course, with this guy, it is impossible for me not to believe. I've got to accept him for what he is, both wolf and magic creature, no questions asked."

Rarjer made a soft bark and turned around to stand beside his mate and their pups, who were lined up in a neat row beside the pool. The big male looked at Kara in anticipation.

Kara said, "Rarjer is telling me it is time for him and his family to go home. I'm going with them and check things out at their cottage den. We'll have plenty of time to talk things over in days to come."

She went around and gave each of them a hug, including Giuseppe. Mimi kissed her cheek and said, "We'll see you back at the villa later. We are all going to need to really sleep in for a couple of days after this!"

Rarjer and his family had already begun the trek back through the tunnel to their den. Kara followed them. Farah nuzzled Mimi and Toby farewell, and then followed up the tunnel as far as her own den-cave.

At last, Kara and the wolves arrived at the large cavern behind the cottage. Kara opened the secret door into the closet and then gently pulled open the pantry door into the little house. She was relieved to see nothing was too badly disturbed there after the battle.

The wolves set about nosing and examining their home. They found a few bits and pieces of clothing to indicate some kind of raucous had occurred here. Kara gathered these into a pile and lit a fire to them in an old fire-pit by the back slope.

She scattered fennel all around the house and grounds, making blessing gestures and saying words of banishment to rid any evil still lurking there. She came upon a single hawk feather and pocketed that. "It's good to keep a piece of the enemy to use in incantations against them if needed sometime in the future" she said aloud, speaking to no one in particular. Idly, she wondered how she knew this. She didn't recall reading anything like that in the journal.

When she came back into the cottage she found that the mother and cubs had already settled themselves into their corner and two of the pups were wrestling. The third puppy, the one who had been more seriously injured, came limping over to her and Rarjer. It was carrying something in its mouth and dropped it at Kara's feet. It was a tiny scrap of torn deer hide.

She picked it up and examined it, then looked toward the nursing nest. She noticed a few stones piled against the wall. The puppy waddled back to the corner and pawed at that cairn.

Kara had the distinct sense that the pup was telling her to look there. But she didn't dare to intrude on the female wolf's protected space. Rarjer barked once at his mate. She raised her head from a nap, looked around and moved away from the corner. Her cubs bounced and played around her legs.

Kara went to the stone pile and gently removed the top rock. Looking into the crevice, she saw a little bundle wrapped in doeskin. She backed away from it, as if fearful that she was trespassing on buried treasure. Rarjer came and poked his muzzle into the hole and pulled out the bundled object and dropped it at her feet.

Obviously, I am meant to see this. How did the animals know it was here? Kara's thoughts tumbled over and over. *How do these things keep happening to me without any direction on my part? Who is guiding me, and why? I thought the weird stuff would be over once we got rid of the evil guy.*

"What am I supposed to do with this?" she asked, knowing the wolves wouldn't tell her. "Maybe there is some information in the Grimoire. Gina said it gives answers to questions, depending on the need." She sat down on a rock outside the cabin entrance and pulled the old journal out of her backpack.

She held the little bundle in her hand and imagined that it was warming up. *Just my own excitement, heating up my body,* she told herself. But she didn't feel ready to open the package. *What am I scared of? It can't be anything bad.*

Turning the book pages at random, she stopped at a drawing of a map. It showed the tunnels and all the secret places. *Funny I missed this all the times I've been reading this notebook.*

On the map, the area of the ruined cabin was glowing subtly. A tiny beam of light fell on it and Kara looked up to see Tinkle sitting near her shoulder on a bush. "Go ahead, open Sophia's present." said the fairy impatiently.

Kara opened the bundle slowly, her heart beating hard against her breast. Rarjer sat watching intently, his tongue lolling in excitement. The package unwrapped with some difficulty, but gradually a shape began to emerge. It had the weight and bulk of a palm-sized stone. But it was carved in the form of a female figure.

As the last of the wrapping unfolded it revealed a shimmering carved crystal image of a warrior goddess. She wore a short tunic and knee-high boots. Her hair was cropped short and she wore a kind of Robin Hood cap with a feather jauntily protruding from it. She carried a bow and arrows slung across her shoulder. A wolf stood at her side and a raven sat on a branch overhanging them both.

Kara examined the exquisite sculpture and tears came to her eyes. *This amulet feels very familiar.* Her memory arose clear and certain in her mind.

This figure of Diana Huntress/ Lady of the Beasts had lain against her own breast throughout her life as great-great-great Aunt Cecelia, the War-Witch.

Kara looked about her at the cottage and its surroundings.

For a moment it all appeared as it had been when she, as Cecelia, had built it. Memories flooded Kara of living here with wolf companions and of fighting against the Malandanti from the church.

She remembered with some humor her escape from arrest and the consequent killing of the evil priest and his guards by her wolves and cat.

And she remembered another life when two little girls came to live with her here, and how they all learned to know the magic of the world in which they live still. So many lives woven together of endless strands.

Kara pulled a leather thong from the tie of her backpack and strung it through the opening of the figurine, tying it around her neck so it lay against her breast. She could feel it warmly pulsing and knew herself to be at peace. The moon slipped beneath the sea, as dawn began to creep up from the mountains behind them. Rarjer nuzzled her neck and they lay down together on the soft grassy knoll to sleep and dream.

Melanthus, the raven, watched from a tree overhead while Kara dreamed of sitting in a great Circle of Beings, with Aunt Sophia, listening to endless tales of their lineage and its long magical and eventful past.

THE END

TIME LINE OF ANCESTRAL AND HISTORICAL LINES WITHIN THE STORY:

5000 to 3000 BC: Indus Valley period. Dravidian descendants of all nature-based spiritual traditions. Precursors of Shiva and Shakti, divine partners. Equal power of feminine and masculine deities: Moon Goddess and Horned God, Aum and Uma.

3000 to 1500 BC: Sumerian/Babylonian period of temple dancer priestesses. Worship of Ishtar, Innana, Isis, Ashtara, and the many varied names for the original Mother Goddess in different cultures of the era. Early biblical Abraham and Sarai-Hagar connection.

1500 to 1200 BC: Egyptian period. Integration of Hebrew group with original Egyptian-Dravidian lines.

1200 to 1000BC: Canaanite/ Middle Eastern Hebrew period. Biblical heroines preserve goddess worship and old nature traditions in secret.

1000 BC to Current Era: Dispersion period. Original Dravidian Gypsies out of India spread westward: north to integrate with Celtic-Gaelic and Germanic groups; south to Anatolia and Balkans and to the Mediterranean isles of Cyprus and Crete. Eventual integration in Italy with native Villanovan tribes to develop the Etruscan civilization.

THE RIMINI ANCESTRAL LINE OF STREGARIA WITCHES:

1.**Dianhea** circa 700 BCE Legendary. First "wandering healer" came to Italy from Crete. Brought the Nature traditions of stag, wolf, and goat gods. Integrated these with Villanovan magic traditions.

2. **Tanaquil,** circa 600 BC: the fabled first Etruscan Queen. Has close ancestral connections with Dianhea.

3 **Tana** circa 500 BCE. Surviving grand-daughter of Tanaquil. Mystery figure said to run in the wilderness with animals. May have dug the tunnel from the grotto to meadow rock.

4. **Cyna** circa 200 BCE. Amazon warrior, came from the north country to join the Etruscans in fighting against the Romans

5. **Fariah** circa 30 AD. Peasant woman who befriends the legendary refugees from Palestine on their way to France.

6. **Sylvia** circa 100 AD. Fariah's daughter, traveled to France as handmaiden to Magdalena, the secret bride of the Avatar, Jesus. Has connections to the Rosicrucian and Templar mysteries of the European Dark Ages.

7. **Anasasia** circa 1250 AD. Descendant of Sylvia. She was a healer who returned to Italy from France. Was instrumental in the teaching and training of Aradia

8 **Aradia** circa 1300 AD. "Beautiful Pilgrim" of Stregaria legend in Italy. Her parentage is unknown. She is credited with the revival of the shamanic Nature traditions among the pagan peoples, following years of religious suppression.

9 **Karamena** circa 1350 AD. Daughter of Aradia, who was said to return to the original home site of her mother after many years. She may have added the tower structure and its tunnel. She was a "war witch"¼ and may have worked to help end the Black Plague in Italy

10. **Amelia** circa 1400 AD. Said to have been raised in the wilderness by wolves after parents died of the plague. Believed to be of the line of Aradia's daughter, Karamena. She rose to fame and fortune as a courtesan in Rome and developed powerful connections. She eventually purchased the villa and added the main sections of the larger house and courtyard.

11. **Maria** circa 1500 AD. Grand-daughter to Amelia, she was a warrior-priestess during the Inquisition period. She added to the villa and reinforced its tunnel to the grotto, as well as constructing other hiding places for those escaping the vigilantes of that period. She was ultimately burned as a witch.